CHETCO COMMUNITY PUBLIC LIBRARY
3 0010 00126 2487

WITHDRAWN

D1005795

BLOODLINE

Also by MARK BILLINGHAM

Sleepyhead
Scaredy Cat
Lazybones
The Burning Girl
Lifeless
Buried
Death Message
In the Dark

BLOODLINE

Mark Billingham

MULHOLLAND BOOKS

LITTLE, BROWN AND COMPANY

NEW YORK BOSTON LONDON

Mulholland Books / Little, Brown and Company
Hachette Book Group
237 Park Avenue, New York, NY 10017
www.hachettebookgroup.com

First United States Edition: July 2011
Originally published in Great Britain by Little, Brown Book Group, August 2009

Mulholland Books is an imprint of Little, Brown and Company, a division of Hachette Book Group, Inc. The Mulholland Books name and logo are trademarks of Hachette Book Group, Inc.

Library of Congress Cataloging-in-Publication Data
Billingham, Mark.
Bloodline / Mark Billingham.— 1st U.S. ed.
p. cm.
ISBN 978-0-316-12666-3
1. Thorne, Tom (Fictitious character)—Fiction. 2. Police—England—London—Fiction. 3. Serial murders—England—London—Fiction. 4. Serial murder investigation—Fiction. I. Title.
PR6102.I44B56 2011
823'.92—dc22 2010041543

10 9 8 7 6 5 4 3 2 1

RRD-C

Printed in the United States of America

For David Shelley

BLOODLINE

Prologue

Debbie and Jason

"Come on, pigeon! Let's go blow at the trains." Debbie Mitchell tugs at her son's arm, but he pulls hard in the opposite direction, towards the chocolate Labrador the old woman is struggling to control. "Puff-puff," Debbie says, blowing out her cheeks. "Come on, it's your favorite..."

Jason pulls away harder, strong when he wants to be. The noise he makes is somewhere between a grunt and a whine. Anyone else might think he was in pain, but Debbie understands him well enough.

"Dog," he says. "Dog, dog!"

The old woman with the Labrador smiles at the boy—she has often seen the two of them in the park—then makes the same sad face as always when she looks at his mother.

"Poor thing," she says. "He knows I've got some treats for Buzz in my pocket. He wants to give him a few, don't you?" The dog hears this, pulls harder towards the boy.

"Sorry," Debbie says. "We need to go." She yanks at Jason's arm, and this time his cry is one of pain. "Now..."

She walks fast, glancing over her shoulder every few steps, urging Jason along. "Puff-puff," she says again, trying to keep the terror from her voice, knowing how easily he picks up on such things. The boy starts to smile, the dog quickly forgotten. He runs alongside her making chuffing noises of his own.

The dog is barking somewhere behind Debbie as she hurries away. The old woman—what was her name, Sally? Sarah?—meant well, but on any other day Debbie would have said something. She would have smiled, concealing her irritation, and explained that Jason was nobody's poor anything. That there was no happier child alive, no child more cherished.

Her precious boy. Nine next birthday, with hair on his legs already and an extra-large Arsenal shirt. Who will almost certainly never be able to feed or dress himself.

"Train," Jason says. Tries to say.

She hurries across the lower field, past the bench where they usually sit for a while, where they have an ice-cream sometimes in hot weather, then Jason runs ahead as they move onto the football pitch. They've been coming here for a couple of years and, as she hurries towards the familiar tree-line that borders the railway tracks, it strikes her that she doesn't even know what the place is called; if it even has a name. It's not Hampstead Heath or Richmond Park—there had been a flasher active for weeks the previous summer and sometimes the local kids lit fires at night—but it was theirs.

Hers and Jason's.

She checks behind again and keeps moving. Walking, fighting the urge to run, fearing that if she does, someone will see and try to stop her. Seeing no sign of the man she's watching out for, she picks up her pace to catch Jason. He's stopped in front of the goalposts to take an imaginary penalty, same as always. He does it whether there's a game on or not, and the boys who play here are used to seeing him charging onto their pitch and flapping around by the goal, waving his arms about like Ronaldo. Sometimes they cheer and none of them laughs or pulls faces anymore. Debbie could kiss each one of the little sods for that. Brings them cold drinks now and again, or a few cut-up oranges.

She takes Jason's hand and nods towards the bridge, a hundred yards ahead and to the left.

They move quickly towards it.

Normally they'd have come the other way, through the entrance opposite her own place, which would have taken them across the bridge on the way in. There would not have been any climbing on plastic chairs and scrambling over her friend's garden fence.

But this was not a normal day.

When she looks around again, she can see the man on the far side of the football pitch. He waves and she fights the urge to shit herself on the spot. He couldn't reach them in time, she thinks, even if he ran. Could he? The fact that he is just walking, though, the confidence in his easy stride, terrifies her more than she ever thought possible. Convinces her that she is doing the only thing she can. She had known even before she'd heard him talking on the phone. She'd seen it in his eyes and in the dreadful red stain beneath his jacket.

The man waves at her again and starts to jog.

On the bridge, Jason stops at his usual spot and waits for her, knowing that she will help him see the train when it comes. He looks confused when she moves to his side. He puffs out his cheeks and waves his arms.

There was a metal safety-barrier once upon a time, but bit by bit it had been pulled down, as soon as those with nothing better to do had covered every inch of brickwork with graffiti.

Who had shagged who. Who was a poof. Who had been there.

She puts a hand on Jason's shoulder, then starts to drag herself up, ignoring the pain as her knees scrape against the bricks, and carefully inches her belly across the top. She takes a few fast breaths, then slowly lifts one leg at a time, up and over until she is sitting. She doesn't dare look down; not yet.

She looks around to make sure that nobody is watching and it is then that she hears the voice of the real policeman. He is somewhere nearby on the far side of the bridge, coming from the other direction. His voice is cracked and raw as he shouts her name, and she can tell that he is running. He keeps on shouting, searching, but Debbie turns away.

Too late, she thinks. Much too late.

She reaches down to pull Jason up, her heart lurching at his smile of excitement. She's always lifted him before, just high enough so that he can see over the edge, watch the train as it thunders beneath them.

This is a whole new adventure.

She cries out with the effort of hauling him up and fights back the tears as he settles down, dangles his legs and snuggles up close to her. He feels the vibration before she does, lets her know in a series of gulps and shouts.

Debbie feels her guts turn to water and looks up to see the train rounding the bend in the distance. The southbound Tube from High Barnet. She knows it will slow a little just before the bridge as it approaches Totteridge and Whetstone station. Still fast enough, though.

Debbie scrabbles for her son's hand and squeezes. She leans down and whispers soft, secret words, knowing—despite any number of expert opinions—that he understands her. He points and yells as the train gets closer, louder. That smile that kills her.

Debbie closes her eyes.

"Puff-puff," Jason says, blowing at the train.

PART I

BRAND-NEW HEARTACHE

One

"... IS NOT viable."

The woman let her words hang for a few seconds, having passed across the thick roll of kitchen towel, switched off the machine, then turned back to pass on the news while Louise was still wiping the gel off her belly.

There were a few statistics then: percentages and weeks and numbers out of ten. Some stuff about how common this was, and how it was far better happening now than further down the line.

Thorne hadn't really taken much of it in.

Not. Viable.

He'd watched Louise nod, blinking slower than normal and buttoning her jeans while the woman talked for a minute or two about practicalities. "We can go through the details a bit later on," she'd said. "After you've had some time to yourselves."

Was she actually a doctor? Thorne wasn't sure. Maybe some kind of "scanner technician" or something. Not that it really mattered. It obviously wasn't the first time she'd said those words; there hadn't been a pause or even a hint of awkwardness, and he would not have expected one. It was probably best for all concerned to be businesslike about these things, he'd thought. He should know, after all. Best just to say what needed saying and move on, especially with back-to-back appointments and plenty more happy couples waiting outside.

That phrase though...

Afterwards, they sat in the corner near the water-dispenser, facing away from the main part of an open-plan waiting area. Four plastic chairs bolted together. A nice, lemon-colored wall and children's drawings tacked onto a cork board. A wicker table with a few magazines and a box of tissues.

Thorne squeezed Louise's hand. It felt small and cold inside his own. He squeezed again, and she looked up; smiled and sniffed.

"You OK?" she asked.

Thorne nodded, thinking that, as euphemisms went, it was a pretty good one. Bland yet final. Probably softened the blow for most people, which was, after all, the point.

Not viable.

Dead. Dead inside you.

He wondered if he should try it for size himself, trot it out the next time he had to meet someone at a mortuary or knock on some poor sod's door in the middle of the night.

Thing is, your husband ran into some drunken idiot with a knife in his pocket. I'm afraid he's... no longer viable.

Fine, so it made the victim sound like an android, but that detachment was important, right? You needed the distance. It was that or a few more empty wine bottles in your recycling bin every week.

Softening the blow for you just as much as for them.

I'm sorry to have to tell you that your son has been shot. Shot to non-viability. He's as non-viable as a doornail.

"Tom?"

Thorne glanced up at the small nudge from Louise, watched as the woman who had performed the scan came across the waiting area towards them. She was Indian, with a wide streak of red through her hair. Somewhere in her early thirties, Thorne guessed. Her smile was perfect: sorrowful, but with a spring in its step.

"OK, I think I've managed to find you a bed."

"Thank you," Louise said.

"When did you last eat?"

"I've not had anything since breakfast."

"That's good. We'll try to get the D and C done straight away." The woman handed Louise a sheet of paper, told her how to get to the ward she needed. Then she looked at Thorne. "You might want to go home and pick up a few things for her. Nightdress, whatever..."

Thorne nodded while the woman talked about Louise needing to put her feet up for a couple of days. Kept on nodding when she said that they should both take things easy, that there were phone numbers on the sheet for people they could talk to, if that was what they wanted.

He watched her walk back towards her room, turning to call the next couple inside when she was at the door. There was a TV mounted high on the wall in the opposite corner. A middle-aged couple was being shown round a villa in France or Italy, the wife saying something about how colorful the tiles were.

"D and C?"

Louise was studying the instructions on her piece of paper. "Dilatation and curettage."

Thorne waited, none the wiser. It sounded horrible.

"Scraping," Louise said, eventually.

A thin woman in green overalls pushed a trolley stacked with cleaning equipment along the corridor towards them. She stopped alongside the wicker table, took a rag and plastic spray-gun from her trolley and squirted one of the empty chairs. She looked across at Thorne and Louise as she wiped.

"What are you crying for?"

Thorne studied the woman for a few seconds, then turned to Louise, who was staring at the floor, folding the paper over and over. He was very hot suddenly, could feel the short hairs prickling at the back of his neck and the film of sweat between his hand and Louise's. He nodded to the sign on the door of the Antenatal Scanning Suite, then snapped his head back to the cleaner.

"Take a fucking guess," he said.

* * *

It took Thorne nearly fifteen minutes to drive the mile or so from the Whittington Hospital to Kentish Town, but at least the journey gave him time to calm down a little. To stop thinking about the heave in Louise's chest when that cleaner had spoken to them. About wanting to stuff that rag in the woman's stupid mouth.

She'd looked at him like he was being rude, for Christ's sake!

Back at the flat, he threw some food into a bowl for Elvis and stuffed the things Louise had asked for into a plastic bag: a clean T-shirt; bra and panties; a hairbrush and a few bits of make-up. He stopped at the door on his way out, needing to lean on the wall for a few seconds before walking back into the living room. He dropped onto the sofa hard and sat there, staring into space, for a while, with the plastic bag cradled on his lap.

It felt cold in the flat. Three weeks into September and high time the heating was put back on. Time for the petty squabbles to start again, with Thorne nudging up the thermostat and Louise nudging it back down again when she thought he wasn't looking. Secretive readjustments of the timer. The constant fiddling with radiators.

The silly sit-com stuff that Thorne loved, despite the bickering.

They had been arguing—rather more seriously—since Louise had first learned she was pregnant, about what their long-term living arrangements would be. Though they spent most of their time at Thorne's place, Louise still had her own flat in Pimlico. She was reluctant to sell it, or at least reluctant to accept the assumption that she would. Though they were both keen on sharing a place somewhere, they could not agree which property to put on the market, so they had started talking about selling both flats, then buying somewhere new together, as well as maybe a one-bedroom flat they could rent out.

Thorne stared at the fireplace and wondered if all that would be put on hold now. If lots of the things they'd discussed—some more seriously than others—would be shifted quietly onto the back burner, or become subjects that were simply never mentioned again.

Moving a bit further out of the city.

Getting married.

Quitting the Job.

Thorne stood up and collected the phone from the table near the door, carried it back to the sofa.

They had been talking hypothetically when most of those things had been mentioned; certainly the stuff about weddings and leaving the Force. Just stupid talk, that was all, along with the jokes about not wanting ginger kids and the barmy baby names.

"What about Damien?"

"I don't think so."

"Wasn't his name 'Thorne' in the film?"

"Without an 'E.' Anyway, who says he's going to be a 'Thorne.' Why can't he be a 'Porter'? Come to think of it, who says he's going to be a 'he'?"

Thorne jabbed at the buttons on the phone. He'd only signed out for two hours, so now he needed to let them know that he wouldn't be back until sometime the following day. He'd have been happiest leaving a message, but he was connected straight through to Detective Sergeant Samir Karim in the Incident Room.

"You must be psychic."

"Sorry?"

"The DCI's in the middle of leaving a message on your phone."

Thorne reached into his jacket for his mobile. He'd turned it off in the hospital and forgotten to switch it back on again. By the time the screen had come back to life and the tones were sounding to indicate that he had a message, Detective Chief Inspector Russell Brigstocke was on the landline.

"Good timing, mate. Or bad."

"What?"

"We've just caught a job." Brigstocke took a slurp of tea or coffee. "Nasty one, by the sound of it."

Thorne swore quietly, but not quietly enough.

"Look, I was about to give it to Kitson anyway."

"You were right before," Thorne said. "Bad timing."

"It's yours if you fancy it."

Thorne thought about Louise, what the woman had said about needing to take things easy. Yvonne Kitson was perfectly capable of dealing with a new case, and he had plenty on his plate at work as it was. But he was already on his feet, hunting for a pen and paper.

Elvis was mooching around his ankles while Thorne scribbled a few notes. Brigstocke was right, it was a nasty one, but Thorne wasn't overly surprised. It was usually the nasty ones they put his way.

"Husband?" Thorne asked. "Boyfriend?"

"Husband found the body. Made the call, then ran out into the street screaming the place down."

"Made the call first?"

"Right. Then lost it, by all accounts," Brigstocke said. "Banging on doors, telling everyone she was dead, screaming about blood and bottles. Definitely not what the good people of Finchley are used to."

"Finchley's easy," Thorne said.

"Right, nice local one for you."

Five or six miles north of Kentish Town. He'd be more or less driving past the Whittington Hospital. "I'll need to make a quick stop on the way," Thorne said. "But I should be there in half an hour or so."

"No rush. She isn't going anywhere."

It took Thorne a few seconds to realize that Brigstocke was talking about a dead woman and not about Louise Porter.

"Give me the address."

Two

It was a quiet street, a few turnings east of the High Road. Edwardian houses with neat front gardens and off-road parking. Many, like number 48, had been divided into flats, though this house was now itself divided from its neighbors: a tarpaulin shielding the side-alley, uniformed officers stationed at each corner of the front lawn and crime-scene tape fluttering above the flower beds.

Thorne arrived just before eight, and it had already been dark for almost an hour. It was light enough in the kitchen of the downstairs flat, where the beams from twin arc-lamps illuminated every mote of dust and puff of fingerprint powder, bounced off the blue plastic suits of the CSIs and washed across the linoleum on the floor. A retro-style, black-and-white check, its simple pattern ruined by a few spots of blood. And by the body they had leaked from.

"I think I'm about ready to turn her," Phil Hendricks said.

In the corner, a crime-scene investigator was scraping at the edge of a low cupboard. She barely glanced up. "That'll be a first..."

Hendricks grinned and gave the woman the finger, then looked around and asked Thorne if he wanted to come closer. To squeeze in where he could get a better view.

Thorne doubted that the view would get any better, but he walked across and placed himself between the still- and video-camera operators, opposite the pair of CSIs who were preparing to give Hendricks the help he needed. To add the necessary degree of strength to his gentleness.

"OK, easy does it."

The woman was face down, arms by her sides. Her shirt had been lifted, or had ridden up, showing purplish patches on the skin just above her waist where the livor mortis had started and revealing that her bra had not been removed.

"Something, I suppose," a female CSI said as she walked past.

Thorne raised his eyes from the body and looked towards the single window. There were plates and mugs on the draining board next to the sink. A light was flashing on the front of the washing machine to let somebody know that the cycle had finished.

There was still a trace of normality.

Assuming they didn't get a result in the first few days, Thorne would try to come back at some point. He found it useful to spend time where the victim had lived; even more so if it was also where they had died. But he would wait until he didn't have to weave between crouching CSIs and negotiate the depressing paraphernalia of a crime scene.

And until the smell had gone.

He remembered some movie where the cop would stand in the houses where people had been murdered and commune with their killer. Was this where you killed them, you son of a bitch? Is that where you watched them from?

All that shit...

For Thorne, it just came down to wanting to know something about the victim. Something other than what their last meal had been and what their liver weighed at the time of death. Something simple and stupid would usually do it. A picture on a bedroom wall. The biscuits they kept in the kitchen cupboard or the book that they would never finish reading.

As for what went on in the mind of the killer, Thorne was happy knowing just enough to catch him, and no more.

Now, he watched as what remained of Emily Walker was moved, saw the hand flop back across the leg as it was lifted and turned in one slow, smooth movement. Saw those strands of hair that were not caked in blood fall away from her face as she was laid down on her back.

"Cheers, lads."

Hendricks worked with a good team. He insisted on it. Thorne remembered one CSI in particular—back when they were content to be called scene of crime officers—handling the partially decomposed body of an old man no better than if it were a sack of spuds. He'd watched Hendricks pushing the SOCO up against a wall and pressing a heavily tattooed forearm across the man's throat. He couldn't recall seeing the two of them at the same crime scene since.

The cameramen stepped forward and went to work. When they'd finished, Hendricks mumbled a few preparatory notes into his digital recorder.

"How much longer, Phil?" Thorne asked.

Hendricks lifted one of the dead woman's arms; began bending back the fingers of a fist that was closed tight. "Hour and a half." The thick Manchester accent stretched out the pathologist's final word, flattened the vowel. "Two at a push."

Thorne checked his watch. "Right."

"You on a promise or something?"

Thorne did his best to summon the right expression, something conspiratorial and devilish, but he wasn't sure he'd managed it. He turned to see where Detective Sergeant Dave Holland had got to.

"She's got something in her hand," Hendricks said.

Thorne turned back quickly and bent down to get a closer look, watched as Hendricks went to work with his tweezers and lifted something from the victim's fist. It appeared to be a small square of plastic or celluloid, dark and wafer thin. Hendricks dropped it into an evidence bag and held it up to the light.

"Piece of film?" Thorne asked.

"Could be."

They stared at whatever was in the bag for a few more seconds, but both knew they would only be guessing until the Forensic Science Service laboratory had finished with it. Hendricks handed the bag over for the evidence manager to log and label, then carefully fastened polythene wraps around both the victim's hands before moving further up the body.

Thorne closed his eyes for a few seconds, let out a long breath. "Can you believe I had a choice?" he said.

Hendricks glanced up at him. He was kneeling behind the victim's head and lifting it so that it was resting against his legs.

"Brigstocke gave me the option."

"More fool you."

"I could have let Kitson take it."

"This one's got your name on it," Hendricks said.

"Why?"

"Look at her, Tom."

Emily Walker was... had been early thirties or thereabouts, dark hair streaked with a little gray and a small star tattooed above one ankle. She was no more than five feet tall, her height emphasizing the few extra pounds which, judging by the contents of the fridge and the magnet on the door that said "ARE YOU SURE YOU'RE HUNGRY?," she was trying to lose. She wore a thin necklace of brown beads and there was a charm bracelet around one wrist: dice, a padlock, a pair of fish. Her shirt was denim. Her skirt was thin cotton, the same pillar-box red as the varnish on her toenails.

Thorne looked across at the sandal that had been circled on the lino close to the fridge. At the decorative bottle a few feet away, with what looked like balsamic vinegar on the inside and blood and hair caught in a few of the glass ridges on the outside, and beyond, to the light still winking on the front of the washing machine. His hand drifted up to his face, fingers moving along the straight, white scar on his chin. He stared until the red light began to blur, then turned and wandered away, leaving Hendricks cradling Emily Walker's head and talking quietly into his Dictaphone.

"There is nothing holding the plastic bag in position over the victim's head. Assume that the killer kept it in place around the victim's neck with his hands. Bruises on neck suggest he held it there with a great deal of force until the victim had stopped breathing..."

Holland was standing out on the patio at the rear of the house, watching half a dozen uniforms combing the flower beds. There were arc-lamps out here too, but this was only an initial sweep and more officers would be back at first light to conduct a fingertip search.

"So, no forced entry then," Thorne said.

"Which means she knew him."

"Possibly." Thorne could smell cigarettes on Holland, wanted one himself for a second or two. "Or she answered the door and he produced a weapon, forced her back inside."

Holland nodded. "Let's see if we get lucky with the house to house. Looks like the kind of street where there's plenty of curtain-twitching."

"What about the husband?"

"I only had five minutes before they took him to a hotel up the road," Holland said. "In pieces, much as you'd expect."

"Trying too hard, you reckon?"

"How d'you mean?"

"Sounds like he wanted everyone in the street to see just how upset he was. After he'd called us."

"You heard the 999 tape?"

"No." Thorne shrugged. "Just..."

"Just wishful thinking?" Holland said. "Right?"

"Yeah, maybe." It was getting a little chillier. Thorne shoved his hands inside the plastic suit and down into the pockets of his leather jacket. "Be nice if it was... a simple one."

"I can't see it," Holland said.

Nor could Thorne, if he was being honest. He knew only too well how domestic violence could escalate; had seen the ways a jealous boyfriend or a domineering husband could lose it. He blinked, saw the flop of the arm as the body was turned. Spots of pillar-box red against black-and-white squares. Not a simple one...

"Maybe he was just that upset," Holland said. "How many of these have we done?"

Thorne puffed out his cheeks. There was no need to answer.

"Right. And I still can't imagine what it must be like. Not even close."

Holland was fifteen years younger than Thorne. He had been working alongside him for more than seven years and though the fresh-faced newbie was long gone, Thorne still relished the glimpses of someone who hadn't been totally reshaped by the Job. Holland had looked up to him once, had seen him as the kind of copper he would like to become, Thorne knew that. He knew equally that Holland was not the same as he was... not where it mattered, and that he should be bloody grateful for it.

"Especially when it's a woman," Holland said. "You know? I see the husbands and boyfriends and fathers, how it hits them, and it doesn't matter if they're hysterical or furious or sitting there like zombies. I've got no bloody idea what's happening inside their heads."

"Don't knock it, Dave," Thorne said.

They both looked across at laughter from further down the garden, where one of the officers had obviously stepped in something. Watched as he scraped the sole of his shoe across the edge of the lawn.

"So, where were you skiving off to earlier, then?" Holland asked.

"Sorry?"

"When all this kicked off."

Thorne cleared his throat.

Louise had been fine about him taking the job on, when he'd popped into the hospital to drop off her stuff. She was already in bed, working her way through a copy of *heat* and trying to tune out the incessant chatter of a woman in the bed opposite. He'd asked if she was sure. She'd looked at him like he was being stupid and asked why she wouldn't be. He'd told her to call if she wanted anything, if she needed him. She'd told him not to worry and said that she could get a taxi back when it was all over, if she had to.

"Dentist," Thorne said. "An hour with the Nazi hygienist. The woman's like something out of *Marathon Man*."

Holland laughed. Said, "Is it safe?"

"You told Sophie you're back on the fags?" Thorne asked.

Holland shook his head. "Got a glove compartment full of extra-strong mints." He leaned down and spat into a drain. "Stupid really, 'cause I'm bloody sure she knows. Just doesn't want a row, I suppose."

Holland and his girlfriend were another couple who had been talking about getting out of London, and about Holland giving up the Job. Thorne wondered if that was something else that was not being mentioned for fear of reigniting an argument. He had always been convinced that Holland should stay where he was, but he would never have said so. If Sophie so much as got wind of Thorne's opinion, she would fight tooth and nail to do the opposite.

So he kept his mouth shut, content that Holland was still there.

"We'll get the official ID done first thing in the morning," Thorne said. "Then bring the husband in for a chat."

"Fair enough."

"You never know, we might get lucky."

Holland snorted, nodded across to where the uniformed officer was now working at the sole of his shoe with a twig, flicking out the shit. "That kind of lucky," he said.

They both looked up as a plane passed low overhead, lights blinking, on its way to Luton. Thorne watched it move fast across a clear sky and swallowed hard. Eight weeks earlier, he and Louise had gone to Greece together for their first proper holiday as a couple. They had spent most days lying by a pool reading trashy books and done nothing more culturally demanding than work out how to ask for beer and grilled squid in the local taverna. They'd both tried hard not to talk about work and had laughed a lot. One day, Louise had rubbed cream into Thorne's shoulders where he'd got burned, and said, "This is as far as it goes for me in terms of non-sexual intimate contact, all right? I'm not into squeezing other people's blackheads and I will not be wiping your arse if you break both your arms."

She'd bought the pregnancy testing kit on their final morning there. Used it just before they'd gone out to dinner that last night.

* * *

Thorne was sitting in the car when Hendricks came out.

He'd checked his phone and tried both flats, but Louise hadn't got back yet and there were no messages. He'd listened to the radio for a while then called again to no avail. Louise's mobile was switched off and Thorne guessed it was too late to ring the hospital.

Hendricks walked around to the passenger side and got in. He'd changed out of the protective suit and was wearing black jeans and a skinny-rib sweater over a white T-shirt. "Just about done," he said.

Thorne grunted.

"You OK?"

"Sorry...yeah." Thorne turned and looked. Nodded and smiled.

A skein of red and blue ink was just visible above the neckline, but most of Phil Hendricks' tattoos were hidden. Much to the relief of his superiors, a good few of the piercings remained out of sight, too. Thorne was happy to have been spared the graphic details, but knew that some had been done in honor of a new boyfriend, one for each conquest. There hadn't been a new piercing for quite a while.

It was not what many people expected a pathologist to look like, but Hendricks was the best Thorne had ever worked with; and still—despite the many ups and downs—the closest friend he had.

"Fancy a pint later?" Thorne asked.

"What about Louise?"

"She'll be fine."

"No." Hendricks grinned. "I mean she'll be jealous."

"We'll make it up to her," Thorne said. In truth, he was the one who had suffered from jealousy. He and Louise had been together almost a year and a half, having met when Thorne was seconded to help out on a kidnap case she had been working, but it had taken her only a couple of weeks to get as close to Phil Hendricks as Thorne had managed in ten years. There were times, especially early on, when it had been disconcerting; when he'd found himself resenting them their friendship.

One night, when the three of them were out together, Thorne had got pissed and called Louise a "fag-hag." She and Phil had laughed, and Phil had said how ironic that was, because Thorne was the one acting like an old queen.

"Yeah, OK then," Hendricks said. He looked towards the house, from which officers had begun to drift in twos and threes. "Mind you, if I'm going to be elbows deep in that poor cow first thing in the morning, I'd better just have the one."

"Well, I'm having way more than one," Thorne said. "So we'd best go to my local. I'll give you a lift."

Hendricks nodded, let his head drop back and closed his eyes. Thorne had given up trying to find any decent country music and had tuned the radio in to Magic FM. It was nearly ten o'clock, and 10cc was winding up an uninterrupted hour of easy-listening oldies.

"He brought his own bag," Hendricks said.

"What?"

"The bag he used to suffocate her. He knew what he was doing. You can't just grab some carrier bag out of the kitchen—they're a waste of time. Most of them have got holes in, so your vegetables don't sweat or whatever. You want something air-tight, obviously, and it needs to be a bit stronger, so it won't get cut to ribbons by your victim's fingernails, if she's got any." Hendricks tapped his fingers on the dash in time to the music. "Also, with a nice, clear polythene bag, you can see the face while you're doing it. I think that's probably important."

"So, he was organized."

"He came prepared."

"He didn't bring the vinegar bottle, though."

"No, I'm guessing that was improvised. First thing he could grab hold of to hit her with."

"Then he gets the bag out once she's down."

Hendricks nodded. "Might even have hit her hard enough to do the job before he had a chance to suffocate her."

"I suppose we should hope so."

"I wouldn't bet on it," Hendricks said. "You ask me, the bottle was just to make sure she wasn't going to struggle too much. He wanted to kill her with the bag. Like I said, I reckon he wanted to watch."

"Jesus."

"I'll know tomorrow."

The windows were beginning to steam up, so Thorne turned on the fan. They listened to the news for a couple of minutes. There was nothing to lift the mood even slightly and there was nothing in the sports round-up to get excited about. The football season was still only a month or so old and, with neither of their teams in action, none of the night's results proved particularly significant.

"Six weeks until we stuff you again," Hendricks said. A committed Gunner, he was still relishing the double that Arsenal had done over Spurs in the north London derbies the previous season.

"Right..."

Hendricks was laughing and saying something else, but Thorne had stopped listening. He was staring down at the screen of his mobile, thumbing through the menu and checking he hadn't missed a message.

"Tom?"

Making sure he still had a decent signal.

"Tom? You OK, mate?"

Thorne put the phone away and turned.

"Is Louise all right?" Hendricks waited, saw something in Thorne's face. "Shit, is it the baby?"

"What? How d'you know...?" Thorne pushed back hard in his seat and stared straight ahead. He and Louise had agreed to tell nobody for the first three months. A good friend of hers had lost one early on.

"Don't be pissed off," Hendricks said. "I forced it out of her."

"Course you did."

"To be honest, I think she was desperate to spill the beans." Hendricks looked for a softening in Thorne's demeanor but saw none. "Come on, who else was she going to tell?"

Thorne glanced across, spat it out. "I don't know, her mother?"

"I think she might have told her as well."

"Fuck's sake!"

"Nobody else, as far as I know."

Thorne leaned down and turned off the radio. "This was why we agreed we wouldn't say anything. In case this happened."

"Shit," Hendricks said. "Tell me."

When Thorne had finished, Hendricks began telling him that these things usually happened for good reasons, that it was better now than later on. Thorne stopped him. Told him he'd heard it all already from the woman who'd done the scan and that it hadn't helped too much then, either.

Thorne saw Hendricks' face and apologized. "I just didn't know what to say to her, you know?"

"Nothing much you can say."

"Need to give it time, I suppose," Thorne said.

"Tell her to call me whenever she likes," Hendricks said. "You know, if she wants to talk about it."

Thorne nodded. "She will."

"You, too." He waited until Thorne looked over. "All right?"

They sat in silence for a minute. There was still plenty of activity at the front of the house—vehicles coming and going every few minutes. Half a dozen spectators were crowded on the opposite side of the road, despite the best efforts of the uniforms to keep them away.

Thorne let out an empty laugh and smacked his hand against the steering wheel. "I told Lou I was going to get rid of this," he said.

"Your precious Beemer?" Hendricks said. "Bloody hell, that's a major concession."

Thorne's 1971 "Pulsar"-yellow BMW had been a cause of much amusement to many of his colleagues for a long time. Thorne called it "vintage." Dave Holland said that was just a euphemism for "knackered old rust-bucket."

"Promised I'd get something a bit more practical," Thorne said. He tugged at the collar of his jacket. "A family car, you know?"

Hendricks smiled. "You should still get rid of it," he said.

"We'll see."

Hendricks pointed to the front door, to the metal trolley that was emerging through it, being lifted down the step. "Here we go..."

They got out of the car and walked slowly across to the rear of the mortuary van. Hendricks talked quietly to one of the mortuary assistants, ran through arrangements for the following morning. Thorne watched as the trolley was raised on its concertina legs and the black body-bag was eased slowly into the vehicle.

Emily Walker.

Thorne glanced towards the onlookers: a teenager in a baseball cap shuffling his feet; an old woman, open-mouthed.

Not viable.

Three

LOUISE CALLED from a payphone in the Whittington at a little after 8 a.m. just as Thorne was on his way out of the door. He felt slightly guilty at having slept so well, and did not need to ask how her night had been.

She sounded more angry than upset. "They haven't done it yet."

"What?" Thorne dropped his bag then marched back into the sitting room, like he was searching for something to kick.

"There was some cock-up the first time it was scheduled, then they thought it would be late last night, so they told me there was no point in me going home."

"So when?"

"Any time now." There was some shouting nearby. She lowered her voice. "I just want it done."

"I know," Thorne said.

"I'm bloody starving, apart from anything else."

"Well, I can tell you where I'm off to this morning, if you like," Thorne said. "That should kill your appetite for a while."

"Sorry, I meant to ask," Louise said. "Was it a bad one?"

Thorne told her all about Emily Walker. As a detective inspector with the Kidnap Investigation Unit, Louise Porter was pretty much unshockable. Sometimes, she and Thorne talked about violent death and the threat of it as easily as other couples talked about bad days at the office. But there were some aspects of the Job that neither wanted to bring home, and while there was often black comedy to be shared in the grisliest of stories, they tended to spare each other the truly grim details.

Thorne did not hold back on this occasion.

When he had finished, Louise said, "I know what you're doing, and there's really no need."

"No need for what?" Thorne asked.

"To remind me there's people worse off than I am."

Two hours later, as unobtrusively as possible, Thorne reached into his pocket, took out his phone, and checked to make sure that it was switched to SILENT.

"I think we're ready."

There were times when you really didn't want a mobile going off.

The mortuary assistant drew back the sheet and invited Emily Walker's husband to step forward.

"Are you able to identify the body as that of your wife, Emily Anne Walker?"

The man nodded once and turned away.

"Can you say it, please?"

"Yes. That's my wife."

"Thank you."

The man was already at the door of the viewing suite, waiting to be let out. It was customary, after the formal identification, to invite the next of kin—should they so wish—to stay with their loved one for a while, but Thorne could see that there was little point on this occasion. Suffocation could do as much damage to a face as a blunt instrument. He couldn't blame George Walker for preferring to remember his wife as she had been when she was alive. Presuming, of course, that he wasn't the one responsible for her death.

Thorne watched Walker being led down the corridor by two uniformed officers—a man and a woman. He saw the slump of the man's shoulders, the arm of the female officer sliding around them, and remembered something Holland had said the day before: I've got no bloody idea what's happening inside their heads...

As if on cue, Dave Holland came strolling around the corner, looking surprisingly perky for someone about to attend a post-mortem. He joined Thorne just as Walker was turning onto the staircase and heading slowly up towards the street.

"I know you said you wanted him in later for a chat," Holland said. "But I reckon we can leave it awhile."

"Oh, you do?"

"He's still all over the shop, and we should really let him have a bit of time with his family."

It was at such moments that Thorne wished he had the ability to raise one eyebrow, like Roger Moore. He had to settle for sarcasm. "I'm listening, Sergeant."

Holland smiled. "We got a result with the curtain-twitchers."

"Let's have it."

"Old bloke across the road claims he saw someone coming out of there an hour or so before Emily's husband got home."

"And he's sure it wasn't Emily's husband."

"Positive. He knows George Walker by sight. The bloke he saw had a much narrower build, he says. Different color hair, too."

"You got him knocking us up an E-fit?"

Holland nodded. "Gets the husband off the hook, you ask me."

"I wasn't," Thorne said. "But it's a fair point. We'll have him in tomorrow."

A door opened halfway along the corridor and a familiar-looking shaved head appeared around it. "In your own time," Hendricks said.

Thorne nodded and loosened the tie he'd put on for the identification.

Holland wasn't looking quite so chirpy as they walked towards the open door.

Other places had different arrangements, but at Finchley Coroner's Mortuary a narrow corridor ran between the Viewing Suite and the Post-Mortem Room, so the bodies could be moved quickly and privately from one to the other. From soft furnishings and a comforting color scheme to a white-tiled room with stainless-steel units where comfort of any description was in short supply.

However much its occupants could have done with some.

Hendricks and Holland caught up a little, having been too busy for chit-chat the night before. Hendricks asked after Holland's daughter, Chloe, about whom he seemed to know more than Thorne did. Thorne found this rather depressing. He hadn't exactly been holding his breath when it came to Holland and his girlfriend choosing a godfather, but there had been a time when he'd sent presents and cards on birthdays and at Christmas.

Thorne listened to the pair of them rattling on—Holland telling Hendricks how big his daughter was getting, still only pushing four, and Hendricks saying what a fantastic age that was, while he moved the scissors and skull-key to within easy reach—and it niggled him. He was still trying to remember the date of the girl's birthday when Hendricks began removing Emily Walker's clothing.

Middle of September?

While Hendricks worked, he related his findings into the microphone hanging above his head. Holland made notes. This précis would be all the investigation had to go on until the full report arrived, but often it would be more than enough for the likes of Tom Thorne, until and if the likes of Phil Hendricks were given their chance to go through the details in court.

The science and the Latin...

"Major laceration to back of head, but no fracture to the skull or sign of significant brain injury."

When Thorne was not being called upon to concentrate, when it was just about observing medical procedures he'd seen far too many times before, he did his best to zone out. To block out the noise. He'd long since got used to the smell—meaty and sickly sweet—but the sounds always unnerved him.

"Damage to thyroid and cricoid cartilages... Major petechial hemorrhaging... Bloody froth caked around victim's mouth."

So, Thorne sang in his head. Hank Williams, Johnny Cash, Willie Nelson, whatever came to him. Just a chorus or two to take the edge off the bone-saw's whine and the solid snap of the rib-cutters. The gurgle in the windpipe and the sucking as the heart and lungs were removed from the chest as one single, dripping unit.

Ray Price today: "My Shoes Keep Walking Back to You."

"No indication of pregnancy... No signs of recent termination... Death due to manual asphyxia."

There's people worse off than I am.

Towards the end, with organs weighed and fluids collected, Thorne asked about time of death. When it came to finding a prime suspect, it often turned out to be the most important factor.

"Late afternoon," Hendricks said. "Best I can do."

"Before five?" Holland asked.

"Between three and four probably, but I'm not swearing to it right now."

"That fits." Holland scribbled something down. "Husband claims to have arrived home a little after five o'clock."

"He out of the picture, then?"

"Nobody's out of the picture," Thorne said.

"OK."

Thorne saw the expression on Hendricks' face, and on Holland's as he looked up from his notebook. "Sorry..."

He'd been looking at the stainless-steel dishes that now contained Emily Walker's major organs and thinking that she'd finally shifted those few extra pounds she'd been so worried about. His eyes had come to rest on her feet, bloated and pale; on the red nail varnish and the star above her ankle. When he'd spoken, he'd snapped without meaning to, the words sounding snide and spiky.

Holland looked at Hendricks, stage-whispered conspiratorially: "Wrong side of the bed."

Thorne could feel himself growing edgier by the minute. He told himself to calm down, but it didn't work, and walking out with Holland ten minutes later, he found it hard to control his breathing and the flush of it in his face. Sometimes, he felt fired-up coming out of a post-mortem, confused or just depressed more often than not, but he could not remember the last time he'd felt quite so bloody angry.

He had been turning his phone back on before he was out of the post-mortem room and by the time he emerged through the mortuary's main entrance onto Avondale Road, he could see that he had three missed calls from Louise. He told Holland he'd catch him up.

It was the voice she used when she'd been crying. "They've still not done it."

"Christ, you're kidding!"

"I don't know what to do," she said.

He turned away, looking across the North Circular and avoiding the stares from a couple at the bus-stop who had heard him shout. "What did they say to you?"

"I can't find anyone who can tell me what's going on."

"I'll be there in fifteen minutes," Thorne said.

She burst into tears as soon as she caught sight of him, pushing through the doors at the far end of the ward. He shushed her gently, drew the curtains around the bed and sat down to hold her.

"I just want it... out of me," she said. "Do you understand?"

"I know."

They heard the voice of the woman in the bed opposite coming from the other side of the curtain. "Is everything OK?"

"It's fine," Thorne said.

"Do you want me to get someone?"

Thorne leaned closer to Louise. "I'm going to get someone."

He prowled the corridors for five minutes until he found a doctor on the next floor up and told him that something needed to be done. After shouting for a minute or so then refusing to budge while the doctor made a couple of calls, Thorne was back at Louise's bedside with a soft-spoken Scottish nurse. She made all the right noises, then admitted there was nothing she could do.

"Not good enough," Thorne said.

"I'm sorry, but this is standard practice."

"What is?"

"Your partner's just been unlucky, I'm afraid." The nurse was flicking through the paperwork she'd brought with her. She waved it in Thorne's direction. "Each time the procedure has been scheduled, another case has taken priority at the last minute. Just unlucky..."

"She was promised it would be done last night," Thorne said. "Then first thing this morning."

Louise lay back on the pillow with her eyes closed. She looked exhausted. "Two hours ago they said I was next in."

"It's bloody ridiculous," Thorne said.

The nurse consulted her paperwork again, nodding when she found an explanation. "Yes, well, we had someone come in with a badly broken arm, I'm afraid, so—"

"A broken arm?"

The nurse looked at Thorne as though he were simple. "He was in a considerable amount of pain."

Thorne returned the look, then pointed at Louise. "You think she's enjoying herself?"

Alex was stuffing a last piece of toast into her mouth when Greg came into the kitchen. He nodded, still tucking in his shirt. She grunted, waved, and went back to the story she'd been reading in the *Guardian*.

"Hope you've left some bread," Greg said, flicking on the kettle. He heard another grunt as he walked to the bread-bin, then a mumbled request for an apology as he moved to the fridge. "Oh, right, as if you would have scoffed it all..." He scanned the inside of the fridge, looking in vain for a yoghurt he knew had been there the day before. Kieron, the flatmate who had moved out at the end of the previous year, had a habit of polishing off the last of the communal bread, milk or whatever, as well as eating stuff that had never been his in the first place. Now Alex was shaping up to be almost as bad. But Greg was more inclined to forgive his own sister, and she did leave the bathroom smelling a lot nicer than Kieron had done.

She pushed the paper away when he finally brought over his tea and toast and sat down. "You're going in early."

"Twelve o'clock lecture," Greg said. "Henry the sodding second. And it's not really what the rest of the world would call early."

"Feels early enough to me."

"What time did you get in?"

"I don't know," Alex said. "Not stupidly late. But a bunch of us ended up in some place in Islington where they were necking these lethal-looking vodka shots."

"They were necking?"

Alex grinned. "Fair enough, I necked a few." She pointed as Greg shook his head and slurped his tea. "You can't get all big brother-ish, matey. Not with some of the things you get up to."

Greg blushed, which annoyed him, then he got even more annoyed when Alex giggled knowingly and he blushed some more. "Look, you've only been here two weeks, that's all I'm saying." He cut her off when she opened her mouth. "And don't tell me to 'chillax' or whatever. You're not twelve."

"I'm making friends," she said.

"Well, you need to pace yourself. Oh yeah, and maybe do some work." He struck his chest theatrically. "I know, mental idea..."

"Like you said, I've only been here two weeks." She reached across, tried and failed to grab a piece of his toast. "And, you know... it's drama. It's not like there's a lot of work to do."

"How thrilled was the old man when you got a place here? When you told him you were moving in with me?"

She shrugged.

"And how pissed off would he be if he knew you were caning it every other night?"

Just when it looked as though Alex was about to shout, or storm off, she produced the same butter-wouldn't-melt smile she'd been turning on for eighteen years. "You're just jealous because you got lumbered with a proper course, with proper lectures," she said. "Henry the sodding second."

"Dull as fucking ditchwater," he said.

They both laughed, and she made another, more successful grab for the toast. Greg called her a sneaky bitch. Alex called him a tight-arse, then got up to make them both some more.

"You going to be in the Rocket tonight?"

Alex turned from the worktop, pulled a mock-horrified face. "After what you just said?"

"I'm just letting you know I'll probably be in there."

"Right. Probably." She pointed accusingly, with a knife smeared in butter and Marmite. The Rocket complex on Holloway Road was the student union of the Metropolitan University's north London campus. It was also home to one of the city's trendiest clubs and until very recently had not been a place her brother had been known to frequent very often. "That's three times this week."

"So?"

"Making a bit of a habit of it, aren't you?"

He shrugged. "The drink's cheap."

"Right, so it's not like you've got your eye on anyone, or anything like that?"

Greg blushed again and stood up. He told her he was running too late for more toast, that he needed to get ready. She shouted after him, told him he could eat it on the way. He shouted back: "Yeah, if I want to get killed..."

Five minutes later, he was wheeling his bike onto the pavement and doing his best to finish the toast Alex had thrust into his hand at the top of the stairs. That was often the way it went. However much their father thought Greg would be keeping an eye on his little sister, she was the one who usually ended up doing the looking after. Fussing and checking up on him, and generally behaving like the mother they didn't have.

As he climbed onto the bike and waited for a gap in the traffic, he glanced up and saw her waving from her bedroom window. She pressed her face against the glass like a child. He waved back and cycled away, heading for the Hornsey Road, the Emirates Stadium glorious against the gray sky ahead of him.

Greg raised a hand to wave again, in case Alex was still watching.

Unaware of the eyes on him.

On both of them.

Four

Though what was inside their heads remained largely a mystery to Dave Holland, he had seen the way that those directly affected by violent death could seem altered physically. It was as if they had been hollowed out by it; or, as in the case of George Walker, shrunken slightly. Walker was six two or three and thickset, but sitting opposite him in the Interview Room at Colindale station, Holland saw a man who seemed almost slight.

"Won't be too much longer," Holland said. "It really helps us to get everything down on tape, you know?"

The Murder Squad was based five minutes away at the Peel Centre, but the brown, three-story building that housed the offices was no more than the administrative HQ. While investigations were orchestrated from Becke House, officers needing the use of interview rooms, custody suites or good old-fashioned cells would usually make the short journey up the road to Colindale.

"Anything I can do," Walker said.

Holland nodded. He had no way of knowing what George Walker had sounded like before his wife was murdered, but now even his voice seemed small. "So, the day before yesterday, you came home at the usual time?"

"Twelve forty-five, give or take."

"And stayed for an hour or so."

Walker nodded, then said, "Yes, an hour," when Holland prompted him to speak for the benefit of the tape. He was a teacher at a school close to where he and his wife lived, and Holland had already established that he came home for lunch every day.

"School meals not got any better, then?"

"They're pretty good actually," Walker said. He'd been staring at the tabletop, picking at the edge of it with a thumbnail. Now, he looked up and directly at Holland. "I just enjoyed going home."

"Wish I could do the same," Holland said. "The canteen here's bloody atrocious—"

The door opened and Thorne walked in. Holland announced his entrance for the tape, then paused the recording while Thorne made his apologies to Walker for being late. Walker told him not to worry about it.

"Traffic's a nightmare," Thorne said.

He had popped into the Whittington en route and caught the tail-end of the Friday morning rush hour. They had finally performed the D and C the previous afternoon but had kept Louise in overnight. She had eaten an enormous breakfast and was in better spirits than at any time since she and Thorne had been told about the miscarriage. Thorne could not explain why, but it had made him oddly nervous.

"I just want to get home now," she had said.

He had told her he would do his best to pick her up at lunchtime, or to let her know if there was a problem.

In the Interview Room, once Thorne had sat down, Holland quickly filled him in on what had been covered so far, and they resumed recording George Walker's statement.

"Tell us about when you got back after school," Thorne said.

Walker cleared his throat. "It just felt wrong the minute I came through the door," he said.

"Wrong?"

"Different..."

"This would have been what time?"

"Just before five," Walker said. "I run a chess club after school on a Wednesday. Otherwise it would have been earlier."

Thorne glanced over at Holland, made sure he saw the significance, then nodded to Walker to continue.

"I caught a whiff of something, which was...the blood, obviously. There was a vase on the floor in the hall, and water everywhere. She must have tried to fight him off, don't you think?"

"We're still trying to put it all together," Holland said.

"So, I was calling Emily's name out in the hall, and then I walked into the kitchen. Well, you saw it."

"And you phoned us straight away, didn't you?" Thorne glanced down at his notes, although he knew the time very well. "We've got the call to the emergency services logged at four fifty-six. You sounded very calm."

"Did I? I think I was just in shock." Walker shook his head, breathed noisily for ten seconds, then said, "I can't even remember calling."

"What about afterwards?" Thorne asked. "Do you remember running out into the street? Knocking on your next-door neighbor's door and shouting about the blood?"

More shaking of the head. "Sort of." Walker's voice dropped to a whisper. "I can't remember exactly what I said...shouted. I can remember my throat being sore afterwards and not knowing why. I was kneeling down with Emily by then, waiting for someone to come. It seemed to be taking ages, you know?" The tears were coming now, but Walker did not seem bothered. He casually lowered his head and pushed them away with the heel of his hand when he needed to. "I really wanted to touch her," he said. "I knew I shouldn't, because it would mess up the evidence or whatever. Seen too many of those TV shows, I think. But I just wanted to hold her hand for a few minutes. To reach inside that bag and tuck her hair behind her ear."

Holland looked hard at Thorne until he got the nod. "Do you want to take a few minutes, Walker?" He pushed back his chair, mumbled something about finding some tissues.

"Actually, I think we can leave it there," Thorne said.

Walker nodded, the gratitude evident in his eyes before he closed them.

As soon as Holland had stopped the tape, Thorne was out of his chair and moving towards the door. "Right, let's see if we can get you a cab organized."

Walker rose slowly to his feet. "The hardest thing was telling Emily's dad," he said. "After what happened to Emily's mother, I mean." He turned to look at Thorne. "How bloody unlucky can one family get?"

"Sorry, I'm not with you," Thorne said.

Walker seemed confused. He looked at Holland, who shook his head to indicate that he was every bit as in the dark.

"Oh, I thought you must have known," Walker said. "My wife's mother was murdered herself, fifteen years ago. Emily's maiden name was Sharpe."

Thorne could do no more than say "sorry" again. As a matter of course, Emily Walker's name had been run through the CRIMINT system to see if she had a criminal history, but there was nothing on record. A tragedy in her family's past would certainly not have been considered relevant criminal intelligence.

Walker was still looking from Thorne to Holland and back, as though he were expecting the name he had mentioned to be recognized. He reached for his jacket and, when he spoke, it was clear he was well used to what he was saying being the end of a conversation.

"She was one of Raymond Garvey's."

They watched Walker's taxi pull away, and began walking in the other direction, back towards the Peel Centre. It wasn't quite ten yet. The morning was mild, but there was the lightest drizzle in the air.

"I made a call before he came in," Holland said. "He was back at school by two. Didn't leave until a quarter to five. I can talk to Hendricks again if you like, double-check to see if he's sure about the timings."

"Don't bother," Thorne said.

They picked up the pace a little in an effort to stay as dry as possible.

"I was thinking about him going back to school after he'd had his lunch," Holland said. "Suddenly had this image of the killer watching him leave, marching straight up and ringing the doorbell. Emily opening it, thinking her old man had forgotten something."

Thorne shook his head. "Times still don't fit."

"Just had that image, you know?"

They walked on, turning left onto Aerodrome Road and falling into step within a few paces.

"I think you were right the other night," Thorne said. "It's somebody she knew. Not well . . . not necessarily, anyway. Maybe he works in a local shop, does next-door's garden, whatever."

"A face she recognizes."

"That's all he needs to be. You heard what Walker said about if it had been a different day. Sounds like whoever killed Emily had been watching, and for a while. He knew their movements, knew when the time was right."

"So he targeted her?"

"Looks that way. He wasn't just ringing doorbells until someone answered that he liked the look of."

"Why Emily, though?" Holland asked.

Thorne looked sideways at him and Holland acknowledged the stupidity of asking the question now, when they had so little to go on. When there were a thousand answers, and none at all. They both knew that the true answer, if they ever found it, would almost certainly give them their best chance of catching whoever had killed Emily Walker. At that moment, Thorne could do no better than a muttered "Christ knows," before jogging across the road and walking quickly towards the main gate.

"That's weird though, isn't it, this Garvey business?" Holland was doing his best to keep up, a few feet behind Thorne. "Before my time, but shit . . . that was a big case, wasn't it?"

Ahead of him, Thorne was waving his ID at the officer inside the control box.

"Did you work on it?"

Half a minute later, it was Holland's turn to wait, light rain blowing into his face, while his warrant card was checked. Thorne was already twenty feet clear of the barrier and moving across the car-park towards Becke House. He didn't appear to have heard Holland's question.

* * *

Thorne had worked on the Raymond Garvey investigation, though not in any significant way. He'd knocked on a few doors, been part of a fingertip-search team one night. At the time, it was the biggest investigation for a decade or more, with hundreds of detectives working to catch a man who would eventually murder seven women. There can't have been too many officers in the Met who had not been involved in some capacity.

Inside Becke House, Thorne walked into the lift and jabbed the button for the third floor, thinking back.

He was an up-the-sergeant's-arse, eager-to-please detective constable back then. Kentish Town CID, the station no more than five minutes' walk from where he lived now.

The lift doors were stubbornly refusing to close, so Thorne stabbed at the button again. He was ashamed that he could remember every detail of a blue suit he used to wear back then and the number plate of the car he'd been driving around in, but not the names of Raymond Garvey's victims.

The door finally slid shut.

Not a single one...

He told himself that it was always the way, especially with a series of killings. How many of Dennis Nilsen's fifteen victims could he name, or Colin Ireland's five? Could he remember any of Harold Shipman's two hundred or more?

Out of the lift, he walked down the corridor, past the Major Incident Room and towards the small office he shared with DI Yvonne Kitson.

It was different with his own cases, of course. He could remember every name, every face; each "before" and "after" photograph. Her mother's name might not have been as instantly familiar as it should have been, but Thorne knew he would never forget Emily Walker's.

Kitson had left a note on his desk about a case that was due in court the following week and some evidence that needed chasing up. Thorne laid it to one side and pulled the computer keyboard towards him. All the way back from Colindale, he had been wondering where the Garvey case notes would have been archived. Now, he decided there was a far quicker way to do a bit of research.

Thorne hit a few keys and logged on to Google. Typed in "Raymond Garvey."

There were over three hundred and fifty thousand hits.

He scrolled past the first half a dozen links, ignoring Wikipedia and something called serialkiller.com, until he found a site that was not advertising a magazine or true-crime shows on satellite TV and seemed more or less reliable. He looked at the list of names. Susan Sharpe, aged forty-four, was number four. She had been attacked on her way home from a gym, bludgeoned to death, as had all the other victims, and been found on a canal bank in Kensal Green, the vast mausoleums and elaborate statuary of its famous cemetery spread out alongside. Thorne clicked on the name and brought up a picture. He saw no immediate resemblance to Emily Walker, then reminded himself that he had never seen Emily alive.

Raymond Anthony Garvey had murdered seven women in four months. He might have killed many more had he not been arrested after a simple pub brawl in Finsbury Park. Had a sample of his DNA taken after that incident not matched that found on two of the victims. It was the kind of coincidence that would have crime-fiction writers accused of laziness, but good luck played a bigger part in cracking such cases than most senior police officers would care to admit.

Garvey, who always refused to talk about his motives, was given five consecutive life sentences, and was told by the judge that he would die in prison. That happened a lot sooner than anyone expected, as he was diagnosed with a brain tumor twelve years into his sentence and succumbed to it six months later.

Thorne looked again at the picture of Raymond Garvey—the bland, blissful stare of an ordinary psychopath—before highlighting the names of the women he had murdered. Just after he'd clicked PRINT, the door opened and Russell Brigstocke walked in.

The DCI dropped his sizeable backside onto the edge of Thorne's desk and glanced at the images on the computer screen. He nudged at his glasses. "Holland told me about that. What are the bloody chances?" He pushed his fingers through what had once been a pretty impressive quiff, but was now getting decidedly thin.

"Yeah." Thorne knew that his own appearance had changed just as much. There was still more gray hair on one side than the other, but a lot more of it everywhere. He logged out of the website, Garvey's face giving way to a blue screen and a Met Police logo: the reassuring words "Working Together for a Safer London."

"Thirty-six hours into this one already, Tom," Brigstocke said. "Where are we?"

The DCI could interpret Tom Thorne's expressions and his curt body language as well as anyone. He recognized the twitch in the shoulder that meant "Nowhere." The puff of the cheeks that said, "Barring our killer handing himself in, you won't be standing outside Colindale station making triumphant announcements to the press anytime soon."

"What's happening with the FSS?" Thorne asked.

The Forensic Science Service lab in Victoria was busy examining all the trace evidence gathered from the crime scene: hairs, fibers, fingerprints. They were analyzing the bloodstain pattern in the hope of creating an accurate reconstruction of the crime. They were trying to identify the fragment of celluloid found clutched in Emily Walker's hand.

"I'm chasing," Brigstocke said. "Same as I always am. Tomorrow, with a following wind, but more likely Sunday."

"What about the E-fit?"

"Have you seen it?"

Thorne nodded. The curtain-twitching neighbor had clearly not witnessed as much, or in as much detail, as he had first claimed. "I'm not holding my breath," he said.

"Right. I don't think it's going to help us a great deal either, but what do I know? Jesmond wanted it out there on the hurry-up, so it's out. It's in the *Standard* today, and some of the nationals. *London Tonight,* too."

Brigstocke was every bit as transparent as Thorne himself, and Thorne caught the roll of the eyes that translated as, "Waste of fucking time." Of course, Superintendent Trevor Jesmond would want the E-fit distributed as widely as possible, to show that his team was making progress. It did not seem to concern him as much as it should—with a picture of the killer that looked as though it had been drawn by a chimpanzee—that precious time and manpower would now be wasted taking, logging and filing hundreds of pointless calls, mental or plain misguided, proclaiming that the person the police were looking for was everyone from the man next door to Johnny Depp.

The superintendent's overriding concern was always how he came across on screen or in print. He would be doing his bit to camera outside Colindale station later that day. He would dispense the simple, shocking facts, emphasizing the brutality and the horror of what had been done to Emily Walker and letting it be known that any steps necessary would be taken to bring her killer to justice.

Thorne had to give the man his due. He couldn't catch a council-tax dodger if his life depended on it, but he did righteous indignation pretty damn well.

"It's someone she knew," Thorne said. "Someone who'd been watching. She'd seen him around, spoken to him, whatever."

Brigstocke nodded. "Let's get bodies into every shop she went to regularly, the nearest supermarket, the gym she visited. Let's take a good hard look at friends and workmates. Interview all the neighbors again."

"Phil reckons he came prepared." Thorne picked up the post-mortem report that Hendricks had delivered the previous afternoon, flicked through it. "I've got a feeling he'd been 'preparing' for a while."

Brigstocke groaned. "How bloody long have I been doing this?" he said. "And yet hearing stuff like that still depresses me." He eased himself up from Thorne's desk and walked to the window. "I mean, I'm not saying it would be any better if her old man had caught her playing away from home and smacked her over the head with something. I know she wouldn't be any less dead. But Jesus..."

"It should depress you," Thorne said. "When it doesn't—"

"I know, time to retire."

"You turn into Trevor Jesmond."

Brigstocke smiled. He picked up the piece of paper that had been spewing from the printer when he'd walked in. He looked down at the list of seven names. "This anything we should be looking at?"

"Don't see why," Thorne said. "Garvey died in prison three years ago."

Brigstocke flapped the sheet of paper, as though he were fanning himself. "Just one of those freaky things."

The DCI nodded his understanding. The pair of them had worked a case only a few months before in which a man had been beaten to death in front of his family after confronting a noisy neighbor. It transpired that twenty years earlier, and only two streets away, exactly the same thing had happened to that victim's father.

"One of many," Thorne said.

As it turned out, with a briefing that overran by twenty minutes and a Crown Prosecution Service lawyer who refused to get off the phone, lunchtime would have been a tricky time for Thorne to get away. But by then it did not matter: Louise had already called to say that she would be making her own way back to the flat. That she felt OK and needed to get out.

Driving back at the end of the day, Thorne felt nervous, as though he and Louise had had an argument. He ran through the conversations they might have when he got home, but they all went out of his head the moment he stepped into the silent flat. When he saw her lying on her side in the darkened bedroom.

"It's OK," she said. "I'm not asleep."

It was only eight o'clock, but Thorne got undressed and climbed in beside her. They lay still for a while, listening to a motorbike revving up in the street outside, and a song Thorne couldn't quite place drifting down from the flat upstairs.

"Do you remember the Garvey killings?" he asked.

She grunted and he wondered if he had woken her up, then she said, "I was at college, I think. Why?"

Thorne told her about Susan Sharpe. How a mother and daughter had been murdered, fifteen years apart. It was quiet now upstairs and Thorne still wasn't sure what the song had been.

"You're doing it again," Louise said. "Trying to make me feel better."

"I wasn't, I swear."

"And all you've succeeded in doing is making yourself feel old."

Thorne laughed, for the first time in a few days. He pushed up close behind her and slid his arm across her stomach. After a few seconds he felt awkward and began to wonder if she would want it there, so he took it away again.

Five

As PER the standard system of rotas and rest days, Thorne spent seven Saturdays out of every eight at home. Normally, a Saturday morning would be taken up with sleeping far later than usual, nipping out for a newspaper then coming home for a gloriously unhealthy breakfast. Since Louise had come into his life, these were no longer always solitary activities, and thankfully the same was true of the sex, which could occasionally be squeezed in between the fry-up and *Football Focus*.

This Saturday, three days after Emily Walker's murder, all rest days had been canceled and overtime approved where necessary. Thorne sat in his office at Becke House, not looking through statements, ignoring the reports on the desk in front of him, wondering instead if the possibility of sex had now become remote.

When would it be all right to talk about it? Just how much of a self-centered bastard was he being, even thinking about it?

He looked over to the desk opposite, where Yvonne Kitson was working considerably harder than he was. She had been taken off a domestic murder that was all but done and dusted, and drafted in to bolster the top end of the team. Thorne was grateful to have her on board. Kitson was one of the best detectives they had, her achievements that much more impressive considering her circumstances, past and present. For several years she had been a single mother of two, her marriage having collapsed after a messy affair with a senior colleague that had also resulted in her formerly smooth progress through the ranks coming to a shuddering halt.

She glanced up from her desk, saw Thorne looking. She dropped her eyes again, turned a page. "What?"

Once, when neither had been laid for a while and it was debatable which was the more drunk, there had been the mildest of flirtations between the two of them, but they were long past that.

"Saturday," Thorne said.

Kitson scoffed: "Never mind the bloody Tottenham game, or a morning under the duvet with Louise, or whatever you were thinking about missing. Some of us should be watching our sons playing rugby. I'll have to be even more of a taxi service than I am already to make up for this."

For a few moments, Thorne thought about telling her what had happened to Louise, getting a female perspective on it. But he just smiled and went back to the reports in front of him.

A minute later, a ball of paper bounced off his desktop and onto the floor. He bent to retrieve it and stared at Kitson. She shrugged, denying all knowledge.

Thorne unwrapped what turned out to be a transcript of that morning's calls to the Incident Room. The published E-fit had generated a good deal of attention, and while the Press Office was handling the understandable media interest, the team itself had to deal with any information from the public. Thorne and Brigstocke had clearly underestimated the extent to which the picture would inspire some of the city's more community-minded nutcases.

"I wouldn't mind coming in," Kitson said, pointing to the sheet of paper in Thorne's hand, "if I didn't have to spend all morning sorting through that shit."

"Got to be done, though," Thorne said.

They all knew it. Everyone on the team routinely joked about procedure and bitched about paper-pushing, and 99 percent of the time, with a primary lead as shaky as their E-fit, nothing would come from this kind of work, but you had to double- and triple-check, just in case. Nobody wanted to be the one who missed the vital piece of information tucked away in a long list of crank calls. The clue hidden in the crap. In an age where the inquiry into the inquiry was commonplace, arse-covering had become second nature. It began before the victim was cold and would continue until the judge's gavel came down.

It didn't stop the whingeing, though.

"Not a single name on there more than once," Kitson said.

"You're wrong." Thorne ran his finger down the list, stopping to beckon Holland inside when he saw his face come around the door. "Three different people phoned to let us know they think it looks like the bloke who runs the garage in *EastEnders*."

"We should arrest him anyway," Kitson said. "For crimes against acting."

Thorne looked up at Holland.

"Had a call I think you might be interested in," Holland said.

"Don't tell me. The killer looks like someone in Emmerdale."

Holland dropped a scrap of paper onto Thorne's desk: a scribbled name and number. "He's a DI in Leicester. Someone up there saw Jesmond on TV last night talking about the Walker murder and thought it sounded familiar."

"Sounded what?"

"So, this DI was calling to check the details we didn't give out to the press. See if they matched up with a murder they caught a few weeks back."

"That doesn't sound good," Kitson said.

Thorne was already dialing...

Once the pleasantries were out of the way, DI Paul Brewer told Thorne that the body of Catherine Burke, a nurse aged twenty-three, had been discovered three weeks earlier in the flat she had shared with her boyfriend, on a quiet street behind Leicester City's football ground.

She had been struck on the back of the head with a heavy ornament and then suffocated with a plastic bag.

"It was the suffocation bit that got the old antennae twitching," Brewer said, the East Midlands accent not as thick as Thorne had been expecting.

"When your superintendent mentioned it on the box. Wasn't me that saw it, but as soon as I heard I thought it would be worth following up. You know, just to make sure." He sounded pleased with himself. "Looks like I was spot on."

"Three weeks ago, you said?"

"Right."

"And?"

A chuckle. "And . . . brick wall, mate. We've got a description of a bloke she was seen talking to outside the hospital the day before, but we've had sweet FA off that. She was an occasional drug user, tablets mostly, nicked them from her own hospital as it turned out, but that's led us nowhere. To be honest, it was all going stone cold until your one turned up."

"Stroke of luck," Thorne said.

Brewer said something else, but Thorne was too busy mouthing obscenities at Kitson and Holland.

"What about forensics?"

"That was the easy bit," Brewer said. "Looks like she scratched him when he had the bag over her head. We dug plenty of blood and skin from under her nails, so we can match the bastard up as soon as we make an arrest."

Thorne scribbled "GOT DNA" on the piece of paper and pushed it across the desk for Holland and Kitson to see.

"You still there?"

"So, how are we going to work this?" Thorne asked.

"Not a clue, mate," Brewer said. "I know it won't be anything to do with me, so it don't matter what I think. My guv'nor's probably on the phone to your guv'nor as we speak, carving it up. Politics, budgets, all that shit. We just do what we're told, right?"

"Right . . ."

"Just so you know . . . I'm not bothered about territory, anything like that," Brewer said. "No need to worry about any of that crap. We can sort out who gets the credit once we've caught him, fair enough?"

Thorne knew that, whatever opinion he was rapidly forming about DI Paul Brewer—Job-pissed and probably disliked by all his colleagues—he was going to have to get along with him. He thanked him for his help, praising his initiative and insisting that the credit would most definitely go where it was due. He called him "Paul" as often as he could manage without gagging, promising him a night on the town when they eventually got together and trying to sound pleased when Brewer promised to take him up on the offer.

"It's from an X-ray, by the way," Brewer said.

"What is?"

"The piece of plastic in her hand." Brewer sounded pleased with himself again. He waited. "There was a piece of plastic, right?"

"An X-ray of what?"

"They can't tell us that just yet. There's a few letters and numbers on it but they can't make sense of them. If we're lucky, your piece might help."

When Thorne looked up he saw the expressions of confusion from Holland and Kitson who had only heard his side of the conversation.

"X-ray?" Kitson whispered.

Thorne put a hand over the mouthpiece, told them he'd be another minute. Brewer was saying he was on his way into a meeting but that he'd try to call again later. That his was a large Scotch and water.

"Just before you go," Thorne said. "Is Catherine's mother still alive?"

"What?"

"Her mother."

"No. Both parents dead, and an elder brother who was killed in a car accident a few years ago. Took us a while to trace a blood relative."

"How did she die?"

"Sorry?"

"How did the mother die, and when?"

"No idea," Brewer said.

"Could you find out and get back to me?"

"I suppose so."

"Cheers, Paul, I appreciate it. What kind of Scotch do you like?"

"What's all this about?"

"Probably nothing," Thorne said. He looked up and locked eyes with Kitson. "Just covering my arse."

* * *

Brewer had phoned back a few minutes before the briefing was due to start, and apologized for taking so long. He told Thorne that he'd spoken to Catherine Burke's boyfriend, who had confirmed that her mother had died of cancer when Catherine was a young girl. Thorne had thanked him, unable to decide if he felt disappointed or relieved.

"Oh, and by the way, any single malt will do nicely," Brewer had said.

Thorne passed the news on to Brigstocke outside the door of the Briefing Room as the troops were filing in. The DCI glanced up from the notes he had been working on for the last hour.

"Worth a try," he said.

Thorne watched as unfamiliar faces drifted past; nodded to one or two of those drafted in quickly from other teams. "So, how's this going to pan out?"

"We take it from here," Brigstocke said.

"Really?"

"Well, no, not officially, but in terms of money and manpower we're way more capable of doing it than they are. So, off the record, we get to run things."

"And off the record, what happens if we mess up?"

"Then, obviously, it was always a fifty–fifty operation and the blame for any operational glitches gets shared out equally."

"Sounds fair," Thorne said.

Inside, it was standing room only. Muttered conversation no more than the preferred alternative to silence. One phone call had changed the complexion of the case entirely and suddenly the atmosphere was as charged as Thorne could remember in a while.

There weren't too many like this.

Loss of life was never treated lightly, not if you looked beyond the banter and the off-color jokes to what was in the eyes of the men and women at a crime scene. Thorne had met clever murderers and profoundly stupid ones. Those who had lost it and lashed out and those who had enjoyed themselves. Some had made him angry enough to come close to murder himself, while for others he had felt nothing but pity.

There were as many shades of killer as there were ways to end a life, but while it was Thorne's job to catch them, the murderer was always taken seriously.

And when he murdered more than once...

"Right, thanks for gathering so quickly," Brigstocke said. "There's a lot to get through."

From the back of the room, Thorne watched the notebooks open, heard fifty ballpoints click. He glanced at the door as a handful of latecomers hurried in, half expecting to see Superintendent Trevor Jesmond make a well-timed and inspirational appearance.

"As some of you know already, we received a call this morning that has changed the focus of the Emily Walker inquiry. I've spent most of the day since then on the phone to various senior officers from the Leicestershire constabulary..."

While Brigstocke spoke, Thorne thought about control; the exercise of it. Emily Walker's killer had been meticulous in his preparation, in waiting to make his move and in the use of the bag to suffocate her. Now, there was every reason to believe that the same man was responsible for the death of Catherine Burke. She too had been discovered at home, with no sign of forced entry, so it seemed likely that he had planned her murder every bit as carefully as Emily Walker's.

A man who waited and watched and then killed twice in three weeks.

"So, the investigations into these two killings will proceed separately for the time being," Brigstocke said. "With as much cooperation between ourselves and the boys in Leicester as is required..."

Thorne felt his mouth go dry. Twice in three weeks...as far as they knew.

"...and if, as seems likely, they turn out to be linked, then we will have the necessary protocols in place."

By and large, the briefing was about practicalities from then on, as Brigstocke outlined the way forward. Neither force would want to risk the other screwing up their investigations, so it had been agreed that each would have "read only" access to the other's HOLMES (Home Office Large Major Enquiry System) account. As the Met team's office manager, DS Sam Karim would be responsible for all case information inputted into their account and for liaising daily with his opposite number in Leicester.

"Not a problem," Karim said.

"Especially not if his other half's a 'she,'" someone added.

It was a "delicate" situation, Brigstocke said, and "potentially fraught," but he trusted his team could handle it.

If his team needed any more reasons to try to make things work, Brigstocke waited until the end to give them the best one of all. He nodded, then turned to the screen behind him as the lights were flicked off. Many in the room had seen the picture of Emily Walker, but none save Brigstocke and his DIs had seen the photo of Catherine Burke that had been emailed across a few hours earlier.

The pictures had been taken from different angles, but projected next to one another, the similarity was evident... and horrifying. Though the limbs were splayed differently and there was a little more blood in one bag than the other, Thorne guessed that all eyes in the room would be drawn, eventually, to the faces. To the shock and desperation etched into each woman's chalk-white skin, just visible through plastic fogged with her dying breath.

When he had finished talking, Brigstocke left the lights out and waited for each officer to walk out past the pictures on the screen.

Thorne was the last to leave.

"They're nothing like each other physically," he said. Brigstocke turned and the two detectives stood in the semi-dark, staring at the screen. "So, if we're looking for a connection, it's not like he's got a type."

"If it's the same killer," Brigstocke said.

"You think it might not be?"

"I'm just saying we don't know for sure."

"Come on, Russell, look at them..."

Brigstocke gave it a few more moments, then turned away, walked across the room and switched the lights back on. "The forensics report came in," he said. "I haven't had a chance to go through it properly, but they're confirming that the celluloid fragment is a piece cut out from an X-ray." He continued before Thorne could ask the obvious question. "No, they don't know what it is either, but there are some very decent prints on it and they're not Emily's. We've got DNA, too. Some hairs on her sweater. Might not be the killer's, of course, but we've eliminated the husband, so if our sample matches the one from Catherine Burke..."

"They'll match," Thorne said.

"Sounds like you're counting on it."

"He's got plans, this bloke," Thorne said. "It's probably the only way we're going to catch him."

"As long as we do."

Thorne leaned back against the wall and stared at the dozens of empty chairs. Already the men and women who had just left them would be settling down at computers and picking up phones; doing everything that could reasonably be done. But Thorne was beginning to sense that real progress was going to depend on the man they were after giving them something more to work with.

"I might be wrong," Thorne said. "It might be piss-easy. One look at the stuff these Leicester boys have got and everything could get sorted."

"Christ, I hope so," Brigstocke said.

Thorne hoped so too, but he could not shake the feeling that this was one of those cases where a break would mean another body.

Six

THORNE PICKED up a takeaway from the Bengal Lancer on his way home. He hadn't bothered phoning ahead with the order, had looked forward to the cold bottle of Kingfisher, the complimentary poppadoms and the chat with the manager while he was waiting.

Louise was slumped in front of some celebrity ice-skating program when he got back. She seemed happy enough, a fair way into a bottle of red wine.

"Every cloud," she said. She raised her glass as though she were toasting something. "Nice to have a drink again."

Thorne went through to the kitchen, began dishing up the food. He shouted through to the living room, "You should," then pushed the empty cartons down into the bin.

When he turned round, Louise was standing in the doorway. "Should what?"

"Should... have a drink... if you want. Relax a bit."

"Get pissed, you mean?"

Thorne licked sauce off his fingers, stared at her. "I didn't mean anything, Lou..."

She walked back into the living room and, after a moment, he followed her with the plates. They sat on the floor with their backs against the sofa, eating off their laps. Thorne poured himself what was left of the wine; a little over half a glass.

"Whoever killed the woman in Finchley," he said. "Looks like he's done it before."

Louise chewed for a few more seconds. "That Garvey thing you told me about?"

"Well, that girl, yeah. She's not his first."

"Shit..."

"Right, all I need."

She shrugged, swallowed. "Might be exactly what you need."

The food was as good as always: rogan josh and a creamy mutter paneer; mushroom bhaji, pilau rice and a peshwari nan to share. Louise ate quickly, helping herself to the lion's share of the bread. Almost done, she moved her fork slowly through the last few grains of yellow rice. "Sounds like you're going to be busy."

Thorne glanced across, searching in vain for something in her face that might give him a clue as to how she felt about it. He hedged his bets. "It's a hell of a big team, so we'll have to see."

"OK..."

"Listen, shall I open some more wine?"

"I really don't mind."

Thorne looked again and saw nothing to contradict what she'd said. He carried the plates back to the kitchen and fetched another bottle. They settled down on the sofa and watched TV in silence for a few minutes, Louise laughing more readily than Thorne when a former glamour model went sprawling on the ice. Once the show had finished, Thorne flicked through the channels, finally settling on a repeat of *The Wild Geese,* a film he had always loved. They watched Richard Burton, Roger Moore and Richard Harris charging about in the African bush, the three just about believable as aging mercenaries.

"I talked to Phil," Thorne said. "I meant to say."

"Did you tell him what happened?"

"I didn't have to." Thorne waited to see if she would pick up on it, say something about having confided in Hendricks about the pregnancy. "He said you should call him, you know, if you want to talk."

"I spoke to him last night," she said.

"Oh, right."

"He was really sweet."

On the television, Harris was begging Burton to shoot him before he was hacked to death by the enemy, but the shouting and gunfire were little more than background noise.

"Why did you tell him you were pregnant?" Thorne asked. "I thought we'd agreed to keep it a secret."

Louise stared into her glass. "I knew he'd be chuffed."

"We decided we wouldn't, though, just in case this happened."

"Right, well, it has happened, OK? So arguing about whether I should or shouldn't have told anyone is a bit pointless now, don't you think?" She shuffled along the sofa, a foot or so away from him, and lowered her voice. "Christ, it's not like Phil's going to run around announcing it."

There were a few grains of rice and some crumbs on the carpet. Thorne inched away in the other direction and started picking them up, collecting them in his palm.

"I honestly wouldn't have minded if you'd told anyone," Louise said.

"I did think about it."

"Who would you have told?"

Thorne smiled. "Probably Phil."

They moved back to each other and Thorne asked if she'd mind if he turned off the TV and put a CD on. Normally she might have rolled her eyes and insisted that it was one of hers, or repeated a joke she'd heard from Holland or Hendricks about Thorne's dubious taste in music. Tonight she was happy enough to nod and stretch out. Thorne put on a Gram Parsons anthology and returned to the sofa, lifted up Louise's legs and slid in underneath. They listened to "Hearts on Fire" and "Brass Buttons," poured out what was left of the wine.

"So, what did Phil say?"

"Stuff you'd expect, really," Louise said. "How there's usually a good reason for these things and how the body knows what it's doing. Knows when there's something wrong." She took a healthy slurp of wine and was struggling suddenly to keep a straight face.

"What?"

"He said it might well have been because the baby was going to look like you." She was laughing now. "That a miscarriage was the preferred option."

"Cheeky bastard."

"He made me laugh," she said, closing her eyes. "I needed that."

She began to drift off soon after that and Thorne was not too far behind. He was sound asleep before ten-thirty, with Gram and Emmylou singing "Brand New Heartache," the clink of cutlery from the kitchen as Elvis licked the plates clean, and Louise's feet in his lap.

The band playing at the Rocket earlier that evening had been fantastic, easily as good as any of the so-called indie bands Alex had heard in the charts recently. They had something to say, and decent songs, and there was a bit more about them than the right kind of skinny jeans and nice arses. Of course, it didn't hurt that the guitarist was a dead ringer for the lead singer from Razorlight...

She loved the heat and the noise; how it felt being in a crowd. She'd been soaked in sweat each time she'd gone outside for a cigarette, and shivering by the time she'd finished it. Afterwards, when the band had packed up, they'd set up some decks and the dance music had started. Some of her friends had stayed on, and were still there as far as she knew, but she'd been about ready to head home by then.

What was it Greg had said about caning it?

She pushed open the door to the flat and listened for voices.

Alex had seen her brother earlier in the bar, but only for a few minutes. Long enough for him to tell her he'd rather die than watch a band called The Bastard Thieves, and for her to clock the figure with whom he was exchanging the lingering, lustful stares. There'd been no sign of him once the gig had finished, but she wasn't surprised.

She guessed he'd decided to get an early night.

There were lights on upstairs, but she couldn't hear anything and wondered if perhaps she'd interrupted something. If they'd heard her coming in and were lying there in Greg's bed, giggling and whispering to each other.

She climbed the stairs, singing softly to herself and keeping a good grip of the handrail. At the top, she threw her coat across the banister then stood there for a few moments, pissed and stupidly gleeful.

Then she crept along the corridor to Greg's door.

There was no light coming from underneath. She pressed her ear to the flaking wood, but couldn't hear anything: no giggles and certainly no creaking bed-springs. She reached down and slowly turned the handle. The door was locked.

Alex turned and walked back towards the kitchen, her steps not quite as gentle as she thought they were, trying to decide if she could be bothered making the cheese on toast she was suddenly craving.

She felt genuinely pleased for Greg, and hoped, even if it turned out to be no more than a one-night stand, that he at least enjoyed himself. That he took full advantage.

Her brother did not get lucky very often.

MY JOURNAL

28 September

I'm tired, of course, more or less all the time, because there's an awful lot of rushing about, keeping all the balls in the air, but when each new challenge has been successfully met, when a tick goes next to a name, there's a buzz which makes me forget how wiped out I am and makes every ounce of blood, sweat and tears worth it.
And there's been plenty of all three!
I was thinking earlier about something my father said. He told me once that setting goals and achieving them had been the only thing that had got him through some of the tougher times towards the end. Reading a book all the way through, finishing a crossword, whatever. Obviously, bearing in mind his situation, they were small things, things which the rest of the world would take for granted, but they meant a hell of a lot to him at that time. These goals I've set for myself are rather grander, I can see that. A bit more difficult to set up and pull off. But, Christ, the feeling when it all comes together is like nothing on earth. After it's done—even though I'm already thinking about the other places I need to be and the people I need to be when I get there—I just feel so fired-up and full of it. So desperate to get back and get the words down, to describe how it all went, that I'm scribbling away on these pages before I've even bothered to wash off the blood.

* * *

"Journal," not "diary," and that's deliberate. A collection of thoughts and ideas and reflections on this weird bloody world. How we end up where we are. Something to be read one day and hopefully enjoyed. Not just what I had for breakfast or watched on TV or any of that.

* * *

The brother and sister thing could not have gone a lot better.
Students have it pretty bloody easy, if you ask me. I know they moan about paying back loans and all that, but most of them seem happy

enough to spend every night in the bar getting wasted. It's an easier life than most, I reckon. Actually, the brother wasn't much of a party animal, not like some of them, but after a while it wasn't the drink he was coming back for anyway.

He wasn't hard to tempt!

I could see straight away what he'd be attracted to. Just holding the stare for a few seconds longer than normal. The whole "bit of rough" thing. By the time he plucked up the courage to come over and say anything, it was a done deal and we were on the way back to his place quickly enough after that.

The sister had made breakfast for the two of us. I found the tray outside his door afterwards. That was sweet, I have to admit. She knocked first, then I heard the door open and the slap of her bare feet on the stripped floorboards.

He was face down and I was lying across the bed, naked but with the sheet covering the things she didn't need to see. I knew she'd stopped, was taking it all in, trying to make sense of what she was seeing, work out what had happened. It was really hard to stay still, to control my breathing as much as I needed to.

I heard her say her brother's name and "Oh my God" a few times. Whisper it.

She went to her brother first and touched him, his shoulder or arm. I heard her breath catch and she started to cry and, when I knew she was looking down at me, I opened my eyes.

Bang! Like a dead man coming back to life.

I stared straight up into her baby blues, all wet and big as saucers. She opened her mouth to scream then, sucked in a nice big breath, but my hand was on her neck quick enough to squeeze and stop it.

By the time I was out of the bedroom the tea was cold and I didn't take more than a bite or two of the toast. I was enjoying the thought of them getting all worked up about DNA from the spit and teeth marks in the toast, all that.

None of it will matter in the end.

Seven

Like all other officers, Thorne was told not to leave important documentation in plain view when he was away from the office. Ancillary staff were instructed not to interfere with workstations while cleaning. However, as neither party adhered particularly closely to best practice, Thorne spent the first half hour of his Monday morning at Becke House searching for several vital scraps of barely intelligible scribble, then carefully reorganizing his desktop into the shambolic clutter of paper that passed for a filing system, albeit one that collapsed if someone left a window open.

Or shut the door too quickly.

"Shit!"

"Sorry," Kitson said. She walked to her desk, smiling as she watched Thorne bend down to pick up the papers that had been blown to the floor. "I don't know, maybe if you used staples or paperclips?" She eased off her jacket and dropped her handbag, then continued as though addressing a young child or a very stupid dog. "Or went completely crazy and typed things up. On. Your. Computer."

Thorne groaned as he straightened up and again as he dropped back into his chair. "You're a bloody genius," he said.

"It's just common sense." Kitson took the lid from the takeaway coffee she had brought in with her, spooned the froth into her mouth. "Unfortunately, most men aren't exactly blessed with too much of that."

"Oh, right," Thorne said. "Are we talking about me or Ian?" The name was as much as Thorne knew about the boyfriend Kitson had been seeing for several months, but after her much-discussed fall from grace, he could hardly blame her for keeping her private life as private as possible. "Poor sod screwed up over the weekend, did he?" Her smile told Thorne he was right on the money.

"I'm just saying, if women ran things..."

"Be better, would it?"

"...the world wouldn't be in such bloody chaos."

"Except once a month," Thorne said. "When things would go extremely tits up."

Kitson's smile widened around the plastic spoon. "How was your Sunday, smart-arse?"

Thorne had spent most of the previous day alone, which had suited him well enough. Louise had driven down to see her parents in Sussex and although Thorne got on perfectly well with both of them, she hadn't bothered to ask if he wanted to come along. If Hendricks was right, and Louise had told her mum about the pregnancy, she probably preferred to be on her own when she broke the news that there no longer was one.

He had not seen the need to ask.

He had made himself a toasted ham and cheese sandwich for lunch, then watched Spurs grind out a piss-poor goalless draw against Manchester City. Louise got home just before he had the chance to be bored all over again by Match of the Day 2 and they spent what was left of the evening arguing about when she was going back to work.

She had rung her office from the hospital that first afternoon, telling them she had a stomach bug, and had decided that four days off sick was more than enough. Thorne disagreed, said he thought she needed longer. Louise told him that it was her body and her decision to make, that she felt as fine as she was ever fucking-well going to, and that she was going back first thing on Monday.

Thorne had left an hour earlier than usual this morning, to beat the traffic and to avoid a repeat of the argument. He looked up at the clock on the wall above Kitson's desk. Louise would be getting to Scotland Yard, where the Kidnap Unit was based, around now.

"My body, my decision..."

He dropped his eyes, nodded at Kitson. "My Sunday was pretty quiet," he said.

•

Once the team had gathered for the morning briefing, it quickly became apparent that others connected to the twin inquiries had been considerably busier than Tom Thorne over the previous thirty-six hours.

"We've been able to match the DNA sample gathered from beneath the fingernails of Catherine Burke in Leicester to that taken from hairs on Emily Walker's clothing. So we're now officially looking for the same individual in connection with both of these murders." Russell Brigstocke took a moment, looked from face to face.

Said, "One killer."

Karim moved his fist from beneath his chin and raised a finger. "Are we releasing this?" he asked.

"Not yet," Brigstocke said.

"And we know the Leicester lot won't, do we?"

"They know they're not supposed to." Brigstocke shrugged. "Look, an inquiry like this means there's obviously double the chance of something being leaked. Some idiot in uniform out to impress a reporter he's trying to get into bed, whatever." He raised his hands to quiet the predictable reaction. "So, all we can do is try to keep the lid on at our end. We all know how the press works, how mental things can get if they catch a sniff of a serial killer." He scanned the faces again, pausing for a second or two when he reached Thorne's, before carrying on.

Thorne knew that Brigstocke was at least half right. The tabloids would certainly go to town. While the broadsheets would use the phrase sparingly and probably use inverted commas, the red-tops would show no such restraint. Same with TV: the BBC would at least want to be seen to avoid sensationalism, while for the likes of Sky News and Channel Five those two words would become something of a mantra.

He also knew very well why Brigstocke had sought him out to push home his point. He guessed that, were he to Google his own name, he would find it cropping up on more than one of those websites he had come across the previous week. His name, alongside those of the men and women he had hunted.

Palmer. Nicklin. Bishop.

One who took the lives of strangers because he was afraid not to; a man who got others to murder for him; a killer whose unluckiest victim did not die at all...

Thorne's mind was yanked back from its wandering as the lights went out and an image appeared on the screen.

"The FSS in Leicester sent us the fragment of X-ray found on Catherine Burke's body." Brigstocke pointed up at the screen. "And we can see how it fits alongside the piece that Emily Walker was holding." The small black pieces of celluloid had been blown up, and though it was still not clear what had been X-rayed, the magnification clearly showed where the full-sized image had been cut—a jagged line that almost disappeared when they were pushed together. "The fact that the killer left these for us to find would indicate that he wants us to piece them together. Although, as yet, we're none the wiser about these." He pointed to a barely legible series of letters and numbers that ran in three lines along the top of each piece, then nodded to the back of the room.

The slide changed and an image appeared showing the sequence of letters and numbers magnified still further:

VEY48
ADD
PHONY

"Write them down," Brigstocke said. He watched as eyes dropped to notebooks all around the room. "Now, there are obviously pieces missing on either side…"

Next to Thorne, Kitson scribbled and mumbled, "Like a jigsaw puzzle."

"Except we don't have a box with the picture on," Thorne said.

"Right, let's crack on." Brigstocke took one last look at the screen. "But if anyone fancies doing some major arse-licking and spending every minute of their spare time trying to figure that out for us, I'll be extremely grateful."

"Better than a bloody sudoku," Karim said.

Brigstocke smiled. "Not that anyone's going to have any spare time, you understand."

As exaggerated groans broke out either side of him, Thorne stared, unblinking, at the picture. The sequence of numbers and letters.

"As yet, we're none the wiser…"

He imagined the killer working with nail scissors, his face creased in concentration. Pictured him later sweating and bloodstained, carefully laying each piece into a victim's palm and folding the dead fingers around it.

"There are obviously pieces missing…"

Thorne stared at the gaps.

Half an hour later, when the team had dispersed, Thorne and Kitson wandered across to Brigstocke's office for a less formal briefing. For the DCI, daily sessions like this were a chance to catch up with senior members of his team and talk about ways to take the inquiry forward. To air grievances, or talk through ideas someone might be too embarrassed to suggest in a larger meeting. A year or two earlier, the cigarettes would have come out; before that, back in the days of Cortinas and fitting up Irishmen, the secret stash of Scotch or vodka.

When Thorne and Kitson arrived, the door to Brigstocke's office was open. He was on the phone, but as soon as he saw them, he beckoned them inside and motioned for Kitson to shut the door.

Thorne saw the expression on Brigstocke's face and did not bother to sit down. He had a good idea what was being talked about when the DCI said, "You're sure, because this one sounds different." He knew, by the time Brigstocke was talking about pieces of plastic and press blackouts.

Thorne exchanged a look with Kitson, and waited.

Brigstocke hung up and let out a heartfelt groan on a long, tired breath.

"Another piece of the jigsaw?" Thorne asked.

The blood had still not returned to Russell Brigstocke's face. "Two of them," he said.

Eight

THE BODIES of Gregory and Alexandra Macken, aged twenty and eighteen, had been discovered just after 9.30 a.m. by the landlord of their rented flat in Holloway—an Iranian named Dariush—who had come round to fix a leaking radiator. They were informally identified by the elderly woman in the flat downstairs, who claimed to have heard them coming home on Saturday, two nights earlier, but had not seen them since.

"They came back at different times, and there were definitely two male voices earlier on." She was very insistent about that, while also making it clear that she didn't like to stick her nose into other people's business. Later, when she was tearful, she said, "Nicer than your average students." She made sure the uniformed officer wrote that down. "Didn't make a racket and always said hello. Even fed my cat when I went to stay with my sister."

Both victims were found dead in the larger of the flat's two bedrooms. Gregory was discovered naked on the bed, while his sister, who was wearing pajamas and a dressing-gown, was found on the floor. Both had slivers of dark plastic in their hands, and head wounds that were clearly visible through blood-spattered plastic bags.

Within an hour, the CSI team had set to work. A uniformed WPC from the local station did her best to comfort Dariush in preparation for taking his statement, while a family liaison officer was sent to talk to the next of kin and inform them that they would be required to identify the bodies formally the following day.

If they felt up to it...

"I never understand why anyone would choose to do that," Thorne said. "I mean, most of us have to do it at one time or another, but why would you sign up for a job where all you do is deal with other people's misery? Where you have to... absorb it?"

"Because you're empathetic?"

"Because you're what?"

"You give a toss."

"All the time, though?" Thorne shook his head and swallowed a mouthful of coffee. "I'd rather face somebody with a gun."

"You should think about retraining," Hendricks said. "The dead ones are no bother at all."

It was almost six o'clock. After more than seven hours at the crime scene, Thorne and Hendricks had left the flat as evening fell and walked the few hundred yards to a coffee bar on the Hornsey Road, to kill time while they waited for the bodies to be brought out.

"How much longer has the brother been dead?"

They had taken a corner table without needing to discuss it, both well used to staying as far away from other customers as possible whenever they found themselves in a bar or restaurant and there was shop to be talked.

"Ten, twelve hours, maybe," Hendricks said. "The sister's been dead around a day, so he would have been killed more like thirty-six hours ago."

"So, Saturday night and Sunday morning?"

Hendricks nodded and took a slurp of tea. "Good film that. When Albert Finney was still gorgeous."

"You think he's gay?" Thorne asked.

"Albert Finney?"

Thorne ignored his friend and waited. He had been thinking about what the downstairs neighbor had said and was working out a timeline.

The girl had not been killed because she had interrupted someone in the act of murdering her brother.

The killer had waited for her.

"Look, I'll be able to tell you if anything sexual went on tomorrow," Hendricks said. "Who did what to who, and for how long. Macken was definitely gay, if that helps."

"Gaydar work on corpses, does it?"

"He had Armistead Maupin and Edmund White on his bookshelves and Rufus Wainwright on his CD player."

Thorne had heard of Rufus Wainwright. "I'll take your word for it."

"The killer might well be gay too," Hendricks said. "But if you ask me, he's whatever he needs to be. Does whatever he has to do to get through the front door."

"Then whatever he has to do once he's inside." Thorne finished his coffee, spoke as much to himself as Hendricks: "He . . . adapts."

"I'm not sure we'll ever know exactly what happened," Hendricks said. "How he got the girl in there, whether he was hiding. But this time he brought two plastic bags with him."

"Two bags, but just one blunt instrument," Thorne said. They had found a heavy glass bowl by the side of the bed. There was hardened candle-wax in the bottom of it and what looked like brain-matter and dried blood caked across the underside. "He plans things carefully and he thinks on his feet."

Hendricks nodded. "He's good at this."

A waitress came over and asked if they would like more drinks. Hendricks said that he was fine, but Thorne ordered another coffee, happy enough to sit there for a while.

"What does he do for twelve hours?" he asked.

"What does who do?"

"Our man, after he's killed the boy."

"Maybe he sleeps," Hendricks said. "Reads a book. Has a wank." He shrugged. "I know what it looks like inside these nutters' heads, but don't ask me what goes on in there."

Thorne leaned back in his chair. "Has a wank?"

Hendricks grinned. "A lot of these are sexual, right?"

Some were, certainly, but Thorne had already decided that these killings were not sexually motivated, and not only because of a lack of evidence. A violent death was never treated as something ordinary, but when it was about sex or revenge or money, there could at least be some level of understanding. When it was about none of these things was when it got scary.

And Thorne was starting to feel afraid.

They both started at the sudden banging on the window, turned and saw a drunk who had tottered past once already, pressing his big red face against the glass. Thorne looked away but Hendricks began to smile and waved at the man. The waitress, who was hovering at a nearby table, apologized and moved towards the door, but the drunk, having blown one final kiss at his new best friend, was already lurching away along the pavement.

Thorne stared across the table.

Hendricks grinned and turned up his palms. "Like I said, empathy..."

There was another knock at the window, and this time Thorne turned to see Dave Holland on his way in. Thorne tried to finish his coffee quickly as Holland reached the table. "They bringing them out, then?"

"No, but you might want to get back over there anyway," Holland said. "Martin Macken's arrived and he's kicking up a fuss." He looked at the coffee in Thorne's hand as though he could have done with a strong one himself. "The father."

The road had been sealed off to traffic, causing considerable congestion in the surrounding streets, which was exacerbated by drivers slowing down at either end of the road to rubberneck. Had there been a match at the Emirates Stadium, a huge area of north London could easily have been reduced to gridlock.

Outside the Mackens' flat the street was nose-to-tail with police and CSI vehicles, so the blue Saab driven by the family liaison officer had pulled up opposite, between the generator lorry and a small catering van dispensing sandwiches and hot drinks.

Thorne figured that the Saab was the car he was looking for, as that was where the noise was coming from. As he and the others neared it, he could see a young, plain-clothes officer and several others in uniforms trying to mollify a man who was screaming and fighting to get across the road.

The man he guessed was Martin Macken.

Twenty feet from the car, Thorne took Hendricks to one side and told him to get back inside the flat and delay the removal of the bodies. As Hendricks walked quickly across the road, Thorne introduced himself to Martin Macken and said how sorry he was.

Macken could not possibly have heard over the terrible noise he was making and, after trying again, Thorne could do no more than stand by and wait for him to draw breath or drop dead with the effort. The man was fifty or so and had clearly looked after himself, but now he was coming apart in front of Thorne's eyes. Hair that would normally have been kept neatly swept back was flying back and forth across his face as he raged and the tendons were rigid in his neck. His lips were thin and white, spittle-flecked. His eyes darted, wild and bloodshot, as he strained towards the house opposite and howled for his children.

"Please, Macken..."

Suddenly, he seemed distracted by movement at the front door and stopped struggling. Thorne gave the nod and moved forward, while the officers, each of whom had been staring at his own shoes while using the minimum of force to restrain the man, stepped back.

"I'm Detective Inspector Thorne, Macken."

Red-faced and breathing heavily, Macken pointed at the figure moving to the front door of the house where his children had lived. "Who's that?"

Thorne swallowed as he watched Hendricks disappear inside. That's the man who'll be cutting up your children in the morning. "It's just one of the team, sir. Everyone's doing all that they can."

Macken's gaze moved to the first-floor windows, a moan rising from the back of his throat. The men in uniform tensed, as though he might try to rush across the road at any moment. When it became clear that he would not, the liaison officer, a Scottish DS named Adam Strang, moved up to Thorne's shoulder.

"I tried to tell him to stay where he was," Strang said, "that we wouldn't need him until tomorrow, but he wasn't having any of it. He just marched out of the house and went and sat in the back of the car. I had to go back in and switch the lights off..."

Thorne nodded his understanding and took another step closer to Macken. "Why don't you get back in the car, sir?"

Without taking his eyes from the window, Macken shook his head.

"Don't you think you'd be better off at home?"

"I want to see my kids." The man's voice was low and hoarse, well-educated.

"I'm afraid that's not possible just yet." Thorne put a hand on his arm. "Why not let us take you back to..." He looked around.

"Kingston," Strang said.

"Someone can stay with you and... your wife, is it?" From the corner of his eye, Thorne saw Strang shaking his head, but it was too late.

Macken snapped his head round and stared hard at Thorne. His mouth fell open as though a dreadful image had suddenly been recalled and there was something desperate in his eyes; a plea, a prayer. "Not after Liz," he said. "Not after what happened to Elizabeth."

Thorne looked at Strang.

"Macken's wife, I think, sir." Strang lowered his voice. "He's been banging on about this all the way from Kingston."

"Jesus, no. Jesus, Jesus..."

"Is your wife all right, Macken?"

"Partner, not wife. We never saw the need to get married."

"What happened to her?"

"Liz was killed," Macken said, simple and sad. "Fifteen years ago. Murdered, like her children."

Thorne had felt it begin as soon as he'd asked the question and seen the look on Macken's face. The tingle, feathering the skin at the nape of his neck, starting to spread before Macken had even finished speaking.

Somewhere behind him, he heard Holland mutter, "Bloody hell-fire."

The fact that they had never married explained why "Macken" had not registered with Thorne earlier in the day; the children's surname taken from their father and not shared with their dead mother. Now, he remembered the seven names on the list of Raymond Garvey's victims: "Elizabeth O'Connor" had been third from the top.

Thorne spoke her killer's name quietly, and could only watch as Martin Macken's face collapsed in on itself and he fell back, moaning, against the side of the car. "Jesus... Jesus... Jesus..."

Thorne was already reaching for his phone and walking away fast, aware of Strang calling after him, asking what he should do about Macken. Scrolling through the phone's contact list, he marched past Holland, told him he'd better get in touch with his girlfriend to let her know he was going to be home very late.

Then Holland was shouting after him as well.

It was easy enough getting through to the Incident Room in Leicester, but it took some cajoling, then a minute or two's concentrated shouting and swearing, to get Paul Brewer's home number.

"In a hurry to arrange that drink?" Brewer asked.

"I'm coming up to Leicester tonight," Thorne said. "And I want to talk to Catherine Burke's boyfriend. I need you to sort that out for me."

"Sort it out?"

"Make sure he knows I'm coming. Make sure he stays in, and waits up."

"Christ, is this about Catherine's mother?" It sounded as though Brewer were suppressing a yawn. "I told you, I already spoke to him about that."

"I know you did, Paul," Thorne said. "The problem is, he lied."

Nine

THERE WAS a for sale sign outside the two-bedroom flat that Jamie Paice had, until three weeks before, shared with Catherine Burke. Thorne was staring at it as the door was opened and a young man in jeans and a Leicester City shirt began ranting about how late it was, and how he couldn't see what was so important. How he was really sick of answering questions when he'd only just buried his girlfriend.

Thorne introduced himself and Holland. Said, "Coffee would be nice."

They followed Paice upstairs, and while he went straight on into a small kitchen, Thorne and Holland turned into a living room dominated by a black leather sofa and matching armchairs. A blond woman in her twenties sat cradling a bottle of beer in front of a large plasma television. After a brief staring contest, she reluctantly turned off the TV and introduced herself as Dawn Turner.

"I'm just a friend," she said, without being asked. "I was a friend of Catherine."

Thorne nodded. She was wearing a cap-sleeved T-shirt that did her no favors, with a transparent bra-strap visible on each shoulder. It was sweltering in the room. Thorne and Holland took off their jackets and sat down on the sofa.

"It's been really hard for Jamie," Turner said. She put her bottle down by the side of her chair. "Last few weeks."

"I'll bet," Thorne said.

They had made good time getting out of London and even with Thorne keeping the BMW at a well-behaved seventy-five all the way, they had hit the outskirts of Leicester within an hour and a half of leaving Holloway. It was pushing ten o'clock by the time Jamie Paice sauntered into the living room with two mugs of coffee and fresh beers for himself and his "friend." As he dropped into the armchair he took a good, long look at his watch.

"I'm doing you a favor here, to be honest," Paice said. "So this better be important. Doesn't look like you're here to tell me you've found the fucker who killed Cath."

Thorne smiled, as though he simply hadn't heard him. "Selling the place, Jamie?"

Paice looked across at Turner and shook his head in disbelief. "That what you came all this way to ask me? You want to make an offer?"

"Just interested. I saw the sign."

"We were planning to sell anyway. Me and Cath had looked at a few places already when she was killed."

"The police thought that might have had something to do with what happened," Turner said. "They reckoned whoever killed her might have come round pretending to look at the flat. I think they checked with the estate agents and that."

"I'm sure they did," Thorne said.

Holland shuffled to the edge of the sofa and looked at Paice. He nodded towards Turner. "Did you ask your friend round when you knew we were coming?" he asked.

"Why would I do that?"

"A bit of moral support."

Paice said nothing, took a swig from his bottle.

"So, she was here anyway?"

"Brewer said there was something you wanted to talk to me about." Paice leaned back in his chair and spread his arms. "Can we get on with it?"

"You were shopping in town when Catherine was killed," Holland said.

"Christ, are we going through this again?"

"Looking for a computer game you wanted, that's what you said. But you didn't buy anything in the end."

"It's not what I said. It's what happened."

"This is stupid," Turner said. "The police checked all that an' all. Went to the shops Jamie went into."

"We could always check again," Thorne said.

"Do what you bloody like," Paice said. "Maybe I should be talking to a solicitor, check out how much I can sue you bastards for."

"A solicitor might be a good idea," Holland said.

"What?" Paice suddenly looked furious and began rocking slowly in the chair, his knuckles whitening around the neck of his beer bottle.

"It's all right, Jamie." Looking daggers at Holland as she went, Turner moved across and sat down on the arm of Paice's chair. She laid a hand on his shoulder and told him that he needed to calm down; that getting worked up wouldn't do any good, or bring Catherine back.

"She's telling the truth," Holland said. "And it's about time you did."

Thorne had been happy to sit there and let Holland get stuck into Jamie Paice. They knew very well that his alibi checked out, and they had not driven a hundred miles because they thought he'd killed Catherine Burke or anyone else. But for some reason he had lied to Paul Brewer, they felt sure about that, and in these situations it always paid to put the subject firmly on the back foot.

Holland had made a good job of it, and not for the first time. Thorne had told him once, a year or so back, how impressed he had been. Holland had laughed, then told Thorne that when it came to making people feel uncomfortable, he'd learned from the master. "I don't mean watching you in interview rooms or anything," Holland had said, enjoying himself. "Just, you know, how you are with people... all the time."

"You were asked how Catherine's mother had died," Thorne said. He waited until Paice was looking at him. "And you talked a lot of rubbish."

"When Brewer rang and asked, you mean?" Paice seemed genuinely confused. Turner was squeezing his shoulder, trying to say something, but he wouldn't let her speak. "I told him. I don't understand."

"You said Catherine's mother died of cancer."

"Right, same as her dad. He died a few years ago, stomach cancer I think, and her mum died when Cath was a kid. I'm not sure what sort—"

"Why are you lying?"

"I'm not. She died of cancer."

"No," Thorne said. "She didn't." He was as certain as he could be that Catherine Burke's mother had been murdered fifteen years before, just as the mothers of Emily Walker and Alex and Greg Macken had been. There was nobody named Burke on the list of victims that was folded in Thorne's pocket, but nor was there a Macken or a Walker. There were any number of reasons why the surnames of parent and child might not match, but the link between the four most recent murder victims could no longer be in any doubt.

"This is mental," Paice said. He shifted forward, trying to get up, but was pressed gently back into his chair.

"It's true, Jamie," Turner said. "Cath's mum was murdered by a man named Raymond Garvey."

Paice looked up at her, and as soon as he had placed the name, he began shaking his head. "You're kidding? He killed loads, didn't he?"

"Seven," Turner said. She looked at Thorne, received a small nod of confirmation. "Cath's mum was the third or fourth, I think."

Paice took a long pull on his bottle, held the beer in his mouth for a few seconds before swallowing. "So, why didn't she tell me? Why was there this made-up cancer story?"

"She just got sick of it," Turner said. "People wanting to know what it was like. I mean, what did they think it was like?" She was talking to Holland and Thorne as much as to Paice now, tearing pieces of the label from her beer bottle, balling them up in her palm. "She used to get pestered by people writing books about it and making TV documentaries. There was even one bloke she used to go out with who she reckoned... got off on it. Sickos, you know? So, a few years ago she just decided she'd had enough. Changed her name, moved to a different side of the city and never talked about it to anyone. I'd known Cath since we were at school, but I was the only one she still spoke to who knew what had happened when she was a kid. Apart from me, nobody had a clue. Nobody at work. Not Jamie."

Thorne looked at Paice. "How long had the two of you been together?"

Paice looked shell-shocked. "A year and a half." He moved the bottle towards his mouth, stared at it. "Christ..."

"Why 'Burke,'" Holland asked.

Turner lobbed the rolled-up pieces of the label into a wicker wastepaper basket in the corner. "It was her mum's maiden name," she said. "She never really had anything of her mum's after she died. Her dad drank quite a bit afterwards, and ended up flogging anything he could find to pay for it. Her mum's name was about the only thing of hers that Cath could keep."

Thorne knew they were just about done. He glanced down towards his jacket, which he had dropped onto the floor by the side of the sofa. "How old was she when it happened?"

"Eleven," Turner said. "Our first year at big school." She closed her eyes for five seconds... ten, then stood up and moved back to her own chair. "It really messed her up. Forever, you know?"

"The drugs, right?"

"Well, who wouldn't?"

Reaching for the jacket, Thorne saw the eyes of the man in the armchair drift down to his feet and knew that Jamie Paice had been more than happy to keep his girlfriend company; to get out of it with her on whatever pills Catherine had managed to smuggle out of the hospital.

"Garvey killed Catherine's mum while she was sunbathing," Turner said. "Climbed over a fence and battered her to death in broad daylight." She looked at what was left in her bottle, then finished it quickly. "Catherine found her in the garden when she came home from school."

Fifteen minutes later, a mile or so from the M1, Holland said, "Should be back by midnight with a bit of luck."

"I think it's probably best if we stay over," Thorne said.

"What?"

"Have a couple of drinks, get our heads down, then head back first thing."

Holland looked less than thrilled. "I didn't warn Sophie."

"Well, we're both in the same boat." Thorne slowed down and began studying the road-signs. "We passed a place on the way in. Be handy for the motorway in the morning."

"Shit... I haven't got any overnight stuff."

"We can get you a toothbrush from somewhere," Thorne said. "And don't tell me you've never worn the same pair of pants two days running."

"It's mad though," Holland said. "We're only an hour and a bit away from home."

"I'm tired."

"I'm happy to drive, if you want to sleep."

"I want to stay over," Thorne said.

It was somewhere between a Travelodge and a reform school, with wood-effect plastic on every available surface, pan-pipe music coming from speakers too high up to rip off the wall and a worrying smell in the lobby. They checked in fast and tried not to breathe too much. Thorne did his best to be pleasant and jokey, failing to elicit a smile from the woman behind the desk, then as neither he nor Holland could face seeing his room without at least one drink inside them, they moved straight from the sumptuous reception area into what passed for a bar.

It wasn't yet eleven o'clock but the place—half a dozen tables and some artificial plants—was virtually empty. Two middle-aged men in suits were huddled at a table by the door and a woman in her early thirties sat at one end of the bar, flicking through a magazine. There was no sign of any staff.

"Joint's jumping," Holland said.

After a few minutes, a balding bundle of fun in a plum-colored waistcoat materialized behind the bar and Thorne bought the drinks: a glass of Blossom Hill for himself and a pint of Stella for Holland. He asked about ordering some sandwiches and was told that the kitchen was short staffed.

They carried their drinks to a table in the corner, Thorne grabbing half-eaten bowls of peanuts from the three adjacent tables before he sat down.

"They're covered in piss," Holland said.

Thorne already had a mouthful of nuts and was brushing the salt from his hands. He looked across and grunted, "What?"

Holland nodded down at the bowl. "From people who go to the bog and don't wash their hands. I saw a thing on *Oprah* where they did these tests and found traces of piss in bowls of peanuts and pretzels, stuff they leave out on bars."

Thorne shrugged. "I'm hungry."

Holland helped himself to a handful. "Just telling you," he said.

The piped music had changed to what was probably Michael Bolton, but could also have been a large animal in great pain. The wine went down easily enough, though, and Thorne enjoyed the banter when Holland commented on the fact that he was drinking rosé. Thorne informed him that Louise had started buying it, that according to an article he'd seen, it was now extremely trendy.

"Extremely gay," Holland said.

Thorne might have said something about that kind of comment upsetting Phil Hendricks, were it not exactly what Hendricks would have said himself. Instead, he pushed his empty glass across the table and reminded Holland it was his round. A few minutes later, Holland returned from the bar with another glass of wine, half a lager and four packets of piss-free crisps.

"Don't you feel a bit guilty?" Holland asked. "About Paice, I mean. He obviously didn't know about the Garvey thing."

"I don't know about 'obviously.'"

"Did you see his face?"

Thorne took a few seconds. "Maybe he and his new girlfriend cooked that story up."

"Why would they do that?"

"Buggered if I know."

"Well, they deserve Oscars if they did." Holland downed what was left of his pint and poured the half into the empty glass. "Anyway, who says she's his girlfriend?"

"It was the first thing I thought, I suppose," Thorne said. "As soon as I walked in."

Holland shook his head. "Never occurred to me. Some people have got nasty, suspicious minds."

"Difficult not to."

"That make you a good copper, you reckon?" Holland smiled, but it didn't sound as though he was joking. "Or a bad one?"

"Probably just one who's been doing it too long," Thorne said.

Holland leaned forward to see if there were any crisps left, but all the packets were empty. "So, how long was it before you stopped giving people the benefit of the doubt?" he asked.

"That's the jury's job, not mine," Thorne said.

"Seriously."

"I don't think I ever did... ever do." Thorne took a mouthful of wine. It was a little sweeter than the one Louise bought from Sainsbury's. "If you start off assuming that everyone's a twat, you're unlikely to be disappointed." He glanced towards the bar and saw the woman looking in their direction. He smiled, then turned back to Holland. "All right, I suppose I do feel a bit guilty," he said. "And stupid, for thinking this business with Jamie Paice might have been important."

"It might have been," Holland said. He held up his glass. "And right now we'd be toasting our success with something a bit more expensive." He swilled the beer around, stared into it. "We've got to chase up everything, right, even if it is stupid, until we get lucky or this bloke makes a mistake."

"I'm hoping he's already made one," Thorne said. "I don't want to see any more pieces of that X-ray."

A few minutes later, Holland asked, "So, why are we really here?"

"I'm not with you."

"Sitting in this shit-hole instead of being at home in our own beds." The look on Holland's face made it clear he was expecting to hear about how Thorne was in the doghouse with Louise, or trying to avoid some tedious dinner with her family and friends. Hoping to hear something he could laugh at or sympathize with; shaking his head in disbelief at the silly shit their girlfriends put them through. "It's fine," he said. "You don't have to say."

Thorne was struggling to answer the question. There was some reason for his reluctance to go home that he could not quite articulate, but which nevertheless made him feel horribly guilty. He would not have felt comfortable sharing it with Holland, or anyone else, even if he had been able to find the right words. "I told you," he said, happy to exaggerate the perfectly timed yawn. "I'm just knackered."

"Fair enough." Holland stood up and said that he was ready to turn in.

They arranged to meet for breakfast at seven. Holland said he would set the alarm on his phone. Then, instead of walking with Holland towards the lifts, Thorne contradicted himself by announcing that he was staying up for one more: "It'll help me sleep."

"Have a couple," Holland said. "You'll sleep like a baby."

Thorne could guess where it was going, but just smiled, letting Holland get to the punchline.

"You'll wake up crying because you've pissed yourself."

Thorne walked to the bar and ordered another glass of wine. The woman sitting a few stools along put down her magazine. "Your mate abandoned you, has he?"

"I've got a dirty, suspicious mind, apparently," Thorne said. He nodded towards the optics. "You want one?"

The woman thanked him and moved across. She asked for a rum and Coke and when she spoke it was obvious that it was not going to be her first. She was pale, with shoulder-length dark hair, and wore a cream denim jacket over a shortish brown skirt. The barman in the plum-colored waistcoat, whose name tag said Trevor, set about pouring the drinks and raised his eyebrows at Thorne when the woman wasn't looking.

"I'm Angie," she said.

Thorne shook the woman's outstretched hand and felt himself redden a little as he told her his name.

"What business you in then, Tom?"

"I sell nuts," Thorne said. "Crisps, nuts... I'm basically a snack salesman."

She nodded, smiling slightly, as though she wasn't sure whether to believe him. When the barman had put down the drinks she picked up her glass and waited until he'd moved away. "Listen, Tom, it's almost midnight, and we can sit here getting hammered if you want. Or we could just take these up to your room."

She did not take her eyes from his as she sipped her drink. Now Thorne felt himself really redden. He could also feel the blood moving to other parts of his body and was grateful that he was sitting down.

He had called Louise earlier from the car-park, at the same time as Holland was speaking to Sophie. She'd said she had no problem with him staying over; had even sounded slightly annoyed that he would think she might have. She'd said that she'd be happy to get an early night and when he'd asked how her first day back had been, she'd told him it was fine; that he had been worrying for nothing.

"I've... got a girlfriend," Thorne said. He nodded, like it was self-explanatory, but the woman just stared, as though waiting for him to elaborate. He was trying to swallow, dry-mouthed, thinking that he didn't really fancy her very much and wondering how he would be reacting if he did. "You know, otherwise..."

The woman raised her hands and spun slowly away on her stool. "Not a problem."

Thorne was still nodding like an idiot. She'd said it the same way that Louise had: casual and frosty. He opened his wallet and took out a ten-pound note to pay for the drinks; turned when he heard the woman cursing.

She pointed to the warrant card, shaking her head. "I can normally spot you bastards a mile away."

From the corner of his eye, Thorne could see Trevor smirking as he dried glasses at the end of the bar. Realizing now that the woman's proposition had been a purely commercial one, Thorne did his best not to look overly shocked.

"Don't worry about it, love," he said. "I'm not local, and if it makes you feel any better, I think my professional radar's working about as well as yours." He listened to the music for a few seconds, drumming his fingers on the bar, then he raised his glass. "Cheers, Angie."

"It's Mary, actually."

"Slow night, Mary?"

"Cata-fucking-tonic," she said.

Ten

THEY HIT the rush hour coming out of Leicester, ran into the tail end of another as soon as they got within commuting distance of London, and the drizzle didn't help. When Brigstocke called just before ten, they were still twenty miles from the city, and still regretting the hideously greasy breakfast they'd eaten two hours earlier.

"Should have just had the muesli," Holland said.

Thorne turned down the radio. "And you take the piss out of rosé?" He pressed the button on his phone that activated the loudspeaker, and passed it to Holland. It was the closest he came to hands-free.

"How did it go with Paice?" Brigstocke asked.

"Nothing to get excited about," Thorne said. "Catherine Burke never told him about her mum, that's all."

"Worth checking though," Brigstocke said. "Providing your expenses claims aren't too stupid."

"There might be a claim later on for food poisoning," Holland said.

Brigstocke told them that Hendricks was due to perform the first of the Macken post-mortems later that morning, and that, as they had already confirmed a DNA match, he'd asked FSS to prioritize the examination of the two newest X-ray fragments, to see if they could get any more information.

"Every chance, I reckon," Thorne said. "He's leaving them for us to find, so he must want us to know what they are."

"Or waste our time trying to find out," Holland added.

Another phone had started ringing in the background and there was a hiatus while Brigstocke answered it; then a minute or two of muffled conversation over the loudspeaker.

"Is that what you think?" Holland turned to Thorne. "He's leaving them for us. It's not... ritualistic?"

Before Thorne could say that he had no idea, he was distracted by the car behind. "Look at this idiot up my arse," he said. He stared hard into his rear-view, stepping on the brake a few times until he thought the driver behind had got the message.

Brigstocke was back on the line, asking them how far away they were, then telling them not to bother coming into the office. "Get yourselves straight down to the Holloway Road," he said. He explained that they had done a door-to-door across some of the university accommodation first thing and managed to track down a few of the students who had been at the Rocket Club on Saturday night. "We may as well save ourselves some time and interview them all together."

"Makes sense," Thorne said. It would also be a chance to see the last place where anyone, save for their killer, had seen Greg or Alex Macken alive.

Brigstocke had an even stronger reason. "Several of them say they saw the brother talking to a man in the bar who he may have left with later on."

"Sounds promising," Holland said.

"Well, I don't know how sober any of them were, but between them, there's a chance of getting a proper description. With luck... we might do even better than that."

Thorne looked at Holland. "Cameras."

"Smart-arse," Brigstocke said. "Yeah, Yvonne's going down to see if there's any decent CCTV."

"Probably have to wade through hours of students throwing up on the stairs and shagging in dark corners," Holland said.

Thorne laughed. "I'm sure there'll be plenty of volunteers."

"I think I'll save that footage for myself," Brigstocke said, before he hung up. "Keep it to show the wife when my eldest starts banging on about going to university."

A few miles further on, the traffic thickened approaching the turn-off for the M25 and Thorne had to take the BMW down into first gear. He smacked the wheel harder than he might in time to the song on the radio.

"Why don't we shoot up the hard shoulder?" Holland asked.

Thorne explained that they would be through the jam quickly enough once they got past the junction. That the students weren't going anywhere, and that he didn't really fancy getting done by one of the cameras and spending weeks writing letters to prove that he was on legitimate police business.

"Just an idea," Holland said.

Thorne checked his mirror and eased the car into the inside lane, thinking about it, knocking the wipers up a notch as the rain grew heavier. Coming down in needles suddenly, from a sky the color of wet cement.

Bearing in mind what they looked like now, pale and half dressed with hair like shit, Thorne could barely imagine how the students sitting in front of him had looked when uniformed coppers had banged on their doors at seven-thirty that morning. Even as he thought it, watching while Holland took down their names, Thorne could hear Louise making some crack about him turning into his father. Back before his dad had died, of course, and before the Alzheimer's had really kicked in. Back when the old man could still string a sentence together without upsetting too many people.

Louise had never met Thorne's father, but she knew enough about the man to enjoy teasing Thorne about how much his habits and attitudes were now becoming like those of his dad. Thorne tried fighting his corner, but could never muster a great deal of conviction.

A few weeks before, she'd said, "It'll probably get even worse, now that you're actually going to be a sodding dad!"

"Greg doesn't come in here much, not normally." The speaker was a young woman with blond hair cut very short and a ring through her bottom lip that Phil Hendricks would have been proud of. "Don't think I saw him in here at all last term."

"I saw him once." A tall, skinny boy with a scrubby beard. "Didn't look like he was enjoying himself much."

There were nods and murmurs of agreement from the rest of the group. Seven of them were gathered in a corner of the main bar at the Rocket Club: four girls and three boys. A few stared into takeaway coffees and three of them passed a large bottle of water between them. The place stank of beer and the uncarpeted area of the floor around the bar itself was sticky with it.

"Greg preferred to stay at home and study," Holland said. "That it?"

The skinny boy shrugged. "Yeah, he worked pretty hard, but he wasn't mental about it or anything. I think he just hated the music in here."

"He liked jazz," the blond girl said. "Weird Scandinavian stuff. We used to take the piss 'cause it sounded so shit."

Thorne tried to hide a smile. A taste in music that others thought dubious was something he and Greg Macken had obviously shared. "So, why was he here on Saturday?"

"And the Saturday before that," the boy said. "Been in here a few times, since the start of term."

"Right. So what was different?"

There were a few seconds of silence, save for some slightly awkward shifting of feet and slurpings of coffee. An overweight Asian girl with a purple streak through her hair smiled sadly as she reached forward for the bottle of water. "He had the hots for this bloke," she said.

"The man some of you saw him talking to?"

A few of them nodded.

Thorne well understood the hesitation. It was strange how the stuff of everyday gossip became something far harder to discuss when the person it concerned had been murdered. "You saw him in here with the same bloke before last Saturday?" he asked.

The Asian girl said that she had. "I think he came in the first couple of times to keep an eye on his sister, you know? Then he saw this guy he fancied, so he kept coming back."

"You saw them talking before?"

"No, not talking. Not until Saturday."

"What happened on Saturday?"

"I think it just took Greg that long to pluck up the courage."

"He wasn't exactly...confident." The girl with the lip-ring started to cry. The boy with the beard moved his chair closer and draped an arm around her shoulders. "Probably needed to get a few drinks inside him first."

Thorne nodded. Gay or straight, eighteen or eighty, he knew how that worked. But whatever shyness had held Greg Macken back until Saturday evening, Thorne was struck by just how confident his killer had been. Happy enough to stalk his victim, then wait for him to make the first move.

"Was Greg drunk, do you think?" Holland asked. "By the time he left?"

The Asian girl shook her head. "A bit of Dutch courage, but that's about it. I spoke to him half an hour before I noticed he'd gone and he sounded fine." Her head dropped. "He was...excited."

The post-mortem would tell them how much Greg Macken had drunk on the night he died. Thorne was also interested to see what the toxicology report had to say. It had been suggested that the killer might have slipped something into Macken's drink—Rohypnol or liquid ecstasy maybe—though Thorne wondered, if that was the case, why the killer had felt the need to smash Macken's head in before bringing out the plastic bag.

"So, did anyone see them leave together?"

The blond girl said that she couldn't swear to it. "But, you know, Greg wasn't here and neither was the bloke he'd been talking to."

"I saw them by the door," the skinny boy said. "Next time I looked, they'd gone, so I just assumed..."

Thorne held up a hand to let them know that it didn't matter too much.

If the CCTV panned out, it wouldn't matter at all. "Tell me about this bloke," he said.

"He was older than most of the people in here," the Asian girl said. "Thirty-ish, I reckon."

Thorne asked if that was unusual, and the students explained that anyone could pay to come in on nights when there were bands playing. Besides, there were always a few mature students around.

"He looked . . . sure of himself," the blond girl said.

The skinny boy agreed. "I thought he looked like a right cocky sod, to be honest."

The Asian girl said he'd seemed relaxed, happy even, and eventually admitted—though she couldn't look anywhere but at the floor as she did—that if Greg hadn't been so obviously interested, she might have made a move herself.

The students began to give a more detailed physical description; the three who had got the best look at the man edged closer to the table as Holland took notes. While they argued about the color of the man's shirt and how far off the collar his hair had been, Thorne took a seat next to a girl who had not spoken at all.

She had long dark hair and wore a sensible coat. She looked about fourteen.

"I take it you didn't see much," Thorne said.

"I wasn't here," the girl said. Her voice was quiet, Home Counties. "I'm a friend of Alex. We were next door watching the band." As soon as she'd said the name, her lip had begun to tremble and Thorne was reaching into the pocket of his leather jacket for tissues. The girl beat him to it, pressing a crumpled wad into the corner of each eye and speaking through delicate, childlike sobs. "We were supposed to be having lunch on Sunday," she said. "A bit optimistic, considering how hammered we both were by the time we'd left, but that was the plan. A big Sunday roast in some pub somewhere. Alex could have eaten for England, you know?" She dropped her hands into her lap, squeezed the tissue between them. "I felt so rough the next day that I never even got round to calling her."

"Come on," Thorne said. He didn't bother telling her that any such call would have gone unanswered.

"Then, you know, she didn't come in on Monday morning. I never spoke to her again." Her hands moved back to her face, and when she finally took away the sodden lump of tissue there was a shiny string of snot between her nose and her fingers. She kept very still as Thorne leaned across and wiped it away.

Once a consensus of sorts had been reached on the description, the students were allowed to go, with a reminder for them to get in touch should they remember anything else. As they trooped slowly out, they passed Yvonne Kitson on her way in, and Thorne saw her entrance earn more than a casual backward glance from the skinny boy with the scraggy beard. Kitson saw it too, and did not seem displeased.

"Careful," Holland said. "That's only a notch above kiddie-fiddling."

"Is it?" Kitson's face was the picture of innocence. "So neither of you fancied the blonde?"

Neither of them said anything.

Kitson smiled and sat down. "Right, we've got no cameras in the bar, unfortunately, but they're on all the staircases, in the main lobby and at the front door. So, we should have something to go through by late afternoon." She reached into her handbag and began reapplying lipstick. "Did we get a decent description?"

"We got one," Thorne said. "Different from the one the Leicester boys were given, and different from the one we got from Emily Walker's neighbor."

"So, they're all unreliable."

"That's always a possibility."

"Or we've got someone who makes an effort to change his appearance."

Holland looked from one DI to the other. "What's that all about, then? Part of the kick he's getting, do you reckon?" He shook his head as though he were answering his own question. "Maybe it's one of those multiple-personalities things."

"No chance." Kitson shook her head and dropped the lipstick back in her bag. “Let his defense team try that kind of cobblers on when the time comes. He probably just enjoys pissing us about.”

“Fine with me.” Thorne picked up the empty cups from the floor and placed them on the table. “They’re usually the ones who get careless.”

“Like Garvey,” Holland said. “He slipped up eventually.”

“Yeah, but there were seven bodies by then,” Kitson said.

Thorne stood, dug into his pocket for the car keys. Said, “This one’s more than halfway to that already.”

Eleven

LOUISE HAD sent him a text when he was halfway between Leicester and London: drive safe. you might still be pissed! Thorne had called at lunchtime, after they'd wrapped things up at the Rocket, but she was busy and a little brisk on the phone. Another text arrived just before five, as he and Holland were walking into Brigstocke's office to review the CCTV footage: sorry about earlier. another takeaway 2nite? can't be arsed 2 cook. early night? Taking his seat next to Brigstocke, Thorne sent back a smiley face that almost matched his own.

It was the best he had felt all day...

While Thorne had been in Leicester talking to Jamie Paice and in Holloway interviewing students, the team had been following those lines of inquiry that had become pressing since the link between the victims had been determined beyond all doubt. All checks thus far had eliminated any of Raymond Garvey's former friends and established that he had no living male relatives, with an elderly uncle in a care home in Essex the only blood relative of any kind that anyone had been able to trace.

They talked through possibilities, while Kitson set up her equipment. "So, some kind of copycat then?" she suggested.

"They're not copies," Holland said. "Not exactly. Garvey bludgeoned all his victims to death."

"You know what I mean, Dave."

"All killed outside as well."

"Some twisted, fucking... homage then, whatever you want to call it."

"Yeah, feasible, I suppose. I mean, it's easy enough to find out who all Garvey's victims were."

"It's a piece of piss," Kitson had said. "There were at least two documentaries and there's loads of books out there."

Kitson and Holland had looked at Brigstocke. Brigstocke looked at Thorne.

"Maybe," Thorne had said.

He had seen plenty of these books, their garish jackets—black and blood-red the favored colors—jumping out at him on that first trawl through the websites devoted to Raymond Garvey and others like him. He had already returned to one such site and ordered a couple of the less sensational volumes. Could it really be that simple, though? Was the man responsible for four brutal and meticulously planned murders just some wannabe psycho looking to emulate one of his heroes? A killer trying to inspire a few garish jackets of his own. "Maybe..."

Now, they were going to get their first look at him.

Kitson had spent the afternoon transferring the tapes from the Rocket Club onto DVD; trawling through hours of footage; highlighting any clips that might be useful; and finally burning them onto a separate disc. With Thorne and Brigstocke ready to watch, she picked up the remote from the trolley on which she'd wheeled in the TV and DVD player.

"Right, we've got three clips of Greg Macken and the man he picked up in the bar of the Rocket Club on Saturday evening."

"I think Greg was the one getting picked up," Thorne said.

"Either way."

"You don't look overly thrilled," Brigstocke said.

Kitson pressed the button and moved to one side. "See for yourself."

The footage was black and white, silent, with a time code running across the top of the screen.

"It's a pretty good picture," Holland said.

"They've just had all their equipment upgraded," Kitson said. "The picture's not the problem."

They were looking along a corridor, with the edge of a staircase on the left-hand side of the screen and a stone banister spiraling down out of the frame.

"These are the main stairs down from the bar on the first floor," Kitson said. A group of four girls came towards the camera, heads nodding, enjoying themselves. "Obviously there's music coming from the room where the band was performing." The girls turned onto the stairs and disappeared out of shot. "Here we go."

They watched as Greg Macken and another man moved out of the shadows at the far end of the corridor and walked straight towards the camera. Thorne could not make out the faces, but he could see that Macken's companion was talking. Macken laughed at something the other man said. Thorne moved his chair towards the screen in anticipation of his first good look at the killer.

"Don't get too excited," Kitson said.

At that moment the man let his head drop, then turned away from the camera.

"Fuck..."

"Gets worse," Kitson said.

The image froze, then jumped to a shot of the building's lobby: a wide expanse of gray stone with stairs running up on either side towards the coffee shop, the dining halls and the upstairs bars.

"We pick them up coming into the lobby five minutes after we last saw them."

"Where were they for five minutes?" Brigstocke asked.

"Maybe one of them needed the toilet. A quick snog? Who knows? Here they come..."

The slight figure of Greg Macken and his taller, better-built friend appeared at the bottom of the right-hand staircase and began walking towards the camera. The man had dark hair, wore jeans and a denim jacket, but Thorne still could not make out the face in any detail. As they reached the point where the features were becoming clearer, the man put a hand on Macken's shoulder. He leaned in to whisper something, then angled his face away from the camera.

"He knows where all the cameras are," Thorne said.

Kitson nodded as she moved on to the final clip. The camera above the main entrance picked up the couple as they stepped outside, almost immediately after the previous camera had lost them. This time the face was already turned from view, and stayed like that until the man was some distance away. The last image, which Kitson left frozen on the screen, was a nice, clean shot of the back of his head as he and Macken walked away along the pavement.

Kitson tossed the remote back down on top of the trolley.

Brigstocke got up and moved to the chair behind his desk. "He'd been in there quite a few times, that's what some of the students said, right?"

"Right," Thorne said. "Letting Macken get a good look at him while he got a good look at where all the security cameras are."

"Why go to all that trouble?" Holland said. "We know he's changed his appearance anyway."

Thorne thought Holland was probably right, but they could not be certain. As Kitson had suggested earlier, the discrepancies in the witness statements could simply be down to the normal lack of reliability when it came to stranger–stranger descriptions. The fact was that very few people could commit a stranger's appearance to memory, to the extent that some coppers did not even bother noting such things down. Thorne himself had lost count of the number of times a heavy-set six-footer had turned out to be a short-arse who'd need to run around in the shower to get wet.

But whatever the reasons, the three descriptions they had tallied in only two respects: the man was in his late twenties or early thirties and was six feet tall. "He knows he's been seen," Thorne said. "And I don't think he's too worried about that. Getting caught on camera's something else, though. He doesn't want to take that risk."

"It's probably a ten-minute walk from the Rocket back to the Mackens' flat," Kitson said. "We might have got him on three or four more cameras between the two."

Brigstocke told her to chase it up, as it was his job to do. Kitson said she already was, even though, based on what they'd just seen, it would probably be a waste of time.

Thorne shook his head, said he knew it would be. He stared at the screen. "I think we can forget what I said about him getting careless."

There was a knock and Sam Karim put his head around the door, waving a slip of paper. "The FSS have been on," he said. "They've put the bits of X-ray from the Mackens together with the other two."

Thorne stuck his hand out for the piece of paper.

"They're getting a proper scan organized," Karim said, handing it over. "They'll email that across in an hour or so, but meantime they said they'd fax over what they've got already and we can call if we've got any questions."

Thorne grunted a "thanks" as he squeezed past Karim into the corridor, then turned towards the Incident Room. A minute later, when he had reached the corner of the room where the fax machine sat, he called the FSS lab in Victoria and asked for the doctor whose name Karim had scribbled down.

"Bloody hell, that was fast, I haven't even sent it yet." Doctor Clive Kelly asked Thorne to hold on. After a rustle of papers and some slightly tetchy muttering Thorne heard a series of tell-tale beeps. Then the doctor came back on the line: "Right, it's on the way."

"I'm standing over the fax machine," Thorne said.

"Not that I could tell you where it is while it's on the way," Kelly said. "These things are a mystery to me."

The fax machine hummed into life and a sheet of paper started to appear. "You're supposed to be the scientist," Thorne said.

Kelly laughed. "Not my specialty," he said. "You give me a document and I'll tell you where the paper came from and when the ink was produced and, if I'm having a good day, I might even tell you how many times the bloke who wrote it scratched his arse. But me putting that document on a machine and pressing a button and you taking it out of another machine in a room miles away... that's just bloody witchcraft."

As soon as the fax had been received, Thorne took the sheet from the tray and stared down at the new and extended sequence of letters and numbers:

VEY48
ADD597-86/09
SYMPHONY

Said, "What am I looking at?"

"Let's start at the bottom," Kelly said. "That's the easy bit. 'Symphony' is just a type of MRI scanner. It's basically the name of the machine that did the X-ray. It's not strictly speaking an X-ray, of course, as it uses magnetic resonance as opposed to radiation, but—"

"X-ray of what?"

"Still can't tell you that, I'm afraid. But we know where it was done. See the second line?"

"I'm looking..."

"We thought the numbers might be some Health Service reference or other, and it turns out to be the area code for Cambridge University Hospitals NHS Trust. And the three letters—ADD—that's the hospital itself." Kelly waited, as though expecting Thorne to start guessing.

"Right...?"

"Addenbrooke's."

"In Cambridge?"

"Easy when you know the answer, isn't it? There isn't too much more we can tell you, I'm afraid."

Thorne said it was OK, that he didn't really need any more. At forty or so miles away, it was not the nearest hospital to Her Majesty's Prison Whitemoor, but Addenbrooke's had a worldwide reputation when it came to neurosurgery. Now Thorne knew exactly what kind of X-ray the pieces of plastic had been cut from.

"That first line's still got us all racking our brains," Kelly said.

VEY48

Thorne thanked Kelly for his help, then said, "I think '48' is probably the age of the patient when the X-ray was done."

"Easy when you know the answer."

"And 'VEY' are the last three letters of his name."

PART II

CRITICAL INCIDENTS

Afterwards

Sally and Buzz

Sally puts down the phone for the third time that day and walks slowly back to her armchair. Buzz is asleep in front of the gas fire, twitching like he's dreaming of chasing cats or something, and she has to step across him to get to the chair. She reaches down to tug at his soft brown ears, which he loves, before she sits down.

She's been ringing every day since it happened, trying to get some information. "Wasting my time," she told her friend Betty. "Nobody wants to tell me anything." She talked to the police on several occasions in the days immediately afterwards and gave a full statement in the end, but now they speak to her as though she were annoying them. Like they have far better things to do, which always makes her laugh.

It wasn't like she was asking for anything they weren't allowed to tell her, not as far as she knows. She just wants to know what's happening. If there is going to be a court case of some sort, because somebody has to be blamed for what happened, surely?

They just fobbed her off. Trotted out the same old line about enquiries being ongoing. She could almost hear the sigh in the voice of whichever policeman happened to be manning the phones that day.

"Oh Christ, it's that silly old woman from the park again..."

A car door slams somewhere outside and Buzz is up, tearing across to the door, barking while she flicks through the TV channels and tells him not to be so silly. Afterwards, he comes back and lays his head on her leg, his tail going ten to the dozen.

"I know," she says. "I'm sorry, Buzzy-Boy. Not just yet, eh?"

The dog is getting fatter, she can see that, and it's her fault. She hasn't been out of the house since it happened, and Betty can't walk him, not with her legs. Sally's daughter has taken him out a couple of times, but Buzz misses the daily visit to the park. They both miss it.

She's got as far as the front gate a couple of times, but her legs have started to tremble and she's had to go back inside.

"It's hardly surprising," Betty says. "It's a hell of a shock, getting caught up in something like that."

But Betty's wrong. It isn't shock. It's guilt.

The woman had been in a hurry, that was obvious, hadn't wanted to hang about and chat, but Sally thought there must have been something she could have done to keep them there. If she had only talked to the boy for a bit longer, just a few minutes would have done it. Got him to throw a stick for Buzz, maybe. At the time she'd thought he was quiet, that was all. It wasn't until she read the papers afterwards that she'd found out there was anything wrong with him.

Lord, just thinking about that poor boy keeps her awake most of the night.

The stupidest thing of all was, a few minutes after she'd watched the pair of them hurry away, that policeman's identification card was being waved in her face and she'd been jabbering away ten to the dozen like the silly old cow she was. Telling him he'd just missed them and showing him which way they'd gone.

She should have known something wasn't right as soon as he started running.

Sally gets up and goes to the kitchen, makes herself some tea and takes a packet of digestives from the cupboard. She brings them back to the chair on a small tray that Betty picked up for her in Southend, looks through the TV listings magazine to see if there's one of her quiz shows on.

She'll try to take Buzz out tomorrow, she tells herself, or failing that the next day. The weather forecast isn't too good anyway.

She settles down in her chair. Watches an old episode of Catchphrase *and drinks her tea. She can still feel it in her legs and in her chest, and the tremor in her hand makes the cup shake a little against the saucer.*

Twelve

As THE car turned onto the hospital approach road, Holland said, "I still think we're ahead of the game." It was the continuation of a conversation they had begun in the queue for a taxi, which had itself sprung from a discussion that had started just as the train was pulling into Cambridge station.

"The game being?"

"Catching him."

"Got it," Thorne said. "So, not knowing who he is, where he is or why the hell he's doing this puts us ahead, does it?"

"We do know who the other victims are going to be, though. That's a decent result, surely?"

"Half decent."

The cab was crawling over speed bumps towards the hospital's main entrance and Holland began digging into his wallet for cash to pay the driver. "At the very least we can make sure there aren't any more killings."

"If we can find them," Thorne said. "I mean, it's not looking too clever so far, is it?"

They had quickly established that there were four more likely candidates: the children of those victims of Raymond Garvey whose offspring had not already been successfully targeted. As of that morning, the team had only been able to track down and talk to one out of the four, and had only been able to trace her that quickly because of a criminal record.

"One out of four?" Thorne had been as angry as he was incredulous. "That's piss-poor, Russell. We need to find the other three, fast."

"You think so?" Brigstocke's tone had been every bit as sharp as Thorne's. "Maybe you should be sitting on this side of the desk."

"I'm just saying, we need to concentrate on finding them, getting them into protective custody or whatever."

"Nobody's arguing."

"That needs to be our top priority."

"I'm well aware of that, Tom, which is why I've got everyone except the cleaner working on it."

Thorne had stood in the doorway of Brigstocke's office and nodded, suddenly aware that he might have been coming across as a little self-righteous. "It wasn't a criticism—"

"So, why don't you stop going on like you're the only one who gives a shit and get out there and do your job?"

The cab stopped and Holland passed the money forward, gave a reasonable tip and asked for a receipt. The driver kept one eye on the rear-view mirror as he scribbled. He had clearly been ear-wigging all the way from the station, and when he had torn off the slip of paper and handed it across, he asked Holland if he and his friend were there to arrest anyone.

Thorne climbed out and slammed the door.

"Got anybody in mind?" Holland asked, one foot already outside the car.

The driver grinned. "I could tell you some bloody stories and that's the truth."

Holland slammed his own door then and followed Thorne, caught up with him by a small cluster of smokers gathered outside the entrance. "Is your glass ever half full?" he asked.

They strolled through the automatic doors, walked past a small shop selling magazines and chocolates, soft toys and bunches of flowers that made the average garage look like a Kensington florist's. "You think I should look on the bright side a bit more?"

"Just admitting that there is one might be a start," Holland said.

Once they had passed through the A and E Department's reception area, they stopped to ask directions. Eventually they picked up signs for the Neurological Department and a few minutes later were walking towards the lifts that would take them up to the right floor.

"You got any mints or anything?" Thorne asked.

Holland shook his head. "We could nip back to that shop."

Thorne said it didn't matter. He was not a big fan of the smell, that was all. Bleach and whatever else. He had glanced up at the signs as they'd walked.

Oncology. Dementia Unit. Antenatal Suite.

"It's a bloody stupid expression anyway," he said. He tried to keep his voice level. "Surely what's in your glass is a bit more important."

"I suppose."

"What if it's a dirty glass and it's half full of hot piss?"

They finally found the room they were looking for behind a busy ward, at the far end of a corridor with a shiny gray floor and paintings on the wall that looked as though they had been done by patients still recovering from head injuries. The sign on the door said "Neurosurgical Secretaries" and, on entering, Thorne and Holland were confronted by three women who turned in unison and stared. Holland let them know, in a quieter voice than Thorne was used to, that they had an appointment. The eldest of the women stood up and walked past him to a door that was all but hidden by an enormous filing cabinet. She knocked, and after a few seconds' muttered conversation, Thorne and Holland were shown into Doctor Pavesh Kambar's office.

Thorne nodded back towards the secretaries' room. "They all yours?" he asked.

"I share them," Kambar said. He spoke like a newsreader on Radio 4. "There's something of a pecking order."

"Are you talking about the doctors or the secretaries?"

"Both." Kambar nodded the same way that Thorne had. "But it's rather more fierce out there."

Kambar was a fit-looking man in his mid-fifties. His hair was thick, silvering, like his well-trimmed mustache, and the dark suit and polished brogues, though understated, were clearly expensive. By contrast, his office was windowless, no more than a quarter the size of the one shared by the secretaries, and there was only one chair other than his own. Thorne took it, leaving Holland to lean back a little awkwardly against the door. A year planner was mounted on the wall, while Holland's head rested at the same level as a model of the human brain that sat at the end of a bookshelf, its different sections molded in brightly colored plastic: blue, white and pink.

Thorne turned and looked from Holland to the model. "It's probably a damn sight bigger than yours," he said.

While Thorne told Kambar about their journey up, and the doctor bemoaned the vicissitudes of the London to Cambridge rail service, Holland dug into his briefcase for a photocopy of the pieced-together X-ray fragments. He handed it over. "What we talked about on the phone."

Kambar nodded, studied the picture for a few seconds. He turned to his computer and punched at the keyboard. "And this is where it comes from..."

Thorne shifted his chair a little closer and peered at the screen. There were three images which, at first glance, appeared identical: a cross-section of a brain, gray against a black background, with a white, almost perfectly round mass towards the bottom.

"I printed one out for you," Kambar said. He opened a drawer and took out what looked like a large X-ray. "These days all the images are digital, stored on disc, but we still occasionally use film if we need to." He fastened the X-ray to the light box that ran the length of the wall above his desk and studied it, as though he had never seen it before.

"So what happened to the original?" Thorne asked.

"There was no original as such," Kambar said. "As I explained, the scans are stored on computer."

Thorne pointed to the photocopy lying on Kambar's desk. "So where did they come from?"

"Well, nobody would have had any reason to print one of these things out before I did," Kambar said. "So, my guess is that they're from one of the series I printed out and gave to Raymond Garvey a few weeks before he died. Every patient is fully entitled to keep copies of all their medical records." He pointed as Thorne stared at the images. "The white mass is the tumor, obviously."

Holland had moved forward. "Looks enormous," he said.

Kambar made a fist. "That big."

"How long did you treat him?" Thorne asked.

Kambar fiddled with a pencil as he took them through a potted history of Garvey's diagnosis, treatment and, ultimately, his death. Holland made notes and Thorne listened, his eyes drifting occasionally to the pictures, stark against the light box. The simple white shadow, round and smooth, looked like nothing.

"About three and a half years ago, Garvey had what looked like an epileptic fit in his cell at Whitemoor, gashed his head open on the side of his bunk. Turns out he'd had a few similar episodes, so they took him to the district hospital in Peterborough and did a CT scan. They would only have had the vaguest idea of what they were looking at, but we're image-linked to most of the other hospitals, so they were able to ask us to have a look. We had... more than a vague idea. He came here a few weeks later for an MRI."

Kambar stood up and took the plastic brain from the shelf. "He had a massive tumor at the base of the frontal lobe. What's called a benign meningioma."

"Benign?" Holland said. "I thought it was the malignant ones that killed you."

Kambar was turning the plastic brain over in his hands. "They'll kill you slightly quicker, that's all. If a benign tumor grows big enough, the inter-cranial pressure will almost certainly be fatal. That's why we needed to operate. Here..." He lifted the model with one hand and pointed with the other to a pair of narrow parallel strips at the back. "These are the olfactory grooves."

"That's smell, right?" Holland asked.

Kambar nodded. "Garvey's tumor was sitting right there. A whopping great olfactory-groove meningioma." He looked at Holland. "In fact, issues with the patient's sense of smell are often among the earliest symptoms. Garvey claimed he had been having problems for many years. Smelling burning or petrol for no reason. Smelling nothing at all, more often than not. Sadly for him, his tumor did not present fully until long after these problems began, by which time it was far too late."

Thorne took the model from Kambar and held it for a few seconds until he started to feel a little foolish, then passed it over for Holland to put back on the shelf. "So, you operated?"

"Not for several months," Kambar said. "The inter-cranial pressure was building, no question, but there was no reason to think he was in any immediate danger. Anyway, it took him a few weeks to make up his mind. It was a high-risk procedure."

"But he still decided to go ahead."

"He did a good deal of hard thinking," Kambar said. "Took advice from some of the people he was close to. Not that there were lots of them, of course."

"Not too many likely to miss him," Holland said.

"Quite."

"So he died on the table?" Thorne asked.

"Shortly afterwards," Kambar said. "An extradural hemorrhage. He never really woke up." He switched off the light box, took down the X-ray and handed it to Thorne. "You can keep this, if it will be useful."

Thorne looked at the three pictures of Raymond Garvey's brain, the tumor that had grown within it. Garvey had brutally murdered seven women and, though it had happened earlier than he might have liked, he had been granted a relatively peaceful death. Now, three years on, someone was killing again. But why? On his behalf? In his name? Someone had left pieces of this very picture for the police to find and they still had no idea how it had come to be in his possession, nor what connected him to Raymond Garvey.

"Any idea who he might have spoken to?" Thorne asked. "Those people you said he was close to."

Kambar thought for a few moments, chewed the end of his pencil. "There were a couple of other prisoners, I think. Other vulnerable ones, like him."

"I don't suppose you can remember any names?"

"I'm sorry."

Thorne turned to Holland. "Maybe we should get over to Whitemoor this afternoon."

Holland smiled. "You angling for another overnight?"

"And the son, obviously," Kambar said.

"We'll make it back tonight—" Thorne stopped. He watched Holland's eyes go to Kambar, saw the confusion on his face, then spun around in his chair. "Sorry, what?"

"Yes, thinking about it, his son probably ended up with all Garvey's things," Kambar said. "The X-rays and so on, after the funeral."

"Garvey had no relatives," Thorne said. "Well, there's an elderly uncle somewhere, but certainly no son."

Kambar pulled a face, as if he were struggling with a particularly cryptic crossword clue. "Well, there was definitely someone claiming to be his son. Someone who made my life rather a misery for a number of weeks after Garvey died. Leaving all sorts of messages, ranting on my answering machine. I'm pretty sure the same went for the governor at Whitemoor. Pestered the poor chap for ages."

"What was his name?"

"Anthony Garvey."

"'Anthony' was Ray Garvey's middle name," Thorne said. "Sounds iffy to me." He sat back, shaking his head. "No... can't be." He looked at Holland, who could do no more than throw up his hands.

"Well, Garvey thought he was his son," Kambar said. "This man visited him several times a week for years. He had hundreds of letters from Garvey, too."

"What do you mean he made your life a misery?" Holland asked. "Did he blame you for what happened to his father?"

"Not so much that," Kambar said. "Although he obviously wasn't happy about the consequences of the operation. No, he thought there should be a retrial—"

Thorne sat up very straight. "What?"

"He wanted me to give evidence on his father's behalf."

"Why on earth would there be a retrial? There was never the slightest doubt that Garvey was guilty."

"Never the slightest doubt that he committed the murders, certainly."

"I'm not with you."

"Anthony Garvey was convinced that, were there to be a retrial, his father's conviction would be overturned. They had been talking about it ever since Garvey was first diagnosed." He jabbed the tip of his pencil at the X-ray in Thorne's lap. "They were convinced that the tumor had altered his personality; that effectively he had not been himself when he had killed those women. He wanted me to clear his father's name."

Thorne looked again at Holland, who was scribbling furiously. He glanced up, shrugged and returned to his notebook. Thorne turned back to Kambar, but could not think of anything to say. The information was still settling, the different strands becoming tangled as quickly as he tried to tease them out.

"You still haven't said what this is all about," Kambar said. "Raymond Garvey has been dead for over three years."

Holland stopped writing. "I'm sure you understand that we're not really at liberty to go into details."

"Of course." Kambar looked a little embarrassed, began to straighten some papers. "Just curious, that's all. It would be nice to know what was going on."

"You're at the back of a very long queue," Thorne said.

Thirteen

The Addenbrooke's staff canteen was no more pleasant a place to eat lunch than its equivalent at Becke House. The food was probably a little better, as was the standard of conversation at the tables, but even on the top floor, which was dedicated to administration, there was no escaping that hospital smell.

Bleach and whatever else.

They carried their trays to a table in the corner, put down plates and cutlery, a bottle of still water and a can of Diet Coke. Both had plumped for the lasagna, though the doctor had chosen to accompany it with a green salad, which had almost, but not quite, prompted his visitor to put back his chips.

"What will your colleague do for lunch?" Kambar asked.

"Not sure," Thorne said. They had rung through to make an emergency appointment with the governor at Whitemoor and, once it was confirmed, Holland had taken a cab back to Cambridge station. From there, it was a thirty-minute train journey to the small station at March, which was a short taxi ride from the prison.

"He might get there in time to eat with the governor."

"Maybe," Thorne said. He guessed that Holland would prefer to make other arrangements. As far as smells that stayed with you long after you'd left the premises went, there wasn't much to choose between a hospital and a prison. "He'll probably just grab a sandwich on the train."

Thorne and Kambar began to eat.

"Is it possible?" Thorne asked. "This change of personality business."

"Oh, personality change is certainly possible. I've dealt with a number of cases. But to the degree where you might murder someone?"

"Where you might murder seven someones."

"This is almost a Jekyll and Hyde thing we're talking about."

"So?"

"I was... dubious."

"You're not saying it isn't feasible, then?"

"Almost nothing is hard and fast where the brain is concerned," Kambar said. "It's nigh-on impossible to rule out anything completely, but there was no way I would have been willing to say that in a court of law."

Thorne began picking up chips with his fingers. "I think I get it," he said.

"Good. The lasagna's better than normal today. It's usually solid."

Thorne knew plenty of doctors and scientists who would have trotted happily up to the witness stand in search of notoriety or a hefty fee. Who would have said that, although such a thing was unlikely, they could not say for certain that it had not happened. People of that sort—many of whom were virtually professional expert witnesses—were gifts to defense barristers seeking to get the likes of Raymond Garvey off the hook. Such testimony was almost designed to plant the seed of reasonable doubt within the mind of even the most skeptical juror.

The relatives of those murdered by Garvey should have been very grateful to Pavesh Kambar.

"These cases you've dealt with," Thorne said, "how do these changes happen?"

Kambar raised his hand to demonstrate and it looked as though he might stab himself in the forehead, until he remembered and put down his fork. "The frontal lobe is what controls our cognition," he said. "It's where the brain's natural inhibitors are, where all the levels are set. It's what makes us who we are."

"And a tumor can change that?"

"Any foreign body, or any injury that affects that area. If the brain gets damaged, the personality can be affected. Altered."

"I read something in a paper once," Thorne said. "This woman suffered a massive head injury in a car accident and when she woke up she was speaking in a completely different language."

Kambar nodded. "I've seen similar cases reported," he said. "But I'm not convinced. I think those kinds of things make good stories."

"So, what sorts of changes have you seen?"

"Shy people who can suddenly become extremely gregarious. It's usually a question of inhibition, of barriers coming down. Alcohol works in the same way in that it disinhibits the frontal lobe. Imagine someone who is very drunk, but without the falling over and the slurred speech. There are no . . . niceties, you know? Social graces go out of the window, the mark is overstepped."

"I've seen that," Thorne said.

Kambar shoved the last forkful of pasta into his mouth and waited.

Ignoring what was left of his lunch, Thorne found himself telling this man he had known for only an hour about the Alzheimer's that had blighted his father's final years and a few of his own. About the old man's bizarre obsessions and the lifestyle that had grown increasingly erratic and disturbing. Kambar told him that the disease acted on the brain in precisely the way he had been describing.

"People think it's all about forgetting people's names or where you've left your keys," Kambar said. "But the worst thing is that you forget how to behave."

Thorne laid down his cutlery. Straightened it. "What about the whole genetic thing?"

Kambar nodded, understanding what he was being asked. "Look, it's far from being definitive, but only something like fifteen percent of patients with Alzheimer's had parents who suffered from it; and even then the strongest genetic link is with the rarest forms, like early onset. We're not talking about that, right?"

Thorne shook his head.

"The fact that your father had it might increase your own susceptibility a little, but no more than that." Kambar smiled. "Dementia is very common, though, and chances are you'll get it anyway, so I'd stop worrying."

"Sometimes it was good," Thorne said. "With my dad, you know? There was this one afternoon we were all playing bingo on the pier and he just lost it. Started swearing and shouting, proper filth, and everyone was upset, but I was pissing myself. And he knew it was funny. I could see it in his face."

"I'm glad it wasn't all gloom and doom," Kambar said. "How was it at the end?"

Thorne suddenly found his appetite again. He had discovered only recently how the fire in which Jim Thorne perished had started; the part he had played in the death of his own father. He had not even felt able to share the truth with Louise. He heard Kambar from the other side of the table telling him that it wasn't a problem, that he had not meant to pry.

Thorne started slightly when Kambar's beeper went off. He got up and shook the doctor's hand when it was offered. "You've been a great help. Thank you."

"I wish I could tell you I was off to perform some vital brain surgery," Kambar said. "But the truth is I've got a squash game." He reached inside his jacket and rubbed his stomach. "Should have eaten lunch a bit earlier."

"That was my fault."

"It's not a problem."

"Someone's killing the children of his victims," Thorne said suddenly.

"Sorry?" Kambar pulled his cryptic crossword face again.

Thorne could see a small blob of sauce at the edge of the doctor's mustache, a thin streak of it just below his collar. "The children of the women that Raymond Garvey murdered." Thorne suddenly felt a little dizzy and guessed he'd stood up too quickly. He took a couple of seconds, hoping that Kambar would think the pause was for his benefit. "Whoever had those fragments of Garvey's brain scan has already killed four people."

Kambar looked as though he wished he had never asked. He puffed out his cheeks, said, "Fuck."

The surprise was clearly evident on Thorne's face.

"It's a medical term," Kambar said. "One you reserve for when you hear something that makes you feel like a hopeless quack with a pocketful of leeches."

"I use it pretty much the same way," Thorne said. "Just more often."

"There are so many things that can mess up the brain, but most of them we can do nothing about." Kambar shook his head, the resignation etched in lines around his mouth. "Sometimes the damage is... invisible."

"Enjoy your game," Thorne said.

When the doctor had gone, Thorne walked over to the counter again. He bought a coffee and a thick slice of cheesecake, took them back to the table. From the window, there was a spectacular view across the flat, green fenland: Grantchester huddled a little to the north; the spires of Cambridge just visible a few miles away to the east; and the pulsing gray vein of the M11 halfway to the horizon.

Thorne looked out, savored his dessert and tried to remember exactly what his father had shouted that day on the pier. Based on what Kambar had told him, his father could probably have committed murder with a fair chance of getting away with it. It's a shame his dad had never known that. He was a crotchety and unforgiving old sod sometimes, especially in the last few years. He'd probably have drawn up a decent-sized hit list.

"Garvey's son thinks his father was wrongly imprisoned, and that the tumor might have been found earlier if he hadn't been in prison. So he blames the world and his wife for his father's death."

"I'm still not convinced this nutcase is Garvey's son," Thorne said.

"Sounds like Garvey was, though."

"OK, for the sake of argument..."

"So, the child of the killer starts killing the children of the victims. It makes a kind of sense when you think about it."

"Sense?" Thorne said.

"You know what I mean."

Thorne was walking slowly around the small branch of WHSmith at

Cambridge station, waiting for the 3:28 to King's Cross and driven back inside by the wind knifing along the platform. He kept the phone close to his mouth as he talked, so he could whisper when he and Brigstocke got to the meat of it.

"Twenty-six Anthony Garveys in the UK," Brigstocke said. "Could be better, but could be a hell of a lot worse."

Thorne had spoken to Brigstocke earlier in the day, after the initial meeting with Kambar. Holland had also checked in with the DCI, having met with the governor at Whitemoor, so now it was Thorne who needed bringing up to speed.

"I think we're wasting our time," Thorne said.

"You're not convinced. Yeah, you said."

"Even if he is Garvey's son, I think the name is dodgy. If it was genuine, there'd be records. We would have known about it."

"Still got to check them out, Tom."

"I know," Thorne said. He was sure that, whoever this man was and whatever his parentage, he himself had chosen the name he had used when visiting Whitemoor and pestering Pavesh Kambar. But he also understood that, as far as the investigation went, arses always had to be covered, and it was easy to criticize when you weren't the senior investigating officer.

"We've discounted half of them since you and I spoke earlier," Brigstocke said. "So it shouldn't take too long."

"What about the potential victims?"

"Not doing quite so well there. Still missing those three."

"Missing?"

"One is apparently on a walking holiday, but his wife can't tell us much more than that, or doesn't want to, for some reason. The other two have both slipped off the radar thanks to one thing and another. We'll find them, though."

"As long as we find them first," Thorne said.

There was a pause, voices in the background. Thorne had stopped in front of the men's magazines, and his eyes drifted from *Mojo* and *Uncut,* past *FourFourTwo,* to the covers of *Forum* and *Adult DVD Review* on the higher shelves.

"What do you think about this personality change business?"

"Have a guess," Thorne said.

"But Kambar didn't deny that it was possible?"

"Anything's possible."

"Right."

"Right, and we shouldn't discount the possibility that Garvey was actually a werewolf, or maybe the unwitting victim of a gypsy's curse. For Christ's sake, Russell..."

"Look, a man who's already murdered four people believes it, so what we think doesn't really matter."

"You haven't said what you think."

"I'm keeping an open mind," Brigstocke said. "You should try it sometime."

"It wasn't you that put Garvey away, so I don't know why you think you've got to sit on the fence."

"Steady, mate."

"Sorry—"

"It's our motive, Tom, so we need to take it seriously. OK?"

Thorne picked up a copy of *Uncut* and wandered towards the till. There was a small queue, but he still had five minutes before the train was due. "I didn't get a lot of sleep last night," he said.

"What time do you get into King's Cross?"

"Half four-ish."

"Go straight home," Brigstocke said. "You had an early start and you wouldn't get back here until after five anyway. Just make sure you're the first one in tomorrow."

"You sure?"

"It's up to you. I mean, if you want to spend a couple of hours ringing up our dozen remaining Anthony Garveys..."

"See you in the morning."

"I'll call if anything turns up."

Right, Thorne thought. Like the body of one of the three missing victims-in-waiting.

* * *

Thorne took another swig from the can of beer which, thanks to Brigstocke, he had been free to purchase and enjoy. Opposite him, a young woman, blond with bad skin, was leafing through a copy of *heat*. Every so often she looked up from the glossy pages and stared at the beer in Thorne's hand, as though the consumption of alcohol on a train was right up there with smoking crack or getting your dick out on a list of unacceptable public behavior.

They were sitting in the train's "quiet" carriage, but it wasn't as if he was drinking particularly noisily.

Raising the can to his lips, Thorne caught another dirty look and toyed with offering her a drink. Or belching as loudly as he could. Or letting her know just what he thought about every stick-thin brain-dead waste of DNA in her magazine, and that any moron who enjoyed gawping at photos of paparazzi fodder stumbling out of nightclubs or climbing out of limos with no knickers on was in no position to pass judgment on anybody. Then he thought about what Louise would say. He remembered that she occasionally flicked happily through *OK* and *heat,* albeit while she was having her hair done or sitting in a doctor's waiting room.

He waited until the woman glanced up again, then smiled until she quickly dropped her eyes back to the magazine.

Makes a kind of sense.

People dying because of who their mothers were; killing because of who their fathers might have been. Thorne swallowed his piss-weak lager and supposed that it made as much sense as anything else in a world where being famous counted for so much. Where what you were famous for didn't matter at all. A world where couples who weren't fit to look after hamsters dragged six kids round the supermarket. Where some women popped out babies like they were shelling peas, while others didn't find it quite so straightforward.

"Any more tickets from Cambridge?"

Thorne had missed the inspector first time round while he'd been busy at the buffet. As soon as his ticket was punched, he stood up to make a return trip, crushing his empty can as noisily as possible as he squeezed out of his seat. Then tossing it back onto the table.

At the end of the carriage, a man was jabbering into his mobile. He was laughing, a hissy half cough, and telling someone how something was "just typical" of someone else. It wasn't loud so much as annoying.

Thorne stopped at the man's table and snatched the phone from his hand, nodding up at the sign: a picture of a mobile with a red line through it. He pushed the button to end the man's call, and reached round quickly with his other hand to take out his wallet. The man said, "What the fuck do you—?" then stopped when he saw the warrant card.

Thorne walked on towards the buffet car in a far better mood.

Louise didn't get home until an hour after Thorne.

"You know what it's like," she said. "You take a couple of days off and there's shed-loads to catch up on." She told him she was enjoying getting stuck into things, having something else to think about. She was in a good mood.

Thorne suggested that she should put in for some overtime, as work was so obviously agreeing with her.

"It's about getting things in perspective," she said.

Louise made them spaghetti with bacon, onions and pesto and afterwards they sat in front of the TV for a while. She said, "I do want to talk about what happened, you know. I think we should."

"We have talked about it."

"No, we haven't. Not how we feel about it." She smiled. "It's been bloody deafening, tell you the truth."

"What?"

"The sound of you walking on eggshells."

Thorne stared at the television.

"How do you feel?" Louise said.

"I don't know," Thorne said. "How you'd expect. Upset."

"You've not said anything."

Thorne felt uncomfortably warm. "I don't think I've had enough time to . . . process things."

"Fine. Good. That's OK."

They watched a little more television, then went to bed. They lay and cuddled, and when Louise fell asleep Thorne read for a while; a few more chapters from one of the true-crime books he'd bought online.

Raymond Garvey had supported Crystal Palace and kept pet rabbits as a boy. He had enjoyed tinkering with motorbikes and had battered his first victim to death with half a house-brick.

When Thorne had switched the light out, he turned onto his side, feeling Louise come with him, pressed soft into his back, and the guilt bubbling up in him like acid reflux.

Fourteen

H.M.P. Whitemoor

"I CAN'T get over how hard they make it getting in here."

"It's a damn sight harder getting out."

"They take everything off you, check your stuff. All these doors you have to go through."

"So you don't smuggle anything in."

"Like what?"

"Cigarettes is the main thing. Drugs. People still manage it, though."

"OK."

"Sorry for... staring. I can't believe you're really here."

"Did you not believe me, when I said I was coming?"

"It's just so out of the blue, you know? I never expected... I never thought you'd find out."

"I wasn't meant to. Nobody would have told me."

"So, how—?"

"There were some old letters in the loft, some official stuff, at my auntie's place. I asked her and she started to cry, so I knew it was true."

"And how did you feel when you found out?"

"Pissed off. With her, I mean... with Mum, for not telling me."

"She never told me, either. About you."

"I know. I found the letter you wrote to my auntie. I know why you did what you did."

"Oh, Jesus..."

"It's fine, really. I know how it made you feel, Christ—"

"It's not fine."

"I think I'd have done the same thing."

"I always presumed you'd hate my guts. That's why I never tried to get in touch or anything."

"From when I was six or seven or whatever, she said you were dead. That my 'father' was dead. Told me he was an engineer. How could she do that?"

"I was an engineer, for British Telecom. Before..."

"I'm not sorry she's dead. You don't have to worry."

"You look different to the photos you sent."

"God, they're ancient. From when I was at school. I'll send you some more recent ones, if you want."

"You not at school anymore?"

"What's the point?"

"Long as it's not got anything to do with me, with finding out who I was, I mean. If you've got exams, anything like that, you should probably finish them."

"You look different, too. I saw a few pictures on the internet, some old newspapers. There's that one they use in all the books."

"Everybody piles on the weight in here. I don't get as much exercise as other prisoners... normal prisoners."

"That's really unfair."

"They keep the special ones apart from the rest. Ex-coppers, nonces, all that sort."

"You're not that sort."

"It's fine, I'm used to it."

"Why are you smiling?"

"It's funny, she never told you about me, then she goes and gives you my middle name."

"No, she didn't. She gave me a stupid name. I changed it as soon as I found those letters. Not legally or anything, but I'll probably get round to that."

"Up to you."

"Doesn't matter. I'm Anthony from now on, whatever."

"It's nice."

"Second name too: Anthony Garvey."

"That's got a ring, definitely."

"Tony's all right, I don't mind that."

"Sounds good. Younger, like."

"So, you don't mind if I visit again?"

"Are you going already?"

"No, don't worry, there's ages yet. I was just checking it would be OK."

"Better than OK."

"For me too."

"Yeah... Tony sounds really good..."

Fifteen

BRIGSTOCKE WAS upbeat at the morning briefing, but then he did not have a great deal of choice. Progress—unspectacular yet tangible—was being made, but the DCI's mood would have been much the same even if it were not. As senior investigating officer and team leader, he could never be seen banging his head against the wall, telling the troops that the investigation was going nowhere and that everything was turning to shit.

It was one of the reasons why Thorne had resisted the step up; why, despite Louise's encouragement, he had not taken the chief inspector's exams. The extra money would have been welcome, of course, and there was a much better parking space attached to the rank, but the putting on of a brave face, however much the circumstances might demand it, was not something he was good at.

"You learn all that stuff," Louise had said.

But Thorne had not been persuaded. "I don't want to learn it," he had said. "And I'd most likely punch the first tosser to give me a funny handshake."

After the briefing, Thorne walked back into the Incident Room with Holland. He waited while Holland made them both coffee and let his eyes drift across to the large whiteboard that dominated one wall. Below photographs of the four victims to date, the board was divided in half, with a thick, not-quite-straight line of black felt-tip running down the middle. On the left-hand side were listed the seven women murdered by Raymond Garvey; and opposite, their children. Red lines linked the mothers' names with those of their sons and daughters.

Thorne looked at the list of names on the right-hand side of the board, their ages and the dates on which they had died, where relevant. A roll-call of those already killed and those they had to presume would be targeted by the killer:

Catherine Burke (23 yrs) 9 Sept. (Brother, Martin, killed in car accident)
Emily Walker (33 yrs) 24 Sept.
Gregory and Alexandra Macken (20 yrs/18 yrs) 27 Sept.
Andrew Dowd (31 yrs)
Deborah Mitchell (29 yrs)
Graham Fowler (30 yrs)
Simon Walsh (27 yrs)

Along the bottom of the board were three E-fits, based on the descriptions given by Emily Walker's neighbor, the witness who had seen a man talking to Catherine Burke and the students who had watched Greg Macken get picked up in the Rocket Club. Under each was the name "Anthony Garvey." Whether Thorne was right to doubt its authenticity or not, it was the only name they had to go on when it came to the identity of their prime suspect.

Holland appeared at Thorne's shoulder and handed him his coffee. Thorne stared into the plastic cup.

"No milk in the fridge, so I had to use the powdered stuff."

"We're going to have to start leaving notes on the cartons," Thorne said. "Like those students."

Holland nodded towards the whiteboard. Said, "What d'you reckon it is with Dowd and his wife, then?"

Andrew Dowd was the man Brigstocke had mentioned the day before; someone who, according to his wife, had set out to go walking in the Lake District a few days before and with whom she had had minimal contact since. She claimed not to know the place he had been headed, the names of any hotels or B&Bs he had been intending to stay in or even how long he had planned to be away. There had been predictable concern for Dowd's safety, until officers had spoken to his wife, after which they decided it was only his marriage that was almost certainly dead. She had told them that Andrew had gone with very little notice, that he had taken his mobile phone but not his charger and that he had called only once, the evening of the day he went, to let her know he had arrived safely. Using cell-site technology, the team had confirmed that the call was made from Keswick, which was where local searches were now focused. A text message had been sent to Dowd's phone asking him to contact the police urgently, but since that first call either the handset had been switched off or the battery was dead.

"They've obviously had some kind of enormous row," Thorne said. "She doesn't want to admit he's just walked out, so she's making out like it's no big deal, like he does this regularly. Cuts himself off for a few days, so he can find himself, whatever."

"He wants to find himself a new wife," Holland said. "The one he's got sounds like a nightmare."

"No one knows what goes on behind closed doors." Thorne saw the sideways look from Holland. "Charlie Rich. 1973."

"What about the other two?" Holland asked.

If either of the two men whose names were below Dowd's on the list possessed mobile phones, then they were pay-as-you-go, as there was no trace of any contracts. No trace of anything.

Simon Walsh had lived at seven addresses in the previous eighteen months, signing on at half a dozen different benefit offices before dropping out of the system. His only existing relative, an aunt, claimed not to have heard from him in ten years; and a friend who had last seen him six months previously said he thought Walsh might have become addicted to anti-depressants. Without being told why they were looking for him, the friend added, somewhat ironically, that he was always expecting to hear that Simon had been found dead somewhere.

According to Graham Fowler's estranged wife, he had been sleeping rough somewhere in southeast London for at least two years, after an increasingly severe alcohol problem had cost him first his job, then his family. There was nobody of that name registered at any of the established day centers or night shelters.

"Well, I can't see us finding either of them through credit-card receipts," Thorne said. A few years before, he had spent a period undercover, living on the streets of the West End in an effort to find the man who was killing rough sleepers. He had met plenty like Simon Walsh and Graham Fowler, men who had slipped through the cracks by accident or design. "They both sound like people who don't particularly want to be found."

"That might be what saves their lives," Holland said. "I mean, if we can't find them..."

Thorne looked at the remaining name, which had been circled again and again in red felt-tip, as if in exasperation. "Not that finding them is the end of the problem."

The one person on the list of potential victims that they had been able to track down was proving to be something of a handful. Despite repeated conversations and visits from family liaison officers, Debbie Mitchell was refusing to so much as consider the possibility of entering protective custody.

"Well, she's not all there, is she?" Holland said.

"She's got problems."

"And there's this business with her kid."

Debbie Mitchell was the single mother of a child with severe learning difficulties. She had been arrested on three occasions for soliciting and on several more for possession of Class A drugs.

"It's weird, this drug thing," Holland said.

"What thing?"

"Catherine Burke did a few; now Debbie Mitchell. I should think there's every chance with Walsh and Fowler, too."

"Not weird really," Thorne said. "Not when you think about what they've all got in common. You ask me, the weirdos are the ones who aren't drug addicts or alcoholics."

The office moved all around them, while they drank their coffees and stared at the board, as though the marker-pen lines and scribbles were symbols in some complex equation, the answer to which might suddenly present itself if they looked hard enough.

Three hours later, Thorne was standing in front of another board, looking at the list of lunchtime specials on the menu at the Royal Oak. Until recently, in what passed for the team's local, "special" might have applied to almost any food that was vaguely edible, but a new landlord had radically improved standards. An ex-copper himself, he knew that even police officers demanded more than shit and chips at lunchtime. It was still far from being a gastropub, but it had finally become something more than a last resort.

Thorne placed his order and took a Diet Coke and a bitter lemon back to a table by the fruit machine. He slid in next to Yvonne Kitson. They touched glasses and drank, their expressions making it clear that they would prefer a pint of strong lager and a cold white wine, respectively.

"Later," Kitson said.

Thorne picked up a beer-mat and began methodically tearing it into tiny pieces. "This case is breaking new ground," he said. "It's a 'who-didn't-do-it.' "

Kitson smiled, happy to play along. "Go on then, who didn't do it?"

"Well, since you ask... It wasn't a primary school teacher in Doncaster, it wasn't a photocopier repairman and keen amateur boxer from Wrexham, and it certainly wasn't a seventy-eight-year-old ex-merchant seaman who's retired with his wife to Portugal. It's lovely weather there today, by the way, he told me so several times. He and his wife were planning to have lunch out by the pool."

"Three of your Anthony Garveys?"

"My morning so far."

"Got to be done."

"Oh, I know," Thorne said. "And I'm loving every vitally important minute of it. I've been eliminating people from my enquiries like there's no tomorrow. Putting lines through their names and ticking them off, just to be on the safe side, you know? Eliminating all day long. I am... the Eliminator!"

Kitson sipped her drink. "Fine, but I didn't hear you coming up with any bright ideas this morning."

Thorne finished ripping up the beer-mat and nudged the pieces into a nice, neat pile. He had nothing much to say and even if he had, seeing Russell Brigstocke turn from the bar and wave at them, he would probably have kept it to himself. Using basic mime techniques, he and Kitson were able to transmit their desire for more drinks, and once Brigstocke had bought them, he joined them at the table.

"Have you already ordered?"

Two nods.

Brigstocke took a long drink of sparkling water and sat back. "I just lost fifteen minutes of my lunch-hour thanks to Debbie Dozy-Bollocks."

"Still being difficult?" Kitson asked.

"You know an FLO named Adam Strang?"

Thorne nodded, remembering the Scotsman from the Macken crime scene.

"Well, he spent most of this morning trying to talk sense into her, but she's not having any of it. She's just point-blank refusing to go anywhere."

"How much has she been told?"

"Not everything, obviously. Enough, though, or at least it should be."

"What are the other options?" Kitson asked.

Brigstocke shook his head, like he was sick of thinking about it. "I'm reluctant to stick a car outside twenty-four hours a day just because she's being stupid."

"Can we install a panic button?"

"Not enough," Thorne said. "I don't think Emily Walker or Greg Macken would have had time to push one."

"So, what else can we do?" Brigstocke asked. "Arrest her?"

Kitson flicked a bright red fingernail against the edge of her glass. "That shouldn't take too long, looking at her record."

A waitress arrived with the food: lamb casserole for Thorne and fish pie for Kitson. Brigstocke stared down unenthusiastically at the bowl of pasta he was given, then pointed at Thorne's plate.

"I fancied that, but somebody had just ordered the last one."

"The quick and the dead," Thorne said.

They ate for a minute or so without talking, until Thorne said, "Why aren't we involving the press with this?"

Brigstocke swallowed quickly. "I thought we went through this earlier on." He looked to Kitson for validation.

She nodded. "Keeping quiet about the serial thing."

"Right," Brigstocke said.

"I'm not talking about that," Thorne said. "Why aren't we getting photos of Dowd and the others in the papers, on the box, whatever? We can get something out of them for a change."

This time Brigstocke took his time swallowing and answered quietly. "That's . . . tricky." He looked around. Many of the team were eating at nearby tables.

Thorne pushed his plate aside and leaned closer to Brigstocke, just as one of the trainee detectives chose that moment to come over and spend five minutes pumping all his loose change into the fruit machine. There was nothing more said about the case until he had finished. Thorne made a comment about the machine being tight and watched the trainee walk away. Then turned back to Brigstocke.

"Tricky, you said?"

"I was talking to Jesmond," Brigstocke said.

Thorne winced theatrically at the mention of the superintendent's name. "I'm sorry."

"Somebody has to. Anyway, there appears to be a strong feeling that using the press in the way you're suggesting might not be a good idea."

"Why not?"

"Because it may alert the killer to the fact that we're onto him."

"Is that a problem?"

"They think it might be, if we want to catch him."

"So, we want to catch him more than we want to protect the people he's trying to kill?"

Brigstocke sighed. "Listen, I know."

"That's mental," Thorne said. "He must already know we're onto him. He left the bits of X-ray, for Christ's sake. He wants us to put it all together."

"I'm just letting you know what I was told, all right?"

"On top of which, I can't see this bloke just packing his bags and buggering off because he sees a few photos in the paper."

"Point taken."

"I don't think he's the type to stop."

"Look, there's no point getting arsy with me. I'm just telling you, there's a... tension, between the different... priorities."

"Surely the first priority has to be protecting the potential victims?" Kitson said.

"Tell that to Debbie Mitchell." Brigstocke turned to Thorne. "In fact, you can tell the superintendent, seeing as you feel so strongly about it. They're talking about putting a critical incident panel together."

"I'd rather stick needles in my eyes," Thorne said. He had sat on such a panel a couple of times before, struggling to look interested while diplomats in uniform droned on about media strategy, and had sworn that he would never do so again.

"Right, in which case you should get off your high horse and stop giving me grief." Brigstocke took one last mouthful of pasta and pushed back his chair. "Fair enough?"

Neither Thorne nor Kitson ate too much more after Brigstocke had left and let the waitress take away the plates the next time she was passing.

"High horse?"

"High-ish," Kitson said.

"Come on, I'm right though, aren't I?"

"I don't think he disagrees with you, but there's not a great deal he can do about it. Rock and a hard place, all that."

There was still fifteen minutes before either of them was due back at Becke House. Thorne drained his glass. "So, do you really fancy spending the rest of the afternoon ringing up people you know haven't killed anyone and asking them if they've killed anyone?"

"You finally had a bright idea?"

"What you said about arresting Debbie Mitchell."

"I was only half joking."

"Let's take a drive over there. You never know, if we push it, we might get her to assault one of us."

Kitson took a compact from her handbag and reapplied her lipstick. "I'll toss you for it in the car," she said.

Sixteen

Totteridge was a leafy north London suburb with a bona fide village at its heart, where men who owned or played for football clubs lived with their suspiciously expressionless wives. A few minutes away towards Barnet, however, you would find yourself in a noticeably less well-heeled area just shy of the Great North Road, where most of the footballers were the sort who kicked lumps out of one another on Sunday mornings, smoking in the center circle at halftime and heading straight for a fry-up at the final whistle.

Debbie Mitchell lived on the top floor of a three-story block on the Dollis Park Estate, a sprawl of sixties and seventies mixed-tenure housing in the shadow of Barnet FC's ground. From the window of the small, smoke-filled living room, Thorne could just make out the floodlights of Underhill, the corner of the stadium's main stand.

"It must get pretty busy on match days," Kitson said.

"Hang on a minute, this is Barnet we're talking about," Thorne said. "They'd probably think the four of us was a pretty decent crowd."

Only Kitson smiled as Thorne turned back to the window. Looking the other way, he could see the main road, the green belt rolling away beyond a petrol station and an enormous branch of Carpet Express.

"Vision Express I can just about understand," he said, pointing. "Even

Shoe Express, at a push. You know, you lose a shoe, you're late for a party, whatever. But who could possibly need a carpet... really fast?"

"What's he on about?"

"I mean, in how much of a hurry does someone have to be?"

One of the two women sitting close together on the sofa nodded towards Thorne, then turned to address Kitson, who was perched on the edge of a dining chair near the door. "I get it," she said. "They've not got anywhere with the sensitive ones, or the ones who marched in here shouting the odds, so now they've sent the copper who thinks he's a bloody comedian."

Nina Collins was a good few years older than Debbie Mitchell, early forties, probably, and she had done most of the talking since Thorne and Kitson had arrived. She had opened the door, told them she was a friend of Debbie, her best friend, and that Debbie was inside, trying to get some rest and keep Jason calm. That she was frazzled, and who the hell wouldn't be, with coppers ringing up every ten minutes telling her she had to get out of her home?

"I suppose you've come to have another bash," she'd said, blowing cigarette smoke at them, before turning and walking back inside.

In the living room, Thorne turned from the window again and shrugged. "As a matter of fact," he said, "quite a few people tell me I'm pretty funny."

Collins stubbed out her cigarette. "They're wrong," she said.

Thorne dragged a footstool across and sat down on it in front of the television. He looked at the two women. Collins was short and large-breasted, with black hair tousled into spikes, red at the tips when it caught the light. She wore a tight, striped rugby shirt that showed off her chest and there was a softness in her face, at odds with the body language and the brittle, Benson & Hedges voice. (Later, when there were new cases to worry about, Thorne would confess to Kitson, after a couple of pints, that he'd secretly quite fancied Nina Collins.)

"He's got a point," the woman next to Collins said. "It is a bloody stupid name. The carpets are seriously cheap, though, I'll give them that."

Debbie Mitchell was taller and skinnier than her friend. Her hair was long and dirty-blond, cut very straight on either side of a face that was drawn and blotchy, the foundation failing to hide an angry cluster of whiteheads around one nostril. She was barefoot, with her legs pulled up beneath her and one arm trailing over the edge of the sofa, in almost permanent contact with the boy playing on the carpet at her side.

"He seems happy," Kitson said.

Collins turned as though she'd forgotten Kitson was there. "He is happy. He's always happiest when he's with his mum."

"Does he have any kind of... carer?"

"Just me," Mitchell said. "There's just us."

Jason was tall for his age—eight, according to his mother's file—and the pajamas he was wearing looked a year or two too small for him. He pushed a large plastic train—the sort a slightly younger child might ride around on—up and down in a straight line along the side of the sofa. It was obviously a game he played a lot. There were track marks worn into the brown carpet.

"What about school?" Thorne asked.

"He goes to a special place three days a week," Mitchell said. "Up in Hatfield. I have to stay with him, though, because he screams the place down if I'm not there."

Collins held up two fingers. "Twice Social Services have taken Jason away from her and every time it's been a nightmare for him." Mitchell shook her head, eyes down, as though she didn't want her friend to continue, but Collins raised her hand again, determined to have her say. "Supposed to be for his own good, being separated from his mum, and of course he bloody hates it." She reached across and squeezed Mitchell's hand. "Every time she's cleaned herself up and sorted her life out, though, haven't you, darling?"

"We're fine now," Mitchell said.

"Three bloody buses and a train to get out to Hatfield," Collins said. She shook her head, disgusted. "You'd think the council would lay on some sort of transport, wouldn't you? But they're too busy funding lesbian play centers and that sort of shit."

"We don't mind," Mitchell said. "It's always an adventure, providing the weather's OK." She looked round at Kitson. "He doesn't get bored like other kids, you know?"

"Is it autism?" Kitson asked.

Mitchell shrugged. "They don't think so. I don't think they know what it is, tell you the truth, and we've given up worrying about it. Whatever it is, nobody can do anything about it, so we just get on with things."

Thorne watched as the boy pushed his train back and forth, his chin quivering as he made barely audible "chuffing" noises. He had the same wide blue eyes as his mother, though his lips were fuller, redder. When he smiled, which for no reason that was obvious he did every minute or so, his front teeth slid down over his bottom lip and he moved them quickly from side to side. There was no way of knowing if Debbie Mitchell did the same thing, as Thorne had yet to see her smile.

"How much does he understand?" Thorne asked.

Nina Collins was lighting up again. "Bloody hell, are you pair coppers or social workers?"

"I just don't want to upset him," Thorne said. "When we get started."

Mitchell shook her head, like it was OK, but her hand drifted across to her son's head, moved through his hair.

"You going to tell us about this man again?" Collins said.

Thorne nodded. "What have they told you so far, the sensitive coppers and the shouty ones?"

Mitchell took a deep breath. "They talked about this weirdo who might want to hurt me because of what happened to my mum."

Thorne nodded again. "Right, and they probably said stuff like, 'We have reason to believe that you might be in danger.' "

"Something like that."

"Well, here's the thing. There's no might about it, OK? Not if you stay where you are."

Kitson moved her chair forward. "You mustn't underestimate the man we're talking about here, Debbie."

"She's had weirdos like this floating around all her life," Collins said. "Wanting to know about what happened to her mum, getting some cheap thrill out of it or something."

"This particular weirdo has already killed four people, Debbie," Thorne said. "Four people whose mothers died the same way yours did."

Collins' hand was in her hair, pulling at the spikes. "They never said four..."

"A couple, I thought," Mitchell said. "You know, that might have been by this same man."

Thorne looked at Kitson. He wondered who had taken the decision about what this woman should be told. Had they deliberated over how many previous murders they could mention? Was two deemed to be OK and three unacceptable? It seemed ridiculous, not least because one should have been enough to send anyone scurrying for cover without looking back. But whatever was preventing Debbie Mitchell from doing the sensible thing, and however much trouble he might be in for taking a unilateral decision, Thorne could see no point in pussyfooting around.

"Would you like to know how he did it?" Thorne asked.

"No." Collins had gone noticeably pale.

"Exactly how he stalked and murdered four people, what he used to kill them. Would that make you take this seriously? Get you off your arse and make you start packing?"

"It wouldn't make any difference," Mitchell said, raising her voice. "We need to stay here."

The women had moved even closer together. Thorne could see that Jason had stopped playing with his train and was on his knees by the side of the sofa, pulling at his mother's hand, trying to rub it against his cheek.

"Are you worried about Jason?" Kitson said. "Is that the problem? Because you wouldn't be separated."

Mitchell started shaking her head, but it wasn't clear if she was answering the question or just didn't believe what Kitson was telling her.

"We have special accommodation designed for families."

"No."

"You need to get out—"

"He got into their houses," Thorne said. "Don't you understand? They all thought they were safe and he got inside and murdered them."

"I'll look after them," Collins said.

Thorne flicked his eyes to her. "What, even at night, Nina? You'll be working, won't you?" Thorne had checked Collins' record and seen that she'd had more arrests for soliciting than Debbie Mitchell. He watched her blink, glanced across in time to see something pass across Kitson's face, and felt a stab of guilt; felt the wind leak out of him. However stupid and stubborn these women were being, it was clear that Nina Collins was hugely attached to Debbie Mitchell and her son; that her affection for them was fierce and unconditional. "Look, I'm just saying..."

When Collins came back at him, her voice had dropped a little. The nerves were evident in the staccato drags on her cigarette and the stutter as she blew out the smoke. "Can't you look after us?"

"That's what we're trying to do," Thorne said.

"We can't go," Mitchell said. She was staring at Jason, watching the teeth move across his bottom lip as he squeezed her hand. "You don't understand. He needs routine. We both do. It's the only way we can manage to keep everything on an even keel, you know? The only thing that stops it all going to pieces."

In the desperation that had masked her face, Thorne caught a glimpse of what was driving her. He could see that her terror in acknowledging the threat—the crippling fear of change that could see a spiral back into drugs and might conceivably cost her custody of her child again—was even greater than her fear of the man who wanted to kill her.

"He would be so unhappy," she said.

Thorne understood, just, but it didn't matter. "How happy would he be if you were dead?"

Mitchell suddenly cried out in pain and yanked her hand away from Jason's mouth, her knuckles having caught on the boy's teeth as he squeezed and kissed it. His face was frozen for a few seconds in shock and she quickly got off the sofa to comfort him, but he was already starting to whimper and turn back to his plastic train.

Collins stood up too. "That's enough, I reckon," she said. She waited for Thorne and Kitson to get up, then ushered them towards the front door.

Kitson stopped and turned at the end of the hallway. "Please try and talk some sense into her, Nina."

Collins reached past her and opened the door. "What would make sense is for you lot to stop pissing about and catch this nutter. All right, love? Then we wouldn't need to be having this conversation, would we?"

"For Jason's sake," Thorne said.

Collins all but pushed them both out onto the front step and stared Thorne down, her swagger returned. She said, "I liked you better when you were telling your shit jokes."

Then she slammed the door in their faces.

"Looks like it's got to be an arrest then," Kitson said, as they walked towards the car.

Thorne shook his head and moved quickly ahead of her. "Last chance," he said. He opened the door of the BMW, reached inside for a large brown envelope and walked back past Kitson, towards Debbie Mitchell's front door.

"Tom . . . ?"

He said nothing when Nina Collins opened the door. Just pushed the envelope into her hand and wheeled away. He was halfway back to the car when he heard the door close behind him.

Kitson stared at him as he turned the ignition over. "Was that what I think it was?"

"Impossible to answer that," Thorne said. He held up his hand to stop her speaking again, as if it might help the engine catch. "I have no idea what you think it was."

Seventeen

Back at the office there were still a few Anthony Garveys to trace and eliminate. There was paperwork for the DVLA and assorted credit-reference agencies to be completed as part of the hunt for Graham Fowler and Simon Walsh; liaison with forces in the north in an effort to track down Andrew Dowd. So, in terms of excitement, there was nothing to match the small wager that Thorne and Kitson had made with each other on the way back from Whetstone.

"By the end of the day, I reckon," Kitson had said.

"No chance."

"I'm telling you. Collins is the type who likes to have her say."

There was every chance Kitson was right, but Thorne was in the mood to argue that white was black. "Tomorrow," he'd said. "Earliest, if at all."

"Tenner?"

Being of a mind to argue—"chopsy," his father used to call it—was one thing, but this was cold, hard cash. Thorne had read somewhere that the buzz of gambling lay in the fear of losing far more than in the possibility of winning, and having recently kicked an online poker habit, he'd been looking for something to make his heart beat a little bit faster. "You're on," he'd said.

With fifteen minutes until going-home time, Sam Karim put his head round the door to say that Brigstocke wanted a word, and Thorne's heart-rate increased for all the wrong reasons. "How are you going to spend the money?" he asked on his way to the door.

"I'm saving up for shoes," Kitson said. "Do you want to go double or quits?"

"On what?"

"Another tenner says Spurs lose tomorrow."

At home against Aston Villa. Should be guaranteed at least a point. It was Spurs, though...

"I think somebody's bottle's gone," Kitson said.

Karim was still standing in the doorway. "The guv'nor did say now."

"Stick it up your arse," Thorne said. "Both of you."

"I think maybe you should make another appointment to see that brain doctor," Brigstocke said. He leaned back against the edge of his desk, arms folded.

Thorne said nothing. It was usually best just to sit there and take it.

"Tell him to have a look, see if he can find one."

Brigstocke had moved on from the straightforward, high-volume bollocking—he had done that while recounting his fifteen-minute phone conversation with Nina Collins—and was now onto the sarcasm. Before long he would be into the last phase, which Thorne enjoyed the least: the one where the pitch dropped and the tone became one of sadness and disappointment, as though the offense for which he was dishing out the dressing down had actually wounded him. Thorne knew that Brigstocke had learned this "you've let me down, you've let yourself down, you've let the whole school down" approach from Trevor Jesmond, who considered himself a master of it. Thorne had been on the receiving end many times, had looked suitably chastened at the slowly shaking head and the puppy-in-need-of-a-home expression, but in Jesmond's case he always relished it, working on the principle that if he was upsetting the superintendent, he was clearly doing something right.

"Mitchell was terrified," Brigstocke said. "Poor woman's shitting herself, according to her friend."

"That was the idea."

"Oh, thank Christ for that. There I was thinking you were showing her confidential photographs of all the murder victims because you were an insensitive idiot who was gagging to get back into uniform. Have you still got a pointed hat?"

"Not all the victims," Thorne said.

"What?"

"It wasn't all the victims. Just the Mackens."

"Well, that's OK then."

Thorne couldn't prevent the faintest of smirks washing across his face. "Just a sample."

"Jesus, Tom..."

"Did it work?"

Brigstocke stared at him for a few seconds, as though toying with one last cathartic bout of shouting, before walking behind his desk and sitting down. "Debbie Mitchell's moving in with Nina Collins," he said. "It's only a couple of streets away—"

"Doesn't matter, as long as she moves."

"She wants to stay close to the park, she says. It's the kid's favorite place, apparently."

"Well, she can forget about that for a while."

"Plus, the kid knows Nina, so there shouldn't be too much disruption. I understand he doesn't respond well to... upheaval."

Thorne told Brigstocke he was right. He remembered the boy's smile, how easily it appeared and how astounding it was, considering that upheaval was something he had lived with for a long time. "So, I'm not in the shit then?"

It was Brigstocke's turn to smirk. "Oh, don't worry, if Collins or Mitchell decides to make any sort of official complaint, I'll give you up like a shot."

"You're a pal," Thorne said.

"Yes, I am." Brigstocke looked down to the papers on his desk, as though he was good and ready for Thorne to leave. "Or I would have given you up already."

Thorne recognized a cue and turned for the door, but Brigstocke called him back.

"You were wrong about Anthony Garvey," he said.

"Yeah?"

"Don't know about the name, but we can be pretty sure he's Raymond Garvey's son."

Thorne nodded. "The DNA..."

"We had Garvey senior's on file, obviously, so we ran a match with the sample we got from under Catherine Burke's fingernails. We can be ninety-nine percent sure they're father and son."

"Ninety-nine percent?"

Brigstocke knew that Thorne understood why they could not declare it a 100 percent match, but he said it anyway, enjoying the moment. "To be certain, we need to know who the mother was." The look, before Brigstocke dropped his eyes back to his paperwork, said, "Now we're done."

Walking out into the car-park, Kitson—ten pounds richer—said, "You remember the argument with Brigstocke in the pub? That stuff about the 'tension' between the need to catch the killer and the need to protect the potential victims."

"I think that's when his bad mood started," Thorne said. "That, or the fact that I got the last lamb casserole."

"Seriously."

"What?"

"I was thinking. Didn't it seem like nobody was trying very hard to get Debbie Mitchell out of that house?"

"Well, she certainly took some shifting."

"You managed it, though. How come nobody else did?"

It was cold and starting to rain. They waited under the concrete overhang outside the rear entrance to Becke House, Thorne's car fifty yards to his left and Kitson's further away in the other direction.

"You saying they were happy to let her stay there as some kind of bait?" Thorne asked.

"Well, it wasn't like they had to plan it or anything. I mean, she didn't want to leave, so maybe someone thought, Let's use this to our advantage."

"Then we can't be blamed if it all goes tits up."

"Right," Kitson said. "They stick a few unmarked cars around the place, set up an observation point, cameras, whatever."

Thorne was nodding, going with it. "And the brass are pissed off with me, not because of this business with the crime-scene photos, but because they had their next victim sitting there waiting for the killer on a plate, and I went and ballsed it up."

"Maybe." Kitson was wearing a gray hooded top under a leather jacket. She raised the hood, stared out into the drizzle. "I'm just thinking out loud. It's been a long day."

"You've had sillier ideas," Thorne said.

"You think so?"

"For sure." Thorne turned to her and held the look to let her know that he meant it, before allowing the smile to come. "We're definitely worth a point against Villa tomorrow."

"You should have taken the bet then," Kitson said.

The ALERT tone on Thorne's mobile sounded. He fished the handset from his pocket. The text was from Louise: celebration drink with team after work. won't be 2 late. X.

"Fancy grabbing a drink?" Thorne asked. Kitson looked at her watch, but he could see it was a gesture as much as anything. "Quick one in the Oak?"

"I'd better not. The kids, you know."

"Why are you still talking to me?"

"See you tomorrow."

"Not sure I'll be in," Thorne said. He was pressing buttons on his phone, deleting the message from Louise. "Got a meeting in the center of town mid-morning, so we'll see how it goes."

"Monday, then..."

Thorne grunted a "yes" and watched Kitson jog away towards her car. After a few moments, he stepped out into the rain and began to walk towards his.

Later, sinking into the sofa, his eyes scanned the living room, taking in the patch of damp by the side of the window and the bits on the carpet that were not the fleck in its weave. Not for the first time, he contemplated getting a cleaner. He listened to Charlie Rich singing "A Sunday Kind of Woman" and "Nothing in the World," letting his eyes close and his mind wander, the music fading into a mix that included the less tuneful voices of Russell Brigstocke and Yvonne Kitson, the hectoring rasp of Nina Collins and the scream of Martin Macken, howling like feedback against the sugary strings and soft waves of pedal-steel.

Thorne thought about Jason Mitchell, the concentration and the quiet "chuff-chuff" as he pushed his train back and forth. The smile, sudden as a slap. He couldn't tell if the boy even knew he was smiling and wondered where in his brain the problem lay.

White, pink or blue?

Would somebody like Pavesh Kambar be able to point to his handy multi-colored plastic model and say, There, that's where the trouble is, that's where the wiring is faulty? Or perhaps he would say that it wasn't faulty at all, that it was a different kind of wiring he hadn't been trained to deal with, one that he simply couldn't fathom. A feeling-useless moment, maybe. Time to pull out that rarely used F-word.

White, pink or blue.

Pillar-box red against black-and-white squares. Brown specks on the carpet and wallpaper by the window yellowing and greasy, like the business side of a sticking plaster when you've torn it off.

The CD finished, so Thorne got up, removed the disc from the player and put it away. The phone was on its cradle near the front door. He picked up his wallet from the table, took out a card and dialed the number scribbled on it.

"Hello?" The voice was wary, cracked.

He checked his watch: just after nine, not too late to call. He wondered if she was alone. "It's Tom Thorne."

"What do you want?"

The words sounded as if they'd taken some effort, like she'd just woken up or been drinking. He looked at the can of lager in his own hand and pushed the thought from his mind. "I didn't mean to frighten you," he said. "With the pictures."

"Yes, you did."

"All right, but just enough to make you leave."

"Just enough? Like you can measure it?"

"I'm sorry."

"They made me feel sick. What if Jason had seen them? Have you any idea . . . ?"

"I didn't know what else to do," Thorne said. "I got into trouble for it, if that makes you feel any better."

There was a pause. "It does a bit."

Thorne laughed, expecting her to join in, but she didn't. "When are you going to Nina's?"

"First thing tomorrow," Mitchell said. "I'm trying to pack."

"It's a bloody nightmare, isn't it?"

"This isn't a fortnight in Majorca, though, is it?"

Thorne was starting to wish he hadn't called, wondering what on earth had possessed him. Not that he had imagined Debbie Mitchell would give him an easy ride. "You on your own?"

"Yeah. Nina's . . . at work."

"He will come, you know?" Thorne took a sip of beer. "If we don't catch him. You've done the right thing." He heard the click of a lighter, the pause as she inhaled.

"I suppose."

"Listen, you can always call if—"

"Are you going to catch him?" Her voice no longer sounded tired. " 'If we don't catch him,' you said. How likely is that, d'you reckon, this bloke getting away with it?"

"We're doing everything we can."

"On a scale of one to ten?"

Thorne thought about it. Five? More? Said, "How's your hand?"

"Sorry?"

"It was bleeding earlier." Thorne looked up at the sound of keys in the front door. "I think you caught it on Jason's teeth."

"It's fine."

"I was trying to say you can call if you're worried about anything."

"What? You, or just 999?"

"Me. If you're... anxious, whatever." He could hear the inner door opening as he gave Debbie Mitchell his mobile number, then heard it close while he waited for her to write it down and read it back to him.

"Anyway..."

"Right, I'll leave you to your packing," Thorne said.

"OK."

Louise came through the lounge door. Thorne raised a finger, mouthed, "One minute," as she walked past him towards the kitchen. He thought about saying something like, "Say hello to Jason," but decided it would sound cheesy and insincere, so he just said, "Bye, Debbie."

He followed Louise into the kitchen and was about to say, "You caught me on the phone to my girlfriend" when she turned from the fridge with a bottle in her hand and he saw her expression.

"What?"

"Nothing, it's fine."

"I thought you'd be a bit later," Thorne said. "Obviously not much of a celebration."

She poured herself a large glass of wine and leaned back against the worktop. "Obviously." She held out the bottle towards him, asking the question.

He raised his can, answering it. "That snotty DCI turned forty again, did she?"

Louise took a drink, like she needed it. "It wasn't a birthday."

Thorne shook his head. "I just presumed..."

"Lucy Freeman's pregnant," Louise said. Another drink, the swallow giving way to a wobbly kind of smile. "She kept it very quiet. Like you're supposed to."

"Shit."

"No, really, it's OK. I'm happy for her." She stared past him, swilled the piss-colored wine around in her glass. "I need to be happy for her."

"Don't be stupid."

"I mean it. I just need to crack on, you know? I can't get stupid every time I see a pushchair outside a shop or feel upset if I run into someone who's up the duff."

"I know," Thorne said, not knowing at all.

"It's just...hard. It's like when you're a teenager and you get dumped and every song on the radio feels like it's about you."

Thorne nodded. "All By Myself" by Eric Carmen had torn his heart out when he was fifteen. "I Know It's Over" by the Smiths did it again ten years later. Hank Williams singing "I'm So Lonesome I Could Cry" could still do it.

"I'll deal with it," Louise said. "I'll have to, won't I? She sits at the next desk, for God's sake. I've got a big pile of baby magazines I can take in for her."

"Don't."

"A pack of three newborn Babygros she can have as well. Shouldn't have bought them really, but I couldn't resist."

Thorne stepped across to her and took the glass from her hand. "Come here."

A few seconds later, she lifted her face from his neck when a phone started to ring in the next room. She started to pull away, but Thorne held her close.

"It's your mobile."

"It doesn't matter," he said.

"Answer it."

"It's fine."

Louise broke the embrace and walked into the living room. Thorne lobbed his empty beer can into the bin. He heard her answer and say, "Just a minute." They crossed in the kitchen doorway, Thorne taking the phone as Louise held it out to him.

He recognized the caller's voice, the precision in it. "I was just thinking about you," he said.

Pavesh Kambar laughed. "Well, obviously you were in my thoughts too, Inspector. Hence the call. Great minds and all that."

Thorne waited. The only other person he knew who used the word "hence" was Trevor Jesmond. "Hence the importance of correct procedure." "Hence the fact that I'm suspending you from duty..."

"I thought of somebody you should speak to," Kambar said. "A writer."

"OK."

"The name is Nicholas Maier."

"Let me grab a pen..." He found one on the table near the door, pulled a scrap of paper from inside his wallet.

Kambar repeated the name, spelling it out, and Thorne scribbled it down. Kambar told him that the writer had contacted him two years previously, a year or so after the death of Raymond Garvey, claiming to be doing research.

Another searing true-crime masterpiece, Thorne thought. He didn't recognize the name. Though he couldn't remember who had written the two books he had sent away for and was currently reading, he was sure neither author was Nicholas Maier.

"This chap was writing a book, or updating one he'd already written, something like that. He called me several times, came to the hospital on more than one occasion. He certainly knew everything there was to know about Raymond Garvey's condition and wanted to get my take on it."

"Your take?"

"Did I think the tumor might have changed his personality?"

"Same thing the son was banging on about?"

"That's why I'm calling really," Kambar said. "He claimed to have got his information from the son."

"He'd been in contact with him?"

"So he said. He talked as though he'd been commissioned as Raymond Garvey's official biographer or something."

Thorne was drawing a line under the name, going back and forth over it. "So, you refused to speak to him?"

"Of course." Kambar answered as though it was a particularly stupid question. "Once I knew what he wanted, yes, of course. He made substantial offers, but I told him what he could do with his money. He was sure I would come round eventually. That sort always are, aren't they? He left me his card. Would you like the details?"

Thorne took down phone numbers and an email address, then thanked Kambar for taking the trouble to call.

"It's not a problem," Kambar said. "When we met, you seemed convinced that this man claiming to be the son was very important. Might well be the man you are looking for."

"It certainly looks that way."

"In which case this writer is definitely someone you should be talking to."

"Maier told you he knew him?" Thorne asked. "That they'd spoken?"

"Oh yes, very definitely," Kambar said. "The way Maier told it to me, he was more or less Anthony Garvey's best friend."

MY JOURNAL

3 October

It's not always easy, certainly not in a city like London, where almost anyone can get lost without even knowing it, can become anonymous, but most people want contact with others. They crave intimacy. I probably crave it just as much as anyone else, but I gave up on all that a long time ago. The fact that everyone else seems to need it makes my job easier, that's all I'm saying.

It makes it simple to get close to other people's lives. You just have to watch and figure out the best way in. If someone's a nurse, for example, you can pretty much bet that they care. So you run into them a couple of times. Maybe you're a junkie who's trying to kick the habit and you know that they'll sympathize. You become a face they know, someone they trust, right until the moment they see the rock coming down or whatever.

You watch. You get to know routines, patterns. What time Hubby comes home from school to have his lunch. When the time comes to pay a call on the wife, you're just that bloke who she's spoken to in the supermarket or wherever a couple of times. She isn't wary, like she should be. You're a face across a busy student bar, or a man who cleans the family car once a week. Eventually you're invited in for a coffee and you get familiar. You can figure out timings, habits, the fact that the man you're after and his wife are fighting like cat and dog.

You find your angle.

It's starting to get trickier now, but I always knew it would. I found the easy ones, got them out of the way first; geared myself up. Obviously, the police will have put the pieces together by now (literally, I should imagine) and will have worked out what's happening. That's all fine, though. Now they can do the hard work for me. They can find the ones I still haven't been able to track down.

Hopefully, that's the bit they haven't worked out yet.

* * *

Dug into the cash again and moved into a new place, a fairly tidy one-room flat, near a station, same as the others, which makes it easier to travel. King's Cross this time. Even though it's only for a few weeks at a stretch, I like walking around each area, getting to know the streets a bit. King's Cross is supposed to be pretty rough, with the prossies and the drugs, but so far I like it. Nobody gives you a second look, which is fine by me. It's like what I said before about people becoming anonymous. That's what everyone seems like round here. It's another thing which makes my life easier.

* * *

The newsagent was banging on about the Macken murders this morning, when I went in for fags. Still loads of stuff in the paper. Family snapshots, all that. Nothing connecting it with the others, though, which is probably just the police playing their cards close to their chests. The bloke in the shop was getting all worked up. He didn't quite get as far as saying they should bring back hanging, but near enough. They were so young, he kept saying, their whole lives ahead of them. Why does it matter how old they were? I just don't get that. Like the young have any more right to life than anyone else. Like it's more tragic than if some pensioner tumbles down the stairs.

"Bright futures," that's what it said in the paper. The newsagent kept stabbing at the Sun or the Mirror or whatever it was and shaking his head at how sad it was. How unfair. All that's been taken away from them, he said.

Stolen.

Like years spent in prison for something that wasn't your fault. Like a normal life. Like the right to walk around without being spat at or beaten up and not spending twenty hours a day trying to deal with the headaches, going quietly mental in your cell.

In the end I just nodded and took my cigarettes and walked out of there. Thinking that he had no bloody idea what "fair" was. Thinking about my part in other people's futures, bright or otherwise.

Thinking all sorts of lives can be stolen.

Eighteen

THORNE HAD arranged to meet Carol Chamberlain at the Starbucks near Oxford Circus, having taken care to specify which of the umpteen branches in the area he meant. Thanks to the Northern Line, he was fifteen minutes late, and as Chamberlain had already finished her coffee by the time he arrived, they decided to walk. It was a bright, dry Saturday morning and Oxford Street was teeming. Four days into October and many people were obviously keen to get their Christmas shopping done nice and early. The shops were already tinseled-up and piled high with tat, the predictable music spilling out of the doorways.

Slade, Wizzard, the Pogues. Cliff bloody Richard.

"It's utterly ridiculous," Chamberlain said.

"Don't get me started," Thorne said.

Thorne had first met Carol Chamberlain four years previously, when her intervention in an inquiry that had been going backwards had provided the much-needed breakthrough. She had been out of the Force five years by then but working for the Area Major Review Unit, a new team that was utilizing the invaluable know-how and experience of retired officers to take a fresh look at cold cases. The Crinkly Squad, many had called it, Thorne included, until he'd met Chamberlain. Decked out with a blue rinse and furry slippers and pulling a tartan shopping trolley through the streets of Worthing, where she lived, she might have looked harmless, but he had seen her work. He had seen her extract information from a man half her age in a way that had sickened him. Sickened him almost as much as the fact that he had watched and said nothing, because even as he had smelled the man's flesh burning, he had known it needed to be done.

They had not spoken about the incident since.

Much had changed for both of them since a case that had taken its toll on each in different ways and had ultimately cost Thorne's father his life. They did not speak about that, either. Though it was always there, a shadow between them, they just got on with taking the piss, same as any other two coppers, despite the differences in age and experience.

Negotiating the crowds, Thorne talked her through the inquiry; the link between two series of murders fifteen years apart. She remembered the Garvey case very well, she told him, having worked for a number of years with the SIO. She had been close enough to have watched a few of the early interviews.

"He never said why he did it, did he?" Chamberlain said. "Like Shipman. Never gave any reason for it. They're always the worst."

"Maybe there wasn't a reason. Maybe he just liked it."

"There's usually something, though, isn't there? With most of them. The voice of God telling them to do it. A message from the devil in a Britney Spears song. Something."

"Well, this one's certainly got a motive," Thorne said. "Or thinks he has. He wants us to know exactly why he's doing it."

"OK, forget what I said. They're the worst."

They carried on towards Tottenham Court Road, crossing Oxford Street at Chamberlain's insistence so they could walk in the sunshine. He told her about the search for the three missing sons of Raymond Garvey's original victims, and about the phone call from Pavesh Kambar.

Thorne had done some checking and discovered that Nicholas Maier had written a book about the Garvey case that was published a year before Garvey's death. He had picked up a copy of *Battered—The Raymond Garvey Killings* from his local Waterstone's in Camden before catching the Tube. On first glance, it looked much the same as the ones he had bought online. The same pictures, the same semi-salacious blurb on the back of the jacket. He fished the book from his bag and showed it to Chamberlain.

"When are you seeing him?" she asked.

"Monday," Thorne said. "He emailed me back from his 'lecture tour' in America. He gets back tomorrow."

Chamberlain pulled a face.

"I know. They teach this stuff in universities over there. Serial Killers 101, whatever. Said something in his email about it paying for his next holiday. Also said he'd be happy to meet me."

"I don't like the sound of that."

Thorne laughed, knowing very well what she meant. He was always suspicious of anyone who seemed overly pleased to see a police officer. It wasn't his job to be popular.

"I mean, I know you," Chamberlain said, "and even I'm not happy to see you."

They crossed back over the road and cut down into Soho Square. Though it wasn't exactly warm, there were plenty of people gathered on benches or sprawled on the grass with books. They squeezed onto a bench next to a cycle courier who was finishing a sandwich. He got up and left before he'd swallowed the last mouthful.

"So, what do you need?" Chamberlain asked.

"We need to know where this bloke comes from. It's looking very much like he's Garvey's son, so let's start with trying to find out who his mother is. It doesn't sound like she was in contact with Garvey."

Chamberlain was still holding the book. She lifted it up. "Why don't you ask your new best friend?"

Thorne took it back. "I've skimmed through and there's nothing about any son in there. I think Anthony Garvey made contact with him after his father had died."

"You think he wants Maier to write another book? Go into all this brain tumor stuff?"

"I'll find out on Monday," Thorne said. "Meanwhile, you can start digging around, see what you can come up with. All the descriptions put him at thirty-ish, so he was born fifteen years or so before Garvey started killing. You up for it?"

Chamberlain nodded. "Well, this or the gardening? It's a tough choice."

"AMRU not keeping you busy, then?"

"They couldn't afford me and the hypnotherapist."

"Sorry?"

"The brass thought it would be a nice idea to try some regression therapy on a few witnesses, see what they could remember."

"Right. 'I think I used to be Marie Antoinette,' all that."

"They reckon this bloke got some witness to come up with a number plate she'd forgotten. I don't know..."

"Jesus." Thorne never ceased to be amazed at what people could waste resources on in an effort to make a splash. "Things are rough when you get bumped off a case for Paul McKenna."

Chamberlain smiled. For a while they sat in silence, watched the comings and goings. A skinny, rat-faced teenager was moving among the groups on the grass, asking for money, meeting each refusal with a glare. A chancer. He looked at Thorne, but showed no inclination to try his luck.

"Someone who's definitely not happy to see you," Chamberlain said.

She asked about the hunt for Andrew Dowd, Simon Walsh and Graham Fowler, and why they had not turned to the media for help. Thorne told her what Brigstocke had said about the emphasis being on catching their man, and Kitson's theory that they were using Debbie Mitchell as bait.

"Nothing surprises me," Chamberlain said. "It's all about the result, right?"

"They'll get one they really don't like if they're not careful," Thorne said. He explained that they were doing their best to trace the missing men through conventional channels—credit cards, mobile-phone records, good old-fashioned donkey-work—and getting nowhere. "Dowd's away trying to find himself, if his wife is to be believed. The other two are off the radar altogether. Homeless, maybe; drifting for sure. All of them have got... problems."

"Sounds like they've all got one very big problem."

Thorne nodded, watched the rat-faced kid arguing with a community support officer who was trying to move him on. "It's not really a shock, though, is it? That they're all screwed up in one way or another."

"We all carry our pasts with us," Chamberlain said.

"Yeah, well, maybe that hypnotherapist's onto something."

"Carry them around like bits of crap in our pockets." She sat very still, patted the handbag on her lap. "We know that better than most, don't we?"

Thorne didn't look at her. The skinny teenager was wandering away now, shouting and waving his arms. The CPSO laughed, said something to one of the people lying on the grass. "How's Jack?" Thorne asked.

"We had a cancer scare," Chamberlain said. "Looks like we're OK, though." She glanced across at Thorne and spoke again, seeing that he was struggling for the right thing to say. "What about Louise? You know, I'm not convinced you haven't been making her up."

Chamberlain and Louise had never met. Thorne himself had not seen Chamberlain in over a year, although he made a point of trying to call her as often as he could. He felt oddly guilty.

"She's busy," Thorne said. "You know how it is."

"Two coppers together. Always a big mistake."

It suddenly struck Thorne that he had no idea what Chamberlain's husband did; or used to do, before he retired. There was no way to ask without making it obvious. "You're probably right," he said.

They sat for another minute or two and then, with a nod to each other, got up and moved through the square, walking out towards Greek Street and into the heart of Soho.

"I'll send over all the stuff later," Thorne said. "And a copy of the original Garvey file."

"A nice bit of bedtime reading."

"What is it normally, then, Catherine Cookson?"

She flashed Thorne a sarcastic grin, then slowed to stare through the window of an arty-looking jeweler's. She leaned in close, trying to make out the prices on the labels, then turned to Thorne and said, "Thanks for this, by the way."

"It's not a problem."

"I know you could have found someone closer to home."

"I couldn't think of anyone better."

"I presume you mean that the nice way," she said.

"Do you want me to walk you back?"

"Don't be daft."

Chamberlain was staying at a small hotel in Bloomsbury at which the Met maintained a constant block-booking of half a dozen rooms. It was used for visiting officers from other forces, relatives of victims who had nowhere else to stay, and occasionally a high-ranking officer who, for one reason or another, did not fancy going home.

"Be nice staying in a hotel for a while," Chamberlain said.

"Make the most of it," Thorne said. He felt himself redden slightly, remembering the last night he had spent in a hotel; the misunderstanding at the bar.

"I'll get some sleep at least," Chamberlain said.

"You never know, you might pull."

"Jack's snoring's been driving me batty."

"With a bit of luck there might be some Ovaltine in the mini-bar."

"Shut up."

It was "winner stays on" at the pool table in the upstairs room of the Grafton Arms, and it took the best part of an hour before Thorne and Hendricks got a game against each other. The table was being dominated by an oikish type in a rugby shirt, who beat both of them easily before losing to Hendricks by knocking in the black halfway through the frame. Hendricks beat the rugby player's mate, then showed no mercy to a teenage Goth, who stared admiringly at the pathologist's piercings and looked as though she didn't know one end of a pool cue from the other.

"You're ruthless," Thorne said, as Hendricks fed in the coins.

"I think she fancied me," Hendricks said. "It clearly put her off her game."

"Pool's not the only thing she knows sod all about, then."

"Fiver on this, fair enough?"

Thorne fetched a couple more pints of Guinness from downstairs while Hendricks racked the balls. The bar was rammed, even for a Saturday night, but it was only two minutes' walk from Thorne's flat and the familiarity was comforting. The Oak was a Job watering-hole, and, as such, would never be somewhere he could completely relax. It wasn't as though anybody in the Grafton knew his name, and there were no wry philosophical types propping up the bar, but Thorne enjoyed the nod from the barman and his step towards the Guinness tap without having to be told.

"I'm in the wrong job," Hendricks said, bending down to break. "A bloody lecture tour?"

Thorne had told him about the email from Nicholas Maier. "You teach, don't you?"

"Yeah, and what I make in a month wouldn't pay for a weekend in Weston-Super-Mare."

"You do it for the love."

Hendricks had knocked in a spot. He moved around the table, chalking his cue. "Maybe I should write this one up as an academic study: 'Man kills children of his father's victims, the pathological implications then and now,' that kind of thing. I could get something like that published anywhere, I reckon. America, definitely."

"Go for it," Thorne said. He knew Hendricks didn't mean it. He looked down at his friend's heavily tattooed forearm as Hendricks lined up a shot and remembered it pressed across the throat of that insensitive CSI. "If you need someone to carry your bags on the lecture tour, you know..."

It was Thorne's turn at the table. Hendricks took a drink, smiled across the room at the Goth girl, who was sitting in the corner with two friends. "The bloke's book any good?"

Thorne had spent the afternoon reading *Battered,* with one ear on the radio's football coverage. "Nothing that isn't in any of the others, as far as

I can make out. Nobody interviewed that hasn't said their piece plenty of times before. Usual pictures: Garvey and his bloody rabbits. That's what most of these books do, just rehash old material. Money for jam."

"Not going to trouble the Booker Prize judges, then?"

Thorne missed a sitter and went back to his drink. "Why do people read this stuff?"

Hendricks knocked in a couple of balls. "Same as all these misery memoirs," he said, without taking his eyes off the table. "You go into Smith's, it's wall-to-wall books about kids who've been locked in cellars, people who've had eighteen types of cancer or whatever."

"I don't get it."

"People enjoy knowing there's someone worse off than they are. Maybe it makes them feel . . . safer, or something."

"It's cheap thrills, if you ask me," Thorne said. He watched as Hendricks fluked his penultimate ball. "You jammy bastard."

"Pure skill, mate."

Hendricks left the final spot over a pocket with the black placed nicely in the middle of the table. With four balls still to pot, Thorne tried to do something clever and nudge the black onto the cushion. He made a mess of it, leaving Hendricks with a simple clearance.

"Maybe people read these books to find out why," Hendricks said. "The ones about Garvey and Shipman and the rest of them. They want to know why those things happened."

"You're giving them way too much credit."

"I'm not saying they know that's what they're doing, but it makes sense if you think about it. It's the same reason they turn these people into monsters, talk about 'evil' or whatever. It makes it easier to forget they're just builders and doctors and the bloke next door. It's not the killers themselves anyone's really frightened of. It's not knowing why they did it, where the next one's coming from, that terrifies people."

Hendricks had yet to play his shot. Thorne was aware that the next player up, a spiky-haired kid sitting on the Goth girl's table, was looking daggers from the corner, waiting for them to finish talking and wrap up the game. "They can read about Ray Garvey all they want," Thorne said.

He was remembering the conversation with Carol Chamberlain. "No 'why' with him. He didn't even kill any of his pet rabbits."

When Hendricks had polished off the frame, the spiky-haired kid stepped forward and picked up his coins from the edge of the table. Hendricks laid down his cue, told the kid he was taking a break, and followed Thorne back to their table, leaving the next player in the queue to take his place.

"So, maybe there's something in this tumor business? The personality change."

"Kambar says not."

"Hypothetically, though," Hendricks said.

"It's rubbish."

"Let's say you've got some severe tic or whatever, something that makes you thrash around."

"I think you've finally lost it, mate."

"You accidentally hit someone in a crowded bar. They smash their head open, die from a severe bleed on the brain. That can't be your fault, can it?"

"It's not the same thing."

"I know, I'm just saying. It would be... interesting, legally."

"If by 'interesting' you mean it would make a lot of smart briefs a shitload of money, then yes, probably. Like they don't make our lives hard enough as it is." Thorne drank and watched the pool for half a minute. "Anyway, like I told you, Kambar reckons it's rubbish."

"Well, he's the brain man," Hendricks said.

The spiky-haired kid cleared the table. The rugby player came forward, took the cue from the loser and fed his money in without a word.

"Even if there was anything in it, Garvey's son hasn't got a sodding tumor."

"Maybe he thinks he has," Hendricks said.

"Sorry?"

"There's plenty of research suggesting that some of the factors contributing towards the development of certain tumors can be inherited."

"You're winding me up."

Hendricks shook his head, drained the last of his pint. "Mind you, there was also a study that said being left-handed might be a factor, so..."

"That's all we bloody need," Thorne said. "Some slimy brief requesting that his client's murder charge be thrown out on the grounds that he's cack-handed."

Hendricks bought another round, after insisting that Thorne hand over the money he'd just won off him. They shared crisps and pork scratchings, watched the rugby player sink two long balls in succession.

"I used to be good at this game," Thorne said.

"You've lost your edge, mate. That's what domestic contentment does for you."

It was the first time that anything pertaining to Louise had entered their conversation. Hendricks had spent the day with her, wandering around the shops in Hampstead and Highgate before lunch at Pizza Express. Thorne had stayed at home with Maier's book and 5 Live for company. Spurs had lost to a needless, last-minute penalty and Thorne's frustration had been only marginally tempered by the smug message he had been able to leave on Yvonne Kitson's answering machine, about the bet he had wisely failed to take.

"You and Lou have a good time today?" Thorne asked.

Hendricks stared at him. "Didn't you ask Lou?"

"Yeah, she said she enjoyed herself."

"So, why—?"

"There wasn't much chance to talk when she got back, you know. Not in any detail. She said she was tired, just wanted to crash out."

"We did do a fair bit of walking," Hendricks said.

"How's she doing?"

Hendricks stared again.

"Jesus." Thorne banged his almost empty glass down on the table. "I can't believe I've got to sit here asking you how Lou is."

"You don't have to. You could go mad and ask her."

"I have."

"And...?"

"She says she's fine, but I'm not sure I believe her. This woman at work getting pregnant must have really cut her up, but she's making out like it's not a big deal."

"Maybe it isn't," Hendricks said. "She's tough as old boots is Lou. Well, you know."

"I'm not sure I know anything," Thorne said. He finished his beer. "What do you think, Phil?"

"I think... it's only been, what, a week and a bit? I think she probably wants a bit of space. For you to stop treating her like she's got a terminal illness."

"Did she say something?"

"Yeah... that, basically."

"Christ."

"And she said the same thing about you. That you say you're fine, but she doesn't know whether to believe it."

The spiky-haired kid potted the cue-ball. The rugby player pumped his fist, bent to retrieve the white and lined up the first of his free shots.

"Sorry you're getting caught in the middle of this," Thorne said.

"Not a problem, mate." Hendricks handed the empty glasses to a passing member of the bar staff. He turned back to Thorne. "Are you fine?"

Thorne nodded, said that he was, but the look he received in return suggested that he'd been a little too quick about it. He could not be honest, not completely. He could not tell Hendricks, or anyone else, how he felt; that it tasted burned and bitter in his mouth. "You just get on with it, don't you?"

"I suppose," Hendricks said.

"What about you? Any new piercings on the horizon?"

It took Hendricks a few seconds. Things had been edgy between them—as far as this kind of conversation was concerned—for a while, since a case the previous year had driven a wedge between them. Hendricks had been targeted by the man Thorne was trying to catch and had almost been killed while cruising a series of gay bars. With Louise's help, they had got back on a more or less even keel quickly enough, but Hendricks' sex life had remained a touchy subject. "I'm doing all right," he said, eventually. "No permanent piercings." He smiled. "Just the odd clip-on."

He asked if they were going to get any more drinks and Thorne said he was about ready for the off. "You stay and have another one if you want," he said. "I'll go back and get the sofa-bed ready. Louise might still be up, so..."

Hendricks eyed the pool table again, where the game had finished and the winner was looking for anyone willing to take him on. He told Thorne he wouldn't be long. "I can't go without trying to beat that arsehole in the rugby shirt again," he said.

"Don't bother playing pool," Thorne said. "Just stick a couple of the balls in a sock and twat him."

"I'm seriously thinking about it," Hendricks said, getting to his feet. "Listen, if I'm not back in an hour, I've gone home with that girl who looks like Marilyn Manson, all right?"

Nineteen

NICHOLAS MAIER lived in Islington, on the ground floor of a terraced Georgian house in a quiet square behind Upper Street. Thorne parked in a residents' bay and stuck a "police business" badge on the dash of the BMW. The spell of good weather was holding.

Thorne and Holland were shown through to a large sitting room while Maier went to fetch coffee. The carpet was gaudy but clearly expensive, and the bookshelves either side of the fireplace were well stocked, though on closer inspection several contained nothing but multiple copies of Maier's own books. The room was immaculate. There were elaborate flower arrangements in matching Chinese vases on two corner tables and the vast plasma screen above the fireplace was gleaming and dust-free. Aside from a large ginger cat asleep on a chair next to the door, there was no sign that Maier shared the flat with anyone else.

"And he had a pot of coffee on," Holland said. "I like it when people make an effort."

"No effort at all," Maier said, nudging the door open and carrying a tray across to a low table. His voice was deep and perfectly modulated, like a late-night radio host. "I only got back from the States last night, so I haven't had a lot of time to run around tidying up. My office is probably a bit more cluttered than this, but I'm not generally a big fan of mess."

"It's a nice place," Holland said.

Maier pointed them both towards the sofa, began pouring the coffee. "Scribbling keeps the wolf from the door," he said.

"Obviously." Thorne nodded, impressed, but shared a knowing look with Holland. He'd done some checking and knew very well that Nick Maier had inherited the property from his father, a wealthy businessman who had died while Maier was still taking his journalism degree.

Maier asked them both how they took their coffee and slid a plate of biscuits across the table. He was wearing khakis and an open-necked salmon-pink shirt, brown suede moccasins without socks and a touch too much gold jewelry. He looks like an upmarket estate agent, Thorne thought.

"You've got a decent color on you," Holland said.

"Weather was very nice over there, when I wasn't stuck inside bloody lecture theaters."

"Where?"

"The West Coast," Maier said. "LA, Santa Barbara, San Diego. Have you been?"

Holland shook his head.

"Thanks for seeing us so quickly," Thorne said.

Maier reached for a biscuit and sat back. "You could hardly expect someone who does what I do not to be curious." He looked from Thorne to Holland and held up his hands. "So...?"

Thorne told him about his conversation with Pavesh Kambar, the phone calls and visits the doctor had described. The relationship Maier had suggested he'd had with Anthony Garvey.

"I hardly think I pestered him," Maier said. "But in terms of what I was trying to write, Doctor Kambar was an important person to talk to, so I... persisted. That's the kind of job I have. The kind of job you have, too, I should imagine."

"Tell us about Garvey," Thorne said. "Junior."

"My grand folly, you mean."

"Sorry?"

Maier held up a hand again, as though to say he'd get there in his own time. He finished eating his biscuit, brushed crumbs from the front of his shirt. "Well, I'd written a book about the Raymond Garvey murders."

Thorne pointed at his briefcase. "I've got a copy."

"I can sign it for you if you'd like, though I'm guessing that isn't the main reason why you're here. Worth at least a fiver on eBay." Maier laughed, but his attempt at self-deprecation was about as convincing as Thorne's fake smile. "The man I later learned was Raymond Garvey's son read it and got in touch with me."

"And this would have been when?"

"Perhaps six months after Garvey died, so about two and a half years ago, I think."

"How did he contact you?"

"He emailed my website. From an internet café, if you'd like to know. I checked. We exchanged a few emails and he told me there was something he thought I'd be interested in, so I gave him my home number. He called and, after a while, he told me what he wanted. He was right, of course. I was very interested."

"Did you meet him?"

"Sadly not. It was all done by phone and email."

"He gave you all this guff about the brain tumor, did he?" Holland said. "The personality change stuff."

Maier nodded, like he'd been expecting the question. "Look, Anthony believed it, which was the important thing."

"Doesn't matter if you don't?" Thorne asked.

"I'm just there to tell the story," Maier said. "And whatever you think, it was a hell of a story. The possibility that one of the most notorious killers of the last fifty years had not been responsible, in the strictest sense of the word, for what he did. How could I ignore that?"

"I presume you asked for proof?" Thorne said. "That Anthony was who he claimed to be."

"He sent me some letters, or copies of letters that he'd received from Raymond Garvey over the years he'd been visiting him in Whitemoor." Maier saw the look on Thorne's face. "You're more than welcome to see them. As far as Ray Garvey was concerned, Anthony was his own flesh and blood."

Holland leaned forward and placed his coffee cup on the table, careful to use the coaster provided. "So, he asked you to write another book, bringing this new... development to light?"

"Correct."

"Did he seriously think they'd reopen the investigation? With his father dead?"

"All he told me was that he wanted to get the truth out there."

Holland shook his head. "I'm sure you were planning to talk to some of the relatives of the women Garvey killed. You know, seeing as the truth was so important."

"It never got that far," Maier said.

Thorne threw a look across at Holland; the signal that he wanted to take over. "What happened after you agreed to write the book?"

"Well, I went to a publisher, obviously. Never has the phrase 'they bit my hand off' been more appropriate. They were more than happy to stump up the money."

"Money?"

"Anthony wanted forty-five thousand pounds for the story. For the use of his father's prison letters, interviews with him, that sort of thing. All sadly premature, of course, since Doctor Kambar refused to play ball. He would not even go as far as to say that the tumor might have changed Garvey's personality. Without any medical evidence, we had nowhere to go. It all fell apart rather quickly after that and, needless to say, I was no longer flavor of the month with the publisher."

"Sorry." Thorne did his best to look as though he meant it.

Maier shrugged. "Had to make do with ghosting for a while after that. Did a couple of senior coppers' autobiographies as it happens. Everyone's got a story or two to tell. I should imagine you've got more than a few, Inspector."

"Did you not think to talk to Kambar before you handed over the money?"

Another shrug. "It wasn't my money, was it? Besides, we needed to strike while the iron was hot. He might well have gone to somebody else."

Thorne saw a possibility. "I'm guessing you paid the money into some account or other?"

"Sorry, no. It was paid in cash."

"What? Used notes in a brown paper bag?"

"A holdall, actually, in the ticket office at Paddington station. If you ask me, I think the publisher quite enjoyed all the cloak and dagger. On top of which, everybody knew that it would make the most fantastic opening to the book: photographs of the illicit pick-up, the shadowy son of a serial killer, all that sort of thing."

"You took pictures?"

"They sent a photographer along, yes, lurking among the commuters. I've got them in the office somewhere, if you want to have a look."

"Could you . . . ?"

"Yes, of course." Maier got up and walked towards the door. He smiled as he passed Thorne. "I dug them out before you came."

Thorne said nothing.

"Don't get too excited, though. It wasn't Anthony Garvey who picked the money up."

Holland waited until Maier had left the room and said, "He loves himself, doesn't he?"

"If he'd already got the photos out," Thorne said, "he knew what we wanted to see him about."

"You didn't give him any hints?"

Thorne shook his head. "Just said we wanted a word with him in his professional capacity. Help with an ongoing investigation. Usual old shit."

They helped themselves to a couple more biscuits while they waited for Maier to return. He was talking as he re-entered the room.

"Of course, we couldn't do anything while the money was being picked up. Like I said, we didn't want him to go running off to someone else. I asked him who the girl was afterwards, obviously."

Thorne took the photographs that Maier was brandishing. Half a dozen black-and-white ten-by-eights. A woman in her early twenties, jeans and a puffa jacket. She looked distinctly nervous. The photographer had caught her full-on as she looked around, approaching the bag that had been left by the counter. More shots: a final check that nobody was paying too much attention; bending to pick up the holdall; side-on as she walked towards the exit.

"Who did he say she was?" Thorne asked.

Maier was standing behind the chair, staring at the photographs over Thorne's shoulder. "Some girl he'd been seeing. Said he paid her a hundred pounds to pick up the bag, that he guessed we'd want some 'coverage' and that he preferred to remain anonymous. A shame, but I wasn't too disappointed, the shots were still usable. I asked him for a name and he said it didn't matter. That she was already out of the picture."

Thorne handed the photographs to Holland. "What happened after you'd got nowhere with Kambar?"

Maier returned to his own chair. "Well, even though we knew it was second best, we tried a number of other neurologists, but we got very much the same result. We couldn't get any kind of... authentication. So, in the end, I had to tell Anthony that, without it, the publisher was refusing to go ahead with the book."

"How did he take that?"

"Not well," Maier said. "There was a lot of shouting, a few very abusive emails, which was rich, considering that I'd been every bit as shafted as he had. I'd already done a fair amount of background work, started mapping out the book, working. All a waste of bloody time in the end."

"How did you leave it?"

"Well, the last time I spoke to him he was a damn sight calmer. I think perhaps his mood had been tempered slightly by the fact that he knew there was no way they could get the cash back off him. He said he was considering other options. All very mysterious, but I wished him luck with whatever they were. What else could I say?" Maier adjusted the crease in his khakis and twisted his cuffs until they were as he wanted them.

"Jesus." Thorne could only shake his head in disbelief, and watch as the author raised his arms again, like it was a funny old world.

Maier leaned back in his chair and crossed his legs, a knowing expression creeping across his face. "So... how many has Anthony killed so far? Four, is it?"

Thorne was stunned. He struggled to respond quickly, his difficulty compounded by the pleasure Maier clearly gained from the hesitation.

"Look, it's no big mystery," Maier said. "I spent long enough studying the Raymond Garvey killings, so the names of the victims did rather jump out of the newspaper at me, even though they were all reported as separate murders. Now, Catherine Burke's brother died years ago in a car accident, if my memory serves, so, by my reckoning"—he counted off his fingers—"that means Anthony has another four to go. I presume you've warned them all?"

"I'm not sure what you're expecting me to say." Thorne shrugged as though it were no big deal. "You'll understand I can't tell you any more than you already know."

"If there is any more."

"On top of which, we'd be very grateful if you kept what you know to yourself."

"Not go running to the press, you mean?"

"Not go running to anyone."

"I appreciate why you're keeping the media in the dark on this one," Maier said. "As far as the link between the murders is concerned. But someone will get wind of it eventually, you do know that? A good serial-killer story will sell a lot of papers."

"And books," Holland said.

Maier seemed to enjoy the dig. "Hopefully."

"So, we understand each other?" Thorne asked.

"Well, I understand you, certainly, but you need to bear in mind that I have a living to make."

Thorne waited, hoped that the sound of his teeth grinding wasn't carrying.

"All I'm saying is that when you are in a position to talk a bit more freely, or if there are any major developments as far as what Anthony's up to, I would hope that I'd be the first person you'd talk to. The first person without a warrant card, at any rate." He leaned forward for the final biscuit. "How's that sound?"

Thorne watched Maier chew, the weak chin working, thinking that he had the sort of face you could not be satisfied with punching just the once. He said, "Sounds fine."

Maier nodded and reached towards the tray again. "There's plenty more coffee in the pot."

Ten minutes later, creeping slowly north along the Holloway Road, Holland said, "I was thinking about how Anthony Garvey lives, you know?"

Thorne swore in frustration at the traffic, then glanced across.

"I mean, he can't be holding down any sort of proper job, can he? Not without leaving traces and certainly not if he needs to move about, tracking his victims. I reckon that cash he screwed out of Maier is exactly what he needs to do this."

"That phrase Maier used," Thorne said. "Garvey was 'considering other options.'"

"Shit, they as good as funded him." Holland stared out of the side window for half a minute. "And that tosser's going to end up getting a book deal out of it."

Thorne was only half listening. He was thinking about the girl in the photographs and something else Maier had said. The precise words Garvey had used.

Out of the picture.

Twenty

H.M.P. Whitemoor

"WHAT'S THAT mark on your face?"

"I'm fine."

"Christ, I thought you were... protected in here. A vulnerable prisoner."

"Unfortunately, it's not just nonces I'm stuck on the wing with. All sorts are vulnerable in here, need to be kept separate. An ex-police officer gave me this. Made him feel better for a few days, I suppose. Got a few people off his back."

"It's a fucking zoo!"

"It's not supposed to be pleasant. Mind you, we have got a PlayStation now..."

"I was thinking, you know, about what it's going to be like when you come out."

"That's not happening, Tony, I've said."

"No harm in thinking about stuff we could do."

"What, you and me in the park, kicking a sodding ball about?"

"You've got to be optimistic."

"You're talking stupid."

"I'm not going anywhere, that's all I'm saying."

"Good. That's good."

"There must be places you fancy going, though, things you want to see."

"Oh, yeah. Inside of a pub would be nice. A decent pair of tits that aren't on an eighteen-stone armed robber."

"I don't know how you can laugh."

"You've got to."

"I certainly didn't get that from you. A sense of humor, I mean. I can't remember the last time I found anything very funny. I see people watching TV, pissing themselves at some stupid sitcom or whatever, and I just don't... see it."

"You've had a hard time of it, that's all."

"Did I laugh when I was little?"

"I wouldn't know, would I?"

"Not really little, I mean, but when you saw me?"

"I can't remember. It was only a couple of times."

"We all know whose fault that was."

"Don't start all that."

"What?"

"Gives me a headache when you talk about your mother. I'm serious. Last time I puked up after you'd gone."

"I've told you, I'm fine about it. It wasn't your fault."

"Course it was my fault. All those women. No excuses."

"It's what you get for keeping secrets."

"Can we talk about something else?"

"I don't mind."

"You seeing anyone?"

"What, like girls?"

"Girls, boys, I don't know."

"Fuck off, Dad."

"So?"

"On and off. Nothing serious. What's the matter?"

"Still does my head in. When you call me that. Dad."

Twenty-One

If a sliding scale of news was topped by being told you'd won the lottery, with a diagnosis of cancer at the bottom, the phone call Thorne received the previous evening would run the cancer diagnosis a pretty close second. Brigstocke had spoken quickly and without hesitation, not wanting to give Thorne a chance to start shouting, or crying, until he had finished.

"Remember I mentioned they might convene a critical incident panel? Well, it's tomorrow at ten o'clock. They'd like you to be there, so you might want to dig out a suit. Sorry, the suit..."

"Like me to be there as in I have a choice?"

"Like you to be there as in what do you think?"

"You don't reckon I could be spending my morning a bit more productively? Trying to find the girl in Maier's photo, maybe? It's just a thought."

"Tom—"

"Having a wank?"

"Don't shoot the messenger."

"I was thinking more 'strangle.'"

"Just don't piss too many of them off, OK?"

"Now you're really pushing it."

"Have a nice evening."

"I was," Thorne said.

Now, twelve hours later, Thorne was sitting at a highly polished, blond-wood table in an overheated conference room at Scotland Yard. There were six other people around the table, each with a notepad and a pair of freshly sharpened pencils in front of them. There were water jugs and glasses near either end. Thorne smiled through the minute or two of small talk, wondering how people would react if he let his head drop onto the table or asked for a cold beer, and waiting for the powerful smell of bullshit to start rising on the thermal of hot air.

The Association of Chief Police Officers was responsible for bringing such panels together, and its representative, the Area Homicide Commander, was chairing the meeting. Alistair Johns was a short, stocky man in his early fifties, with a permanently pinched expression, as though he were always walking through heavy rain. He brought the meeting to order, making sure that everyone around the table knew one another. Aside from Trevor Jesmond and Russell Brigstocke, there was a surly-looking DS named Proctor from the Community Relations Unit and a woman named Paula Hughes, who Thorne gathered was a civilian press officer. Another woman, a WPC whose name he failed to catch during a stifled yawn, was taking the minutes. Thorne caught her eye. She looked as though she'd had enough already, or perhaps she was thinking about the work that lay ahead: typing up her notes, circulating endless emails and preparing a bound report for everyone from the Commissioner to the Mayor.

"We need to crack on," Johns said. "Obviously this is an ongoing inquiry and I'm grateful to DCI Brigstocke and DI Thorne for taking the time to be here."

Thorne looked across at Brigstocke, who suddenly appeared to find the tabletop uniquely fascinating.

"But we may well be looking at problems down the line, as far as the public perception of our handling of the case goes, so we need to take a few decisions now. Start preparing answers for some of the questions that are bound to be asked, whether we get a result or not."

"We'll get a result," Jesmond said. He nodded towards Brigstocke, whose interest in the tabletop seemed only to increase. Jesmond's confidence was to be expected, of course; the last thing Johns wanted to hear was doubt or uncertainty. A bit of gung-ho positivity always went a long way with the brass.

The smell of bullshit was kicking in nice and early.

When Thorne had first heard about critical incident panels, he had presumed that they were convened as a result of terrorist incidents and the like, but he had quickly discovered that they were little more than forums for the mitigation of bad publicity; to discuss cases that were likely to attract criticism from the press or community groups. They were little more than damage-limitation exercises. Often, they were all about getting your retaliation in first.

"We need to talk about the media," Johns said. "How we use, or don't use them as the inquiry moves forward. Obviously, we've kept our powder dry as far as the serial elements of these killings is concerned."

"Dry-ish." Thorne spoke instinctively and held the stare when he caught a look from Jesmond that suggested he should have kept his mouth shut. "At least one journalist has already put it together."

Johns glanced down at his notes. "Nicholas Maier. But he's assured you he understands the importance of discretion."

"He understands that we'll feed him information about the case to keep him quiet. If he's lucky, maybe enough to get a book out of it."

"Not much we can do about it," Brigstocke said.

Jesmond launched into a tirade about Nicholas Maier and his "ilk" making a living out of the suffering of others. He called them "hacks" and "leeches," said that they were no more than a few links up the food chain from the killers themselves. There were nods and appreciative murmurs from all but one person around the table. Jesmond's comments had sounded heartfelt, but Thorne knew that the only thing the Superintendent was really passionate about was his own progress up the greasy pole. The two men exchanged glances again, and Thorne smiled like a good boy. He could not help wondering which hack would be ghost-writing Jesmond's autobiography a few years down the line.

"We will be keeping a close eye on Maier," Johns said. "But obviously our main focus this morning is on the hunt for our three potential victims." He glanced down at his papers. "Andrew Dowd, Simon Walsh and Graham Fowler."

"As far as that goes, we feel the time might have come to start circulating pictures," Brigstocke said.

Thorne looked across at his DCI and felt a surge of admiration for the man. He had been worryingly non-committal on the way into the meeting and Thorne would not have put money on which way he was liable to jump.

"You'd be ready to move quickly on that?" Johns asked.

Brigstocke nodded. "The photos of Fowler and Walsh are long out of date, but they're the best we've got: an old driving license shot of Walsh from the DVLA and the most recent photo that Fowler's father was able to find. We should be able to get some good ones of Andrew Dowd from his wife as soon as we're given the word."

"If she hasn't cut them all up," Jesmond said. "Sounds like a bit of a bitch."

Johns looked towards Paula Hughes. She had a mop of brown curls and, for Thorne's money, showed a few too many teeth when she smiled.

"We can get them into all the nationals by tomorrow," she said. "And the six o'clock news tonight, if we're quick."

Johns nodded, scribbled a note or two.

"We're still... concerned," Jesmond said. "About alerting Garvey to the fact that we're onto him."

Thorne's sigh was clearly audible to everyone at the table. Heads turned. "I think he's well aware of that," he said. "I think that suits him just fine. Why else would he be leaving the X-ray fragments?"

Jesmond's eyes hardened. "It's extremely dangerous to make any kind of presumption about a man like Anthony Garvey. We're not exactly dealing with a rational mind."

"All the more reason to take no chances."

"I agree completely. So why broadcast pictures of the very people he intends to kill?"

"So we can find them." You fucking idiot. The words sounded so loud in Thorne's head that, for a second or two, he wondered if he'd spoken them out loud. He caught the eye of the WPC taking notes. Clearly, he hadn't needed to.

"We have to at least consider the possibility that we might be helping him."

"I think he knows who he's after." Thorne fought to keep the sarcasm from his voice. "And if we don't do everything we can now, he's likely to find them before we do."

"Why should he be able to do that?"

"He's been searching a damn sight longer than we have." Thorne made sure he had Johns' attention. "And if we don't use these photos, it's going to start looking like he's trying a damn sight harder, too."

Jesmond reddened and tapped his pencil against the edge of the table. It heartened Thorne enormously to see that the sandy hair was a little more wispy than the last time he had seen him, the face a little more veined.

"I'm sorry," Thorne said. "I really don't understand why you're so worried."

"What if we use these pictures in the press and Garvey kills someone?"

"What if we don't and he kills someone anyway?"

"Well, obviously, either scenario is one we'll try to avoid. But we do need to think about which is the least... problematic."

"Problematic?" As Thorne stared at Jesmond, he remembered reading about an American car company that had discovered a potentially dangerous fault on one of its models. After considering their options, the management decided not to alert the public. They had calculated that it would be more expensive to organize a national recall of the affected vehicles than to pay damages to the injured and the relatives of those killed.

More problematic...

"This is what we need to talk about," Johns said. "We don't want to be accused of not doing all we could have done, should this information come to light."

"Which it will," Thorne said.

Jesmond shook his head. "As long as we keep the link between the victims quiet, it's not a criticism that can be leveled."

"The papers will get hold of it," Thorne said. "There are far too many gobshites around, and too many journalists waving checkbooks. And the whole story's going to come out anyway when Maier's next book's published."

Thorne thought he saw concern pass across Jesmond's face, but it was no more than momentary. Jesmond knew that, in all probability, he would have moved on by the time anything damaging emerged. His successor would have to deal with the fallout. Thorne guessed that Johns was thinking the same thing.

Thorne would still be where he was though, as would the families of Catherine Burke, Emily Walker and the Mackens.

Jesmond removed his glasses, began rubbing at the lenses with a handkerchief. "We have allocated another dozen officers to the search for Andrew Dowd and the others. We're liaising closely with all the relevant local forces, whose missing persons units have pretty much dropped all other cases." He slid his glasses back on and looked around the table, making eye contact with everyone but Thorne. "We'll get there."

"I'm giving you another dozen, Trevor," Johns said. He glanced over at the woman from the Press Office, who quickly scribbled it down. Thorne knew that this was information they were only too happy to see in the papers.

"On top of which, we do have another avenue of investigation," Jesmond said.

Johns turned a page. "The young woman in Maier's photograph?"

"Correct." Jesmond turned towards Brigstocke. "Sounds like a very strong lead to me, Russell. If we can track her down, we might get to Garvey before he can get anywhere near Dowd or the others."

"I've got officers on it," Brigstocke said.

"Can we at least run her picture?" Thorne asked. He reached for the water jug, but moved back when he couldn't quite reach it and nobody seemed inclined to help. He looked over at Proctor, the community relations representative who had not spoken at all. Said, "What is it you actually do?"

Johns leaned forward. "Listen, nobody's saying we can't run the other pictures at some point. We're weighing up the options, that's all." He looked hard at Thorne. "I'm sure you understand our position well enough, Inspector. You're not naïve. So, I'll put your tone down to a genuine concern for the missing men rather than pure bolshiness."

"It's probably a bit of both," Thorne said.

Brigstocke cleared his throat. "Tom..."

Jesmond held up a hand and nudged the water jug towards Thorne. "I can't see too much of a problem with running the girl's picture," he said. "Sounds like a good compromise."

There it was. One of the Superintendent's favorite words. Thorne was amazed it had taken so long to hear it.

"Right, we'll go that way," Johns said. "And keep an open mind as far as the other photographs are concerned."

"Absolutely," Jesmond said. His eyes closed as he smiled, same as always.

Thorne poured then sipped his water. It was warm and tasted faintly metallic. "If things should change...?"

"We can move quickly," the Press Officer said.

Thorne did not doubt it. He knew that, when it came to shutting the stable door after the horse had bolted, there was nobody quicker.

Brigstocke had been kept back for a one-to-one with Jesmond, but Thorne wasn't complaining. He was happy to get out of that room and back onto the street, to take a few decent-sized breaths of gorgeous, dirty air.

Sitting on the Tube back to Colindale, his eyes fixed on the ads above the heads of the passengers opposite, Thorne felt the tension ease a little. He let the images drift and sputter in his mind and the ideas raise their voices above the noise of the train; let his imagination run amok.

He imagined Jesmond's face as the contents of the water jug ran down it, and the look on the face of the WPC—equal parts lust and admiration—as she unbuttoned her crisp white shirt and begged him to take her, right there across the blond-wood table.

He imagined telling Martin Macken that the man who had murdered both his children was sitting in a cell, or breaking news of an altogether more terrible kind to a father he had yet to meet.

He imagined Louise, smiling at him across the dinner table, across the bed, across a room in some wonderful house, with paintings on the walls and flowers he could not name in matching Chinese vases.

He imagined her starting to show.

Taking a life seemed a little easier if the person it belonged to was drunk; same as lifting a wallet. It had certainly been the case with Greg Macken — the responses sufficiently dulled and the defenses down, something not quite there in the eyes even before the light had started to fade from them. Watching the man walk away from the pub now, he couldn't say if he was pissed or not, but even a pint or two would blunt the reflexes. He crossed the road and began to follow. Once someone had poured enough alcohol down their necks, you could take almost anything you liked from them with nothing more deadly than a kebab.

That was not to say, of course, that everyone became easier to deal with when alcohol was involved and he knew that as well as anybody. Had his father not been the kind of drunk more liable to throw a punch than blow a kiss, he might never have kicked off in that Finsbury Park boozer, might never have got himself arrested.

Might, arguably, still be alive.

Walking past a crumbling stretch of wall, he bent quickly to pick up a fist-sized rock. He kept his eyes on the figure fifty yards in front of him, watching as the man stepped onto the road when such pavement as there was gave way to muddy verge. He picked up his pace a little, checked his pockets one last time to make sure the bag was there, and the other bits he needed.

When he was no more than a few yards away, he reached into his jacket for his cigarettes, smiling like an idiot when the man looked over his shoulder and miming the striking of a match; thanking him when he saw the nod, then jogging the last few feet between them so as not to hold him up.

"Swap you a light for a fag?" the man said.

Even better...

He thought about his father in those few seconds before he swung the rock, about the yellow fingers knitting themselves together on the metal tabletop and the way his cheeks caved in with every draw on one of those pin-thin roll-ups. The fucked-up teeth showing when he said, "Banning this almost everywhere on the out, aren't they? Banging people up for it. Bloody stupid, considering this is about the only place you can still smoke."

The rock bounced off the man's arm—broke it, more than likely—when he lifted it to protect his face, but the cry of pain was quickly silenced by the second blow. He followed the man down onto the grass and rolled him over, knelt across his chest and hit him several times more, until there was no resistance.

No, not drunk, he thought, but he looked for that dying light anyway, staring at the point where the man's eyes should have been as he reached for the plastic bag.

It was impossible to tell. The face was no more than blood and meat by then.

He drove the rock down into the mess again, a few more times, until it became too slippery to hold.

When headlights began creeping towards him, he rolled the body over the brow of the verge and waited there with it, his heart starting to slow and the damp grass tickling his face as the lorry rumbled past. He picked himself up and wiped the worst of the mud from his jeans. The man's book of matches was lying near the edge of the road and he used one to light a cigarette as he walked back to where he'd parked the car.

Twenty-Two

WEDNESDAY MORNING: two weeks since a schoolteacher had come home from work and found the body of his wife; since a man calling himself Anthony Garvey had begun to make himself known.

Carol Chamberlain wondered if it was too early to pour herself a glass of wine. Despite Thorne's crack about Ovaltine, it was not the kind of hotel where the rooms were furnished with mini-bars, but over the last few nights she had got through a bottle and a half of the Pinot Grigio she'd bought at the local Threshers and kept cool in the bathroom sink.

Knowing what Jack would have to say about it, she decided to wait until dinner, and went back to her notes on the Anthony Garvey case.

Bloody wild-goose chase, by the sound of it, Jack had said. She'd given him a general picture of what she'd been asked to do, not deeming it necessary to mention Ray Garvey's name, and he had still struggled to share her enthusiasm.

"Why should you be able to get anywhere if the cops can't?" he had said.

Because I am a cop, she'd wanted to say. Inside. And I'm bloody good at this stuff.

"How long are you going to be away?"

It was the kind of job that might have suited a private detective—a career move she had considered a few years back, when she'd left the Force. Been pushed out. But she knew she'd hate sitting in cars for hours on end, clogging up the footwell with empty crisp packets and watching nondescript houses in the hope of getting a picture or two of an unfaithful wife or husband.

She'd made light of the hypnotherapist business, but it had not been funny at the time, and she was stupidly grateful to Tom Thorne for the helping hand. It had pulled her back from a cozy future of dog-walking and crosswords. That was a pace of life she might be ready to embrace five or ten years down the line, but not now.

Christ, she wasn't even sixty yet.

Thorne had seemed a little distracted, she'd thought, when they'd met on Saturday. It was hard to tell if there was anything really wrong, though, because, if she was being honest, she could not say that she knew him well enough to discern what was normal. There were too many things they never spoke about, and she always sensed a reaction if she as much as alluded to them.

Sometimes, watching the dog tear along the seafront, or pottering about with Jack in their tiny garden, those events seemed as if they had happened to somebody else. But she was not ashamed of what she'd done. Back then, the need to get a result had overshadowed everything—a single good one being enough to compensate for a dozen cases' worth of frustration and failure. It drove her—something she knew she had in common with Tom Thorne—and even now, staring at the mess of paperwork and Post-its spread out on the bed in front of her, she felt an excitement she had feared had all but bled out of her.

I need to get out of the sodding house a bit more, she thought.

She had spent the day after she'd met up with Thorne going through the case notes from the original Garvey inquiry. She hadn't expected any great revelation, but she had been shocked all over again by the casual brutality of the murders. Like Thorne, she found it hard to swallow that they had been carried out by a man whose personality had been horribly altered; one for whom such terrible actions were wildly out of character.

She had filled her time subsequently on the phone or working at her laptop, making contact with old colleagues, many of whom had been closely involved with the inquiry. She had picked brains and called in favors, telling those who were interested enough to ask what she had been up to since they'd last been in touch.

"You know, keeping my hand in," her stock reply.

At the time of his arrest, Raymond Garvey had been married for seventeen years to his childhood sweetheart. In the wake of the predictable press hounding and after one too many turds through her letterbox, Jenny Garvey had left London and gone to ground, waiting for the man she thought she knew to go to prison, and, later, for her divorce to come through. Chamberlain had traced her to a flat in Southampton. The woman had sounded understandably wary on the phone, but had softened a little when Chamberlain had assured her that she would not be picking at too many old scabs.

She would catch the train down to the South Coast first thing the following morning and see what a chat with the ex-wife threw up. She knew, of course, that Anthony Garvey was not Jenny's child, but without too much else to go on, she had little choice but to see where the conversation led. If she could catch so much as a glimpse of Jack's wild goose.

He would be calling again in a couple of hours. They spoke three times a day, sometimes even more. Often, he would call if she was taking a little longer than usual at the supermarket, but she rarely resented it.

It would be the usual conversation later on.

The night before, she'd asked how he was holding up and he'd told her he was trying to make the best of it, despite the fact that his hip was playing up and he missed her cooking. She made sympathetic noises, but knew damned well that he was living the life of Riley, walking about the house in his underpants and living on takeaways and tinned bitter. It was a little lie, a lovely one. But she'd been spending a lot more time lately thinking about the less than lovely lies they told themselves and each other every day. The years they still had together and the cancer not returning.

"It's strange, love, that's all," he'd said. "With you being away."

Chamberlain did her best to organize the paperwork, made some room on the bed to lie down. Yes, she was away, she decided, so there was no reason why she should not behave a bit differently, too. She picked up the glass from the table next to the TV and carried it into the bathroom.

Despite the scope and scale of the Anthony Garvey inquiry, Thorne, like every detective on the Murder Investigation Team, had other cases on his books. Those inclined to murder a spouse or take a knife to someone who disrespected their training shoes did not hold back simply because there was a serial killer taking up everybody's time. There were also many cases going through the post-arrest stage. There was evidence to be carefully checked and prepared where court proceedings were imminent, and time-consuming liaison with the Crown Prosecution Service. As the trial date neared, a CPS rep might call the detective on an hourly basis to pass on the thoughts and wishes of those trying to keep their clients out of prison.

With little he could do to help in the search for Dowd, Fowler and Walsh, and with Kitson working on the Maier photograph, Thorne had spent much of the morning dealing with his backlog: the beating to death of a thirteen-year-old boy by a gang of older girls in a park in Walthamstow; a couple who had died in an arson attack on a block of flats in Hammersmith. Just after lunch, a CPS lawyer named Hobbs called with depressing news. Eight months earlier, a young woman had been killed during an attempted car-jacking in Chiswick. She had got into her car after shopping, then stopped when she'd noticed a large piece of paper stuck to her rear windscreen. When she'd pulled over and got out to remove it, a man had jumped from the vehicle behind and attempted to steal her car. In trying to stop him, she had been dragged beneath the wheels and, a week after the incident, her husband had taken the decision to turn off the life-support machine.

"It's Patrick Jennings defending," Hobbs said. "And he's confident he can get this reduced to manslaughter."

"No chance," Thorne said.

"Claims he's got a decent crack at it. Reckons it was the woman's fault. He intends to present a heap of Met Police campaign material which urges victims not to struggle, to hand over their property when threatened."

"You're winding me up."

"He's getting bloody good at this. Last month he was defending a kid who tried to take a woman's car by climbing into the back seat while she was paying for petrol."

"Shit, that was Jennings?"

"You see what I'm getting at?"

The trial had caused something of a stir in the papers, not to mention a nasty scuffle on the courtroom steps. The petrol station attendant had seen the boy getting into the car and kept the woman inside while he called the police. It emerged afterwards that the boy had a history of sexual assault, but, with no weapon found, the defense had been able to get the charge knocked down to trespass and he had walked away with a two-hundred-pound fine.

"We need to be careful, that's all," Hobbs said. "Don't give the bugger anything he can use."

"It's not happening."

"Let's make sure it doesn't," Hobbs said. "They're starting to call him Jack-off Jennings."

Despite the work this entailed, along with establishing base-camp at a fearsome mountain of paperwork, Thorne could not get the Anthony Garvey case out of his mind. Not for more than a few minutes, at any rate. Its dark beats, the twisted melody of it. Like the first song you hear on the radio in the morning that stays in your head all day.

Martin Macken's mouth like a ragged wound, howling blood.

A note stuck to Emily Walker's fridge.

Debbie Mitchell's kid, pushing his train up and down the carpet.

And all the time, as he and the rest of the team flapped and fidgeted and waited for something to happen, the nagging worry that they were dancing to Anthony Garvey's tune.

Towards the end of a nine-hour shift, with going home at a reasonable hour starting to look like a real possibility, Thorne ran into Yvonne Kitson on his way back from the toilet.

"I think I've found the girl in the photograph," Kitson said.

His first thought was that Louise had been right, that dinner together was probably optimistic. This was good news, nevertheless. Then he saw the look on Kitson's face. "Fuck..."

"I went through all the missing-persons reports for the six months after the date when the picture was taken. Found a girl who fits the description. She turned up two weeks later. Was... discovered."

"Where?"

"Same place she'd been sent to pick up the money, near as damn it," Kitson said. "Back of Paddington station. Looks like Garvey's got a sense of humor."

"I'm pissing myself."

"I've put a call into the SIO. Got an address for the parents."

"You told Brigstocke?"

"He's out, so—"

"Let me." He took out his phone as Kitson turned back towards the Incident Room, said, "Well done," as he dialed.

Got Russell Brigstocke's voicemail.

"It's me. Just in case you're playing golf with Trevor Jesmond, I thought you could pass on a message. Tell him that his nice, useful avenue of inquiry has just become a cul-de-sac."

Twenty-Three

ALL AT once, Alec Sinclair, a large man in his late fifties with thinning hair and restless hands, fell silent. He had been talking about his daughter Chloe, whose body had been found in a disused tool shed behind Paddington station almost three years earlier.

Struggling for words, he turned to his wife, who was seated next to him, in the cluttered living room of a terraced house in Balham. Miriam Sinclair was probably a few years younger than her husband, but there was gray bleeding through a dye job above her forehead and Thorne guessed the make-up was a little more thickly applied than it might once have been.

"It's nice to talk about her," she said. She smiled at Thorne and Kitson. "But then it all sort of rushes up at you. It's not like you forget what happened or anything."

"I dream about her sometimes," Alec said. "And there are those few seconds when you wake up... before you remember she's dead."

"You sure I can't get you anything to drink?"

"We're fine, thanks," Thorne said.

The couple had asked, of course, as soon as Kitson had called the previous afternoon. Shocked to get the call, so long after the investigation into their daughter's murder had petered out, but as eager as they had ever been to find out if there had been any progress. Kitson had told them that Chloe's murder might well be connected to an ongoing inquiry; then she had checked herself, stressed that the inquiry into Chloe's murder was still ongoing itself, would continue to be until an arrest was made.

"It's fine, love," Miriam had said on the phone. "I know how stretched you lot are, and, I mean, you've only got to open a paper to see there are plenty of other murders. Other families who haven't been grieving quite as long as we have."

"Have you found him?" Alec asked now.

"We don't have anyone in custody," Kitson said. "But we have a number of useful leads, and—"

"The boyfriend." Miriam looked at her husband. "We know it's the boyfriend."

"Right," Kitson said. The officer leading the hunt for Chloe's killer three years before had confirmed that their prime suspect had been the man she'd been reported as seeing at the time of her death. Despite their best efforts, they had never been able to trace him.

"We've got a name," Thorne said. "A description." He didn't say that neither was exactly reliable. "We're doing everything we can to follow these up and obviously we've passed all this information on to DCI Spedding." The man who had been in charge of the original investigation had been delighted to hear from Kitson; happy, he said, to share any intelligence that might take the Chloe Sinclair murder off his books.

Alec Sinclair turned to his wife. "Dave Spedding still gets in touch from time to time, doesn't he?"

"A card every Christmas," Miriam said. "A phone call on Chloe's birthday. That sort of thing."

"I mean, he was very close to us by the end. Close to Chloe, too, in a funny sort of way."

"Hard for him as well, I would have thought," Miriam said.

Thorne nodded. It should be, he thought. The day it stops being hard is the day to get out, to up-sticks and find yourself a nice little pub to run. He said that Spedding seemed like a good man, and a good copper.

"It might sound stupid," Kitson said, "but is there anything you might have remembered since the original investigation? Something that's come back to you?"

"We would have told Dave Spedding," Miriam said.

"I know, and we really don't want to dredge it all up again."

"Would you mind just going over it?" Thorne asked. On the cupboard against the far wall, he could see a collection of photographs in metal frames: the Sinclairs on a beach with two small children; Chloe and her brother cradling a baby monkey at the gates of a safari park; a young man posing proudly next to what was probably his first car. The brother who had lost a sister, the son who had become an only child.

"She was on her gap year," Alec said. "Saving up to go traveling before university. She did some stuff for me at my office for a while, but she was bored to death, so she got the job in the pub. That's where she met this Tony."

"Did she tell you much about him?" Kitson asked.

Miriam shook her head. "She told us he was a good few years older and I think she could tell we didn't really approve."

"Maybe if we'd been a bit more...liberal or what have you, things might have been different." Alec stared into space for a few seconds. "I just didn't want her getting too attached to anyone, not with university and everything round the corner. As it turned out, she started talking about not going at all, about going traveling with this Tony, or moving in with him."

"There were a lot of arguments," Miriam said.

Thorne said it was understandable, that he could see their first concern had been for their daughter. "But you never met him?"

It was a warm morning, but Miriam pulled her cardigan a little tighter around her chest as she shook her head. "She got very secretive about it, told us that it was her life, all that kind of thing." Her smile was regretful, a tremble in her bottom lip. "I could see that in the end there was a danger we'd drive her away, so I asked her to bring him round."

"She told us it was too late for all that," Alec said. "That Tony knew how we felt and she didn't want to put him through the whole trial-by-parents thing."

"It's stupid, looking back," Miriam said. "It was only a few months, but she was completely smitten with him. One day she was talking to us about all the places she wanted to visit and the next thing we wouldn't see her for days on end."

Alec's face darkened. "That's why we didn't even know anything had happened for a few days."

"Can you tell us . . . ?" Thorne asked.

Alec cleared his throat, but it was his wife who spoke. "She'd taken to stopping over at his place more and more."

"Where was that?" Kitson asked.

"Hanwell, I think. At least Hanwell was somewhere she mentioned a few times, and I remember she needed to get a travel-card for Zone Four. We never had the address, though. Obviously, we would have passed it on to the police." She picked at a loose thread on the arm of the sofa. "So, when she didn't come home on the Thursday night, we just presumed, you know . . ."

"We started to get worried by the Saturday morning," Alec said. "I mean, I know we've said there were arguments, but she'd always phone after a day or two. She knew we'd worry."

Miriam tugged at the loose thread until it broke, then balled it up in her palm and closed her fist. "We called the police on the Saturday," she said. "Then, three weeks later, we had the visit."

"There were two of them on the doorstep," Alec said. "I knew it, when the woman tried to smile and couldn't quite manage it."

"Do you know why?" Miriam asked suddenly. "I know you've got a name now, so maybe you've got some idea why he did what he did."

Because Anthony Garvey already had a plan. Because he needed your daughter to get the money to fund it. And once she'd done what he wanted, he had to get her out of the way. He could not afford to have loose ends lying around once his grand scheme of killing was under way, so he stuffed your daughter behind a pile of rusted metal and dusty sacking, curled up among the shit and the silverfish with the back of her skull caved in and a plastic bag tied around her head.

Because he needed to practice on someone.

"It's a bit too early to say," Thorne said, hoping that it didn't sound as piss-weak and pathetic as he felt while saying it.

Kitson glanced at him, but couldn't meet his eye. "We'll come back to you as soon as we know any more."

Thorne could see that the couple had had enough. He thanked them for their time and apologized for making them talk about something that was so painful. Miriam said that it was no trouble, that nothing was too much trouble if it might help find the man who had murdered her daughter. She said she was the one who should apologize for not being a better hostess.

"Did Chloe have a diary?"

"Yes, but only for appointments and things," Miriam said. "I looked through it afterwards... hoping she might have said something. The police had a good look, of course, but it's just 'meeting T,' 'having a drink with T,' that kind of thing. You're welcome to take it, if you want."

"It might be useful for checking dates," Thorne said. "What about a mobile phone?"

"Police looked at that, too," Alec said. "They found it in her bag."

"Do you still have it?"

Miriam shook her head. "Once the police had returned all Chloe's things, Alec took it to one of those recycling places."

"I can't bear waste." Alec reached across and fumbled for his wife's hand. "Can't bear it."

Thorne nodded and looked down for his briefcase. He knew the man was not talking about mobile phones anymore.

Jenny Duggan, formerly Jenny Garvey, had not been comfortable with the idea of Carol Chamberlain visiting her at home, so they met outside a small pub in the city center. Chamberlain was the second to arrive, her train from Waterloo having got in fifteen minutes late, and once she had visited the toilet and got some drinks in, she walked back outside to join Duggan at a table in the sunshine. They were no more than a hundred yards from the Bargate, the ancient monument at the northern end of the old medieval wall. It had served as police headquarters during the Second World War and now housed a contemporary art gallery, but eight hundred years earlier it had been the main gateway to the city of Southampton.

"All very nice," Duggan said, as Chamberlain drew back a chair. "But it's still rough as you like round here on a Friday night."

Chamberlain took a pair of sunglasses from her bag, smaller than the rather oversized pair Jenny Duggan was wearing. Chamberlain found herself wondering if, even now, fifteen years on and in a different city, the woman worried about being recognized.

"I didn't think you were allowed to drink on duty," Duggan said. "Or is that just something they say on TV?"

"I'm not on duty, strictly speaking," Chamberlain said. "I'm retired, actually. Just helping with an inquiry."

"Like a cold-case thing? Like on *Waking the Dead*?"

"I suppose."

"I've always quite fancied the main bloke in that," Duggan said. "Do you know any coppers like him?"

"Not many," Chamberlain said.

They sat there for ten minutes or more, talking about television, the weather, the job doing the accounts for a local furniture firm that Duggan had recently found for herself. Chamberlain knew she was ten years or so older than her drinking companion, but guessed that an impartial observer would have put it closer to fifteen. Duggan had looked after herself, maintaining a good figure and with her hair kept in the kind of shaggy bob that women a lot younger seemed to favor. Chamberlain was a little ashamed at wondering if the sunglasses might also be hiding the signs of having a bit of work done.

Duggan was talkative and relaxed. Chamberlain knew that she ought to be steering the conversation towards Garvey, but she was reluctant to push it, and not only because it was always useful to establish a rapport. She was enjoying their chat about nothing in particular. The sun was warm and the wine wasn't too bad, and any passer-by would have taken them for two friends having lunch or gearing up for an afternoon at the shops.

"So, you didn't get married again?" Chamberlain asked.

"Sorry?"

"You're still using your maiden name."

Duggan laughed. "It's a bloody good job you retired. Married again and divorced again."

"Oh, right."

"Don't worry, this one wasn't a serial killer or anything." She took a slug of wine, swallowed it fast. "Just a selfish pig."

Chamberlain did not know how to react, so said nothing and they stared at the traffic and the shoppers for a minute or more until Duggan said, "Ray never laid a hand on me, do you know that?"

Once again, Chamberlain had no reply.

"Surprising, isn't it, considering what happened later? He was a good husband, more or less. Good at his job, too." She looked away. "Good at killing, as it turned out."

Chamberlain thought about the tumor, about the notion that it had changed Raymond Garvey's personality. Could she and Thorne be wrong in dismissing the possibility so easily? "So, would you say that what he did was out of character?"

"Well, I wasn't... shocked," Duggan said. "When these things happen, they talk to people, neighbors, whatever, and they always say, 'I'd never have believed it' and 'He seemed like such a normal bloke' and all that stuff. But when they told me what Ray had done, I just nodded. I remember the coppers' faces, how they looked at each other, and for a while I'm sure they thought I'd known what he was doing, you know? Looking back, I think there was just something in him... a dark side, which I knew was there but wasn't willing to face up to. Not that I had any bloody idea where it would lead, mind you."

"You couldn't have known that."

Duggan smiled, grateful. "Like I said, there were plenty who thought I did, but how much do you ever really know? I mean, you hear about these cases, horrible stuff, men hiding children underneath the house and what have you, and I'm as bad as anyone, thinking the wives must have known what was going on. No smoke without fire, you know?"

"Did you know he had a son?"

It took Duggan a while to say anything. Chamberlain stared at her, saw an expression of surprise that was no more than fleeting, and knew she was seeing an echo of the reaction from fifteen years before, when Jenny Duggan had been told that her husband had brutally murdered seven women. She could understand why officers at the time had been suspicious.

"I knew there were always other women," Duggan said, finally. "I knew... but I pretended I didn't. Told myself I was just being stupid." She removed her sunglasses and laid them on the table. "You can understand that, right?"

Chamberlain nodded. The less than lovely lies they told themselves and each other.

"He kept all that out of the house, at least. He always came home."

"We're looking for someone who would have been born around thirty years ago," Chamberlain said. "So..."

"Just after we got married."

"Yes."

Duggan nodded, thinking back, staring down at the last of the wine in her glass. "When we were trying for kids ourselves."

Chamberlain waited.

"There was a group of women he worked with at British Telecom," Duggan said. "A couple of them were married themselves, but they were a right bunch of slags. I went to a few nights out early on, but it was obvious partners weren't really welcome. I wondered back then if he might be knocking around with any of them."

"Can you remember any names?"

Duggan said she couldn't, even when Chamberlain pressed her. But she said that she knew someone who might be able to help and told Chamberlain about a friend of Raymond Garvey from when he'd first joined BT. "Malcolm Reece was a wanker," she said. "He used to come round and sit there while I waited on him and Ray, making sandwiches and fetching them beer from the fridge. Sometimes I'd catch him smirking, like he knew something I didn't, and once I got so angry I deliberately spilled tea in his lap." She smiled, enjoying the memory, but not for long. "Even then

I told myself I was imagining it, you know, about there being other women. Convinced myself that it was only Malcolm who was up to that kind of thing. He really fancied himself. I remember one time he grabbed my arse when Ray wasn't looking."

"Sounds like a charmer," Chamberlain said.

Duggan nodded and drained her glass. "Malcolm never went short of female company, that's for certain." She sat back and let the sun wash over her face. "If anyone knows what Ray was up to back then, who with, I mean, he will."

Chamberlain wrote down the name, along with the name of the street where Malcolm Reece had been living in the 1980s. She thanked Duggan for her time, especially as it had involved her taking the morning off work.

"I told them I'd got someone coming round to fix the boiler," Duggan said. "I've got used to telling lies over the years."

As she put her notebook back in her bag, Chamberlain said, "Why didn't you and Ray have kids?"

"We wanted to. I couldn't." Duggan's tone was matter of fact, but Chamberlain could see the pain slide into her eyes before she let her gaze drop to the tabletop. Even after so many years, hearing that Raymond Garvey had fathered a child with someone else had obviously hurt. Chamberlain neglected to say that others had paid a far higher price for her ex-husband's infidelity.

"Do you fancy getting some lunch?" Duggan asked. She pointed across the road to a small Italian restaurant. "I mean, you probably need to get back."

"Well, I'm not in a mad rush." Chamberlain was hungry, and she had thought to buy an open return. And, insignificant as it was in the scheme of things, the pain had not quite left Jenny Duggan's eyes.

Kitson had made an appointment to see Dave Spedding, the DCI on the Chloe Sinclair murder. He was now a superintendent based in Victoria, so after leaving the Sinclair house in Balham, Thorne dropped Kitson off, then carried on towards the Peel Centre.

Driving north through the center of town, he could not stop thinking about the horribly mixed emotions with which Miriam and Alec Sinclair had discussed their daughter. He'd seen enough grief to know that time would eventually tip the balance, that the good memories would one day outweigh the dreadful ones. Slow but steady, it had been like that—was still like that—with his father. There would come a day—though with the man responsible for her death still at large, he had not felt able to tell her parents—when Chloe's name need not be whispered and when mention of her would not drive the air from their lungs like a sucker punch.

When cardigans would not need to be pulled tight on warm days.

In slow traffic on the Euston Road, Thorne flicked through the radio channels, looking for something that would not annoy him too much. He stopped at a classical station, let his finger hover above the button, then moved it away. He could barely tell Beethoven from Black Sabbath, but the music was pleasant, and, despite the car's stop-start progress, his mind began to drift.

But not very far...

He considered Emily Walker's husband, and Catherine Burke's good-for-nothing boyfriend. The father of Greg and Alex Macken and the parents of Chloe Sinclair.

Anthony Garvey's other victims.

For reasons he could not fathom, Thorne imagined them strung along a rope, like life-sized beads on a living necklace. Stuck fast and twisting in the cold and dark, the bodies of their loved ones bloodless alongside them. One dead, one as good as, one dead, one as good as... the vast necklace straining with the weight of them, yet plenty of room still on the creaking rope.

Thorne turned up the music, put his foot down when the road opened up a little.

However their loss had caused each of them to behave—absurdly polite or obstreperous; howling or struck dumb—Thorne knew that the relatives of those Anthony Garvey had murdered were looking in his direction for a particular sort of comfort. Strong arms and warm words were easy enough to come by, but finding the man who was responsible for their pain was down to him and his sort. It would be one step, no more than that, but the first step to easing them from the knotted thread of grief.

He drove through Camden and Archway, up into Highgate as the rain started, then down into Finchley, passing within a few streets of where Emily Walker's body had been found a little over two weeks before. Ten minutes later, approaching Barnet, he turned off the Great North Road, and shortly after that, onto the street where Nina Collins lived.

Thorne showed his ID to the officers in the patrol car that had been stationed outside since Debbie Mitchell had moved in with her friend, and rang the bell.

Collins came to the door and stared at him. "Well?"

"Everything OK?"

She nodded towards the patrol car, flicked her cigarette into the bush at the side of the narrow path. "Apart from having to check with Starsky and Hutch every time I want to go and buy a packet of fags, yeah."

"It's all right, Nina." Debbie Mitchell appeared behind Collins, who sighed and let her past before disappearing back inside.

"I was just passing," Thorne said.

"Good of you."

"Thought I'd check, you know... see how you were getting on."

"Well, I can't go anywhere, and Jason's missing school. Can't be helped, though, right?"

"I'm sorry, but you've always got the option to come into protective custody. It would probably be the best thing."

She shook her head.

"OK, well you can call if you're worried about anything, you know that?"

Debbie Mitchell nodded and folded her arms. "Any joy?"

Thorne took a second or two. "We'll let you know, I promise."

Plenty of room still on the creaking rope.

Thorne's mobile rang in his pocket. "Sorry." He saw the caller ID and walked a few steps away from the front door. "I need to take this."

Holland was a little breathless, speaking from inside a fast car, raising his voice when necessary above those of the other officers traveling with him.

"Where?" Thorne asked, when Holland had said his piece. Listening, he glanced back towards Debbie Mitchell and saw the look on her face reacting to the expression on his own, saw her arms fall to her sides. "Sorry, Dave, say again."

The rain was getting heavier, and as Thorne opened his mouth to talk, he heard her say, "There's been another one, hasn't there?"

He turned to look at her, with Holland still passing on the details, and spotted Jason Mitchell creeping through a doorway down the hall, peering past his mum to see what was happening.

Holland said, "Sir?" and Debbie Mitchell said something else before taking a step back, out of the rain. For a few seconds Thorne remained silent. He could not tear his eyes away from the boy in the hall, wide-eyed and shiny-lipped in red-and-white pajamas, his teeth sliding back and forth across his bottom lip.

MY JOURNAL

10 October

Not sure if they've found him yet, but if they haven't, it can't be very far away. My money's on someone walking a dog. How many times do you read that? Or kids, playing where they shouldn't. I was thinking that, if I had the chance, if I could somehow find out when it was going to happen, I might pop down to have a look at the fun and games. Mind you, unless you don't have a television or you're living in a cave, it's not hard to imagine what it would be like. Dozens of them swarming about in their plastic masks and paper suits, lights and tents and tape, and some chain-smoking detective standing off to one side, shouting at his sidekick or moaning about his boss.

I can't help thinking that if they'd made that sort of effort fifteen years ago, they might have figured out what was really happening a lot quicker. They might have saved a few women's lives and might even have worked out that their "vicious killer" was a man who could not help himself. Who was as much a victim as any of them.

They might have prevented all this.

Even if I did have the chance to get down there and join the gawkers, I'd almost certainly not get to see the body being brought out, but I bet they have an easier job shifting it than I did. It's only when you've tried to move one that you discover why they call it a "dead weight." Lugging him into and out of the car was a nightmare, so it was amazing to watch him slip into the water a bit later, when I'd found the right spot. Then, he looked almost weightless, drifting down into the murk. Graceful.

I'm not really sure why I'd like to go, if I'm honest. It certainly wouldn't be about gloating, nothing like that. I suppose I just want to feel that I'm part of it. That might sound odd, considering that none of this would be happening were it not for me, but it's easy to feel... removed from what's going on. Stating the bloody obvious, I know, but I have to be one step ahead of the game and I can hardly pour my heart out to some stranger in the pub, can I?

It always makes me laugh, reading about "crazed loners." Well, yes, and there's usually a pretty good reason for it! Not that it isn't a major drawback when it comes to humping those "dead weights" around, mind you.

It's not like I'm desperate for attention. I know, so what am I putting all this down on paper for? Well, I suppose that when everything's finally wrapped up, I just want there to be some basic understanding of the whys and wherefores. Not that I'm expecting a great deal on that score, to be honest. There's always the ghouls and the academics, I suppose, and the odd religious nutcase who comes on side with blather about forgiveness. But apart from them, the reaction will be so hysterical that almost nobody will give a toss about the reasoning. All the more reason for me to get it down in black and white then, yes? Besides which, when the Nick Maiers of this world sit down to write their blockbusters, they'll have a little more to go on than usual. Hopefully they'll make a better job of it than they did last time.

* * *

Shock, horror: it's all gone very quiet in the newsagent's these days. He's too worried about keeping children out of his shop and it doesn't take much to knock a story off the front page. Too many kids stabbing each other, too much sleaze. A celebrity scandal or a decent terrorist story will trump an honest-to-goodness murder every time.

Once they find this latest one, though, he's bound to kick off again, waving his rolled-up tabloid like some sword of justice and ranting about how the streets aren't safe. I'd better make a point of going in as soon as I can. With a bit of luck, the self-righteous old bugger might burst a blood vessel while he's handing over my Bensons.

Twenty-Four

"On top of which, the victim appears to have had a sex change quite recently, and been murdered with a priceless, jewel-encrusted crossbow."

"What?"

"Good, so you're still with us, then?"

"Sorry, Phil."

Thorne was feeling the ill effects of sleep deprivation. He had not got home from the crime scene until late the night before, Louise dead to the world when he got in and dead to the world when he'd crept out again, into a street no less dark and damp than it had been four hours earlier.

By eleven in the morning he was ready to go back to bed, a heaviness having settled in his arms and legs. The cold, metal slabs of Hornsey Mortuary were looking every bit as inviting as the comfiest Slumberdown.

"Pro-Plus is good," Hendricks said. "Or Red Bull, though I wouldn't recommend the two together."

"Unless you've got a few cans stashed in one of your fridges, you're not helping."

"It's illegal in France, did you know that?"

"What is?"

"Red Bull. And in Norway and Denmark."

"The French drink absinthe. Doesn't that stuff kill you?"

"God knows, but it makes the heart grow fonder."

It took Thorne a second or two to get it; even then, a sarcastic smirk used up a lot less energy than laughing.

Outside the post-mortem suite, Thorne studied the health and safety posters on the wall. A yawn provided the cover for an unusually delicate fart, as he read up on the ways to avoid AIDS and MRSA, while Hendricks stripped off his protective gown and surgical scrubs and tossed them into a communal bin. Then they walked along the narrow corridor towards the coroner's office, which the pathologist on call could use whenever he was in the building.

"Silent but deadly," Hendricks said.

For a few seconds, Thorne thought that his friend was talking about MRSA, but then he saw the grin. "Sorry."

"Dirty bastard..."

The office was fractionally larger than Pavesh Kambar's but a lot more chaotic. A stack of green lever files was piled up on one of the three desks, and there were sticky notes on each computer screen. Hendricks pulled out a chair for Thorne, then dropped into his own. The Arsenal "Seventies Legends" calendar above the desk was the sole demarcation of territory in the shared space, and Thorne could see that a fortnight from now Hendricks would be attending a seminar on "gene regulation." The date was highlighted in red, beneath a picture of Charlie George, flat out after scoring the winner in the 1971 Cup Final.

Hendricks gestured towards the other desks. "Most of the people who work in here have pet hates as far as the 'customers' go, and it's always been water for me. What it does to the body. I'd take a jumper or a decent car accident any day."

Thorne could not remember too many lovely murder scenes, but on arriving at the canal bank the previous afternoon even he had been grateful that he had not found time for lunch.

They had pulled the body out of the water near Camden Lock, within spitting distance of the shops and bars of the sprawling market, though as yet it was impossible to tell where it had gone in. It lay on the bank beneath a hastily erected tent: one hand formed into a fist, stiff around the expected sliver of X-ray; the other, pale palm upwards and purplish fingertips, as though the victim were black but wearing white fingerless gloves; a shoe missing, a bracelet of weed around the foot; and the belly straining with gas against a waterlogged denim jacket.

There was still a little water trapped inside the plastic bag, which now lay plastered to the man's face, distorting what was left of it even further. Thorne thought it looked like an old cushion. The sodden stuffing leaking out, the material ragged and rotten.

"Somewhere around thirty-six hours in the water," Hendricks said now. "Not that it would have been very pretty beforehand."

"Definitely dead before he went in, then?"

"You saw his face, mate. That wasn't the fish." Hendricks sat back in his chair. "And dead for a few hours before that, I reckon. Four or five at least."

"So he was killed somewhere else?"

"Well, I don't think the killer battered him, stuck a bag over his head and then stood around on the canal bank waving at passers-by."

Thorne acknowledged the inanity of his question with a nod, already thinking that their best chance of working out where he was killed would normally have been provided by forensics. But that was virtually a dead end, those thirty-six hours in the water having ruined more than just the victim's good looks. He blinked away an image of the tattered flesh inside the plastic bag. "Doesn't seem much point in a personal ID," he said. "No birthmarks or anything, and I can't see anyone recognizing him."

Hendricks shook his head. "Good job we don't need one."

"First piece of luck we've had," Thorne said. "Mind you, he was only ever going to be one of three people."

The treatment meted out to the dead man's face made even a check of dental records tricky to say the least and the chances of getting any fingerprint or DNA samples from a reliable source to match with his corpse were almost non-existent. So, the items found on the body itself were liable to be as close as they would come to identify Anthony Garvey's latest victim as Simon Walsh: an old driving license in the back pocket of his jeans; a barely decipherable letter from his aunt tucked inside the protective wallet.

"The aunt's the next of kin, right?"

Thorne nodded.

"How did she take it?"

"Brigstocke got the shitty end of the stick on that one."

"I still don't know how you lot do that," Hendricks said. "Cutting 'em up's a doddle by comparison."

"I'd take a room full of widows and grieving parents any day."

Hendricks shook his head, adamant. "I always know how the dead ones are going to react."

Thorne was about to say, "You get used to it," but Hendricks knew him too well. Knew otherwise. "I think his aunt was pleased that Walsh still had her letter. That he thought about her, you know?"

There was a sudden clatter, and the squeak of rubber wheels outside the door as a trolley was pushed past. It faded quickly, lost beneath the echoing conversation of the mortuary attendants; an everyday cadence.

Hendricks turned to his computer, opened his email browser and scanned his inbox. Thorne watched him, the elaborate Celtic band tattooed around his biceps moving as he pushed the mouse around. "Fancy a couple of days in Gothenburg?" Hendricks asked, peering at the screen. "A seminar on 'image analysis in toxicological pathology' and all the pickled herring you can eat?"

"Why change his method?" Thorne asked. "Why did Walsh get it from the front? And why was he so violent this time?"

Hendricks spun around on his chair. "That's a 'no' to the pickled herring, then, is it?"

"Come on."

"Maybe he's getting cocky, thinks he's good at it."

"Nobody's arguing."

"So, he doesn't feel like he's got to sneak up. I don't know. Maybe he was in a hurry, or didn't have time to get to know this one, like he did with Macken." Hendricks thought for a few seconds. "Maybe he's just getting angrier."

"Why kill him somewhere else, then dump him, though?" Thorne said. "He's never worried about the body being found before."

"Nobody said he didn't want the body found. If he killed him outdoors, he's pretty much got to dump him outdoors, I would have thought. Where else is he going to stick him?"

"Yeah..."

"Even if he'd wanted to use the same MO as before and kill him indoors, it sounds like Walsh might not have been living anywhere Garvey could have done it."

"Yeah... you're probably right," Thorne said. He puffed out his cheeks and let the air go slowly, forcing himself to his feet, though he would have been happy to stay in his chair for a few more hours. Walking towards the door, saying he'd phone later and asking for the report to be faxed across as soon as it was ready, he was aware that Hendricks was still looking at him. Thorne knew that expression well enough—the eyes narrowed behind the glasses—and that Hendricks was concerned about him. Him and the case, him and Louise, he couldn't be sure which, but he was certainly not going to ask.

In the end, Hendricks just said, "You're positive about the Gothenburg trip? They do seriously good vodka in Sweden, you know. And they haven't banned Red Bull."

Back at Becke House, the atmosphere in the Incident Room was strange, as though the workforce at a call center—which today it resembled even more than usual—had been incentivized with a mystery prize that everyone suspected would not be worth winning. The discovery of a body would always light a fire under a team, even one that was becoming used to it, but the urgency seemed somehow perfunctory. The sense of futility was there if you looked hard enough—in each glance from colleague to colleague, in every stab at a keyboard and snatch of a phone from its cradle.

As office manager, DS Samir Karim had been rallying the troops since the call out to Camden the previous afternoon. He found Thorne by the coffee machine, hunting fruitlessly for biscuits.

"Headless chickens," Karim said.

Thorne slammed the door of the cupboard above the fridge. "Not a lot else we can do."

As expected, the wizards at the FSS were twiddling their thumbs, any forensic evidence having been destroyed in the water. There was always the chance that a call might come in from a member of the public who had seen something, either at Camden Lock or at the murder scene—wherever that was—and there were plenty of officers out conducting a house-to-house, but save for the handful of trendy apartments a few hundred yards from where the body was found, it was not a residential area.

"There was a chicken in America who lived for eighteen months without a head," Karim said.

"What?"

"Straight up. Fifty-odd years ago. One of my kids showed me on the internet. 'Miracle Mike the Headless Chicken.' They used to feed it with an eyedropper straight down its neck and it went round fairs and circuses and stuff. A year and a half, running around with no head."

"We haven't got that long," Thorne said.

Brigstocke appeared on the far side of the Incident Room and beckoned him over. Thorne left Karim to continue the search for biscuits and followed the DCI into his office.

"Just had a lovely chat on the phone with Simon Walsh's aunt," Brigstocke said. "Usual bullshit and diplomacy. Telling her that her nephew was the victim of a random attack and trying to convince her that she really doesn't want to come and have a look at him just yet."

"I've been talking about miraculous chickens," Thorne said.

Brigstocke blinked and Thorne gave a small shake of the head to let him know that it wasn't important. Brigstocke walked round and sat behind his desk. "So, as soon as we can find a piece of this poor sod's jaw with any teeth left in it, we'll be looking at dental records to confirm the ID. Got to find his dentist first, of course, so I'm not holding my breath." He suddenly seemed to notice Thorne's appearance for the first time. "Bloody hell, I'm the one with three kids. How come you look so knackered?"

"Mental exhaustion," Thorne said. "Exercising a brain the size of mine takes it out of you, not that you would know. It's a bit harder than helping with the geography homework and making sure your kids have got the right packed lunches."

Brigstocke laughed. "You wait until you've got one, mate."

Thorne studied the dents along the metal edge of the desk, the dust on the shelves of the plastic in-tray. When he looked up again, Brigstocke was pushing a pile of newspapers towards him. "What?"

"We've finally got pictures," Brigstocke said. He pointed as Thorne flicked through the early edition of the *Evening Standard*. "Page five... and they've gone into all the nationals as well. Working on *London Tonight* as we speak."

Thorne looked at the black-and-white pictures of Graham Fowler and Andrew Dowd. Above, a headline read "Police hunt for missing men," while below were a few deliberately vague words about an "ongoing inquiry" and a contact telephone number. The first picture was blurry and long out of date and the second, though it had been provided that day by Dowd's wife, was hardly a definitive portrait. Thorne wondered if they would be of any use at all. Then again, he knew that, barring weddings, few people ever had professional photographs taken and that, if Louise were ever asked to provide a picture of him, there would be not much more than passport shots and a few holiday snaps.

He tossed the newspaper back onto the desk. "Nice that the superintendent finally saw sense. Bit late for Simon Walsh, mind."

"As a matter of fact, Jesmond was still against it."

"You're kidding."

"And a couple of the others who are always up his arse. Way he saw it, to run the pictures now, after Walsh has been killed, is almost an admission that we screwed up. Something people might focus on once everything's done and dusted."

"We screwed up?"

Brigstocke raised a hand. "Luckily, Johns overruled him, so now we can all relax and keep our fingers crossed."

"Is that the best we can do?"

"It's not like we've got leads coming out of our ears, is it? We're no further on after the Walsh murder, and I can't see it panning out with your mate Carol."

Chamberlain had called an hour earlier. Once Thorne had told her about the discovery of the latest body, she'd described her meeting with Ray Garvey's ex-wife and told him about Malcolm Reece, the old friend she was already trying to track down. Thorne had said he would come to the hotel and catch up in person if he could find the time. He had encouraged her, as gently as he could, to work a little quicker.

"Maybe you should pay me a bit more." Chamberlain had sounded miffed. "Or get me an assistant."

"We're stretched for cash as it is," Thorne had said. "It was you or the hypnotherapist..."

Brigstocke stood and walked around his desk. He gestured towards the pile of newspapers. "I reckon those phones are going to go mad this afternoon."

"Let's just hope we don't have too many nutters ringing."

"We should get a decent lunch inside us," Brigstocke said. "It might be a long day."

Thorne nodded. He had not eaten breakfast and needed something to soak up all the coffee he had been pouring down his throat.

"With any luck, the Oak might have that lamb casserole on again." Brigstocke opened the door. "The one you snaffled the other day."

Thorne said that sounded good, but thought they should probably be eating something a little less solid. Something that could be taken through an eyedropper, straight down the neck.

There had been plenty of calls that afternoon; and, despite Thorne's worst fears, a few had sounded promising. There had been more than one sighting of Graham Fowler, two within half a mile of each other in the area between Piccadilly and Covent Garden. A woman who ran a bed and breakfast in Ambleside, a market town ten miles south of Keswick in the Lake District, claimed that a man who might have been Andrew Dowd had been staying with her for a few days earlier that week, before moving on suddenly. She seemed more interested in the as-yet-unsettled bill than anything else.

There had been no shortage of work, the mood in the office a little more positive, but Thorne still managed to get back to Kentish Town before seven and was pleased that Louise had managed to do the same. She was brighter and more talkative than she had been all week. She told him about the latest developments in the case she was working, while he made them both poached eggs and opened the bottle of wine he'd picked up on the way home.

They watched half an old episode of *The Professionals* on G.O.L.D. while they ate, then listened to *The Essential George Jones*—her choice—while Thorne cleared up and Louise leafed through a couple of reports for the following day. If she was still feeling fragile, she was showing no sign of it. She hummed along to "Why Baby Why" and "White Lightning" and seemed happy enough during "The Door"—one of several George Jones numbers that Thorne himself could rarely listen to without swallowing down the lump in his throat.

When they were getting ready for bed, she said, "I had a long chat with Lucy Freeman today."

The pregnant woman in Louise's office. Thorne threw his dirty shirt into the laundry basket, sat on the edge of the bed to remove his trousers.

"I told her I'd got a friend who's just lost a baby."

"What did you do that for?"

Louise shrugged; she didn't know or it didn't matter. She sat in front of the small mirror on the dressing-table in just panties and a T-shirt. "Lucy was really... nice, actually."

"That's good." Good that the other woman was nice. Good that Louise had the conversation and that it went well.

"Your hormones get all mixed up afterwards, which is why I've been getting upset, moody, whatever."

"You've every reason to be upset."

"I'm just saying. That's what Lucy was talking about. She's also got a friend who lost a baby—"

"One in four pregnancies, that's what it said in your leaflet."

"And she didn't feel right again until her due date."

"Sorry?"

"Not properly, anyway. Lucy said that it only really changes once the date you were due to have the baby comes and goes. Said it was just like a switch being thrown. That's when you can... move on."

Thorne nodded, doing the maths as he removed his underpants.

"Thirty-one weeks and I'll be right as rain."

Thorne heard something in her laugh; enough to know that he should go to her. "Come here..."

She got up and turned into his arms, pressed her face into him. He could feel the tension in her, the effort to keep it together.

"It's my fault," she said. Her mouth moved against his chest. "She was only trying to help."

"She didn't though, did she?"

"Not a lot, no." The half laugh again, and then her face was open and moving towards Thorne's, and by the time they were on the bed she was already pulling the T-shirt up over her head.

"Things are still a bit... delicate downstairs," she said. "We'll have to find other things to do."

Thorne grinned.

"Not that," Louise said.

There was nothing too soft or subtle about the things they did to please each other, and despite the emotion that had been crackling between them, it still felt closer to sex than making love.

Like something they both needed.

The ringing of Thorne's mobile pulled him from a dream in which he was moving fast across the surface of very blue water. He looked at his watch in the light from the small screen: 6:12 a.m. It was Russell Brigstocke's name on the display.

"You're up early."

"Some things are worth getting out of bed for," Brigstocke said. "I'm in such a good mood I might pop back between the sheets, start Mrs. Brigstocke's day off with a bang."

Thorne thought about the night before and felt himself start to stiffen. He had hoped that the guilt might have gone, but it was still there, solid and stubborn in his chest.

"Let's have it then."

"Graham Fowler walked into Charing Cross station at eleven o'clock last night with a copy of the *Standard* he'd been planning to sleep on."

"Bloody hell!"

"It gets better," Brigstocke said. "About half an hour ago, they took a call from Andrew Dowd in the Incident Room. Looks like he finally turned on his phone and picked up our message."

"Where is he?"

"Kendal," Brigstocke said. "Where the mint cake comes from. Someone's on the way up there to get him."

Careful not to wake Louise, Thorne pushed back the duvet and stood naked by the side of the bed in the dark. "So, Jesmond and his cronies might get away with it after all."

"We all might."

"Jammy bastards."

Brigstocke laughed. "Us or them?"

"I was talking about Fowler and Dowd," Thorne said.

PART III

A GAME OF SKILL AND STRATEGY

Afterwards

NINA

At the worst moments, when she feels like lashing out, she knows that there's only one man really responsible for what happened, but it's hard not to blame those two extras from The Bill who had been sitting in the car outside. Or that tosser Thorne and his cronies, the ones who'd stuck it there twenty-four hours a day, since the day Debbie and Jason had moved in.

Working from home the way she does, the way she did, a police car on your doorstep is hardly good for business, after all.

She'd always preferred to do business from her own place, and most of the girls she knew felt the same. She felt safer inside her own four walls and in control. But she could hardly expect any of her regulars to come strolling in past a pair of boys in blue, could she, and the money wasn't going to earn itself. So she'd had to make a few more visits to crappy hotels and dodgy flats. A few more hand-jobs in cars, parked up behind the football ground. She'd had to take a few more risks.

And she hardly ever worked in the afternoon, that was what was so stupid! She was rarely up for it, preferring to sleep in after a long night. To keep the days for herself and get slowly geared up for as many punters as she could squeeze in the next evening.

A balding, flabby businessman down from Manchester for some conference or other was the reason why she wasn't there when it happened. Not that her being at home would have made a lot of difference. He got past those two coppers easily enough.

Sick fucker was too clever for all of them in the end.

Worst thing of all was that she'd made a promise to Debbie a week or so before it happened. Told her she'd get clean and sort herself out. Talked all sorts of shit about the three of them getting away somewhere for a couple of weeks once they'd got enough money together. One of those places that was covered up, so the weather wouldn't matter. Somewhere with a decent club for her and Debbie to have fun in the evenings, with a swimming pool and plenty of rides and stuff to keep Jason happy.

"Long as there's a railway line somewhere nearby," Debbie had said. "Somewhere he can blow at the trains."

Christ…

All gone for nothing now, the promise and the plans.

She's been pissing away almost everything she earns on gear ever since that day Anthony Garvey came. It isn't like she needs the stuff more than she used to; she just needs to get out of it more often. She can't face thinking straight and worrying about what the future is going to be like. But it's getting so that however much she does, the high isn't lasting long enough.

Some days, with some punter or other sweating away on top of her, it was like she'd just… wake up, and remember what had happened, and it was all she could do to stop herself screaming and clawing at his neck. Lately, she's found herself taking even more risks. Getting into iffy-looking cars when she knows she should step away; letting an arsehole or two get rough with her, feeling better when it hurts.

Feeling like she deserves it.

Nina stands in front of the mirror by the front door. Slapping on the last bits of make-up before she goes out to work: a head teacher who likes her to talk dirty and who has arranged to pick her up in front of the petrol station.

She checks her bag for condoms, K-Y and tissues, stares at herself.

Rough as fuck, she thinks, knowing that, before, she'd have said it out loud and that Debbie would have laughed. Would have told her that she looked great and that whoever handed over cash for the pleasure of her company that night should be bloody grateful.

She runs fingers through the spikes in her hair and does her best to smile at herself. Says, "God bless."

Fumbling for one of the tissues in her handbag, Nina turns towards the front door.

Twenty-Five

THORNE DROVE south towards Euston, through the skinnier end of the morning rush hour. The headache he had woken up with showed no sign of easing off, and a heated argument about Spurs' lack of form on 5 Live was not helping. Monday morning, and it felt like it.

He had spent the majority of the weekend quite happily on his own, save for an hour or two in the Grafton with Phil Hendricks, Sunday lunchtime. Louise had gone to stay with her parents for a couple of days, got back late the night before and left early in the morning.

"She's on the mend," Hendricks had said in the pub.

"Yeah, she is." Thorne had spoken slowly, careful to avoid stressing the she.

"The pair of you should get away, soon as you can."

"Easier said than done."

"You might have a chance. Now this Garvey thing isn't quite as frantic."

"For you, maybe."

Hendricks had been right, though. Everything had calmed down a little. There were five unsolved murders—six, if you factored in Chloe Sinclair—and there was still a killer to be caught, but there had certainly been a change of focus, now that the last two people on Anthony Garvey's list had been found safe and well.

A small team of specially trained officers had spent the previous two days "debriefing" Andrew Dowd and Graham Fowler. In practice, this meant explaining the threat they had been under as sensitively as possible, emphasizing that they were now completely safe and talking them through their new living arrangements. This had not gone altogether smoothly, according to the reports Thorne had been sent. Neither man had been completely cooperative, with both described as "difficult" on paper and "not quite the full shilling" in a phone conversation Thorne had had with one of the liaison officers.

"Understandable, I suppose." The officer had sounded relieved that his day was over. "Mums murdered, some nutter trying to do the same to them, and it looks like the pair of them are on medication, of one sort or another."

"Is it going to be a problem?"

"We've got Tasers."

Thorne had laughed, but he had seen the havoc that grief, fear and drugs were each capable of wreaking on their own. All three were likely to be a volatile and dangerous combination.

Understandable, I suppose...

He turned into a wide, newly tarmacked street behind Euston station, a little apprehensive about the conversations he was shortly to have with two men he would be meeting for the first time. He wished he had Kitson with him, or Holland. They were both better than he was when it came to putting people at their ease, his own gifts tending towards the opposite.

He pulled up behind a Volvo whose plate marked it out as a Job vehicle that would probably be a damn sight quicker than it looked. He reached for his warrant card as he jogged across the road.

Thinking: Safe, but not particularly well.

It was a bland, two-story building comprising eight service apartments, each one self-contained and accessible only via a secure lobby. Liveried squad cars were not allowed within two streets, local uniforms were under instructions to give the place a wide berth and there were no outward indications that it was anything other than the utilitarian block it appeared to be. Though its occupants' bills were being picked up by the Met, their movements were rather more closely monitored than the hotel at which Carol Chamberlain was staying. Cameras in every hallway relayed pictures back to the desk on the ground floor, rapid-response units were stationed nearby and two plain-clothes officers remained on the premises twenty-four hours a day.

Despite the lack of an obvious police presence, nobody staying there was in any danger of being burgled.

The building had been purchased by the Police Authority to house witnesses in high-profile trials, especially those whose evidence was being given in return for immunity, or against someone who had good reason to ensure it was not given at all. During a major drugs case the year before, the place had become known as "Grass-up Grange," and it had stuck, with one wag going so far as to have a guest book embossed with the name. Each apartment had been occupied back then, and a good many officers had spent long nights playing cards or collecting takeaways. But for now, Grass-up Grange had only two residents.

Thorne entered the code he had been given and pushed open the door to the lobby. The two men who had been talking near the single desk turned as he approached. One face was new to him, but Thorne recognized the other officer as a detective sergeant he had worked with a few years earlier.

"Got the short straw then, did you, Brian?"

Brian Spibey was thirty or so, tall and from somewhere in the southwest. If his premature baldness upset him, he didn't show it, and Thorne admired anyone who accepted the inevitable and got rid of what little remained, instead of endlessly teasing, gelling or, most unforgivable of all, combing over.

"It's not too bad," Spibey said. "There's a pretty fair rota system, so I'm only on three overnights a week."

"And how are they?" Thorne nodded upwards, to where he knew Fowler and Dowd were staying on the top floor.

"Oh, they're not too bad. Started hanging out together, which suits me. Saves us having to keep them entertained."

"They're calmer now, then?" Thorne asked.

"Well, there was a bit of screaming and shouting earlier today. Fowler that was, but I think that's just because he's not used to being stuck in the one place. We gave him another twenty fags and he was right as rain."

The second officer laughed. "Well, as right as he's ever going to be."

Spibey introduced his colleague as Rob Gibbons. He and Thorne shook hands.

"You want to show me, then?" Thorne said.

It was two flights up, the last two rooms at the end of a perfectly straight corridor. The nylon carpet was gray and all but sparking with static electricity. There was a large plastic plant at the top of the stairs and someone had thought to break up the monotony of the pale yellow walls with a few prints, the sort you picked up in Ikea for £4.99 and slapped in a clip-frame.

Thorne thought that if he had to spend any length of time here, he'd probably start screaming and shouting himself.

Spibey nodded towards the penultimate door. "You want some tea or anything?"

"There'll be some in there, won't there?"

"You'll probably have to make it yourself." Spibey punched a four-digit code into the security lock on the door, then knocked.

"What?" The voice was hoarse and high pitched.

"You decent, Graham?" There was a grunt of assent and Spibey smirked at Thorne before he pushed open the door. "Give us a shout when you're ready for the next one," he said.

Fowler was sitting in an armchair angled towards the window and barely seemed to register Thorne's arrival. He was wearing jeans and an oversized sweatshirt, part of a basic wardrobe that had been provided for him, though he had clearly not been too impressed with the shoes or socks. He was smoking and there was an ashtray full of butts on a small table in front of him.

Thorne introduced himself and apologized for not having got across earlier. He sat down on the small sofa. "It's all been a bit hectic. Well, I know that things have been explained to you."

Fowler turned then and stared at Thorne. His hair was dark and down to his collar and a week or so's growth of beard could not disguise the sunken cheeks or poor complexion. He said, "Yeah, they've been explained."

Thorne nodded around the room and did his best to look impressed. "So, this isn't too bad, is it?"

"It's OK."

"Better than where you've been for a while."

"What do you know about that?"

Thorne leaned back, did his best to keep it conversational. He could see that Fowler was jumpy, disoriented. "Well, I'm here to find out, but I know you've been living on the street for a while. I know a bit about how these things happen."

"Yeah?"

"A bit."

Fowler produced a thin smile, clearly unconvinced. He stubbed out his cigarette, leaving the butt still smoldering. Said, "Maybe you should move in here."

"Sorry?"

"I mean, seeing as you know."

"I didn't say that."

"Seeing as your mother was murdered when you were a child." He nodded, mock-serious. "This bloke's probably after you as well."

Thorne cocked his head as if it were a fair point and asked Fowler if he wanted a cup of tea. Fowler shrugged and turned towards the window, then said, "Yeah, all right," as Thorne walked across to the tiny kitchen.

By the time Thorne sat down again and put the mugs on the table, Fowler had lit another cigarette. "Here you go," Thorne said.

There was a small hum of acknowledgment. The window was open a fraction and Fowler's eyes were fixed on the curls and strands of smoke, following each one as it drifted up and away through the gap and beyond.

"Are you on something, Graham?" Thorne asked.

Fowler turned slowly, after a small delay, as though the question had taken a while to reach him. "What do you think?"

"We can get a doctor over."

"Seen one on the first day."

"And?"

"He said he could get me some methadone."

The screaming and shouting that Spibey had mentioned was now even more understandable. "I'll get it organized," Thorne said.

"A few beers would be good, too."

"That shouldn't be a problem."

Fowler nodded, muttered a "ta," and spread his arms wide. "Home from bloody home," he said. Then he smiled, revealing that a number of teeth were missing, top and bottom. "Home from homeless."

"We'll see what Social Services can do about finding you somewhere permanent," Thorne said. "When all this is over."

"No thanks, you're OK."

"You want to go back on the street?"

"I don't like hostels much, anything like that. Too many stupid rules, and some of those places won't even let you have a drink."

"That might be a good idea."

"All a bit late now, mate."

Thorne knew there were others on the streets who thought the same way as Graham Fowler, who for one reason or another had an aversion to any sort of institution. He'd shared space with several when he'd been sleeping rough a few years back. Fowler's attitude explained why they had been unable to trace him through the records of hostels and emergency shelters.

"So, when are we talking?" Fowler asked.

"Sorry?"

" 'When all this is over.' When you catch him, right?"

"Right. I don't know."

"How long's a piece of string, sort of thing?" He nodded eagerly, without waiting for an answer. "Listen, pal, you just keep the methadone and the Special Brew coming, you can take as long as you bloody like." He laughed, then pulled up short when he saw the look on Thorne's face. "Joke, mate, all right? Joke."

"With a bit of luck, we'll be kicking you out of here before they get a chance to change the sheets," Thorne said.

Fowler stood up and tossed his cigarette butt out of the window, agitated again suddenly. "Why's he doing this, anyway? Nobody's said."

Thorne saw no reason to keep him in the dark. If patients had a right to see their medical records, then a man deserved to know why someone wanted him dead. "He thinks that the man who killed your mother should not have been convicted."

"Garvey?" Fowler spat the word out like abuse.

"He believes that Raymond Garvey was not in control of his actions. That it was all because of a brain tumor, and if it had been spotted earlier, he would not have died in prison."

Fowler shook his head, taking it in. "So, why not go through the courts or whatever? Why do this?"

"Because he's seriously disturbed."

Fowler thought about that for a while, then lowered himself gingerly back into the chair, as though he were aching. "Well, when you catch him, I'll make sure I stop by for a chat. Sounds like we might have a fair bit in common."

Thorne realized that he had not touched his drink. He picked up the mug, drank half the lukewarm tea in one go. "I don't suppose you were aware of anyone following you over the last few weeks? Anyone you didn't recognize hanging around?"

Fowler shook his head. "Sorry. I'm not very observant at the best of times."

"Anybody asking after you?"

"Not as far as I know. You could ask some of the boys, if you can find them. Strangers are pretty easy to spot. There's a... look, on the street, you know?"

"Can you give me any names?"

"I can tell you where to try and find them."

Thorne had known that was the best he was likely to get. When it came to those dossing down or shooting up in the shadows every night, there was no such thing as a full name and address. "That'd be good, thanks."

"Say hello from me, will you?" Fowler said. "Tell them I've won the lottery."

Thorne assured Fowler that he would. He stared at the uneven grin, the slightest of tremors around the mouth, and thought that, as far as luck went, the good sort was clearly something that happened to other people.

A few minutes later, he was in the corridor outside, waving at one of the CCTV cameras mounted on the wall. He was on the verge of marching back downstairs and mouthing off about security when he heard Brian Spibey's distinctive burr echoing in the lobby beneath him.

"I'm coming, all right, I can bloody see you! Just I've got a bugger of a sudoku going here..."

Twenty-Six

ANDREW DOWD's apartment was much the same as Graham Fowler's—bland and comfortable—and though Dowd himself seemed a little more at ease than his neighbor, and was certainly better-dressed, in khakis and an open-necked shirt, in another respect his appearance was equally shocking.

"You look... different," Thorne said, remembering the photo Dowd's wife had provided and which the newspapers had printed the previous Friday.

"This?" Dowd shrugged and ran a hand across his shaved head. Thorne noticed the expensive watch around his wrist. "Lots of things are different," he said. "Lots of changes."

"Not just a walking holiday, then?"

"I did plenty of walking."

Thorne nodded, leaned back on a sofa identical to the one he had been sitting on a few minutes earlier. "I've always fancied going up there myself."

"It's nice."

"A good place to get away?"

"I needed to get my head straight."

"Well, you can certainly see more of it," Thorne said.

Dowd smiled, showing a few more teeth than Graham Fowler had.

When Thorne arrived, Dowd had been reading a newspaper, with the radio on in the background. Where Fowler had been jumpy and mercurial, Andrew Dowd appeared relaxed and resigned to his situation, but Thorne guessed there was plenty going on beneath the surface. Shaving his head might just have been a radical grooming decision, but coupled with what Thorne had gleaned about his troubled domestic situation, he was pretty sure that the man had suffered some kind of nervous breakdown.

Not one of Anthony Garvey's victims, but still one of Raymond's.

"Apart from just checking to see how you're getting on," Thorne said, "I wanted a word about your wife."

"Well, 'bitch' is usually the first one that springs to mind," Dowd said. "But I've got plenty more."

Thorne summoned a smile to accompany the thin one Dowd had flashed before he'd spoken. "We want to go and see her."

Dowd's face darkened for a second or two. "Good luck. Make sure you take some garlic and a wooden stake."

Plenty going on beneath the surface...

Having spoken to the officers who had escorted him back from Kendal, Thorne was not surprised by Dowd's attitude towards his wife, but the venom was startling nonetheless; more so, as he spoke so calmly, without losing his temper.

"He didn't even want to see her," one officer had said. "Just told us to take him straight to the station."

Dowd had been adamant that he wanted no contact with his wife. That he would not go home with them to pick up some clothes and that he definitely did not want her informed of the address where he would be staying. He even went so far as to say that, if he'd had his way, she would not have been informed that he'd been found in the first place.

"It might have done her some good to worry," he'd said. "And I would have had something to keep myself amused."

Now, Dowd sat back and closed his eyes, apparently uninterested. But curiosity got the better of him after a minute or two. "Why do you want to see Sarah?"

"Obviously, you know we're looking for a man who calls himself Anthony Garvey."

"I should hope so."

"We think he got close in some way or another to the people he's killed so far." Thorne stopped, saw that Dowd had picked up on the final two words. "To the people he killed."

"Slip of the tongue?" Dowd said.

Thorne pressed on, feeling himself redden a little. "We're fairly sure he was known to them. Probably no more than casually, but known. That he put time into making sure they would be relaxed around him, let him into their homes, whatever."

"How did he do that?"

"We know he picked one of them up in a bar," Thorne said. "He may have got to know another through the hospital where she worked. We're still putting all that together, if I'm honest, but we're pretty sure he gets involved in their lives somehow."

"You think he's involved in mine?"

"Well, it might be that he just hadn't got round to you yet—"

"Jesus..."

"But yes, it's possible. Can you think of anyone who you might have met in the last few weeks?"

"I've met lots of people," Dowd said. "When I was up at the Lakes there were other walkers, people in pubs." He raised his hands, like it was a stupid question. "We meet people all the time. Don't you?"

"OK, someone you might have seen a few times. A new neighbor, maybe. A window cleaner."

Dowd thought for a few seconds. "There's this bloke Sarah found who comes round once a week to wash the cars. He's got one of those little vans with a generator in it, you know?"

"Since when?"

"A couple of months now, I think."

"What's his name?"

"I barely spoke to him, to be honest," Dowd said. "You'd be better off asking Sarah."

"Like I said, we were planning on talking to her anyway."

Dowd grunted and looked away, drummed his fingers on the arm of his chair. The sky outside Graham Fowler's window had been clear, but glancing out of this one, Thorne could see that a blanket of gray cloud was slowly moving to darken the day.

"What's the problem with you and your wife, Andrew?" Thorne asked. When Dowd looked up sharply, he said, "Look, I won't even try to pretend it's got anything to do with the case, but..."

Dowd began fingering the collar of his shirt. He took a deep breath and let it out slowly. "There's no point me kidding you. I'm not the easiest person in the world to live with, all right?"

"You and me both," Thorne said.

"I'm on a fair few tablets which don't help matters. Been on all sorts, more or less since I was a kid."

Thorne remembered the relevant chapter from one of the books he'd been reading. Since Raymond Garvey caved your mother's head in, he thought. Since he dumped her on a patch of waste ground behind a bus station in Ealing.

"But Sarah knows how to push all my buttons. She's a bloody expert at it. It's like she enjoys pushing them... pushing one in particular. You know how some women just get off on winding you up? Sometimes, I think it's the only time she actually feels anything, feels properly alive. Like she thinks her life's shit and the only way she can get her blood pumping is to push and push and push until she gets a reaction. Until she forces me to push back. Well, I'm sick of pushing. I just need to get to a place where she can't reach me, do you understand? Not just in my head, I mean."

Thorne nodded, guessing that he was the first person Dowd had ever said this to, but that he'd been rehearsing it. He suddenly had a vision of the man tramping around the Lakes all day, working out what he'd say to his wife when he had the chance. Getting pissed in the pub each night, trying to forget why he was there. Going back to some damp B&B and reaching for the scissors and the razor.

"One button in particular, you said."

"Kids," Dowd said quickly. "She wanted them and I absolutely didn't."

Thorne blinked. "Tricky."

"Oh, yes. A few days before I buggered off she got pissed and started talking about finding someone who did want them." He folded his arms and dropped his head back. "Maybe that bloke who washes the cars would oblige. A couple of quick squirts..."

"Sorry," Thorne said. He wasn't, not particularly, but it felt like the right thing to say.

When he stood up to leave, Thorne saw Dowd's confident mask slip a little, saw something like disappointment that the conversation was over. There was fear in his eyes, too, as he followed Thorne towards the door.

"You will catch this bloke, right?"

"We'll do our best."

Dowd nodded fast. "Course, yeah, sorry. So, talk to Sarah. See if it leads anywhere. You know, this car-washer business."

"I'll let you know how we get on," Thorne said.

When Thorne was reaching for the door, Dowd stepped close to him. Said, "Why would anyone want to bring kids into a world like this? A sick world."

Certainly a weird one, Thorne thought a little later, as he walked back to the car. When one man asks you to pass on his regards to his mates in the soup queue while another has nothing to say to his own wife.

"How do people get like that?" Louise asked. "Why would they stay together for that long if they hate each other so much?"

"Easier than being on their own, maybe?"

"No..."

"Or it's like he said and some people just enjoy conflict. Doesn't light my candle, but what do I know?" Thorne had told her about his conversation with Andrew Dowd, about the dysfunctional nature of his marriage. He had not bothered mentioning the central disagreement that Dowd claimed lay at the heart of it. That one button in particular.

Louise shook her head. "If it doesn't work, you should get out."

"I'll bear that in mind."

"Good. Because if you start pissing me off, I'll just trade you in for a younger model."

Thorne was on the sofa with a beer. He had been looking through his copy of Nick Maier's book on the Garvey killings, rereading those sections that dealt with the deaths of Andrew Dowd's and Graham Fowler's mothers, and the harrowing chapter that detailed the murder of Frances Walsh, the mother of Simon. Her body was the third to be discovered, though it was later determined that she had been the first victim.

A spot of light entertainment after dinner.

Louise lay on the floor, making a fuss of Elvis, moving a finger back and forth under the cat's chin. Elvis closed her eyes and stretched her neck towards her new best friend. Thorne watched, thinking that Elvis was rarely that affectionate with him. She had been owned by a woman before Thorne got her—albeit one who didn't know the cat was a she—so perhaps that was the reason. Or maybe it was something to do with pheromones, whatever they were. Or maybe the cat just enjoyed winding him up.

"Seriously, though," Louise said, "life's too short."

Thorne glanced down at the cover of the book on the sofa next to him. He wasn't arguing.

"That's one of the things that strikes you when something like this happens. You know, losing the baby. At first you think you've been unlucky, but you can look at it the other way too, start to appreciate what you've got."

Thorne nodded, felt that lump in his chest.

"You OK?"

He picked up the book again. "Just thinking about this stuff, sorry."

"That's another thing," Louise said. "Since it happened, work doesn't seem to have as much effect on me. I don't know if it's because I've had more important things to think about, or if it's just not getting to me in the same way. Do you know what I mean?"

She said something else after that, lying there stroking the cat, but Thorne caught only half of it. It was hard to follow a train of thought with the Garveys rattling around inside his head.

Father and son.

According to Maier's book, the detective leading the investigation had described the murders as some of the nastiest he had ever had to deal with. He talked about the level of violence meted out, how it must have been motivated by an incomprehensible level of hatred.

One powerful bloody tumor, Thorne thought.

It might not have been hatred that was motivating the son, but his killings had been every bit as brutal, and Thorne's desire to find him and put him away was the equal of anything he had felt in many years.

Louise was talking softly now, to Thorne or the cat.

Anthony Garvey might have seen the newspapers, but there was no way he could know that both Fowler and Dowd had been found, or that Debbie Mitchell was safely tucked away. He would still be out there somewhere; searching, growing increasingly frustrated. That might just give me the edge over him, Thorne thought.

Louise sat up, pulled Elvis onto her lap. "This cat loves me," she said.

Thorne smiled and put down the book.

Or it might just make him more desperate.

Twenty-Seven

H.M.P. Whitemoor

"THE EX-POLICE officer again, was it?"

"What?"

"Your face?"

"I fell."

"Right..."

"Seriously, I had some sort of fit and I hit my head on the bunk as I went down. I've got to go and have a few tests. Some kind of scan."

"What, like an epileptic fit or something?"

"Could be, yeah. Could be all sorts. I've had a couple before—"

"What?"

"But this was the first time I got hurt. Good job really or they might not have picked it up."

"Christ."

"I'm OK, really."

"Why didn't you say?"

"I didn't want to worry you."

"What about the headaches, though? Do you get headaches with epilepsy?"

"I don't know."

"I'll go online and have a look."

"I can do it myself, we've got access to all that. Thanks, though."

"We can both do it. Doesn't hurt to get as much information as possible."

"OK."

"It's set off by flashing lights and stuff, isn't it, epilepsy? Strobes and whatever."

"Should be fine, then. Not too many of those in here."

"It's good news, when you think about it."

"What is?"

"They'll have to move you to a hospital, maybe permanently. Got to be better than this."

"I don't know how that works."

"I bet the food's a damn sight better, and there won't be any nutcases hanging about with homemade blades."

"Let's see what happens."

"Might turn out to be a stroke of luck, you never know."

"How's things with you?"

"I'm fine, same as always."

"What about work?"

"Just bits and pieces really. I'm great though, honestly."

"You need to find something permanent, sort yourself out a bit. It's all right messing about when you're a teenager, but you should really think about getting settled."

"I don't see why."

"Don't you want a steady job and a family and all that?"

"I've got family."

"Not just me."

"Look, I haven't found anything I want to do yet, that's all. There's plenty of time."

"Listen, I've got more time than you have, OK, smart-arse? It tends to drag a bit when you've got sod all to do but dig the governor's vegetable patch and take degrees you'll never use. Goes by in a flash out there though, trust me."

"I know, don't nag. I'll find something."

"I was talking to one of the other lads, and he told me you might be able to come along when I go for these tests. You know, as a relative."

"Yeah, course."

"You don't have to. Just it's nice to have a friendly face around when you're lying there handcuffed to a hospital bed. Never been a fan of hospitals at the best of times."

"You don't have to worry about this."

"I'm bricking it, if I'm honest."

"I'll be there, all right? You listening?"

"That'd be good."

Twenty-Eight

ONLY A decade earlier, Shoreditch had been a run-down commercial district; but like its neighbor Hoxton, it had undergone a rapid and radical period of gentrification. Recent years had seen the appearance of seven-figure loft accommodation, private member's clubs, and even an urban golf tournament during which businessmen and media types could dress up in ridiculous clothes and knock specially designed balls around. Young writers set their novels there, and independent movies were shot on the streets. Taxi drivers were no longer reluctant to make journeys there after dark, and they had no shortage of business. While decades of grime had been sand-blasted from Victorian buildings, new developments had sprung up to house bars and nightclubs, with office space for consultancy firms and sleek advertising agencies, such as the one where Andrew Dowd's wife was a director.

She kept Thorne waiting for fifteen minutes, but he was content to drink coffee in the small, crowded bar and watch the world go by; specifically the hordes of immaculately dressed young women with which the streets around Hoxton Square seemed unnaturally blessed. When Sarah Dowd finally appeared to add to their number, she was at pains to point out that she had only ten minutes. With an accounts meeting scheduled for later that afternoon, she could allow herself no more than thirty minutes for lunch.

Thorne might have said that he was fairly busy himself. Or pointed out that she seemed in a hurry to do everything except apologize for being late. "I'll try not to keep you," he said.

She ordered a chicken Caesar salad and a bottle of mineral water. "Sorry I wasn't able to see you at the house," she said. "I don't get back until late, most nights, and we're having some work done, so the place is a bit of a state."

"Not a problem," Thorne said. "Must be a nightmare having builders in."

"Oh, God. You haven't done it?"

"Nothing major. If I want anything to do with cowboys, I'll watch a Western."

"It's just a small extension..."

Thorne hadn't inquired, but he nodded anyway and asked when the work had begun. If the builders had been on site for a month or two, it might be significant. Plenty of contractors were happy to take on casual laborers for the heavy work, which would have been as good a way as any for Anthony Garvey to gain access to his target.

"They started last week," she said. "Hell of a mess, but it helped take my mind off Andrew being missing, to be honest. Can you understand that?"

Thorne said that he could.

"I'd been starting to worry that it would all be finished before he was found. If he was found."

"Well, you can stop worrying."

"Can I?"

Her food arrived and Thorne watched her begin to eat; precise movements of her fork, a sip of water every two or three mouthfuls. He tried to imagine her and her newly shorn husband dining together in the new extension on their already large house in Clapham. Sarah's salary on top of what Andrew made as an investment manager, expensive holidays twice a year, private healthcare and a nice car each. They were the typical young professional couple who had it all, Thorne thought.

Except for a marriage that worked.

When she put down her fork suddenly, Thorne could not tell if she had lost her appetite or if that was as much as she normally ate. Had it been anything other than salad, he might have asked if he could help her out.

"When the police called to tell me he'd been found, they said he didn't want to see me. Well, they were a little more discreet than that, some rubbish about procedure, but I got the message."

She looked very serious, but Thorne got the impression that she was not the sort of person who smiled a great deal anyway. He had certainly seen no evidence of it so far. "Obviously that's none of our business," he said. "Our job was just to find him and keep him safe."

She continued as though she had not heard him. "Then, when they came round to collect his clothes, they wouldn't tell me where he was." She tucked a strand of immaculately styled blond hair behind her ear. "I mean, is he even in London?"

"He's...in London," Thorne said. "I'm sure you understand that it's best to keep the exact location secret. Bearing in mind the nature of the inquiry." It sounded convincing enough as he said it, but he could see that she was not taken in.

She pushed the remnants of the salad around the plate. "I didn't know things were quite that bad," she said. "We'd been arguing, you must know that much."

"Like I said, not our business."

"He's making it your business though, isn't he?"

"Your husband's been under a lot of stress, I know that much. Maybe he thinks it's better for both of you if he just...cuts himself off a bit right now. It makes a lot of sense actually, considering that there has been a serious threat."

"I don't know if you're a good detective or not," she said. "But you're pretty good at bullshit."

"It's a vital part of the job."

"Ever thought of working in advertising?"

Thorne caught the first hint of a smile. "I'm sure the money's a damn sight better," he said.

She shrugged. "It's bloody stressful."

Thorne had to struggle not to laugh. A waitress appeared and asked if Sarah had finished. She picked up her plate and handed it over without looking at the girl. The suggestion of a dessert menu was waved away, and it was only then that Thorne noticed just how thin Sarah Dowd's arms were, the bones sharp at her wrist.

"Andrew was telling me about a man you had working for you," Thorne said. "Someone who came to the house to clean the cars?"

She nodded. "Tony."

Thorne felt a prickle at the nape of his neck. "Do you know his second name?" He asked, knowing that it would certainly not be Garvey, not when he was working for someone to whom the name would be so recognizable.

"He was always just 'Tony,'" Sarah said. "I never asked."

"Tell me about him."

"He just turned up at the house one day touting for business. I told him what we were already paying, he offered to do it cheaper and he did a bloody good job. He had all the equipment in his van—a jet-wash thing, a vacuum, et cetera. Why are you so interested?" A second after she'd asked the question, her face changed; a pale wash of realization. "You think this could be the man who wants to kill Andrew?"

Thorne reached down for his briefcase and took out copies of the three E-fits, based on the various descriptions they had been given thus far. "Could any of these be him?"

She studied the pictures, then lightly tapped a finger against the middle one. "This one isn't a million miles away, I suppose. But he was a bit fatter in the face and he wore glasses. A lot of stubble too, like he was growing a beard."

Thorne put the pictures away, thinking how easy it was to change your appearance. You did not need to be a master of disguise. A beard grown or shaved off. A haircut, a hat, glasses. Factor in the average person's powers of observation and recall and almost anyone could hide in plain sight.

"Did he ever come into the house?"

She seemed to become nervous suddenly, as though she were being accused of something. "I made him cups of tea, we chatted about this and that...yes."

"How long was this going on for?"

"He probably came eight or nine times, so I suppose a couple of months?"

"Then he stopped coming?"

She nodded, getting it. "Around the time Andrew went off. I tried calling the number I had for him, but it wasn't in service." She reddened. "I remember I was pissed off because I had to drive to the garage to wash the car."

"Can you let me have the number?" Thorne knew that it had almost certainly been a pay-as-you-go phone and all but untraceable, but it was worth checking.

"He seemed like a nice enough guy," she said. "Down to earth. Just a... regular bloke."

"What did you talk to him about, when he was in the house?"

"I don't know." She sounded tetchy now. "Holidays, jobs, we just nattered for ten minutes at a time while he drank his tea."

"Did he ask you any questions?"

"Well, you do when you're having a conversation, don't you? Nothing out of the ordinary, though."

"Nothing about your routines, your domestic set-up?"

"No, nothing specific, but he was probably there enough to get a... sense of everything."

"Right."

"I never said anything...told him anything."

"You wouldn't have needed to," Thorne said. Everything he'd learned so far about Anthony Garvey pointed towards a man who was content to watch and listen, until the time was right. "Was Andrew ever there when he came?"

She thought for a few seconds. "A couple of times, I think. He usually came on a Saturday." She began to play with her napkin. "I remember he was there once when we had a major bust-up. I hate it, you know, airing your dirty linen, but Andrew's never shy about speaking his mind when other people are around. He doesn't even notice them most of the time, but if he does, it's like he enjoys having an audience." She took a breath and it caught slightly, and she ignored the strand of hair that fell back across her face. "We were screaming at each other and swearing, and I remember it spilling out into the front porch and seeing Tony outside working on the cars." She paused for a moment or two. "I remember him glancing up and me smiling at him like an idiot, as if to say everything was fine. Like this was all perfectly normal."

Thorne watched her squeezing the napkin, thinking that if Andrew Dowd's version of events was to be believed, a row such as the one she was describing had become perfectly normal. Thinking, as she looked at her watch, then made noises about having to go, that he liked her far more than he had ten minutes earlier, especially when he considered what the rows between her and her husband had been about.

"It's all right," Thorne said. "You didn't do anything wrong."

He ordered another coffee and stayed for ten minutes or so after Sarah Dowd had left. Thinking that the background music—salsa, was it?—was actually pretty good and that, what with his newly discovered appreciation for classical music, perhaps his taste was broadening a little. He wondered if one day he might even grow to like jazz, then decided that was probably pushing it.

Thinking for the most part about a killer who was perhaps the most meticulous, the most organized, he had ever tried to catch.

Had Anthony Garvey ever planned to let Nicholas Maier write his book, or had that been no more than a scheme to extort the money he needed? When did he first draw up his list of victims? How early in their relationship had he decided that Chloe Sinclair was expendable?

Wondering, as he stared at the passers-by, what plans Anthony Garvey was making now, with three of those on his list still alive and well, and with no way to reach them.

On his way out, Thorne was almost knocked flat by a man who then glared at him for daring to be in the way. Thorne said, "Sorry," then wished he hadn't—the typical English response. He winced at the rib-tickling slogan on the man's T-shirt: "If found, please return to the pub."

Walking back to where he had parked the BMW, Thorne decided that if a prick like that was lost, then those who knew him would surely be praying he stayed that way, or that anyone who found him left him exactly where he was.

Twenty-Nine

"I DON'T know how you can stand the smell."

"What?"

"It's like... dried piss and damp, and you're right up close to them."

"You've obviously not been to a post-mortem yet," Kitson said.

Trainee Detective Constable Bridges looked away to hide his embarrassment. He had been assigned to Kitson for the evening, and she could see that he was no more thrilled with the arrangement than she was. It was sensible, though. A night-time trawl around the West End's less glamorous locations was unpredictable, and all six feet three of TDC Bridges was there as back-up as much as anything. Even though Yvonne Kitson could handle herself if it came to it, she supposed that the occasional stupid comment was a small price to pay for feeling safe; and, green around the gills as her companion might have been, he had at least been smart enough to stay back when she was talking to anyone.

That bit of the assignment obviously suited him.

They had already covered Leicester Square and the small streets off Piccadilly Circus, and both were grateful for the mild weather. Kitson had shown pictures of Graham Fowler to anyone who looked as though they might be sleeping rough, and she was ready to produce an E-fit of Anthony Garvey if she got lucky. Thus far, the E-fit had stayed in her bag.

Having spoken to Tom Thorne and picked his brains about life on the streets, Kitson had not expected to strike lucky immediately. The population of rough sleepers around the West End was thankfully not huge, but it was fragmented into distinct cliques—the drinkers, the addicts, those with mental-health issues—and big enough for many of its members to be strangers to one another.

"You shouldn't have to look too hard, though," Thorne had told her. "People can move on quite quickly, or just disappear, but there's a hard core who've been knocking around for years."

Bridges was not quite so optimistic, or understanding. "Even if some of them have seen this bloke," he had said after the first hour, "most of them are too out of it to remember."

They walked down to Trafalgar Square and along to Charing Cross station. An old man with an East European accent, a thin blanket wrapped around his shoulders, shook his head at Fowler's picture, though he was clearly finding it hard to focus. He pointed Kitson further up the Strand, where a soup run would shortly be taking place. "Be many types around there," he said.

Kitson thanked him, though the location was on the list that Fowler had provided anyway, and pressed a couple of quid into his hand.

"You can probably claim that back on expenses," Bridges said, as they walked. "You know, as part of the inquiry."

Kitson ignored him.

The van pulled up just after nine-thirty in a quiet street behind Somerset House, between a small park and the grand building that housed the headquarters of American Tobacco. About two dozen men and women had been waiting, and they moved forward quickly to form a queue as soon as the serving hatch was lowered and the smell began to drift across the road.

Like the man at Charing Cross had said: many types.

Several customers took their soup or coffee and immediately drifted away, but others remained, standing alone and looking as though they preferred it that way, or gathered in small groups on either side of the road. The first few people Kitson approached shook their heads, not interested or unfamiliar with Graham Fowler's face, it was hard to tell the difference.

One man just stared at her and the woman next to him told her to piss off. Much as she wanted to do just that, Kitson persevered until she finally got a positive response from a Scotsman named Bobby who was standing on the edge of a group near the railings that ran alongside the park. He nodded enthusiastically between slurps of tea and jabbed a finger at the picture. "Aye, I know that bloke."

"You sure? His name's Graham Fowler."

Bobby shrugged and peered again at the photo. He could have been anywhere between forty and sixty. "Graham, is it?"

"Graham Fowler."

More nodding. "Aye, I know that bloke."

Others in the group moved across then, and two more men said that they recognized Fowler, too.

"He's all right, he is," Bobby continued. "Had a go at some arsehole who gobbed at me, down by the river."

Another man said he would have punched the arsehole, but agreed that Graham, if that was his name, was a decent sort.

"Not seen him for a few nights," Bobby said.

Bobby's friend nodded at Kitson. "Why d'you think they're going round showing everyone his picture? He's dead as mutton, mate. Probably been done over by that arsehole who gobbed at you."

"That right?" Bobby asked.

"He's fine," Kitson said. "He's just staying with friends." She quickly dug out the E-fit. "We're more interested in this man."

"Bloody terrible photo," Bobby said.

Kitson laughed along with everyone else. "Do any of you remember seeing him, probably hanging around whenever Graham was there?"

Bobby shook his head, but then another member of the group said, "Seen someone with the same eyes. Hair's all wrong but the eyes are spot on. I thought he looked a bit mental, so I stayed well clear."

"When was this?"

"Two weeks ago, maybe. Right here, waiting for the van."

One of the others agreed and said he'd spoken to the man with the small, dark eyes. Kitson asked if he could remember the conversation.

"He was just asking about where various places were, you know . . . shelters and day centers, what times they opened. All that." He took a sip of his coffee. "Said he was new, just getting to know the ropes, so I put him straight. Well, we was all new to this once weren't we, so you try and be helpful. And it doesn't bother me if they've got a screw or two loose."

"Graham was here, was he?"

"Yeah, far as I remember." He finished his drink and turned to head back to the van for more. "Yeah, Graham was probably knocking around somewhere."

"You sure he's not dead?" Bobby asked.

Kitson thanked everyone and put away the pictures. She was turning to leave when a man she had not spotted before came marching across the road in her direction. He was probably mid-twenties, skinny as a stick, with bad skin and dirty-blond hair teased into sharp spikes. His walk was oddly purposeful, and the fact that he was grinning was probably the only reason why Bridges did not step forward to meet him.

"I know one of your lot," he said.

Kitson was wary. "Oh yes?"

"We did a job together once, as it goes. I helped him catch a bloke. You can ask him about it."

"What's his name?"

"Thorne." He stared at her, waiting for some sign of recognition and seeing none. "Been a few years, like, but you don't forget stuff like that. We're talking seriously heavy business." He stepped a little closer. "You know him?"

"Yeah, I know him."

The grin grew wider and Kitson got a good look at what few teeth the boy had left, brown against gray gums. She could almost smell the rot. A junkie's mouth.

"Tell him Spike says hello, yeah? He'll know who you mean." He began rooting in the pockets of his jacket and eventually produced a packet of cigarettes. "Tell him to take care."

Walking away, Bridges was keen to know what the boy had been talking about, but Kitson ignored the question, talking instead about what

Bobby and the others had told her. She said they should be pleased with a good night's work: "It puts Garvey here. Tells us a bit more about the way he does things."

Bridges looked unconvinced. "Doesn't help us catch him, though, does it? Not really sure of the point."

"It's called building a case, all right? Helps us put him away when we do catch him."

"If you say so."

Kitson picked up her speed and moved a step or two ahead of the TDC. The lad was probably able to handle himself, and if she'd been interested she might have said he wasn't bad looking, but she couldn't help feeling she'd got herself lumbered with the superintendent's idiot son.

Bridges grumbled behind her. "It all takes so bloody long."

"You want a job that's quick and easy," Kitson said, "you made a very bad career choice."

"I thought he'd be back by now, to be honest." Louise took another look at her watch and pulled up her legs. "I knew he was going to be late, but it's usually before this. Maybe there's been a break in the case."

Hendricks was sitting at the other end of the sofa. "He'll call if something's happened," he said. He reached down for the wine bottle and poured each of them another glass. "This is a bloody awful case, Lou."

"Why does he always get the bad ones?"

"They seem to suit him."

"Maybe I should be worried about that," Louise said. "If he's going to be the father of my child."

"Don't worry. With any luck, the kid'll get your looks and your personality."

"Right, and his bloody taste in music."

They were talking over an album Hendricks had dug out from the back of a cupboard, a CD he'd left at the flat one time or another, something they both knew Thorne would have hated.

"I've got to say, I was amazed he had it in him at all."

"He was sound asleep at the time," Louise said. "I just helped myself."

Hendricks laughed for a few seconds longer than he might have done with fewer glasses of wine inside him. Said, "So you are going to try again?"

"We've not talked about it, and maybe not yet... but I want to, yeah."

Hendricks drank, holding the wine in his mouth for a few seconds before swallowing. "Funny, I remember sitting here a couple of years ago... well, lying here actually, because I was staying over while I was getting the damp sorted in my flat. I was upset, because I really wanted a kid back then and the bloke I was with at the time wasn't keen, so..."

Louise shuffled across and let a hand drop onto Hendricks' knee.

"I remember telling him about seeing this... exhibition on children's mortuary facilities, this special room all done up to look like a kid's bedroom. I'd seen a kid in there and it was like being kicked in the stomach. Anyway, I was telling him all this and suddenly I was just lying here, crying like a girl. No offense."

"None taken."

Hendricks took another swig, emptied the glass. "Silly soft sod."

"You'd still like to have a child, though?" Louise asked. "'Back then,' you said."

"Yeah, course I would. But now it's just like... if it happens, it happens, you know? There's no point getting worked up about it."

"That's how I feel, I think. I say that—if we get pregnant again I'll probably be going up the wall—but I reckon I'm less stressed about the whole idea now."

"That's good," Hendricks said. "I mean, stress can have a lot to do with... you know."

"How was Tom? When you got upset?"

"Awkward."

Louise nodded, half smiling. "That's how he's been about this. Like he doesn't know what to say. Or he wants to say something but he doesn't know how to get it out."

"He'll get there in the end."

"Yeah, that's him," Louise said. "Awkward. And only happy when he's got some awful murder case to get his teeth into."

"I don't know about happy."

"OK then, comfortable."

Hendricks thought, said, "Yeah, that's about right."

And they sat there and carried on drinking, comfortable enough with one another to say nothing for a while.

Thorne had rounded off a longish day with a quick one in the Oak, which had turned into a couple once Brigstocke and a few of the other lads had turned up. He had not meant to stay quite so long, but was glad he did, knowing now, as he drove back towards Kentish Town, that he had needed to let off a little steam.

It was better for everyone concerned.

He reached across to the passenger seat for his mobile, deciding to compound the fact that he was almost certainly over the limit by committing a second offense. If he was stopped, it would be by one of only two kinds of copper. There were those who would call him all sorts of silly beggar and look the other way and those who did their job properly and would gleefully do him without turning a hair.

He reckoned that fifty–fifty was pretty good odds.

"Are you hands free?" Kitson asked.

"What do you think?"

"I think that if anyone ever asks, I should deny having this conversation."

"Where are you?"

"At home," Kitson said. "Got back about ten minutes ago to a kitchen that looks like a bomb-site and a bloke who's pissed off because he's had two kids giving him grief all evening."

Kitson had already left Becke House for her evening shift when Thorne had returned from his meeting with Sarah Dowd. He had spent the rest of the day being reasonably constructive between long bouts of window-watching. Trying to put together a rough picture of Anthony Garvey's movements in recent weeks, and asking himself why he'd let Kitson handle the rough-sleeper lead while he had been content to drink coffee and do marriage-guidance duty in Shoreditch.

Now, he asked Kitson how things had panned out in the West End.

"Aside from having to work with a tosspot of a trainee, pretty well." She told him about the sighting of a man who was almost certainly Anthony Garvey, who in all likelihood had been following Graham Fowler, waiting to pick his moment.

"I was wondering how he does it," Thorne said. "Pick his moment I mean."

"Maybe he wants to do them in a particular order."

"I thought about that, but he's not doing them in the same order their mothers were murdered."

"No point trying to second guess a nutcase," Kitson said.

Thorne said that she was probably right. He'd wasted too much time trying to do that in the past.

"Oh, and I bumped into a friend of yours."

"Not too many of those about," Thorne said.

"Bloke called Spike. Told me to say hello to you."

Thorne feathered the brake of the BMW as his memory fired a series of unwelcome images into his mind: a network of tunnels; a couple making love inside a coffin-sized cardboard box; a syringe blooming with blood. "Was there a woman with him?" he asked.

"Not that I could see," Kitson said. "He looked pretty far gone, to be honest."

Thorne thought about Spike and a woman named One-Day Caroline, who had loved each other and the drug that was killing them so fiercely. If Caroline had managed to get off the streets—and he hoped that was why she was no longer around—staying away from the one person who might drag her back onto them was probably a good idea. There had been a child as well, a boy. Thorne squeezed the steering wheel, willing himself to remember the name.

"I'll catch up with you tomorrow, then," Kitson said, breaking the silence.

He knew this was why he had been happy to let somebody else interview the rough sleepers. He had no desire to revisit a period of his life that had been so out of kilter, both personally and professionally. No need to step back into the shadows.

"Right. Tomorrow." He jumped a red light at the Archway roundabout, still buzzing with the drink and with those images from his past, and wondering who he was trying to fool. Asking himself if his life now—professionally and personally—was really any better than it had been back then.

He cracked the window to let in some cold air, silently wished Spike well and drove on.

"Tom . . . ?"

Robbie. The kid's name was Robbie.

Thirty

MALCOLM REECE, the man whose name had been provided by Raymond Garvey's ex-wife, still worked for British Telecom, though in the three decades since Jenny Duggan had first met him, he had risen from being an engineer to a service installation manager. He was based in a small office on an ugly industrial park in Staines, a Thames-side town in the London commuter belt that looked as depressing as it sounded.

He was decidedly frosty from the moment Chamberlain walked in.

"Look, I've already spoken to the police once."

"I know," Chamberlain said.

"Told them where I was on whatever dates... bloody ridiculous."

Officers had spoken to Reece a fortnight earlier, as soon as the Garvey connection to the killings had been established. He had been eliminated from their inquiries almost immediately, but the record of the interview meant that Chamberlain had been able to track him down very quickly. "I'm actually here to talk to you about something else," she said.

Reece looked up from his desk, his head almost perfectly framed by a large year planner on the wall behind him. "Well, I haven't got all day, so..."

"Some of the fun and games you and Ray Garvey got up to, thirty-odd years ago."

"Fun and games?"

"I spoke to his ex-wife. She told me the two of you were quite a pair back then."

"I don't know about that."

"Right couple of likely lads, she said."

Reece leaned back in his chair, and gradually a smile that said, "It's a fair cop" spread across his doughy features. Chamberlain smiled back, suitably conspiratorial. Although looking at him now, the only thing Malcolm Reece seemed likely to do was burst the buttons on his pale blue nylon shirt or drop dead from heart failure.

Chamberlain put him somewhere in his mid-fifties, maybe a year or two younger than she was, and it was hard to envisage him as the man whom Jenny Duggan had described as never going short of female company. He was bloated and jowly, with glasses perched halfway down a drinker's nose. He had kept his hair, but it was gray and wiry, the kind she remembered her father having.

"Blimey, you're going back a fair way," Reece said. "And there was a bit more about me then, if you know what I mean."

Chamberlain nodded, thinking: I doubt that.

"I was single, for a start."

"Ray Garvey wasn't, though, was he?"

"Neither were a lot of the girls," Reece said. "Didn't seem to matter much to anyone, though." He took off his glasses and leaned forward. "Look, it wasn't like there were orgies every day, anything like that. We were lucky, that's all. A lot of the girls in the office back then were very attractive and they didn't mind a bit of flirting. We were in our twenties, for God's sake. Come on, you must have been the same."

Chamberlain reddened a little, in spite of herself.

"I mean, that's all it was most of the time, harmless flirting. Every so often you'd have a drink and things might go a bit further, but it was just a bit of fun at work, you know? These days, you as much as tell a woman she looks nice and you get slapped with a, what do you call it... sexual harassment charge."

Thinking that she'd like to slap him in a way that would be rather more painful, Chamberlain told him that she sympathized, that things were even worse in the police force. "So, you and Ray put it about a bit, then?"

"Well, like you said, Ray was married, so he had to be more careful." He unfastened his top button and loosened his tie, enjoying himself. "I was probably more of a naughty boy than he was. I told you though, some of those girls didn't need a lot of encouragement." He grinned. "A couple of gin and tonics was usually more than enough."

"Can you remember any names?"

"The girls, you mean?"

"Sounds like it might be a long list."

"Bloody hell, now you're asking."

"Come on," Chamberlain said, smiling, still playing the game. "I know what you blokes are like. You can't remember to put the bins out, but you can remember the name of every girl you ever copped off with."

"Well..."

"Ray, I'm talking about."

Reece looked disappointed. Eventually, he said, "I suppose he had a few over the years."

"Anyone special?"

Reece thought about it. "Maybe one girl, worked as a secretary. A little bit older than he was, if I remember, and married. Yeah, he was seeing her for a while on the quiet."

"Name?"

"Sandra." He closed his eyes and fished for a surname. When it came to him, he snapped his fingers and pointed at Chamberlain, delighted with himself. "Phipps!" He shook his head. "Bloody hell... Sandra Phipps."

Chamberlain noted down the name and stood to go.

"That all finished when she left, though," Reece said. "She moved away, I think. In fact, there were a few rumors flying about at the time."

"Rumors about what?"

"Well, Ray didn't say much, but I know one or two people thought she might have been up the duff."

Chamberlain nodded, as though the information were of no more than minor interest.

"You on the train?" Reece asked.

She said that she was, and when he offered her a lift to the station she lied and told him that she had pre-ordered a taxi. Reece walked her out of the building and up close, pushing through the swing doors, she noticed that he smelled quite good. As he told her how nice it had been to meet her, Chamberlain thought, just for a second or two, that she could understand what those girls had seen in him thirty years earlier. It was only momentary, though. Walking away, she decided that back then British Telecom must have had a policy of employing young women with particularly poor eyesight or very low self-esteem.

She called Tom Thorne and talked him through the interview, told him that she might finally have a name for Anthony Garvey's mother. He said it would be good to catch up in person and they arranged to meet later on at Chamberlain's hotel.

"I'll see you about seven unless anything comes up," he said.

Then, she called Jack.

Listening to the phone ring out, imagining her husband turning off the TV and taking his sweet time strolling into the hall, she remembered how she had blushed when Reece had asked what she had been like in her twenties. When Jack finally answered, she snapped at him.

"What's up with you?" he asked.

She had blushed not because she had put herself around back then, but because she had not.

Andrew Dowd turned from the window of Graham Fowler's apartment. "You think we're the only ones? The last ones?"

Fowler was sitting on the sofa, a can of beer in one hand and a cigarette in the other. On the table in front of him were the remnants of several previous beers and many previous cigarettes. He shook his head. "There's at least one more," he said. "Those two coppers were talking about it."

"I wonder why he isn't staying here."

"She," Fowler said. "I heard one of them mention a name." He put down his can. "Fuck, you think she's already dead?"

Dowd shook his head and resumed looking out of the window. After half a minute he said, "What if they don't get him?"

"I can put up with this for a while," Fowler said.

"I mean ever." Dowd walked across and dropped down into the small armchair. "They'll give it a couple of months and then, if they haven't got him, it'll just fizzle out. They'll have other fish to fry."

"You reckon?"

"How can we go back to a normal life?"

"Some of us never had one, mate."

"OK, any life, then." Dowd sounded irritated suddenly, or perhaps it was just nervousness. "They'll have to protect us somehow . . . set us up somewhere else. New identities, maybe."

"Like those blokes who blow the whistle on the mafia," Fowler said. "That doesn't sound too bad, tell you the truth."

Dowd shook his head again, then let out a laugh as he picked up the coffee he had been drinking a few minutes before. "You're just about the most optimistic bastard I've ever come across," he said. "Especially considering you've got every right to think life is shit."

Fowler raised his can in a salute. "Things can only get better, pal."

"Let's hope so," Dowd said. "You reckon that bloke Thorne's up to much?"

"Seemed like it," Fowler said. He leaned forward to stub out his cigarette. "There's not a fat lot we can do about it either way, is there?"

They sat for a while, the silence broken only by the noises of the block—the water moving through the central-heating system, the low hum of a generator—and the grumble of the traffic moving along the Euston Road. Fowler took a fresh cigarette from his pack and rolled it between his fingers.

"Did you think about her a lot when you were growing up?" he asked. "Your mum?"

Dowd swallowed, then sniffed. "For ages I just pretended she was still around. My imaginary mum. I wrote her long letters telling her how I did at school, all that. It got better, eventually. What about you?"

Fowler smiled. "I think I just went from being one sort of mess to another," he said. "I felt it every day, you know? Felt like everyone knew what had happened, that they were looking at me like I was some kind of freak. I got into a shit-load of fights at school. They used up all their sympathy in the end and threw me out." He narrowed his eyes, remembering, the cigarette still unlit between his fingers. "Even after I got married, had kids, it was still... difficult, so I found things to help me forget about it, you know?" He nodded towards the empty cans on the table. "Only problem is, those things tend to ruin your life ever so slightly, and you end up replacing one kind of grief with another." He scrabbled for the lighter. "Christ, I'm rambling."

"It's fine."

"Sorry..."

"You ever see your wife or kids?"

Fowler shook his head and pointed at Dowd through the thick fug of smoke. "Listen, you want to make sure you don't lose yours, mate."

"Already lost her," Dowd said. "In all the ways that count."

"Don't be daft."

"I'm serious. I'm taking a leaf out of your book and thinking positive. Making a fresh start once all this is sorted." He got to his feet quickly and clapped his hands together. "Right, I'm making more coffee and I think you should have one."

Fowler laughed and said thanks. He watched Dowd disappear into the small kitchen, then said, "I really do think that copper's OK, you know, Andy. Thorne."

After a second or two, Dowd shouted back, "He might need to be better than that."

As soon as the video had finished, Jason wanted to watch it again, same as always. He tugged at Debbie's arm until she handed over the remote, grinning at the noise of the tape rewinding and settling back down in front of the screen.

Debbie could not bear to sit through it again. She knew every word by heart, every moment when Jason would turn and blow at her, imitating the puff-puff of each and every train. She got up and walked out into the hall, thinking that she could happily throttle Ringo Starr, and that Thomas the Fucking Tank Engine was in serious need of a derailment.

Nina came out of her bedroom just as the theme music kicked in next door. "I can't believe he hasn't worn that bloody video out by now."

"It's wearing me out," Debbie said. "I'll tell you that much."

"He loves it though."

"Yeah, I know... best fifty pence I ever spent. That market up in Barnet, remember?" She watched Nina checking her make-up in the hall mirror. "You going out?"

"Got to work, darling."

"You don't have to. I was thinking, why don't I start giving you something towards the rent?"

"Don't be stupid."

"No, I should."

"Where from?"

Debbie closed the lounge door. Jason would not be able to understand what they were saying, but he was sensitive to tone of voice, and easily upset by any falling-out. "I'll find it."

"Not as easy as I can," Nina said. "I've got three lined up tonight and one always pays me a bit extra." She looked at Debbie in the mirror. "You all right on your own? You're not worried are you?"

"No."

"Those coppers are still sitting out there and you can always ring Thorne if you're nervous."

"I'm fine."

Nina nodded. "I need the money, Debs. You know?"

When Nina had gone, Debbie remained in the hall for a few minutes, doing her best to tune out the sounds from Jason's video in the next room. She would put him to bed as soon as it had finished, and once the screaming and playing up were done with, she'd get an early night herself. It was better than sitting up and fretting, waiting for Nina to get home.

There was no way she could tell her friend how frightened she was. She'd decided years before that the only way to keep it together was never to let anyone see how scared she was. No man, however handy he might be with his fists, not any of those pinch-faced bitches from Social Services, and certainly not Jason. Ever since the police had first come knocking with their serious faces, warning her, she'd been thinking about what it might be like to be separated from him. Not just for a few weeks, but forever. She watched him sleeping, or stared at the back of his head as he knelt in front of the TV screen, and it made her want to be sick.

She got up and pressed her ear to the lounge door, held back the tears as she listened to her son puff-puffing and humming to himself. I'm the Fat Controller, she thought, and Thomas wouldn't know what to do without him.

The Fat Controller can't be shit-scared.

Thirty-One

WHEN THORNE entered the lobby of Grass-up Grange, DS Rob Gibbons was sitting behind the desk, reading a paperback. Thorne glanced at the cover: some fantasy rubbish.

"Dragons and hobbits, all that kind of stuff?" he asked.

Gibbons smiled, clearly unimpressed. "Not really."

"Where's Spibey?"

"Upstairs with the Gruesome Twosome," Gibbons said.

Walking up, Thorne wondered which of the stock answers he could give to Fowler and Dowd when they asked the inevitable question about how the inquiry was going. It was a reasonable question, all things considered, but such conversations were never easy.

Have you found the man who killed our mum/dad/brother/sister?

Why is this taking so long?

When are you going to catch him . . . ?

We're doing our best. We're making progress. There have been several significant developments. Whichever version of "no" and "I don't know" he trotted out, Thorne was always left feeling slightly grubby. He'd talked about it to Louise more than once, and they'd agreed that there was nothing that could be done about it, and besides, wasn't it better to give people who were grieving something to hope for? Perhaps, but it didn't make lying to them any easier.

Any day when a case moved in the right direction was a good one, but they were few and far between, and the really good days, when an arrest—the right arrest—was made, gave hen's teeth and rocking-horse shit a run for their money. Even then, of course, the possibility of a great day lay with the courts. A less than foolproof legal system meant that the best anyone could do at that stage was cross their fingers, move on to the next case and try not to worry.

"If they screw up," Hendricks had said once, "it doesn't mean you did."

"It doesn't matter," Thorne had said. Because it wasn't tricksy barristers or incompetent judges who had to face the toughest question of the lot, was it?

How could that happen?

Thorne stepped onto the top-floor landing. He could hear laughter coming from Graham Fowler's apartment.

So, any chance we might get out of here soon, that you might catch this bloke? You know, the one who's trying to kill us. Not for the first time, Thorne resolved to be as honest as possible, knowing that when the time came he would probably bottle it.

Forensically, they had about all they were ever going to get, and the phone number provided by Sarah Dowd had proved to be as useless as Thorne had feared. Her information, together with the sightings reported by Yvonne Kitson, was helping to put the picture together, but no more than that. Looking at it from almost any angle, Kitson's grumbling sidekick might have had a point.

Thorne walked along the corridor, past the open doors of the vacant apartments. Each one looked clean and ready, should it be needed, and there was the faintest tang of new paint. Thorne wondered if Grass-up Grange was expecting a particularly fussy gangland informant, and then—for no good reason—if it was true that the Queen thought the world smelled of fresh paint. Hers was certainly a sweeter-smelling world than the one he and Phil Hendricks lived in.

The poor old soul did have a lot of waving to do though...

He knocked on the door of Fowler's apartment. Said, "Brian, it's Tom Thorne." Spibey gave him the four-digit entry code and Thorne walked in to find him at a table with Fowler and Dowd, a scattering of poker chips just visible between the takeaway cartons and beer cans. The room stank of curry and cigarettes.

Spibey, who was seated with his back to the door, held up his cards so that only Thorne could see. He was holding two kings and a jack. "Three-card brag. Fancy a few hands?"

Thorne said that he couldn't as he was only stopping by on his way to an appointment.

"Go on," Dowd said. "You might change my luck, help me get some money back off this jammy bastard."

"Pure skill," Spibey said.

"Where's all the money come from anyway?"

Fowler nodded at Dowd. "Well, I came in here with about forty-six pence, but Andy's subbed me."

"And I'm the only one losing," Dowd said.

Fowler slowly pumped his arms in the air, began tunelessly singing "Things Can Only Get Better." It was clear that the empty cans were down to him.

Dowd looked at Thorne, shaking his head. "Like I told you, it's a sick world."

Thorne asked if everything was OK, and Spibey told him it was. Fowler and Dowd nodded their agreement, the two of them sitting there as if it were the most ordinary situation imaginable.

Neither seemed inclined to ask Thorne any difficult questions.

"Go on then, sod off," Spibey said. "I'm about to clean these two out."

"Oh right, your pair of kings."

Fowler and Dowd threw their hands down immediately.

"Bloody hell!" Spibey said.

Thorne grinned. "I'll phone later tonight," he said. "OK?" He would call Debbie Mitchell too, last thing.

Spibey caught up with him at the door. "Listen, Tom, I just thought this would take their minds off things, you know? Any problem?"

"Not as far as I can see," Thorne said. Both men had been far more relaxed than the last time he had seen them, and a few hours' harmless gambling had certainly got Thorne himself off the hook. If it worked with men whose lives had been targeted, he wondered if the chance of a quick flutter might be the key to diluting those awkward moments with desperate relatives.

I'm so confident that we'll catch the man who killed your husband/wife/hamster that I'll give you ten to one against us catching him. Stick a tenner on and it's a win–win...

He decided to bring up the idea next time he saw Trevor Jesmond. See if the twat thought he was joking.

"Have you eaten?"

Thorne suddenly felt guilty. "I grabbed a burger on the way over. Sorry. I thought you'd have had something."

"I can grab a sandwich later," Chamberlain said. "It's fine." She held up her glass of wine. "I'll probably need something to soak this up."

The bar of the hotel in Bloomsbury was nice enough, but no bigger than a large sitting room, so Thorne and Chamberlain, once they'd got beyond the chit-chat, had needed to keep their voices down. The other occupants, a pair of blowzy Midlands girls on the lash, were showing no such discretion. Thorne had twice come close to marching across and letting them know he had no interest in their jobs or boyfriends and suggesting that they might like to take their Bacardi Breezers somewhere else.

"You're turning into a miserable old git," Chamberlain said.

"I was always a miserable git," Thorne said. "I just used to be younger."

"You think it's the Job?"

"Not really."

"That you'd be any less miserable if you worked in Currys?"

"Christ, no."

"Well then."

"A week of that and I'd hang myself with one of their reasonably priced extension cords."

"So, cheer up," Chamberlain said.

She refilled their glasses then picked up the bar menu, tapping her fingers against it in time to the quasi-Celtic folk drivel being piped from the speakers in the ceiling. The girls at the next table laughed and Thorne thought about asking if he could have the drivel turned up a little.

"You think there's anything in what this bloke Reece told you?"

"If it had been himself he was talking about, I'd probably have thought he was full of it. But it sounded... convincing."

"A convincing rumor."

"Got to be worth checking out though."

Thorne knew that, as the inquiry stood, a call claiming that Anthony Garvey was the bastard son of Lord Lucan would be worth checking out. "So, tell me about this woman," he said.

Chamberlain inched forward in her chair. This was what she was being paid for. "Sandra Phipps. Well, Phipps as was. She's been married twice since then. She lives out near Reading somewhere."

Something rang the faintest of bells with Thorne.

"What?"

For a second or two he almost nailed it, but the noise from the adjoining table made it difficult to concentrate. "Nothing. When are you going to see her?"

"Tomorrow."

"She know you're coming?"

"I thought it might be best if I just turned up," Chamberlain said. "If she is Anthony Garvey's mother, I'd rather not give her any time to think about it, cook up false alibis."

Thorne agreed that it was a good idea. He knew how easily the bond between a parent and their child could breed credulity and twist into denial. It was hard to condemn unconditional love, even when it bordered on stupidity, but if it came close to a perversion of justice, a line had to be drawn.

He remembered a woman who had flown at him a few years back, after her son had been jailed for kicking an Asian shopkeeper to death. He'd held her at arm's length until she'd been restrained. Stood there with gobbets of spit running down his shirt, wondering if the woman hated him as much as she hated herself.

And he remembered Chloe Sinclair's mother and the father of Greg and Alex Macken. A different sort of unconditional love.

He knew where his sympathies lay.

"You want me to come with you?" he asked.

"Right," Chamberlain said. "I do all the donkey work and you step in at the finish."

"Not at all."

"You don't think I'm up to it?"

"No, I mean... yes, course I do. I just thought you might want some company." Thorne shook his head. "Bloody hell, you're turning into a touchy old git."

Chamberlain emptied her glass. "Less of the 'old,' you cheeky sod."

"Pardon me." Thorne finished his own wine and sat back for a few moments. He noticed that one of the Midlands girls, despite the grating voice, was not unattractive. He thought about Louise and quickly turned his attention back to Chamberlain. "Course, even if this woman is Garvey's mother, she might well have no idea where he is."

"Or he might be popping round every Sunday with a bunch of flowers. We don't know, do we? At the very least we might get a real name."

"True."

"Maybe more."

"God, I hope so."

"This one's wound you up, hasn't it?" Chamberlain asked.

Thorne took a few seconds to gather his thoughts, which weren't coming quite as quickly or cleanly as usual. "The weird thing is that I'm almost grateful for it. Just when you think you might be getting... desensitized to this stuff, some freak like Garvey comes along and you find there's a bit of you that's still... Shit, can't think of the word."

"I know what you're saying."

"And there's other things... things at home or whatever. They change the way you react to people. Make you angrier, sadder. Jack all your reactions up a few notches so you can't switch off quite so easily."

"What things?"

"It doesn't matter." Thorne shook his head. "I'm talking shite, that's all."

Chamberlain waited, but Thorne waved the subject away as though it weren't worth their time and effort. The music had dropped in tempo, like Clannad on sedatives. They watched the barman flirting with the two girls as he gathered up their empties.

"Are you driving?" Chamberlain asked. She held up the spent wine bottle to let Thorne see how much they'd put away.

"Well, I was." Thorne had driven home the previous night when he shouldn't have, but aside from being a little further over the limit now than he had been then, he didn't feel like calling it a night just yet. "Getting a cab shouldn't be a problem, though."

"Shall we get another bottle, then?"

He had parked in an NCP, which meant that, on top of the taxi fare, he would probably need to take out a second mortgage if he was going to pick the car up the next morning. He could always try claiming it on expenses. "Might as well," he said. "If you're going to order some food anyway."

"We could just go up to my room, if you like."

"Steady, Carol."

"Behave yourself." Chamberlain smiled, enjoying it. "I've got a couple of bottles up there, that's all, so it's free and it's a damn sight nicer than this rubbish. I can always ring down for a sandwich."

They gathered their stuff together and moved towards the lifts. Thorne made sure his voice was raised as he walked, not altogether steadily, past the table at which the Midlands girls were sitting. "Why do women keep asking me to go up to their hotel rooms with them?" he said.

Chamberlain shrugged. "It's a mystery to me."

A minute or so later, Thorne was grinning as the lift doors closed. "Mind you, the last one did want me to pay for it."

Thirty-Two

THORNE PERCHED on the end of the bed while Chamberlain sat in the small chair next to the window. The wine, from plastic bathroom glasses, went down easily enough, though it was hard to say if it was really any better than what they'd been drinking in the bar. Thorne was rapidly reaching the point where he could not have distinguished between Merlot and meths.

The first few glasses were taken up with chat about the case, but it seemed like small talk. They had said all that needed saying downstairs and both had been in the Job long enough to know that speculation was ultimately pointless, even when it was all you had left.

"I'll call as soon as I've spoken to Sandra Phipps," Chamberlain said. "If she does turn out to be Garvey's mother, I'm guessing you'll want a few words yourself."

Thorne nodded, that faraway bell ringing again.

"And if she isn't, do you want me to go back to Malcolm Reece, see if there's anyone else he can think of?"

"Might as well," Thorne said.

"Actually, I think he took rather a shine to me."

"Why wouldn't he?" Thorne spread his arms wide. "Attractive and mature lady, still got both her own hips. You have still got both your hips, haven't you?"

"Both fists as well," Chamberlain said. "And you should watch it, because I reckon you've drunk more than I have, so your reflexes are probably buggered."

"I wouldn't fancy my chances stone-cold sober," Thorne said.

"Long as you know."

Thorne had thought about asking if there was any music, if he could turn on the radio, maybe, but he'd stopped himself. Fuzzy-headed as he was, he was still thinking clearly enough to sense that it might not be...appropriate, or at the very least that the connotations might be embarrassing, for one or other of them. The silences grew longer, or seemed to, broken only by the sound of yawns no longer stifled, and once by the laughter and muted conversation of people entering the room next door. For ten minutes, while Chamberlain talked about life in Worthing, Thorne sat in dread, waiting for those tell-tale bedtime noises to start coming through the walls. Would he and Chamberlain sit there mortified, he wondered, raising their voices and pretending they could hear nothing? Or would they piss themselves like naughty children and hold their plastic glasses to the wall? He poured himself another drink, concluding that, should it come to it, alcohol would clearly be the deciding factor.

With two and a bit bottles accounted for between them, Chamberlain said, "I told you how grateful I was for this, didn't I?"

"Yes, and you didn't have to."

"I meant it, and you know it's not just about the money."

"A chance to stay in a hotel, whatever... I know."

"I needed the break, Tom," Chamberlain said. "We both know the cancer's coming back and I know Jack's only trying to make the best of things, but we're just drifting along, bored and talking rubbish like a pair of stupid teenagers."

"But it's better to be... positive, surely?"

She shook her head, adamant. "The pretending's doing my head in, tell you the truth. He's doing my head in."

Thorne took a deep breath. He was finding it increasingly hard to put the words in the right order. "I don't quite know what you—"

"I'm not saying I want to leave, anything like that."

"OK, because I thought you meant—"

"It's just that I want to slap him silly sometimes."

Thorne was about to laugh, but Chamberlain cut him off.

"Does that sound horrible?"

Thorne could manage no more than a shrug, a puff of boozy breath.

"We were walking the dog the other week," Chamberlain said, "and obviously Jack needs to stop quite a bit and catch his breath. I just have to stand and wait, you know, listening to him wheezing and watching the dog disappear until he's ready to carry on. So I was standing there this one day, thinking, I can run, you know? I can still run." She smiled sadly at Thorne. "Still got two good knees as well..."

Thorne returned the smile.

"God knows where it came from, but I thought, I could just go, right now, turn away from him and leg it all the way up the beach until he couldn't see me anymore. Sprint up the beach for the hell of it, just because I still can, you know? And for a few seconds I stood there next to him, fighting the urge to do it. Listening to the wind and the dog barking somewhere, and the air through his lungs like sandpaper.

"Now you're thinking, Stupid, selfish cow, right?"

"No," Thorne said.

She brought her glass to her mouth and tipped, but it was already empty.

Thorne could feel the pulse ticking in his temple as his eyes drifted away from her, finally settling on the card on top of the television: a menu of the various channels and pay-movies that were available. He scanned the titles, doing his best to focus, with trivial thoughts bubbling up through the gloop of more serious concerns that slopped inside his skull.

Would the Met pick up the tab for the movies?

Was Carol the sort to watch the dirty ones?

He turned to see Chamberlain unscrewing the cap from the wine bottle and said, "I think I should phone for a cab."

Chamberlain nodded and cleared her throat. "I'll do it." She sounded unnaturally bright suddenly, as though she were trying to distance herself from what she had just confessed. She reached for her handbag and pulled out her mobile. "Louise be waiting up, will she?" She smiled, starting to dial. "You should think yourself lucky—"

"We lost a baby," Thorne said.

After a few seconds, Chamberlain put down the phone and moved across to sit next to him. "I'm sorry. I knew there was something."

It came out quickly, the words tumbling from him, and when Thorne had finished, he watched Chamberlain stand and walk to the bathroom, saw her return a few seconds later with a wad of tissues in her hand.

"Here you go."

It was only as he took them that Thorne realized he was crying and he spoke in rapid breaths, screwing the tissues up in his fist; each small sob clearing his head a little, lifting his heart. "Thing is... there was this sort of numbness when we got the news, and I knew Louise was feeling the same thing. But just for a minute or two I didn't feel like it was necessarily a bad thing. I felt... pleased, you know, because I was off the hook." He smiled, sickly and self-mocking. "Because maybe, deep down, I hadn't been sure I was ready to take it all on. Very grown up, eh?" He shook his head when he saw Chamberlain about to say something. "It was just a gut reaction, I know that, like laughing when you get bad news, but it's all I've been able to think about since. Every hour spent on this stupid fucking case. Seeing how cut up Lou's been, how she's just got on with things so that I don't feel bad and... pretending. Carrying this stone in my chest."

After a few seconds that felt like minutes, Thorne heard Chamberlain say, "What about now?"

"I want it," Thorne said. "Not just for Louise, I swear. I want her to feel better, course I do, but... for me." The laugh burst from him on a bigger sob. "I mean, you're never really ready, are you?"

Chamberlain was already holding his hand, and now she lifted it and squeezed it between both of hers. "Sometimes, I think about Jack not being here and I don't feel quite as bad as I know I should. I feel 'off the hook,' too." She nodded when Thorne glanced up. "Those stones in your chest are more common than you think, Tom."

"Christ," Thorne said. "Look at us..."

There was still a little more crying to be done, and comforting. Then Thorne found himself craving sleep, and thinking about his father as he closed his eyes and laid his head on Carol Chamberlain's shoulder.

MY JOURNAL

15 October

It isn't easy to kill someone.
People are not wasps or spiders to be swatted or stepped on without a second thought. It gets easier, that's for sure, same as anything else, but if I've made it sound like the moment itself is anything less than hugely stressful, then I've done something wrong. Before I began all this, back when the idea was starting to take shape, there were times when I wanted to talk to my father about it. About what it felt like. But it never seemed like the time was right and, if I'm honest, it was always a bad idea. I knew he didn't want to talk about it, about what he'd done; and besides, it was not something he was ever in control of, so I'm not sure he would have been a lot of help. I mean, it wasn't like I was going into the family dry-cleaning business, or that he was an ex-footballer with tips to pass on...
We did talk a lot, though, about all sorts of stuff, and he did help me more than he'll ever know. I learned that wasting time is stupid. Believe me, that's a lesson you take on board from someone who's got a lot of it on their hands. I learned, same as he did, that you get judged by what you do, whatever the reason for doing it. And I learned that life is short. Yeah, ironic I know, that last one, bearing in mind that I've done my bit to shorten more than a few! I suppose I'm really talking about getting things done when you've got the chance. Not wanting to grow old while you bang your head against legal brick walls. Not letting it grind you down, the getting laughed at or being told you're obsessed and that maybe you can come back when you've got some "proper medical evidence."
Life is short and sometimes you have to make your point another way. You make an impact or you don't, simple as that.

* * *

It's funny now, living so cheap. I remember that arsehole Maier one time, saying, "We're going to make a fortune." I could almost hear him smacking his lips down the phone, spending the money in his head. And I could hear how shocked he was when I told him I wasn't that interested. I needed enough money, that goes without saying—it's cost a fair old bit putting all this together. But I swear, I never wanted any more than that. Once this is finished, I'd be fine just settling down somewhere quiet. Sitting behind a till, clearing up in the park, whatever. I know that's not going to happen, not without a major change of plan, but it's something I've thought about, that's all. I would be genuinely happy without very much.

* * *

So, onwards and upwards, I suppose. It's been very strange, sitting around on my backside all day, knowing they're waiting for me to do something. The police and the press and maybe even those who know they're still on the list. The last of them, clock-watching and shitting their pants, however reassuring Detective Inspector Thorne and his friends are trying to be. Some bit of me must be enjoying it, though, because I've been ready to round things off for a few days now. Maybe I've been enjoying their uncertainty a little more than is right and proper of me.

Best not keep them waiting anymore.

I don't suppose I'll see the miserable old sod again, but I should set about giving my old mate the newsagent a few more headlines.

I wonder if the Sun's got a typeface big enough?

Thirty-Three

When Thorne stepped out of the shower, Louise was standing in the bathroom. She was wearing a T-shirt under the thin, linen robe she'd bought in Greece. She handed him a towel and sat down on the lid of the laundry basket.

"Early start," she said.

"I've got to go into town, pick up the car."

"After such a late night, I mean."

"I had a few drinks after the shift," Thorne said. He could just remember heaving himself into a dodgy-looking minicab in the early hours. Getting increasingly annoyed as he was forced to give the driver directions. Trying to stay awake.

"I know." Louise stood up and walked to the basin, stared at herself in the mirror, opening her eyes wide. "I woke up in the night and I could smell it on you." She turned and watched Thorne drying himself. "You feeling all right?"

Thorne nodded. "OK...surprisingly." He could not remember ever having drunk so much and feeling so well on it, and was grateful he had been on white, rather than red, wine. There was a headache, and it felt like one of those that would grumble on for a while yet, but in spite of it he was looking forward to the day ahead, the days and weeks. He could remember everything he had told Carol Chamberlain the night before. There was a twinge of embarrassment to go with the bad head, but no more than that. Their conversation might well turn out to be something else they never mentioned again, but he was hugely glad that he had said what needed saying.

He rubbed the towel across his chest. The stone had gone.

"You want me to do you some breakfast?" Louise asked. "A bit of scrambled egg or something?"

"Just some tea. I'm a bit pushed."

"It'll be ready by the time you're dressed." She walked out, calling back as she moved towards the kitchen, "You can eat it in five minutes."

"Thanks." He called after her: "Lou..."

"What?" After a few seconds, she reappeared in the bathroom doorway.

Thorne had wrapped the towel around his waist, and stood there with his toothbrush dangling from his fist. "What that woman said, about not feeling better until your due date..."

Louise pushed her hands into the pockets of her robe.

"It's probably crap anyway," he said. "But even if it's not, it wouldn't apply if you were pregnant again before then, would it?"

She looked at him for a few seconds. "No..."

"Well, then?"

She nodded, like it was no big deal, but her face told a different story. "We could always skip the scrambled eggs," she said.

"I certainly don't have time for that."

"You sure? It doesn't take that long normally."

An hour later, he was leaving Russell Square Tube station and a few minutes after that, he was walking past Chamberlain's hotel. He thought about calling her, then decided it was probably a bad idea. It wasn't eight o'clock yet, and although he had no idea what time she was planning to pay Sandra Phipps a visit, he guessed she had as much to sleep off as he had. He would talk to her later.

He handed over £27.50 at the NCP, making sure to check his change and ask for a receipt. The cashier was brisk and seemed disinclined to chat, which suited Thorne perfectly, a grunt of thanks being about all either man could manage.

"I think I prefer you a bit hung over," Louise had said. "It's a lot quieter."

Thorne smiled, remembering the look on her face as he'd closed the front door, and wondered about stopping somewhere for breakfast, seeing as he'd never got his scrambled eggs. He tuned the car's radio in to Magic FM, turning up an old Willie Nelson track that he liked as he steered the BMW out of the car-park's gloom and into an unexpectedly bright October day.

A day that would grow considerably darker as it wore on, as Thorne learned exactly what Anthony Garvey was planning. As he saw a son outstrip his father.

A day on which more people would die.

When Debbie heard the phone ring, she was busy in the kitchen trying to feed Jason. Before she had a chance to reach it, she heard Nina clattering into the hall, swearing and complaining about being woken so early.

Debbie had already been up an hour or more, but she knew that her friend had been working until late and shouted, "Sorry!" as she struggled to clear up the mess Jason had made. She listened, wiping up egg and juice and toast crumbs. Once she heard Nina start shouting, it did not take long to work out who was calling.

"Yeah, right, but does it have to be so bloody early?... No, we've all been murdered in our fucking beds, what do you think?"

Nina was still grumbling and shaking her head when she walked into the kitchen. She switched on the kettle and sat down at the table opposite Jason. He grinned at her and got the flicker of a smile in return.

"Thorne's only doing his job," Debbie said.

Nina pulled faces at Jason as she spoke. "If he'd been doing it properly, there wouldn't still be a police car outside the front door."

"He seems an OK bloke, though."

"I know what coppers are like," Nina said. "I've done plenty in my time." She got up to make the tea. "Come to think of it, I wonder if either of those two out there fancy a quick one."

They both laughed and Jason laughed in turn. Debbie finished wiping the surfaces and finally sat down. Nina dropped a couple of slices of bread in the toaster, sniffed the milk.

"Listen, I've got a job on this afternoon, is that all right?"

"Does that mean you can take the night off?"

"Maybe. I've done this bloke a few times, that's the thing. He always calls me whenever he's down from Manchester, and he always gives me a bit extra, so..."

"You'd be stupid not to," Debbie said.

"I need to start putting a bit aside as well, you know, if we're going to get away." Nina bent down and nuzzled the back of Jason's neck. "You want to go on holiday, sweetheart?"

Debbie smiled, knowing very well where every penny would be going, and said, "Yeah, that makes sense."

"We should get some brochures," Nina said. "I'll pick some up on the way back from this bloke's hotel. You fancy Majorca?"

Debbie nodded. "Be good if you could give it a miss tonight, though. We can have a night in front of the box. I'll make us spaghetti Bolognese or something."

Brian Spibey was on the breakfast run. He'd dropped off a bacon and egg McMuffin at Fowler's apartment and was on his way along the corridor with coffee and an almond croissant for Andrew Dowd. The smells were making him hungry, and he was keen to get stuck into the bacon sandwich he'd bought for himself that was getting cold down in the lobby. It was funny, he thought, how everyone liked different things for breakfast. That hobbit-fancier Gibbons had been peeling the lid off some poxy pot of muesli when Spibey had headed upstairs.

Thorne had called while Spibey was queuing in McDonald's. He'd apologized for not phoning the night before as promised, explained that he'd been stuck in a meeting until late. Spibey had reassured him that everything was fine, that their guests were alive and kicking, and had tried to sound jokey when he'd told Thorne that there was no need to check up every five minutes.

"I've been doing this a bit longer than you have," he'd said.

Thorne had sounded jokey enough himself. "I doubt that, Brian, but you certainly look as though you have."

Cheeky sod.

He wasn't sure that Thorne had altogether approved when he'd walked in on their card school. Funny, he'd never had Thorne down as any kind of stickler, and it would be a bit rich, bearing in mind some of the stories Spibey had heard about him over the years. Yes, by rights, he and Gibbons should both be sitting downstairs, glued to the security monitors, but Spibey liked to think he had got to know the two men in his charge pretty well and that he knew the best way to keep them relaxed and happy. They both had good reason to be stressed out, after all, and neither was the type for praying or settling down with a good book, he was sure about that much.

He entered the code for Dowd's apartment, knocked and waited. "Grub's up, Andy."

Dowd opened the door and took the cup and paper bag.

"They better find this bloke soon," Spibey said, "else you two are going to end up as a right pair of fat bastards. Me an' all, come to that."

Dowd didn't seem to see the funny side and shook his head. "I don't think Graham could put weight on even if he wanted to. The drugs have screwed up his metabolism."

"Right, fair enough," Spibey said, after a few seconds. "I'll leave you to it." He took a few steps away, then turned as Dowd was about to close the door. "Listen, you up for another game of cards a bit later? Only Graham said he fancied it."

Dowd had already bitten into his croissant. "Yeah, why not? Least he's got some money to play with now."

"I'll have that back, don't you worry," Spibey said.

"We'll see."

"I'm telling you mate, I feel lucky."

"Well, you're the only one round here who does," Dowd said.

Thirty-Four

Her train arrived in Reading just before midday. A simple check of the voters' register had revealed that Sandra Phipps—as she had been called thirty years previously—was not working, and Chamberlain guessed that lunchtime would be as good a time as any to catch her at home. If there was nobody in, she would find some way to kill an hour or two, perhaps see what Reading had to offer in the way of retail therapy, and try again later.

How threatening could a middle-aged woman carrying a couple of shopping bags be?

Waiting on the platform at Paddington, Chamberlain had been aware that this was the place where Anthony Garvey had collected the cash to fund his killing spree. Also where he had disposed of Chloe Sinclair's body. She did not know if it was an ill omen or a good one, but she had focused instead on the possibilities of the day ahead: a positive outcome to the interview; the breakthrough she hoped she would be able to pass on to Tom Thorne.

Looking through her notes on the train, she had been unable to stop thinking about their session the night before. She wondered how the state he had been in—might still be in—had affected his ability to handle the inquiry. Had it weighed him down or fired him up? She knew that personal problems usually had an impact one way or the other, and remembered a spell of a few months, twenty years earlier, when she and Jack had been going through a rocky patch. Afterwards, to satisfy her curiosity, she had checked and been amazed to see that her arrest record had been better than ever.

She hoped it worked out the same way for Thorne.

It was a short trip from Reading station to Caversham, a small district a few minutes to the north of the town on the other side of the Thames. The taxi, whose driver gave a running commentary throughout the journey, crossed a large and ornate bridge into an area that looked more like the center of a chocolate-box English village than a commuter suburb. He finally pulled up—as per Chamberlain's instructions—a hundred yards or so short of a tidy-looking terraced house set back from the road and within spitting distance of the river.

Walking up to the house, Chamberlain could see rowing boats and steamers moored on both sides of the river, and a pair of swans treading water in mid-stream while a group of kids threw bread from the far bank, trying to spin the slices, like Frisbees.

"Got him, right in the neck," one of them shouted.

"See if you can do it again..."

Chamberlain had already decided that, should the worst happen, she would move, a little nearer to London maybe, and that this was the kind of place she would choose. She loved being near the water, and though this stretch of river had a little less character, it was probably a damn sight cleaner than the English Channel.

And some of the people here were under fifty.

The door was opened by a surly-looking girl, aged fourteen or so, who stared at Chamberlain, careful not to open the door too far. Chamberlain remembered her notes. This would be Nicola, Sandra's daughter by her third husband, who would be at work as manager of the local Tesco's. Chamberlain toyed with freaking out the sour-faced little cow by using her name, but instead she just produced her photo ID and asked the girl if her mother was at home.

After a few seconds, the girl backed away from the door, then pushed it until it was almost closed again before disappearing. While Chamberlain waited, hearing the girl's footsteps on the stairs followed by a muffled conversation, she started to believe that this was all going to work out the way everybody wanted. She wondered if the girl knew anything about a half-brother twice her age, a serial killer who might well have babysat her.

The woman apologized as she yanked the door wide. "Sorry... she's not very chatty at the best of times," she said. "And she doesn't like to see me upset."

"Oh, right. Is everything OK?"

The woman cocked her head. "I don't understand. She said you were police."

"I'm working with the police, yes, but—"

"So, you haven't come about..." The woman gave a small shake of her head, seeing the confusion on Chamberlain's face. "Sorry, I just presumed. We've had a death in the family and I thought that's why you were here."

"Oh... I'm sorry," Chamberlain said. "What happened?"

The woman leaned her head against the edge of the door. "One of those things, love. Poor bugger was in the wrong place at the wrong time, that's all, ran into some nutter. We weren't exactly close, if I'm honest, but still, it's a shock."

Chamberlain waited.

"My nephew," the woman said, nodding. "Not even thirty! God only knows when they'll let me bury him, mind you."

Chamberlain cleared her throat and the woman's eyes flashed to hers. "Well, apologies if this is an awkward time, but I actually wanted to have a word with you about Raymond Garvey."

The woman blinked and slowly straightened.

"A name from the past, I know," Chamberlain said. "And this is probably a bit out of the blue."

"Well, yes and no."

"Sorry?"

The smile was somewhere between relief and resignation, and it remained in place as Sandra Phipps took a step back into her dimly lit hallway. "I'd better make us both a drink," she said.

* * *

Gibbons brought up sandwiches and cold drinks for lunch, moaning about being a glorified waiter and looking horrified when Spibey invited him to join the game. Before he left, he pointed out that at least one of them needed to stay on duty downstairs. "You know, do the job we're being paid for."

Now that one is a stickler, Spibey thought.

After an hour or so, Dowd was well ahead, with several well-organized stacks of chips in front of him, and was even able to sub Fowler, who had lost heavily early on to both the other players. Taking the last game into account, Spibey was still down overall, and was keen to exert a little more pressure. Luck was one thing, he thought, but he was far and away the most experienced player at the table. On top of which—he smiled to himself—neither of them was exactly playing with a full deck.

"Just to remind you," he said. "Brag is different to poker and a run beats a flush. You both clear about that?"

Fowler laughed and tossed a few more chips into the pot. "Yeah, fine, but I don't believe you've got either."

"Mind games," Dowd said. "It's the sort of crap they pull on people in interview rooms." He pushed enough chips across the table to match Spibey's bet. "Call…"

Spibey nodded thoughtfully, but was unable to contain a broad grin as he laid down ace–king–queen. The grin became a chuckle as Fowler and Dowd groaned in disbelief and threw away their hands. Spibey gathered in the chips. "You've got coppers all wrong," he said. "We're the honest ones."

Dowd had collected the cards and was already shuffling. "So, tell us honestly then, do you normally catch this kind of killer?"

"Nothing normal about this bloke."

"Do you?"

Spibey was stacking his winnings. "Look, I'm just on babysitting duty. I don't really know the ins and outs of it."

"Come on…"

"You'd be better off talking to Thorne."

"Would he be honest?"

"Probably not."

"You going to deal or not?" Fowler snapped.

Dowd raised an eyebrow at Spibey. "How long since you had your medicine, Graham?"

Fowler stared for a few seconds, unblinking across the table, then calmly reached for his cigarettes. "I'm having all that, mate." He pointed at Spibey's stack. "Every last chip."

"Easy to say when you're not playing with your own money," Dowd said.

"You'll get it back."

"What, you going to sell a few Big Issues?"

Fowler smiled, his mood appearing to change again suddenly. "When they set us up with these new identities, they'll have to give us a bit of cash, won't they? Something to get us started."

"Look, it's all academic," Spibey said. "Because you won't be winning jack-shit." He reached for his cards. "I'm telling you, I've hit a lucky streak."

Fowler lit his cigarette. "It'll change," he said.

Thirty-Five

SANDRA PHIPPS was not a short woman, but she still showed every pound of the excess weight she carried. Round-faced and having done nothing to disguise the gray in her hair, she moved slowly, ushering Chamberlain into a small, overheated living room. "You're welcome to have tea," she said. Her voice was flat and there was the hint of a wheeze in her breathing. "But I think I might need something a bit stronger, so..."

"Tea's fine for me," Chamberlain said.

"It's a bit early in the day, but what the hell."

The woman hovered in the doorway, as though she were waiting for Chamberlain to change her mind. Chamberlain smiled, saw a flash of what might have been fear in Sandra Phipps' eyes and, for the first time since she'd accepted Tom Thorne's offer to get involved in the investigation, began to feel excited.

"You sure?"

"I'm sure," Chamberlain said.

While she waited for Sandra to return, Chamberlain sat in a well-worn but comfortable armchair and took in the room. The tops of the television, sideboard and corner cupboard were cluttered with knick-knacks and photographs. A TV listings magazine lay open on the sofa and a chick-lit paperback was on the small table next to it. A tropical-fish tank had been built into an alcove, its gentle bubbling just audible above the frantic bass-line that had begun to bleed down from an upstairs room. There was certainly no sign that this was a family in mourning: no flowers or sympathy cards on display. The daughter had been wearing black, but even with her limited knowledge of teenagers, Chamberlain guessed it was probably the color Nicola Phipps chose to wear most of the time anyway. The scowl was probably a permanent feature, too.

When Sandra returned—with a mug of tea and a half-empty bottle of wine—there were a few minutes of chit-chat, each woman getting comfortable in her own way. Sandra was horrified, she said, at how unsafe the streets had become in recent years. Chamberlain told her she agreed, and made the right noises when Sandra complained about the extortionate cost of funerals.

Then, Chamberlain got down to it.

She had found it hard to gauge the other woman's reaction to the mention of the name "Raymond Garvey." A long-distant ex-boyfriend was one thing, but when he also happened to be a notorious mass murderer, there were few precedents. Sandra's reaction to the name "Malcolm Reece" was a little easier to read.

"They were a right pair," Sandra said, laughing. "Him and Ray, swanning around like they were God's gift."

"Sounds like a few of you fell for it."

"Yeah, well." She shrugged. "Young and stupid, I suppose."

"How long were you and Ray an item?"

"I don't think we were ever 'an item.' We were both married, so..."

"OK. For how long were the pair of you sneaking into the stationery cupboard for a quick one?"

Sandra smiled, reddening a little. "There was a hotel room once in a while. The odd weekend away."

Chamberlain waited.

"Six months or so, I suppose, on and off. Until he met my younger sister." She smiled again, cold this time, then took a drink. "Frances."

"He started seeing your sister?"

Another shrug. "She was prettier than me."

"Malcolm Reece said something about a baby."

If Sandra heard what Chamberlain had said, she chose to ignore it. "They kept their affair even quieter than me and Ray did," she said. "I only found out by accident and, to be honest, I didn't really want to know too much about it. I was jealous, I suppose, and pissed off with my sister. We didn't talk to each other for quite a while."

Chamberlain said she could understand.

"I even gave Malcolm Reece a bunk-up once or twice, stupid cow that I was. Trying to get my own back at Ray, I suppose."

"So, what about this baby?"

"Not mine," Sandra said.

"Your sister's?"

Sandra took her time, then nodded. "A little boy. Frances and Ray had already broken up for a while by that time. I think Ray's wife was starting to cotton on."

Chamberlain grunted agreement. She remembered Jenny Duggan telling her she'd always known about Garvey's other women.

"Took her long enough, mind you." Sandra drained her glass. "You OK?"

Chamberlain stared at Sandra Phipps, suddenly stunned by the echo of a coin dropping hard. "Frances?"

Sandra nodded again, and seemed to be wondering what had taken Chamberlain quite so long. "Frances Walsh. The stupid thing is, we never really made up properly."

Chamberlain blinked, pictured the pages of notes she'd been studying on the train: a list of Anthony Garvey's victims and a list of the women, long since murdered, who had given birth to them. "Frances Walsh was Ray Garvey's third victim," she said.

Sandra shook her head. "First victim. They found her third, but she was the first to be killed." She leaned forward and picked up the wine bottle. "You sure you don't want one of these?"

Chamberlain shook her head.

Sandra said, "Suit yourself," and began to top up her glass.

* * *

Hendricks breathed heavily for a few seconds then spoke, nice and slowly, in the huskiest voice he could muster. "What are you wearing?"

"You must be really bored."

"Bloody hell, how much more miserable could you sound?"

"Give me another hour or so," Thorne said.

When the lack of progress on a case cast heavy shadows across every brick, rippled black in each pane of its dirty glass, Becke House could quickly turn a good mood bad and a bad mood ugly. Thorne had been more than halfway there, sitting in his office and trying in vain to recapture a little of the morning's optimism, when Hendricks had called.

"Fancy a beer or six later?"

"Tricky," Hendricks said. "I'm in Gothenburg."

"Right. Shit." Thorne had completely forgotten about his friend's seminar. Analysis of something or other.

"You had your chance, mate."

"How's it going?"

"Well, I'd been hoping for wall-to-wall Vikings and bars full of men who look like Freddie Ljungberg."

"I was talking about the seminar."

"Equally disappointing."

"So, these men..."

"More like Freddie Krueger."

Thorne laughed, remembering the last time he had done so, and thought about describing his conversation with Louise that morning, perhaps even telling Hendricks about the one he'd had with Carol Chamberlain the night before.

He never got the chance.

"I'm guessing there's no joy on Garvey, then?"

"Well, he hasn't killed anyone else, not as far as we know, anyway, so it's not like things are any worse."

"I was thinking about the one in the canal."

"Walsh?"

"Right. Remember you asked me why I thought he'd attacked him from the front? Why it was so much more brutal?"

"You said something about him getting cocky or angry." Thorne tucked the phone between his chin and shoulder, began sorting through the mass of unread paper on his desk. "Being in a hurry, maybe."

"Maybe."

Thorne heard something in the silence. "What?"

"What if he wasn't in a hurry?" Hendricks asked. "What if he deliberately took the trouble to make the victim unrecognizable? There's still been no formal ID, has there?"

"No, but—"

"Can we get a DNA sample from that aunt, do you think? Make sure."

"We know who he is, Phil. The stuff in his pocket?"

"Who the hell carries an old driving license around? An old letter?"

"Maybe someone who's off his face on God knows what and is trying to hang on to who he was." Thorne balled up a sheaf of papers he no longer needed, tossed it at the waste-paper bin. Missed. "Walsh was virtually living on the street, as far as we can tell."

"I was thinking about that, too," Hendricks said. "The drugs that showed up in the body weren't what I'd expected."

Thorne told Hendricks to hang on while he found the relevant file on his computer and called up the toxicology report. He opened the document, said, "OK."

"I mean, where does the average dosser get hold of antidepressants?"

Thorne looked through the report. Alcohol had been found—beer and whiskey—and a partially digested final meal, chips and a pie of some description. He scrolled down and studied the list of drugs, traces of which had been found in Simon Walsh's body. Diazepam, Prozac, Wellbutrin. "You can get hold of anything," Thorne said.

"Isn't it normally smack and Special Brew?"

"There comes a time when you'll take whatever you can get your hands on, mate." Thorne remembered the boy called Spike, his eyes glazing over and starting to close even before the needle had slipped from his vein and clattered to the pavement. "I remember one bloke who got off shooting up cider."

There was a pause, then Hendricks said, "Sorry. Spending too much time sitting in hotel rooms thinking."

"Just thinking?"

"Well, I have to admit you get a better class of porn on the in-room movie system."

Thorne laughed again and glanced up to see Sam Karim standing in the doorway. Karim asked if Thorne was speaking to Hendricks, then if he could have a quick word.

"Hang on, Sam wants you..."

Thorne handed over the receiver and rose from his desk. He thought about Simon Walsh's face, what had been left of it. Listened as Karim asked Hendricks if he'd seen a moose yet, and if he would mind bringing him back some duty-free cigarettes.

Fowler was drunk.

He struggled to focus, swiping wildly at the ash that dropped from his cigarette onto the table, as he told Spibey, a little louder than was necessary, that he'd been right about the policeman's lucky streak coming to an end.

"Brag's not a game of luck," Spibey said. "It's a game of skill and strategy."

Dowd laughed. Said, "Where are all the chips?"

"Yeah," Fowler said, triumphant. "Where are all the fucking chips?" He clapped his hands and pointed theatrically at the large piles of chips in front of himself and Dowd, then at the few that remained in front of the policeman.

Shuffling the cards, Spibey just about managed a weak smile, but he knew that Fowler was right. Since lunchtime he hadn't seen a hand, or, if he had, he'd run hard into a better one. He'd watched as Fowler and Dowd had struck lucky time and again and his stack had dwindled to almost nothing.

"You'd better ask your mate downstairs if he can pop out to a cashpoint for you," Dowd said.

Fowler cackled, said, "cashpoint" and knocked a pile of his chips to the floor as he leaned across to high-five his friend.

"Fuck's sake," Spibey muttered.

Fowler bent to retrieve his chips while Dowd told Spibey he should just deal the next hand.

Spibey doled out the cards and was delighted to see that he was holding an ace and two queens, a premium three-card brag hand. He raised big and Dowd quickly folded, but Fowler was content to play blind, which enabled him to call the bet with only half what Spibey had staked. Spibey was all-in and turned over his cards. He watched as Fowler snuck a peek at his hand then began to laugh before sliding them face down across the table to Dowd.

Dowd shook his head and shrugged. "Not your day, Officer," before showing Spibey the 7–8–9 that Fowler had been holding.

Spibey slammed the flat of his hand on the table and Fowler had to lurch forward to stop his beer can toppling over.

"Sorry," Spibey said. "But that's just ridiculous."

Dowd nodded. "It's a bad beat."

"Bad?"

"I need a piss," Fowler said, dragging the chips towards him.

Dowd pushed back his chair. "Who wants tea?"

Spibey had his back to the open window. The sun was warming his neck. Once Dowd had gone into the kitchen area and Fowler had blundered into the small bathroom on the other side of the room, Spibey turned to take a few breaths of fresh air, the creamy fug of cigarette smoke drifting past him before being whipped away on the breeze.

He turned back into the room, reached for his wallet and dug out a twenty-pound note to buy his way back into the game. "Bollocks," he said, quietly.

As he sat shuffling, waiting for Fowler and Dowd to return, Spibey thought about how quickly he had come to despise the two men he'd been forced to babysit. How a couple of hours' harmless gambling could show people in their true light. Only a few days earlier, he had considered them both victims, rootless and terrified. But today, watching, listening to them whine and bray, he had come to realize that they were little more than spongers. Mental cases, the pair of them, taking the piss and living it up at the taxpayer's expense, while the likes of him ran around after them like servants.

Christ, as though either of them copping it would be any great loss to society.

Dowd, who clearly thought he was a bloody comedian, had become unbearably smug; and Spibey wasn't convinced that Fowler was half as drunk as he was pretending to be. What had he put away, four cans of supermarket-strength lager? It was an old card player's trick, and Spibey was starting to wonder if Fowler was not quite the novice he'd claimed to be.

He smoothed out the twenty on the table in front of him, stared down at it. He'd start again, build it up nice and easy into forty, eighty, more. He'd clean the two of them out before the relief shift came on at six.

Arseholes.

He heard the footsteps and glanced up, waved his twenty-pound note in the air, then reached for the cards again, focusing on them as he continued to shuffle. "Skill and strategy," he said.

What he felt, saw, heard—the sensations that assaulted his body and brain in the last thirty seconds of his life—did not come in the order that Spibey might have expected. He saw the blood first—or perhaps he had blacked out for a few moments and it was just the first thing there when he opened his eyes—spattered across the cards that had tumbled onto the table. Red as diamonds and hearts. Then he felt it, soft against his scalp as his fingers fluttered to the wound on the back of his head, and then the pain as the second blow shattered his hand, and the wash of nausea after the third strike, and then the cool of the tabletop against his cheek.

He tried to raise his head and it began to get dark, and he thought that it was probably wooden, with spikes. The thing he had been hit with. Was still being hit with. He heard someone say, "What the hell are you doing?"

and smelled his own piss and felt the sun that was still warm against the back of his neck.

Sunshine that was running, thick and sticky, beneath his collar.

"What the hell are you doing?"

There were a few seconds' silence as the two men still breathing in the room stared across at each another.

Then, Anthony Garvey walked briskly around the table and calmly pushed a chair to one side, the policeman's blood flying from the weapon as he raised it once again.

"You both ran out of luck," he said.

Thirty-Six

It was only when she heard the noise on the stairs that Chamberlain realized the music from the upper floor had stopped. She and Sandra Phipps both looked towards the door as the footsteps grew louder, listened to the sound of someone thundering downstairs and then the short silence before the front door slammed shut.

Sandra puffed out her cheeks and sat back in her chair. "She's upset," she said.

"About your nephew?"

Sandra nodded, half smiled. "Stupid really. I mean, Nicola hasn't even seen Simon since she was little. She'd be just as upset if someone in one of those bands she listens to died. It suits her, if I'm honest."

"What about you?"

Sandra stared at her, as though unsure whether to point out that it was something of an odd question. "I'm . . . sad. It's horrible what was done to him. It doesn't matter that we weren't particularly close, does it?"

Chamberlain said nothing.

"I've still not heard when I can go and have a look at him, get the funeral sorted, anything like that." She swilled the wine around in her glass. "God only knows what kind of state he must be in."

"They'll let you know when they're ready." Chamberlain said what she thought was necessary and no more. She had all the pieces now. She knew who the man calling himself Anthony Garvey was, and she knew what that meant. But she was still struggling to make sense of any of it.

"That's why I got the wrong end of the stick on the doorstep," Sandra said. "I mean, that's what I thought you'd come about."

"About Simon?"

"I thought maybe they were releasing his body, whatever."

Simon Walsh. The son of Raymond Garvey and his first victim. The man the police were looking for and who—Chamberlain now realized—they mistakenly believed had become a victim himself.

"It's why Ray killed her, you know."

Chamberlain's head snapped up. It was as though Sandra Phipps had been able to read her thoughts and she felt the blood rushing to her face. "Sorry?"

"That's what he said, anyway. Because Fran had never told him about the baby. Because he didn't know he had a twelve-year-old son. I'm not sure how he found out, tell you the truth, but he said he just lost it. He went round there to have it out with her and lost control."

"Jesus."

"What?"

"Why the hell didn't you let the police know?" Chamberlain said.

"I didn't know any of this until Ray had been arrested, did I? I didn't know it was him." Sandra was reaching for the bottle again. "All those women were already dead by then, so I kept my mouth shut. It wouldn't have brought any of them back, would it?"

"When did you find out?"

"He wrote to me from prison," Sandra said. "Just the once. Wanted me to know why he'd killed Fran." There was hatred suddenly, glittering in the woman's eyes. "Wanted my forgiveness, if you can believe that."

Seven, Chamberlain thought. Seven women had been murdered because Frances Walsh had kept Garvey's child a secret from him. It made the notion of a changed personality sound even more ridiculous than it had before. "So, why did he keep on killing?" she asked. "After your sister?"

Sandra lifted the bottle onto her lap and stared up at the ceiling. "Christ knows. Maybe something had snapped. I don't know how that mental stuff works. Maybe he was trying to hide the real reason he'd killed Fran... if not knowing about his son was the reason. Maybe he just did it once and liked it. Doesn't really matter now, does it?"

Chamberlain was finding the woman's calm, water-under-the-bridge attitude hard to stomach, but she couldn't, with her hand on her heart, say that it mattered at all. "So, you took Simon? After Frances had been murdered?"

"It was either me or Social Services, so what was I supposed to do? I mean, things had never really got back to normal between me and Fran, all that ancient history with her and Ray. But she never deserved what that bastard did to her. And Simon was family, so I didn't even have to think about it."

"What did you tell Simon about his father?"

"Same as Fran had told him: his dad had died when he was very little, vague stuff about how he'd been an engineer. But what's strange is that he never really asked. Had enough on his plate with what had happened to his mum, I suppose, and he went through quite a tough time at school." She blinked slowly, remembering. "He got angry with her a bit later on, angry with everyone. But that happens to people sometimes, doesn't it?" She poured the last of the wine into her glass. "When they lose someone."

Chamberlain waited for Sandra Phipps to continue, watching the woman's chest rise and fall, listening to its soft wheeze and the gentle bubbling of the fish tank. She started slightly when a mobile phone began to ring, a loud and ludicrously cheery samba.

Sandra leaned across to a small table and snatched up her phone. She stared at the screen for a moment or two and then switched it off. "The old man," she said. "Probably just ringing for a natter. I'll call him back."

"You were saying about—"

"Look, I just wanted things to be as normal for the kid as possible, OK? Last thing I wanted was for him to know who his dad was or what he'd done. I didn't want him feeling like a freak."

Chamberlain fought to keep her reaction from her face. "When did you last see him?"

"He left when he was seventeen," Sandra said. "Ten years ago, that would be." She thought for a second or two. "Yeah, ten. It was pretty sudden, you know, he just told me he wanted to get his own place. I think he just wanted to strike out on his own, find his feet. Understandable." She nodded towards the door. "She'll be off soon enough."

"Did you hear from him?"

"Once or twice. Just to let me know he was all right. He wasn't though, was he? The police told me he was living like a tramp when he died." She took a drink, closed her eyes as it went down. "I've been feeling guilty about that ever since I heard what happened."

"So, why now?" Chamberlain asked. "You've kept all this to yourself for fifteen years."

Sandra shrugged. "Truth doesn't really matter anymore, does it? Not now Simon's dead."

For want of anything better to say, Chamberlain shook her head. Said, "I suppose not."

Chamberlain knew very well that Simon Walsh was not dead, but how could she possibly tell this woman? I know your nephew is not the man they hauled out of that canal with a shattered skull and a face like a squashed cantaloupe. I know because Simon is the one who killed him. Who has killed a great many more...

As far as good news/bad news routines went, it was right up there with the best.

Sandra cleared her throat, sat forward in her chair. The wine she had drunk could be heard in her voice, which was suddenly brighter, louder. "You said you wanted to talk to me about Ray Garvey," she said. "When you got here. You never said why."

"Didn't I?" Chamberlain stood up. That was a conversation for someone else to suffer, someone who still possessed a warrant card. Now she just needed to get out of Sandra Phipps' house as quickly as possible.

She needed to call Tom Thorne.

* * *

Detective Sergeant Rob Gibbons glanced up from his book, as he dutifully did each time he turned a page, looked briefly at each of the three security monitors on the desk in front of him, then went happily back to reading.

To losing himself, and loving it.

The job he did, the stupid, shitty people he had to deal with day in day out, what else was he going to read but fantasy? The likes of that loser Thorne could take the piss all they wanted—dragons and hobbits, my arse—but to Gibbons' way of thinking, the outlandish worlds created in fantasy novels, in the best ones anyway, made a lot more sense than the piss-poor one he lived in. They were pretty much the most popular books in prison libraries too, certainly the ones that got nicked most often, and you didn't need to be a genius to figure out why. Fantasy, along with the true-crime stuff, obviously.

As a habit, reading was a damn sight safer than gambling, Gibbons knew that much, and he knew Brian Spibey had a problem. Hours on end trying to take a few quid off a pair like Dowd and Fowler, how sad was that? He'd been up there since lunchtime, for Christ's sake. Gibbons was happy enough alone with his book, but they still had a job to do, and he was starting to think he'd need to have a quiet word. Either with Spibey or, if he felt like being a real arsehole about it, with someone higher up. That was always a big step, but—

He heard a shout from upstairs and dropped his book; looked up in time to see a shadow cross the screen on one of the monitors, the camera at the end of the first-floor corridor.

He picked up his radio. "Brian, you on the way down?"

A hiss of static.

"Brian? Fuck!"

It hadn't looked like Spibey...

He got up and moved quickly around the desk, his shoes squeaking, stupidly loud as he walked across the lobby. Nobody would come down without Spibey's say-so, would they? They were supposed to stay in their rooms with the doors locked. Had the silly bugger lost it completely and got pissed with them?

He turned onto the stairwell, then stopped and staggered back, the radio slipping from his fingers and clattering onto the marble floor. "Jesus!" He stared up at the man walking slowly down the stairs towards him. The lost look in his eyes and the blood soaking the front of his shirt. "What happened? Jesus..."

"He just went mental. I think you need to call someone."

Gibbons could only nod and swallow, unable to move for those few seconds it took the man to descend the final few steps. Gawping at the blood and the look on the man's face. Seeing far too late the kitchen knife that had slipped from beneath a sleeve into Anthony Garvey's hand.

"Slow down, Carol."

Thorne had only just finished talking to Phil Hendricks when the call came through. He had been joking with Dave Holland, describing some of the pathologist's escapades in Sweden. Now, hearing something in Thorne's voice, Holland hovered near his desk and listened, mouthed, "What?"

Thorne shook his head.

"Are you listening to me, Tom?" Chamberlain sounded annoyed, out of breath.

"Course I am, but you're not—"

"Ray Garvey's son is Simon Walsh."

"That's not possible."

Chamberlain took him through her conversation with Sandra Phipps as quickly as she could: the misunderstanding about her visit and, finally, the revelation that had changed everything. "Garvey had an affair with her sister, and they had a son. She was his first victim, Tom. Frances Walsh."

"Why the hell did he—?"

"He killed her because she never told him about the kid. That's why he killed all of them. It's got sod all to do with any brain tumor."

Thorne was out of his chair, fighting to take it all in. "But Simon Walsh was battered to death. We fished him out of the bloody canal."

"No, you didn't," Chamberlain said.

"There was ID." But even as he was saying it, he knew that they'd got it wrong. He thought about what Hendricks had said and knew that his friend's concerns had been well justified. The idea had always been to leave the body unrecognizable, with the letter and the driving license there to provide evidence that the victim was someone he was not.

But why?

Back when the body had been found, Thorne and Hendricks had also talked about the victim being dumped after being killed elsewhere. Now, Thorne was starting to wonder just how far from Camden that might have been.

"Anthony Garvey is the son of Ray Garvey's first victim," Chamberlain said. "His father murdered his mother, Tom."

Thorne's shirt was plastered to the small of his back. He could feel the pulse ticking in his neck.

"More importantly, though, whoever you pulled out of that canal, it wasn't Simon Walsh."

Thorne told Chamberlain he'd call her later and hung up. He was moving before Holland had a chance to speak. Holland followed him into the narrow corridor, started to ask the question, but Thorne cut him off.

"We need to get rapid-response cars to Euston, as many as you can round up. And an armed-response unit."

"What?"

Whoever you pulled out of that canal...

Thorne knew it could have been only one of two men. That the same applied to the killer himself.

"Now, Dave."

Thirty-Seven

H.M.P. Whitemoor

"You ready for tomorrow?"

"They ran me through the list of what could go wrong."

"They have to do that to cover themselves."

"I know, but you still think about it, don't you?"

"This bloke Kambar sounds like he knows what he's doing."

"Yeah, I suppose. Not got a lot of choice really, have I?"

"How have the headaches been?"

"Bloody typical, isn't it? Last few days I haven't had so much as a twinge. Having something else to think about, maybe."

"You should just think about getting better, about living a damn sight longer."

"Right, when I've got so much to live for."

"Listen, I've been doing a bit more reading up, looking online and stuff, and there's tons about this personality change business."

"Christ, Tony."

"There's documented cases."

"I've told you—"

"You should be excited about this, I mean it. It could get you out."

"That's not going to happen."

"Let me worry about it, OK? You just get well and then I'll show you all the stuff I've put together."

"I don't want you wasting your time."

"I'm not, I swear. After the op I'm going to start talking to people, get a campaign started."

"What people?"

"Writers, journalists, whatever. I'll talk to Doctor Kambar after the operation."

"What about the women who died?"

"That wasn't you. We can prove it."

"What about their husbands and parents? Their children? Don't you think they might want to start a campaign of their own?"

"We can't get . . . sidetracked by that. Innocent is innocent."

"Not to mention —"

"Don't."

"Your own mother, Tony."

"She asked for what she got."

"None of them asked for it."

"It wasn't your fault. It was the tumor. It explains the other women, can't you understand that? You had no control. Not even with her."

"I'm not up to this. Any of it."

"I'm up to it, OK? You don't have to worry about anything."

"Just having my brain cut open."

"I'll be there when they put you under, OK? And I'll be there when you wake up."

"If . . ."

"Don't say that."

"Sorry. It's just . . ."

"It's all right."

"I'm grateful, really I am."

"Don't be stupid. It's what families do."

Thirty-Eight

DEBBIE WAS stepping back from the door before the officer's warrant card had been fully raised. Instinctively, she reached behind her, her hand flapping, beckoning Jason from where she had left him at the foot of the stairs. Her heart lurched; fear, excitement, both.

"Did you get him?"

The detective shook his head and looked away for a second or two, searching for the words. "There's been a . . . development, that's all."

She shouted her son's name, without turning round.

"There's no need to panic, Miss Mitchell."

"What?"

"We just think it's better if someone stays with you for a while. Is that OK?"

Debbie took a tentative step forward, craning her neck to see past the man on her doorstep, looking up and down the street. The nosy cow opposite was watching through a gap in her curtains. She probably had the copper down as one of Nina's clients. Debbie gave him the finger.

"Is that OK, Debbie?" The detective's warrant card was slipped back into the inside pocket of his jacket. "Can I come in?"

Debbie took a few seconds, then nodded and turned back into the house, looking for Jason. She heard the front door close as she walked into the sitting room, moving quickly to where her son was now hunched over a picture book next to the sofa. She knelt down beside him, feeling her heart rate slowing a little as she watched him turning the pages, listened to him mutter and grunt.

"Is there someone else in the house?"

She turned to look up at the figure standing behind her in the doorway. He nodded towards the open door that led through to Nina's kitchen.

"The radio," she said. "It's a play."

The detective nodded and listened to the voices for a few moments. It sounded like an argument. "Pictures are better, right?"

"Sorry?"

"They say that, don't they?"

"Say what?"

"Plays and what have you. That's why they're always so good on the radio." He tapped a finger against the side of his head. "Because the pictures are better."

"I've never really thought about it."

Debbie turned back to Jason, but she supposed that the detective was right. She usually had the radio tuned in to Capital or Heart FM. She was no great fan of the DJs, but she liked most of the music they played and Jason seemed to like it too. She occasionally caught him dancing, though few other people would have called it that. If there was a play on, though, she'd always try to sit and listen. She'd make a coffee and work her way through a packet of biscuits while Jason was glued to his video. Even when it was one of the weird ones, or some old rubbish set in India or Iraq or wherever, it was usually easy enough to get into the story and an hour would fly by without her really noticing.

Because the pictures are better.

They were certainly better than the ones that had been filling her head of late. The man who was coming for her. Nothing in there suitable for a nice, cozy afternoon play...

She heard the detective walking across the carpet and turned just as he squatted down next to her. His knees cracked loudly and he laughed and shook his head.

"Bloody hell, listen to that," he said.

He smelled of sweat and cigarette smoke.

"Who's this, then?"

"This is Jason," Debbie said.

For half a minute or more they both watched Jason moving his fingers across the pictures in his book.

"How old is he?"

"He's eight."

If the officer was surprised, he did not show it. He just watched silently for a few more seconds, then nodded and pushed himself back up to his feet. At that moment, Jason looked up from his picture book and smiled at him.

The detective smiled right back.

Thirty-Nine

THEY HAD already cordoned off both ends of the street by the time Thorne and Holland reached Euston, and a small crowd had started to gather. Residents and passers-by had quickly become members of an attentive audience. They fired questions at the officers keeping them at bay and spread rumors among themselves when their inquiries went unanswered. Thorne played equally dumb. He climbed out of the car, keeping his head down, and flashed his warrant card before jogging away up the street towards Grass-up Grange.

There were a dozen or more emergency vehicles parked haphazardly along the street: vans and cars, marked and unmarked; an ambulance. Someone had already called up a tea wagon, which was never a good sign. As Thorne got close, several armed officers walked towards him, ominously slowly, while others stood at the open doors of a van, handing in weapons and stripping off their gear.

Their presence unnecessary.

Thorne was no great fan of the Firearms Unit—he'd always found too many armed officers to be cocky sods. Of course, most of them had been a little less full of themselves since Jean Charles de Menezes, and he knew, from the looks that were being exchanged—the heavy steps and the slumped shoulders—that he would have no over-inflated egos to deal with today.

He watched a squat and surly CO19 officer toss his helmet onto the grass and start pulling off his body-armor. As Thorne approached, the man took a cigarette packet from his back pocket and said, "Fuck me!" His face was the color of candle-wax.

"How bad?" Thorne asked.

"As bad as it gets."

They both turned as a stretcher was carried out through the open doors and on towards the ambulance. There was a blanket across the body and an oxygen mask was being pressed to the face, but Thorne still recognized the figure of DS Rob Gibbons. He studied the grim expressions of the paramedics, looking for some clue as to the officer's chances, but saw none. Then he hurried towards the building.

Inside, the lobby was buzzing with activity. The tea wagon would not be needed for a while. The CSI team was already moving around purposefully, the rustle of their body-suits competing with the squawk of radios and the barked orders of senior officers doing their best to keep a lid on the panic.

Thorne walked across to where the remaining members of the paramedic team were gathering their equipment together at the foot of the stairs. Holland was only a few steps behind him, and the two of them stood quietly watching for a moment; staring at the long-bladed knife that lay on the bottom step and the blood that had spread, shiny against the marble floor.

"What the hell happened?" Holland asked.

"We had him," Thorne said. "We had him all the time."

"Had who?"

"Anthony Garvey."

"Yeah, I know that." Thorne had done his best to explain as the car had raced from Colindale. Holland had listened, open-mouthed, as Thorne told him what Carol Chamberlain had discovered, spelling out its implications as he urged the driver to put his foot down. "But who?"

Instinctively, Thorne raised his head, looked up towards the rooms where he'd visited the last two men on a killer's list. Where he'd visited the killer himself.

"Sir?"

Thorne turned and nodded at the nervous young woman who had walked across to them. Nodded again, impatient as she introduced herself as the DI with the on-call Homicide Assessment Team, her name going out of his head immediately. "Let's have it," he said.

"Two bodies upstairs." Her eyes flicked momentarily to a notebook. "Detective Sergeant Spibey and a man named Graham Fowler."

"Christ," Holland said.

Thorne said, "Show me."

The woman chatted as they walked up the stairs, the nerves still evident in her voice. She explained that Superintendent Jesmond was on his way, as was the pathologist, who was running later than he might have been, having got caught in traffic. There had been some kind of mix-up, she said, as to exactly who was covering for Doctor Hendricks. Thorne thought of his friend, happily oblivious in some Gothenburg watering-hole, and felt a stab of envy. He looked at Holland. "So, now we know."

Holland nodded. "Dowd."

"The man pretending to be Dowd," Thorne said.

They stood in the doorway of the room at the far end of the corridor, so bland and utilitarian until Anthony Garvey had gone to work. They took in its grisly new design.

Spibey was still in his chair, head down on the slick tabletop. On the other side of the room, Graham Fowler was slumped against the wall, one knee oddly raised, as if he were resting casually, though the blood and brain fragments caked to the side of his face told a very different story. A few feet away, a crude circle had been sprayed on the carpet around a stained and splintered mug-tree, and the three small branches that had broken from it; snapped clean off as it had been brought down repeatedly onto the heads of the dead men.

Thorne watched, his fists clenching and unclenching while the stills photographer moved in as close as he was able to the bodies. He listened as one of the CSI officers said something about the murder weapon, cracked a feeble joke about tea.

Whistling in the dark had never sounded so shrill.

"The superintendent's going to go mental," Holland said.

Thorne nodded, half listening. Thinking back over his conversations with the man they had all thought was Andrew Dowd. Wondering if he had missed something.

"They'll be wanting heads to roll, and sure as shit Trevor Jesmond's won't be one of them."

Thorne had put the man's behavior down to stress and medication. To some kind of breakdown caused by his predicament and the business with his wife. Christ, he'd been an idiot. Been made to look an idiot. "Are you going to catch this bloke?" Dowd had asked, looking him in the eye, right where Thorne was standing. He turned to the female detective, who was standing behind them, talking quietly to one of her junior officers. "We need a description out there now," he said.

She stepped towards him. "It's done."

"Every car in the area, right?"

"Like I said—"

"House-to-house as well, nearest half a dozen streets." He glanced back into the room. "Bastard'll be covered in blood, so he can't have got far without somebody seeing him."

"We think he took DS Spibey's jacket," the woman said. "We can't find it, anyway." She glanced back towards her colleague, looking for a little moral support before continuing. "There's no sign of his car, either. I checked and Spibey definitely drove in, so..."

Thorne stared at her.

"We have to assume our suspect's taken it."

"What about a briefcase?"

It was the woman's turn to stare.

"Briefcase, bag, whatever," Thorne said. "Is Spibey's stuff missing?"

"I've not seen anything."

"Look. For. It."

She turned and headed back down the stairs, but Thorne knew it was pointless. He began shouting as he lurched forward and followed her. At anyone who would listen. At himself. "The killer is almost certainly now in possession of sensitive case-notes and documents." His voice echoed as he got close to the lobby. "Details of surveillance and protection operations. Names and numbers..." He froze for a second and almost stumbled, used the momentum to take the remaining stairs two at a time.

Debbie Mitchell's name.

The address of Nina Collins' flat.

Coming out onto the street, he watched a patrol car pull up and saw two uniformed officers step out. He recognized their faces and felt a spasm in his gut. What had Nina Collins called them? Starsky and Hutch...

"Why the hell aren't you in Barnet?"

The older one leaned back against the car, peered past Thorne at the comings and goings. "We were told to leave and get over here."

His colleague chipped in: "Yeah, he said it had all kicked off."

"Who did?" Thorne asked.

"Detective Sergeant Spibey."

It felt like a punch, and Thorne was still reeling from it as he ran towards the marked BMW that was moving slowly towards him, its driver searching for a parking space. Thorne furiously signaled to the driver that he should turn the car around fast. He blinked to erase the picture in his head as he reached for his radio, shouting about blues and twos.

Debbie Mitchell's face peering through a plastic bag.

Forty

THE BMW raced through traffic in Camden and Kentish Town, then screamed north along the Archway Road. The thoughts were flying equally frantically around Thorne's head as he braced himself against the dashboard, trying to keep his breathing under control and shouting obscenities at any vehicle that did not get out of their way quickly enough.

Obscenities meant, in truth, for the man who had run rings round him.

The body found in the canal must have been that of the real Andrew Dowd. It would be easy enough to get a DNA sample and make a positive ID. The conversation Thorne would soon be having with Dowd's wife would be more difficult. He half expected the woman to sue them for incompetence.

It would be a difficult case to defend.

"Hang on."

Thorne gritted his teeth, trying to look unafraid as the car accelerated through a red light and swerved hard into a bus lane. He glanced across to see the speedometer's needle touching seventy-five.

"Ten minutes away, tops," the driver said.

He remembered what Hendricks had said about the victim being killed elsewhere, then dumped. It was a fair assumption that Walsh—or Garvey, as he now called himself—had followed Dowd to Cumbria and killed him there, then traveled back to London to dispose of the body before heading up to Kendal again and handing himself in to the local police.

As monsters went, this one was brilliant.

The trick had been in not trying to make himself look like Dowd, in so radically changing the appearance of the man whose identity he had stolen. The shaved head had convinced everyone they were looking at a man who had been through a major breakdown and Garvey had used every ounce of knowledge he had gained about Andrew and Sarah Dowd's private life to keep the wife out of the picture. Washing their cars. Watching and waiting for his chance, tucking away the information he would use when the time came. The troubled marriage gave him the perfect excuse once he'd "become" Dowd to avoid any confrontation with the one person who would know he was not who he claimed to be.

As a confidence trick, it was the equivalent of a shoplifter pushing a double bed out through the doors of a department store.

With two people on his list that Anthony Garvey could not track down, he had let the police do the work for him. He had smuggled himself inside the investigation. Fowler had been there on a plate, holed up in the room next door. A sitting duck. It was one policeman's weakness for gambling, the ease with which he had abandoned procedure, that had provided Garvey with the opportunity he had been waiting for, the information he needed.

Had led him to the last victim on his list.

Despite the speed, the noise, the adrenaline fizzing through him, Thorne still tensed when his phone rang. As the car tore down into Finchley, he spent half a minute shouting above the siren to Dave Holland, asking him to check the ETAs of the other units he had ordered to Nina Collins' flat, hoping that they might get there quicker than he could.

"We'll get him," Holland said.

The siren screamed again before Thorne could think of anything to say, so he just hung up. He was tucking the phone back into his pocket when he had the idea.

Garvey had taken Spibey's jacket and briefcase, his paperwork, the ID he had used when talking to the officers outside Collins' flat. So, why not...?

He pulled his phone out again, searched through the memory and dialed the number he had called first thing that morning, the last time he had spoken to Brian Spibey.

The mobile rang three times, four, then it was answered.

"You took your time, Thorne."

Thorne needed a moment to catch his breath. The casual tone, the lightness in the man's voice, sent a shiver through his chest and shoulders. "Is she alive?"

"You might need to be a little more specific."

"Look, I know what this is all about, Simon, and we need to talk about it."

"My name's Anthony."

"Sorry...Anthony. We need to talk about what happened to your father. I think we can get the case looked at again." It was nonsense, but Thorne could think of no other way to reach the man. He winced at Garvey's reaction, the playful mockery in his voice, which made it clear that he thought it was nonsense, too.

"Really? You'd do that for me? After all these bodies?"

Thorne's mouth went dry. These bodies, not those. Was Garvey looking down at the body of Debbie Mitchell even as they were talking?

"Are you still there?"

"I'm still here," Thorne said.

"I suppose you're tracing this."

"No."

"Using cell-site location or whatever."

"No, really." There would not have been time, and there was no point when Thorne knew precisely where Garvey was.

"It's a lot more high-tech these days than when they were blundering around trying to catch my father."

"That's true."

"Not that you haven't been doing a fair bit of blundering yourself."

"I can't argue with that," Thorne said. "But you've been pretty clever."

"Right. The 'we can talk about this' approach didn't work, so now you're trying to flatter me." Garvey sighed. "You're very predictable."

"I'm just trying to save a woman's life."

"You know, it's awfully noisy where you are," Garvey said. "Wailing sirens and what have you."

"Tell me if Debbie's alive—"

"I've got enough of a headache as it is."

"Just get out of there," Thorne said. "If she's still alive, just run. OK? I don't care."

"Makes me think I should get a move on."

"Anthony—"

The line went dead.

Thorne turned to look at the driver, who had not taken his eyes off the road for a moment. At the speed they were traveling, Thorne was more than grateful, but he knew that the man had been listening.

"Five minutes," the driver said.

Thorne could only close his eyes and clench his fists, and hope that Debbie Mitchell had that long.

Forty-One

SHE TOOK another step towards the kitchen, one eye on the doorway that led out into the hall, where the man was still on the phone.

"I need to take this," he'd said, looking down at the phone's small screen and smiling before answering. "You took your time, Thorne." He'd taken a step or two towards the door then, looking at her and shaking his head as if to say, "What a pain in the arse. Just give me a minute."

Debbie had nodded her understanding and signaled to him that she'd make some tea, biting her lip and trying not to let her face give anything away until he stepped out into the hall and lowered his voice.

You took your time, Thorne...

It wasn't what he'd said that was making her insides churn and slop, though she knew that was no way for a detective to talk to his colleague. It was what she'd seen as he'd raised himself up from her side a minute or two earlier. The sudden flash of red where his jacket had fallen open, the slash and spatter of it.

The bloodstain on his shirt.

She could hear him muttering now, a laugh in his voice as she stood on the threshold to the kitchen and beckoned Jason to her. He was still engrossed in his coloring book.

She hissed his name. Got no response.

She called him again, raising her voice a little. When Jason turned his head towards her, she looked to the sitting-room door to make sure she had not been overheard.

She counted to three and took a deep breath, fighting back tears and a desperate need to urinate. "Come with Mummy, Jason..."

He nodded at her.

"Please, chicken."

Jason got up slowly, then, for an agonizingly long few seconds, stood staring at the wall, as though he'd forgotten what he was meant to be doing. Debbie held out her hand and waved. She clicked her tongue and made "puff-puff" noises until, with a spin and a smile, her son was bounding across the carpet towards her.

She almost dragged him into the kitchen and quietly pushed the door closed. She could see straight away that he was agitated, picking up on her terror. But there was no time to calm him.

She eased up the volume on the radio, then bent down to whisper in Jason's ear.

"Let's go blow at the trains," she said.

He beamed and grabbed at her, squeezed away the trembling in her free hand, while the other gently pushed down on the handle of the back door.

Forty-Two

BRIGSTOCKE HAD called no more than a minute or so after Thorne had finished talking to Garvey. The DCI had arrived at Nina Collins' flat with a team of detectives from Barnet station and a unit from CO19 that had been stood down from the scene in Euston and had left before Thorne had.

"How far away are you?"

"Minutes."

"What do you think, Tom?"

Though nominally his senior officer, Brigstocke sounded keen to get Thorne's feedback. Thorne was both gratified and appalled by the courtesy, if that's what it was.

"I think you should go in," he said.

"Shouldn't we hang back a bit?" Brigstocke asked. "Assess things, I mean? He could well be armed."

"There's no reason to think he's got anything," Thorne said. "But it doesn't matter either way. He'll just use whatever he can find. He used a mug-tree back there, for Christ's sake."

"Right."

"Put the fucking door in, Russell. Don't give him the chance."

So, for the second time in less than an hour, Thorne arrived at a crime scene and could do no more than search the faces of those who had beaten him to it for some clue as to how things stood.

If he was too late to change anything.

This time, pulling up hard outside Nina Collins' flat, the prevalent expression was one of bemusement and Thorne felt relief wash over him as he sprinted up the path to be met at the door by Russell Brigstocke.

"Nobody here," Brigstocke said.

The relief was short-lived. Had Garvey taken her? "Any signs of—?"

"No blood. Nothing to indicate a struggle."

"That's got to be good," Thorne said. "Do you think?"

Before Brigstocke could answer, there was a shout from the back of the house. A few seconds later, a plain-clothes officer wearing a stab vest came running down the hall.

"You might want to take a look at the garden."

While the officer was telling Brigstocke what he had found, Thorne moved quickly into the house and out through the open kitchen door. He saw it immediately. A white plastic garden chair had been taken from the end of a matching table on the patio and placed against the fence at the far end of the small garden. There were muddy footprints on the seat. Thorne bent down to take a closer look.

Three different sets.

Wary of destroying evidence, Thorne ran to grab another chair, climbed up and peered over the fence. He could see nothing but an area of scrubland backing onto a row of garages, the ground littered with shards of glass and twisted scraps of metal, an old mattress, the remains of several fires. In the far corner, a dilapidated cross-hatch fence curled around a corner and out of sight.

He jumped back down and tried to think, then reached for his phone.

When she eventually answered, Nina Collins sounded as though she was very busy, but she was still happy enough to let Thorne know what she thought of him.

He cut her off fast, while trying to keep his voice calm. He did not want to scare her, but he needed information quickly. "Debbie's gone," he said.

"Gone where?"

"If you climb over the fence at the end of your garden, where do you come out?"

"What?"

"Where does it go, Nina?"

"Fuck's sake, she's climbed over the fence?"

"Where might Debbie go?"

There was silence for a few seconds, then Nina began to curse again. Thorne told her several times to be quiet, and when she had finished, he could hear a man's voice in the background.

Thorne said, "Where would Debbie take Jason, Nina?" He waited until he could hear her breathing and said it slowly. "If she was frightened."

"I don't know, Christ!" The man was talking again, and Nina's voice was muffled as she put her hand over the mouthpiece and told him to shut up. "The park, maybe."

"The park?" The kid's favorite place. "Are you sure?"

"They go there all the time."

When the man with Nina started to shout, Thorne hung up. As he turned, he saw a woman standing in the garden next door. She was cradling a child and staring at Thorne over the fence.

"It's like a madhouse here," she said.

"Did you see anything?"

She shook her head, then nodded towards the phone in Thorne's hand. "I was listening," she said. "Sorry."

"It doesn't matter."

"Thing is, there's a quicker way."

It had been so easy, there had seemed no other choice, as she had stumbled across the patch of wasteland beyond Nina's garden, through the hole in the fence and out from the tangle of trees into the park. The thought of what might be behind her had driven her forward, compelled her to keep Jason moving, pulling him away from the old woman with the dog and across the football pitches towards the bridge. The certainty had been as total, as all-consuming, as the panic.

Now, though, looking down from the bridge, she was paralyzed by a very different sort of terror.

Rigid with it and helpless.

In her head it had all been so simple, and so obvious. She had not chosen this way of doing it and if she'd been given any option, she would have gone about things very differently. Unable to sleep and listening for Nina's key in the door, she'd imagined the final moments and settled on a long lie-down, with crushed-up tablets and booze, and Jason pressed against her beneath the covers. Drifting away together with the radio on, or maybe the music from Jason's video coming through from the next room. His long, warm body stretched out next to hers.

Knowing nothing. Unafraid.

Next to her now, Jason slapped his hands against the edge of the bridge, grunting with excitement. She opened her eyes and watched the broken snake of the train curl out, the tracks crackling beneath it as the final carriage rumbled onto the straight.

This would be quick, she knew that, but the drop was so terrible and for a few seconds, she was a little girl again, no older than Jason was now. Shivering, her toes curled around the edge of the high board as her father pushed her in the small of the back and told her not to be so stupid. Not to be a baby. She blinked away the tears, staring down at the black lines on the bottom of the pool, wavy beneath that solid block of blue. Leaning back against her father's hand. Closing her eyes and swallowing back the sick feeling.

Was that what was stopping her now, pressing her down against the stone and shredding her heart like wet paper? Or, Christ... perhaps she was wrong. Was she being stupid and selfish? She had been thinking of nothing else since the police had first come to her door to warn her. Had been so sure that it was the right thing.

For both of them.

Jason could not survive without her, she'd always known that. He would have no sort of life with anyone else. Nobody but Debbie could truly understand him or make him happy. Nobody could ever love him as much as she did.

Now, though, with the bricks humming beneath her, the voice that screamed inside her head told her that she was thinking only of herself. How could she possibly know the way things would turn out for Jason? The sort of future that he might have? They were discovering stuff all the time, making medical advances and coming up with new ideas. Finding ways to get through to kids like him.

"Puff, puff..."

Debbie dragged her head around, looked down at Jason, his lips moving, his eyes wide and bright. Fearless. Movement at the edge of her vision told her that the man who had brought them to this was no more than yards, no more than moments, away.

She could smell her own sour stink, feel the rush of wind slapping against a face she knew was blank and bloodless. Like someone who was dying.

Which, of course, she was.

It was then, as she sucked in the strength, that she heard Thorne's voice, hoarse and desperate above the clack-and-grind of the train. He was calling her name every few seconds, first from the street and then from the path, up and away to her right.

His timing is as bad as his jokes, she thought, turning back.

Closing her eyes, her fingers reaching to adjust the tight, thin straps of a long-lost swimsuit.

Her father's hand in the small of her back.

Forty-Three

THORNE HAD followed the instructions that the woman in the garden had given him. He had rushed back through the house and out of the front door, ignoring the looks of those he all but flattened and the questions as he legged it past Russell Brigstocke. He had grabbed the keys to the nearest squad car and floored it. Back onto the Great North Road and south towards Whetstone, counting off the turnings until he'd reached the correct one, then heading downhill into a U-shaped side street.

Looking for the path that ran above the Tube line.

This was the normal way in, the woman had told him, the way that the local kids and dog-walkers usually went, and it would get him into the park a damn sight quicker than the route Debbie Mitchell appeared to have taken. There were a couple of cut-throughs off the same street, she'd said, narrow alleyways between blocks of houses, but this was definitely the way to go if you were looking for someone. It would give him the best view of the whole park as he entered it from above, would take him in across the railway bridge.

Thorne double-parked as soon as he had found the entrance and when he came around the car he saw an old woman with a dog emerging from one of the cut-throughs a dozen or so houses to his left. He ran towards her. He saw the look of alarm on her face as he approached, watched her step towards the nearest front gate and pull the Labrador tight to her leg. Thorne dug into his pocket for ID and began shouting when he was still fifteen feet away.

"Police," he said. "I'm looking for a woman and an eight-year-old boy."

The dog started barking and the woman told it to be quiet.

"Did you see them in the park? She's tall, blond hair."

The old woman fed the dog something from her pocket. "That's right, with her son," she said. "Bless him. He doesn't say much—"

"Was there anyone else with them?"

The woman shook her head, suddenly flustered. "I don't think so, love. I didn't see anybody."

"Where?"

She thought for a few seconds and pointed over Thorne's shoulder. "They were heading towards the bridge, I think." The dog was barking again, in search of another treat. "This was only five minutes ago, but they were in quite a hurry."

Thorne was already running.

Where it left the road, the path was just wide enough for a car, but Thorne could see that it narrowed ahead of him. It ran straight for fifty yards or so, before curving to the right. His view of what was round the corner was obscured by treetops and a block of low buildings where the straight ended.

Thorne shouted Debbie's name.

For half its distance, once it was past the gardens, the path was bordered by garages and other outbuildings at the back of houses. Fences in various states of repair bulged or rose up on either side of Thorne as he ran. Overgrown bushes and small trees gave way to stretches of flaking wood and brick, the graffiti that covered them no more than flashes and washes of color as he sprinted past.

"Debbie!"

My fault, Thorne thought as he ran. My fault, my fault, the words sounding in time with his feet as they pounded against the dirt and loose stones. Or if not, then my responsibility...

He shouted again, heard only his ragged breath, the loose change jumping in his pockets and the cawing of crows high away to his right as he charged towards the curve of the path.

Down to me.

At the end of the straight he kept as close to the right-hand side as possible, trying to cut the corner, but lost his footing as a cat darted from under a gate and he changed direction hard to avoid it. He was sweating and breathless now, felt as though something had torn behind one of his knees, but he could see that the path cut sharply left again only thirty feet ahead of him. Through gaps in the trees he caught glimpses of the Tube line below. He knew that the bridge was around the corner, that he would get the view he needed as soon as he made the next turn.

He could hear a train coming.

He ran, picking up speed as the downhill slope grew more pronounced, as the panic gained momentum equally fast. Scuttling around in his head, dark images and ideas, like trapped rats.

Garvey reaching for a brick and a bag. The boy screaming. Blood in Debbie Mitchell's dirty-blond hair.

Thorne shouted again as he took the final turn, tried to scare away the rats.

There was a series of metal gates on his right as he turned onto the section of path that approached the bridge: yards filled with engines and old tires; a collection of logs and antique lawnmowers; a row of dirty greenhouses and a sign made out of plastic leaves saying, "Whetstone Nurseries." After a few steps, Thorne could see that the woman in the garden had been right. The land swept away below him, granting him a fantastic view of the park. He could see across the treetops to the two football pitches; the parallel foot and cycle paths snaking around them towards a small lake with fields on the far side; and, beyond them, perhaps half a mile from where he stood, the edge of a golf course. But he didn't need the view.

Debbie and Jason were on the bridge right ahead.

Thorne stopped dead when he saw them sitting on the wall. He felt his stomach turn over and his breakfast start to rise up. Should he stay where he was or move towards them? Should he shout or keep quiet? The last thing he wanted to do was startle her. He needed her to stay calm and still, but Christ, the train was coming. Then he saw Garvey jogging onto the bridge from the other side, no more than a few steps from them, and he knew that he had no choice.

He shouted Debbie's name—a warning and a plea—and began to run. He saw Garvey raise his head to look at him, saw Debbie do the same. He ran, with no thought of what he would do when he reached the bridge, his eyes flashing from the figures ahead of him to the train moving fast from his right, then watched in horror as his path was blocked by a metal trailer rolling out in front of him from one of the yards to his right.

Thorne shouted, but the trailer kept coming, piled high with plastic water-butts, bags of compost and potted palms; shunted out of the nursery gates by a miniature tractor whose driver stared at Thorne as he reversed onto the path, stopped and prepared to turn round.

"Get out of the fucking way. Christ..."

For precious seconds, Thorne lost clear sight of the figures on the bridge. When he was finally able to see anything at all, it was obvious that Garvey had reached Debbie and Jason. That there was some sort of struggle going on.

Thorne saw arms grappling for purchase.

Heard Debbie shout, "No!"

He bellowed at the tractor driver and flattened himself against the gate, looking for a chance to squeeze past. When he heard the scream of the Tube train's brakes, he decided to clamber right across the driver's lap, but as soon as he was clear of the obstruction and ready to move again, he could see that there was no longer any need to hurry.

There was only one figure ahead of him now.

To his right, the train had emerged from beneath the bridge, hissing and squealing as it slowed. He could just make out passengers pressed against the windows, eager to see what had happened. Why they were stopping so suddenly between stations.

He took two small steps, then looked down at the tracks to his right.

The bodies could easily have been twin bundles of rags.

Behind him, somebody was shouting. Someone who had seen it happen. The tractor driver, maybe.

Thorne stayed where he was for a few seconds, then gave up waiting for the shaking to stop and walked slowly towards the figure on the bridge.

PART IV

ALL THAT REMAINS . . .

Afterwards

MICHAEL

His wife brings in his dinner: jerk chicken and sweet potato mash, his favorite. He thanks her and picks up his knife and fork, but there's little chance of him eating, and when he turns to see her looking back from the doorway, smiles and says thanks again, he can see that she knows it, too.

He's been picking at his food ever since it happened. He's also been sleeping a lot during the day, which he thinks is strange, because he's always been so active, and when he wakes to find his wife standing over him, he can tell that he has not been sleeping peacefully.

"Shush," she tells him. "Why don't you ask the doctor for something?"

But he doesn't believe in popping pills for this and that; never has. He knows that it will pass eventually; and, anyway, he would worry about what kind of a man he was if he was not changed by it. If he were dreaming sweet dreams and eating like a horse.

"It's always worse underground," another driver told him. "You were lucky in a way. Easier than when you come barreling out of that tunnel into a station, see that flash of color as some nutter jumps at the last minute."

Michael nodded, kept his own counsel, same as always. The man doing all the talking had never had "one under," but he claimed to know plenty of drivers who had.

There was no shortage of war stories. Myths and misinformation.

"Yeah, definitely rougher underground," the man said.

Two, though. Two of them…

"How high's that bridge up there, anyway? Forty, forty-five feet? They were probably both dead before you came along. Nothing you could have done, mate, not a bloody thing. That's something you can rest easy about."

That driver and several others poured whiskey down his neck the day after. He let them, although all he wanted was to go home, crawl between his sheets for a while.

He simply nodded and took another drink.

But he had seen it, seen the woman. Had seen an arm move and seen her raise her head, turn away when the train was almost on her. That was when he had closed his eyes, waiting for the bump. It had been no more, not really, than that time he'd hit a fox on the last run north up to Mill Hill East.

He sits in the front room. The television is on, but the sound is muted. Dinnertime already? It was only half-past ten last time he looked at his watch. He thinks it might be a good sign that the days are moving by a little faster now. The first few felt like they would never end. All the advice and talking in lowered voices.

He needs to ring in and ask when he can come back. Someone from the union came round, but it was all so damned fast and he didn't really take it in. Two weeks' compulsory "rest," was it?

His daughter called the day after and offered to come home, but he didn't want to drag her away from college so told her he was fine. Now, he wishes she was there. He could talk to her in a way he could never talk to Lizzie, which was stupid, but there you go. He knew his daughter would cope with it all better, with how he was.

"It was their choice, Dad," his daughter said on the phone. "You were unlucky, that's all." That was before it all came out in the newspapers, of course. Choice had nothing to do with what happened to that woman and her boy.

He saw the bodies dropping, of course, the arms and legs, the woman's skirt blowing up around her waist. Just enough time for the wrench in his belly before he was on them, bracing himself for it.

There's a mess of papers on the floor by the side of his armchair, and half a dozen paperbacks piled up on the dining table. He's always loved reading, would come home on a Monday with four books from the library, regular as clockwork. Lizzie had gone and fetched this lot for him, told him it would help to take his mind off things, but he only picked at them, same as the food. The books he likes, thrillers and whatnot, don't seem fitting somehow, and he can no more read one of Lizzie's romances than fly.

"All hearts and flowers and kissy-kissy," he said to her once.

"Nothing wrong with that." She pulled a face. "Better than all that blood and badness you seem to like so much."

She comes in ten minutes later and takes away his untouched plate. Says it doesn't matter. He's wondering whose job it is to clean up the front of the train afterwards. Thinking that there's always someone worse off than yourself.

"I think I'll take the paper to bed," Michael says.

He goes up and gets into bed in his underpants, shuts his eyes and hopes there won't be any dreams. He hears a door close somewhere downstairs, feels it through the bedroom floor.

Just a bump. No more, not really, than when he hit that fox.

MY JOURNAL

16 October

So, all over bar the shouting and famous last words time. Last words in these pages at least, whichever way things turn out later. I should probably try to think of something deep and meaningful, but it's hard to focus at the moment, feeling like this. Ironic that today of all days the headache should flare up this badly. I should probably lie down in the dark for a while, but there isn't time. Things are going to kick off soon.

A nice, friendly card game.

All through this, I've been wondering what my father would have said about what I was doing. I can only hope that he would have approved, but I'll never know for sure. He didn't really want to talk about what he'd done, those women that he went inside for. Maybe it was because he didn't understand it, at least not until the tumor was discovered. But either way, he preferred to keep it all to himself and, much as I was desperate to know, I had to respect that. He decided to keep quiet. That's where we differ.

If the worst happens and I end up in the same situation, they won't be able to shut me up. I'll be happy bending any sod's ear. It'll be solitary confinement for me, just to give everyone else in there a rest!

Have I made a point doing this? I think so. Has it changed anything? It's changed me, which I'll probably have to settle for.

Those last words? Well, I suppose it depends on who I'm writing them for. The select few who will ever get to read this. It will probably get read out in court, nice and dramatic, so the more sensitive members of the jury can catch their breath or fight back a tear or two. The juicier bits will almost certainly be picked out as headlines in the red-tops, which will be worth a few quid extra to my old mate in the newsagent's. And I know every page is going to get pored over endlessly later on by the shrinks and the documentary-makers.

Best of luck.

The thing is, though, I'm not sure I care about impressing any of them. Any of you.

At the end of the day, especially a day as important as this one, I can't waste valuable time trying to come up with something profound.

So, fuck it.

Fingers crossed.

Forty-Four

THORNE LAID down the final page of the file; a thick sheaf photocopied from the dog-eared notebook found at Grass-up Grange. The journal dated back to the day of Raymond Garvey's death in Addenbrooke's Hospital after the operation on his tumor. The day when everything had changed.

The day when Anthony Garvey had begun making plans.

Thorne reached for his beer and drank deep from the can. He needed it.

"What's going to happen to Jason?" Louise asked.

"It's down to Social Services," Thorne said. "Foster care in the short term, I suppose."

"Their history's not great with him, though, is it?"

"There's nobody else," Thorne said. Nina Collins had offered to take him, begged to, but she was few people's idea of a fit mother.

Louise lay with her feet up on the sofa, Elvis sprawled across her chest. She reached down, fumbling until she found her empty wineglass. She held it up. "Another one would be nice."

Thorne stood, took the glass and walked into the kitchen.

"Why do you think he did it?" Louise asked.

Thorne bent to take the bottle from the fridge. He blinked and saw

Jason Mitchell's face, the desperation in the boy's eyes as Thorne had reached for him, tried to pull him away; the sound of his repeated "puff-puffing" just audible above the sirens and the squeal of the train's brakes.

"Come with me, Jason," Thorne had said. "Let's go back, see Auntie Nina."

Jason had still been smiling, still blowing imaginary smoke and pointing back towards the bridge, when Thorne had walked him up the path to within sight of the cars and the flashing lights.

"Tom?"

Thorne walked back into the living room and handed Louise her wine. "Sorry, what?"

"Why did Garvey kill himself?"

"Carol reckons it was always part of his plan," Thorne said. "His mother was one of his father's victims. So, he was on his own list."

Louise looked dubious.

"Yeah, I know." One or two lines in Garvey's journal had also suggested that he thought he was dying, that he might soon go the same way as his old man. The post-mortem, carried out as soon as Hendricks had flown back from Sweden, showed that there had been no tumor, that Garvey had been suffering from nothing worse than the occasional migraine. It seemed as though hypochondria had been the mildest of his psychological problems. "It's all speculation," Thorne said. "The truth is, I couldn't give a flying fuck."

He had said much the same to Nicholas Maier when the writer had called, cheerfully reminding Thorne that he had agreed to tell his story in return for Maier's silence.

"We had a deal," Maier had said.

Thorne had told him where he could stick their deal, then had hung up.

Chamberlain's was just one of several theories about what had happened on the bridge. Debbie Mitchell might have struggled for her life, or at least ensured that she took Garvey with her, down into the path of the train. Perhaps Jason had done it, fought in those last moments to save his mother. The only thing that Thorne was sure of, having seen them sitting on the edge of that wall, was that, until Anthony Garvey had caught up with her, Debbie Mitchell had been intending to end her own life and that of her son.

He found it hard to understand, but equally hard to condemn. The love a mother had for her child—especially when she thought he was incapable of living happily without her—was something he could never fully fathom. Unless and until he became a parent himself. He had almost said as much to Louise, then stopped himself, still wary about applying any pressure.

"We should get an early night," Louise said.

"Sounds good."

Thorne knew there was nothing suggestive in her comment. They both needed sleep. Louise was working even longer hours than he was on a messy kidnap case: the family of a building-society manager held while he was forced to enter his branch out of hours and open the safe. Thorne was already busy with two further murders: a domestic and a hit-and-run. Both were brutal and banal and neither was likely to catch the eye of TV news and tabloid editors in the way the Anthony Garvey killings had.

Yvonne Kitson had volunteered to deliver the death message to Sarah Dowd. To break the news that her husband was not the man they had been keeping in protective custody. That the real Andrew Dowd had been battered to death in an unknown location and dumped into the canal at Camden Lock.

Thorne had taken Kitson out for a drink that night and she had seemed glad of it.

"She made me feel like I'd as good as given Garvey the brick," Kitson had said. "Or whatever it was he used to smash her husband's head in."

"Sorry, Yvonne."

"It's fine. I volunteered, remember?"

"Why?"

"You had the kid on the bridge," Kitson said. "We need to spread the misery around a bit."

Now, the misery was being duly dispensed and the Garvey murders were someone else's to worry about. Another team was responsible for wrapping things up and even though there would be no trial, there was still a mountain of paperwork to scale in preparation for those inquests still to be carried out.

Graham Fowler. Brian Spibey.

Rob Gibbons had been luckier—the knife had missed every major internal organ—though he would not be returning to work anytime soon.

Simon Walsh, who called himself Anthony Garvey and later posed as Andrew Dowd, had been cremated quickly and quietly, with only Sandra Phipps and her daughter in attendance. Thorne wondered if there would be many more at the service for Debbie Mitchell in two days' time. He had already booked the morning off, taken his black suit in to the dry cleaner's.

Brigstocke had raised an eyebrow when Thorne had told him why he was booking himself out. "Time to move on, Tom," he'd said.

Thorne had said, "I know," and imagined walking away from the funeral with Nina Collins' spit running down his jacket.

"It's our job to clean up the shit," Brigstocke had said. "That doesn't mean walking about with bits of it stuck to us afterwards."

Time to move on...

Carol Chamberlain had been round for dinner a few nights earlier, with Phil Hendricks making up an unlikely foursome. He'd arrived with the bottle of vodka he'd promised Thorne and unsavory tales of the good-looking Swede he'd finally found on his last night.

It had been an enjoyable evening, with everyone drinking a little more than they should, especially Chamberlain. Thorne was pleased at how well she had got on with Louise, but was surprised that she hadn't gone straight home to her husband as soon as she had the chance. She had told him that she would be going back to Worthing in a few days; that she liked to see things through to the "bitter end." Thorne had not been convinced, but hadn't pushed it.

She'd held him tightly and thanked him before climbing into the taxi she was sharing with Phil Hendricks. Thorne had told her not to be stupid, that he was the one who owed her. "All debts are cleared, Tom," she'd said. "OK?"

"OK," Thorne said.

Then she had lowered the taxi window and nodded towards Hendricks. "If your friend was ever likely to turn, do you think he might go for an older woman?"

Thorne had wished her luck.

Afterwards, he had put on a Laura Cantrell album while he and Louise did their best to clear up. He sang along to her cover version of "The Wreck of the *Edmund Fitzgerald*" while he ferried cups and plates through to the kitchen and Louise loaded the dishwasher.

Ten minutes later, with only half the clearing away done, they were in bed, neither of them willing to get up and turn off the light they'd left on in the hall and the song still rattling around in Thorne's head.

"This baby business," Louise said.

Thorne turned over, leaned up on one elbow.

"There's no reason to rush things, is there?"

He did not know what the right answer was, settled for a hesitant "no."

"We can just wait and see what happens."

Thorne nodded and they looked at each other for a while. Then he turned over again and lay awake, with the words of the song outstaying their welcome as he waited for sleep to take him.

And all that remains is the faces and the names of the wives and the sons and the daughters.

Life and love and murder, kids, whatever.

It was more or less all you could do, he thought.

Wait and see what happens.

Acknowledgments

I AM hugely grateful to Dr. Brian Little, who opened my eyes in more ways than one, and to Dr. Bob Bradford for his patience and expertise. Both helped to make the complex workings of the human brain a little clearer to my own less than perfect one.

I want to thank Michael Pietsch, John Schoenfelder, Miriam Parker, Wes Miller, and the team at Mulholland Books for the faith, support, and enthusiasm that keeps coming around that curve. Feels like home already.

Thanks, as always, to Sarah Lutyens, Wendy Lee and Neil Hibberd.

To Peter, the better half of Will Peterson.

And to Claire, of course. For the title and so much more.

Mark Billingham is a stand-up comedian, an award-winning children's writer, and one of Great Britain's most acclaimed and top-selling crime writers. He has twice won the Theakston's Old Peculier Award for best crime novel of the year, most recently with *Death Message*. He was also awarded the 2003 Sherlock Award for Best Detective created by a British writer. He lives in north London with his wife and two children.